Praise for #1 *New York Times* bestselling author
and *USA TODAY* bestselling author

ROBYN CARR

"This book is an utter delight."
—*RT Book Reviews* on *Moonlight Road*

"Strong conflict, humor and well-written characters
are Carr's calling cards, and they're all present here....
You won't want to put this one down."
—*RT Book Reviews* on *Angel's Peak*

"This story has everything: a courageous,
outspoken heroine, a to-die-for hero
and a plot that will touch readers' hearts
on several different levels. Truly excellent."
—*RT Book Reviews* on *Forbidden Falls*

"An intensely satisfying read.
By turns humorous and gut-wrenchingly emotional,
it won't soon be forgotten."
—*RT Book Reviews* on *Paradise Valley*

"Carr has hit her stride with this captivating series."
—*Library Journal* on the Virgin River series

"The Virgin River books are so compelling—
I connected instantly with the characters
and just wanted more and more and more."
—#1 *New York Times* bestselling author
Debbie Macomber

Don't miss Robyn's next book,
SUNRISE POINT
Available May 2012

ROBYN CARR

REDWOOD BEND

MIRA®

Recycling programs
for this product may
not exist in your area.

ISBN-13: 978-0-7783-1310-6

REDWOOD BEND

For questions and comments about the quality of this book please contact us at
Customer_eCare@Harlequin.ca.

www.Harlequin.com

Printed in U.S.A.

For Jill Shalvis with gratitude
for providing her very own bear with triplet cubs
for this story, and even more importantly, with
heartfelt thanks for a lovely, devoted friendship.

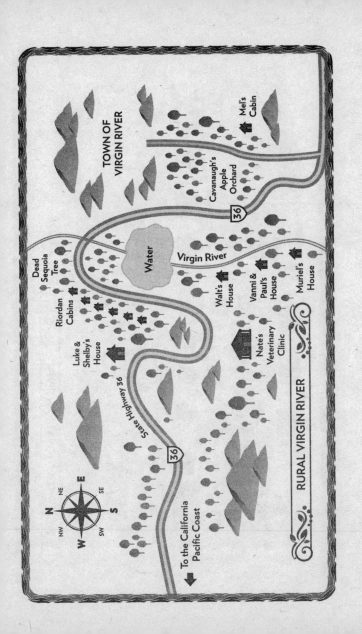

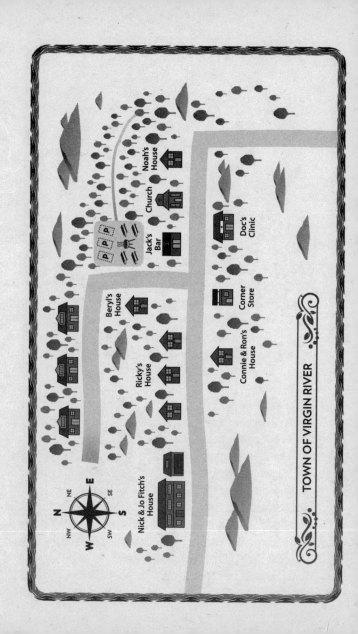

TOWN OF VIRGIN RIVER

One

Katie Malone quit her job and packed up her little Vermont house. The past few years had been tough and the past few months, having been separated from her brother, Conner, her only family, had been awful. In fact, she'd been feeling so alone, she stopped herself just moments before signing on to an online dating service.

But her watershed moment came when she began to have high hopes for a romantic relationship with her boss, the sweetest pediatric dentist who ever lived and a man who had never even kissed her. And guess what? There was a logical reason he hadn't—he was gay. She was the *last* person he wanted to kiss.

It was high time she forgot about men and worked on bolstering her independent spirit with a return to California. One of her twins, five-year-old Andy, said something that nearly drove an arrow through her heart and caused her to realize the whole family needed a fresh start.

She was packing up a box to ship ahead to California when Andy asked, "Do we have to move in the dark again?"

She was stunned. Speechless. Here she had been thinking about kisses and loneliness while her boys were worried about fleeing in the dark of night to some strange, unknown place. A place even farther from family than they were now.

She clutched her little boy close and said, "No, sweetheart! I'm taking you and Mitch to Uncle Conner."

Andy and Mitch were a matched set, five-year-old identical twins. Mitch overheard this and came running. "Uncle Conner?" he asked.

"Yes," she said, suddenly clear on what she had in front of her. She had to get her family together, make sure her boys felt safe and secure. "Right after a little side trip. How does Disney World sound?"

They started jumping for joy, screaming "Yay!" and "Cool!" And then the celebration dissolved to the floor and into a wrestling match. Like usual.

She rolled her eyes and continued packing up.

Last winter her brother had had a devastating experience that had become a family crisis. A man had been murdered behind their family-owned hardware store and Conner called the police at once. He became the only witness in a capital murder case. Shortly after the arrest was made, the hardware store was burned to the ground and a threat was left on Conner's voice mail. This led the D.A. to decide it was in the best interest of their family to separate them. Katie and her boys were spirited off to Vermont for their own protection, about as far from Sacramento as she could get and still stay in the country, while Conner was hidden away in a tiny mountain town in Northern California.

Now it was over. The suspect in the murder had been killed before he could stand trial, Conner was no longer a witness and their family had escaped danger. Now they could get about the business of healing and bonding.

And Conner had met someone in Virgin River, Leslie, a woman he loved. He'd settled in to make a life with her.

Katie would enjoy surprising her brother, but they'd long ago established the habit of talking every day. Conner talked to the boys, if only briefly, at least every other day—the closest thing to a father they had. There was no way she could conceal her travel plans. If Conner didn't suspect, the boys would certainly tell all.

"Summer is almost here," she told Conner. "It's almost June, we're all free to roam and move around now that there's no threat. I have to get my boys back to some kind of stable life. They need you, Conner. I'd like to spend the summer in Virgin River with you, if that's okay. I want to rent my own place, of course, but the boys should be near you."

"I'll come and get you," Conner immediately offered.

"No," she said flatly. "I'm taking the boys on vacation, just the three of us. We've earned it. We're going to Disney World for a few days. I'll have the car shipped from there, then we'll fly to Sacramento and I'll drive up to Virgin River—it's only a few hours. And I love scenic drives."

"I'll meet you in Sacramento," he said.

She took a breath. Conner's overprotectiveness had intensified after their parents' deaths. He was always there for her and she adored him for it, but he verged on bossy and sometimes she had to take a firm hand with him. "No. I'm not a child. I'm thirty-two and very competent. And I want to spend some time with my kids. They've been on shaky ground since the move and we need some fun time together."

"I only want to help," he said.

"And I love you for it. But I'm going to do this my way."

And he backed off! "All right, fair enough."

Katie was momentarily shocked into silence. "Wow," she finally said. "Who are you and what have you done with my big brother?"

"Very funny."

"Although I have the utmost respect for you, I give all the credit for this change to Leslie. Tell her I owe her."

When Katie had escaped to Vermont in March, she had left behind her minivan with the license plate that could identify her. It was to be sold and Conner had arranged for a late-model Lincoln Navigator SUV to be waiting for her in Vermont—a mammoth vehicle that she could barely park. As any carpooling mother might, she had grieved her minivan—it was light and easy to handle and felt like an extension of her body. But she came to quickly love the big, gas-guzzling SUV. She felt like queen of the road—invulnerable; she could see over everything and everyone. She looked forward to some time on the road for reflection, to consider her options. The act of seeing the miles vanish in the rear-view mirror was a good way to leave the past behind and welcome a new beginning.

It didn't take Katie long to get out of town. She had UPS pick up her boxes on Monday, phoned the school and arranged to have the boys' kindergarten records scanned and emailed to her, invited the landlord over to check the condition of the house, and asked her neighbor to come over and help herself to the perishables that would otherwise be thrown out. She arranged to have the Lincoln picked up in Orlando and moved to Sacramento while she and the boys did a little Disney. She packed not only clothes, but the cooler and picnic basket. Her tool belt, which was pink and had been given to her by her late husband, Charlie, went with her everywhere. Armed with portable DVD players and movies, iPads and rechargers, she loaded her monster SUV and headed south.

They got off to a great start, but after a few hours the boys started to wiggle and squabble and complain. She stopped for the bathroom for one when the other one didn't have to go and fifteen minutes down the road, had to stop again for the second one. They picnicked at rest stops every few hours and she ran them around to tire them out, though the only one who seemed tired was Katie. She repaired a malfunctioning DVD player, set up some snacks and loaded them back up to hit the road again.

She couldn't help but wonder how parents did this sort of thing ten, twenty, thirty years ago before portable movies and iPad games. How did they manage without fifth-wheel-size cars with pull-down consoles that served as tables to hold games and refreshments? Without cars that, like cruise ships, had individual heating and air-conditioning thermostats? How did the pioneer mothers manage? Did they even *have* duct tape back then?

Most women, at times like this, would be reduced to self-pity because they were left with these high maintenance, energetic boys, but Katie just wasn't that kind of woman. She hated self-pity. She did, however, wish Charlie could see them, experience them.

Katie met and married Charlie when she was twenty-six. They had a romantic, devoted, passion-charged relationship, but it had been too short. He was a Green Beret—Army Special Forces. When she was pregnant with the boys, he deployed to Afghanistan where he was killed before they were born.

How she wished he knew them now. When they weren't in trouble they were so funny. She imagined they were like their father had been as a child; they certainly resembled him physically. They were large for their ages, rambunctious, competitive, bright, a little short-tempered and possessive. They both had a strong sentimental streak. They still needed maternal cuddling regularly and they loved all animals, even the tiniest ones. They tried to cover up their tears during Disney movies like *Bambi*. If one of them got scared, the other propped him up and reassured and vice versa. When they were forced together, like in the backseat of the car, they wanted space. When they were forced apart, they wanted to be together. She wondered if they'd ever take individual showers.

And just as she'd always griped at Charlie for never closing the bathroom door, she still longed for a little solitary bathroom time. The boys had been in her bubble, no matter what she was doing, since they could crawl. She could barely have a bath without company in the past five years.

So her life wasn't always easy. Was theirs? They didn't seem to realize they didn't have the average family life—they had a mom and no dad, but they had Uncle Conner. She showed them the pictures of their dad and told them, all the time, how excited he had been to see them. But then he'd gone to the angels.... He was a hero who'd gone to the angels...

So Disney World was a good idea. They'd all earned it.

Mickey didn't wear the boys down quite enough. Three days and nights at Disney World seemed to energize them. They squirmed the whole way to Sacramento on the plane and because they'd been confined, they ran around the hotel room like a couple of nut balls.

They set off for Virgin River right after breakfast, but as for the scenic drive to Virgin River, it was dark, gloomy and rainy. She was completely disappointed—she wanted to take in the beauty Conner had described—the mountains, redwoods, sheer cliffs and lush valleys. Ever the optimist, she hoped the gray skies would help the boys nod off.

But not right away, apparently.

"Andy has *Avatar!* It's my turn to have *Avatar!*"

"Christ almighty, why didn't I buy two of those," she mumbled.

"Someone wants soap in her mouth," Mitch the Enforcer muttered from the backseat.

It was hard to imagine what she'd be up against if Charlie were still with them. He had no patience and the filthiest language. Marines blushed when he opened his mouth. For that matter, Katie wanted to shout into the backseat, *I took you to goddamn Disney World! Share the goddamn movie!* "If I have to stop this car to deal with your bickering, it will be a very long time before we get to Uncle Conner's house! And then it will be straight to time-out!"

They made a noble effort, but it involved a great deal of grunting, shoving and squirming.

As soon as she got off Highway 5 and headed for the narrow, winding road that skirted Clear Lake the driving became more challenging. Sometimes it was harrowing. She passed what appeared to be a small dock house or shed that had broken apart in the lake, right off the road, but as she slowed, she saw that it was an RV that had slipped off the road and crashed into the water. She slowed but couldn't stop; there was no place to pull over and behind her were the sirens of first responders.

Once they got to Humboldt County, she turned off the freeway right at the coastal town of Fortuna and headed east on Highway 36, up into the mountains. This was a good, two-lane highway and as she rose into the mountains, the views took her breath away. Huge trees on the mountainsides reached into the clouds, lush farms, ranches and vineyards spread through the valleys below. She couldn't indulge in the views—there were no guardrails, nor were there wide shoulders. And before she'd gone very far up the mountain she found herself buried in the forest on a winding road that broke left, then right, then up, then down. The trees were so large, blocking what little light there was, and her headlights in the rain were a minor help.

Then it happened. She felt a bump, then heard a pop. The big car swerved, then listed to the left and went *kathump, kathump, kathump*. She pulled over as far as possible, but was on a very short straightaway between two curves, so still stuck out into the road a bit. Here's where having the supersized SUV wasn't so convenient.

"Stay in the car, in your seats," she told the boys. And she cautiously exited the car, watching for traffic coming around the curves in either direction. The rain came down in a steady sheet, although it was filtered by the boughs of huge pines and sequoias. Those pine needles didn't do much to keep her dry, however. She shivered in the cold rain and wondered, *This is June?* It had been so warm in Sacramento, she hadn't taken jackets or sweatshirts out of their suitcases. She hadn't accounted for the temperature drop in the mountains.

She crouched, sitting on the right heel of her Uggs, and glared at the traitorous tire in disgust. Flat as a pancake, rubber torn away. What a mess. It wasn't going anywhere, that was for sure.

Katie knew how to change a tire, but just the same, she got back in the car and took out her phone. On a vehicle this size, it could be a challenge. Maybe they were close enough to Virgin River for Conner to help.

No bars. No service. No help.

Well, that certainly diminished her options. She looked into the backseat. "Mommy's going to change the tire and I need you to stay in the car and sit very, very still. No moving around, all right?"

"Why?"

"Because I have to jack up the car where the flat tire is and if you wiggle around it could fall and maybe hurt me. Can you sit still? Very still?"

They nodded gravely. She couldn't have them out of the car, running wild in the forest or along this narrow highway. She shut off the SUV and went to the rear, lifting the hatch. She had to pull out a couple of suitcases and move the picnic basket to open the wheel well cover and floorboard. She pulled out the lug wrench and jack.

The first thing to do was actually the hardest for a woman her size—loosening the lug nuts before jacking up the car. She put her whole body into it, but she couldn't budge a single one. Not even the slightest bit. This was when it didn't pay off to be five foot four and a lightweight. She used a foot and two hands. Nothing. She stood up, pulled a rubber tie out of the pocket of her jeans and wound her long hair into a ponytail. She wiped her hands down her jeans and gave it another try, grunting with the effort. Still nothing. She was going to have to wait for someone to…

She heard a rumble that grew closer. And because today wasn't turning out to be one of her luckier days, it couldn't be some old rancher. Nope. It had to be a motorcycle gang. "Crap," she said. "Well, beggars can't be choosers." And she waved them down. Four of them pulled up right behind the SUV. The one in front got off his bike and removed his helmet as he approached her while the others stayed balanced on their rumbling bikes.

Whew, wasn't he a big, scary-looking dude. Huge and leather-clad with lots of hair, both facial and a long ponytail. He also jingled a little while he walked—there were chains around his boot heels, hanging from his belt and adorning his jacket. With his helmet cradled in the crook of his arm, he looked down at her. "Whatcha got?"

"Flat," she said, and shivered. "I can handle it if you'll just help me with the lugs. I'm in good shape, but

I'm no match for the air compressor torque that tightened 'em down."

He cocked his head and lifted one brow, probably surprised that a woman would know about the torque. He went over to the tire and squatted. "Dang," he said. "Doesn't get much flatter than that. I hope you have a spare."

"In the undercarriage. Really, I can—"

He stood up and cut her off. "Let's just get 'er done. That way the lugs on the spare will be as tight as these."

"Thanks, but I hate to hold you up. If you'll just—"

He completely ignored her, walking back to his bike and stowing his helmet. He pulled a few flat road warning triangles out of his side pocket and handed a couple to riders. "Stu, take these warning markers up the road to that curve. Lang, go back down to that last curve and put these out. Dylan, you can help change the tire. Let's do it."

And then he was walking back to where she stood, still holding the lug wrench. Now, Conner was a big man and this guy was yet bigger. As she stood dripping in the rain, she felt fully half his size. As two bikers rode away with their road markers, the fourth, Dylan, propped up his bike, removed his helmet and came toward them. And her eyes almost popped out of her head. Warning! Major hottie! His black hair was a little on the long side, his face about a couple of days unshaven, his body long and lean with a tear in each knee of his jeans. He walked with a slight swagger, pulling off his gloves, which matched his tan leather jacket, and stuffing them in the back pockets of his jeans, though they were so tight there couldn't be much room for anything. She lifted her eyes back to his face. He should be on a billboard.

"Let's make this easy," Number One was saying to Dylan. "How about you lighten the load a little bit." And then he applied the lug wrench, and with a simple, light jerk, spun the first lug nut, then a second, then a third. Piece of cake. For him.

Dylan approached her and she noticed his amazing blue eyes. He completely ignored her and began to pull things out of the back of the SUV—first a large, heavy suitcase, a smaller one, then the cooler. Meanwhile, the SUV was lifting, apparently already on the jack.

Dylan paused, cooler in his hands, looking down at her. She followed his gaze down. Swell. Her white T-shirt was soaked, plastered to her skin, her pretty little lace bra was now transparent, her nipples were tan bullets pointed right at him. He looked up and frowned. He put down the cooler, stripped off his leather jacket and draped it around her shoulders, pulling it closed.

Nice, she thought. Wet T-shirt display on the deserted road for a biker gang. "Thank you," she mumbled. And she backed away so he could empty the back and get the tire from the undercarriage.

"Must've hit a pothole or something," the first biker was saying. "That tire is done for."

She hugged the jacket around herself and his scent rose, his very pleasant musk combined with rain and forest. It was toasty inside, dripping on the outside.

Robyn Carr

Okay, maybe they weren't Hells Angels. Just a bunch of nut balls out for a ride in the rain?

While Dylan took the spare around the SUV to his buddy, Katie got into the suitcase on top and pulled out a dark, cowl-neck sweatshirt. She put the leather jacket in the back of the car and pulled the sweatshirt over her wet T-shirt. She looked down. Better.

Not long after her clothing adjustment, Dylan came around the back of the car, carrying the useless tire, his long-sleeved shirt glued against his totally cut, sculpted chest. His shoulders and biceps bulged with the strain of carrying the heavy tire. But, God, what a body. He probably shouldn't be out riding in the rain—he should be modeling or working with the Chippendales.

Stop, she told herself. *Great to look at, but I'm sworn off. I'm concentrating on my future and my family.*

After he stowed the tire, she picked up the jacket and held it toward him. "Here you go," she said. "Thanks."

"My pleasure. Hard to believe it's June."

"I was just thinking that."

And then he did the most unexpected thing. He put the jacket down in the back of the SUV and stripped off his soaked shirt; he put the jacket on over skin. Her mouth fell open slightly, her eyes riveted to his body until he snapped the jacket closed. Then she slowly looked up, and he smiled and winked. He walked back to his bike, shoved the wet shirt in a side pocket and returned to the back of the SUV just as it was lowering onto a new tire.

Dylan began to reload the SUV and for a second she

was just mesmerized, but then she shook herself and began to help, every once in a while meeting his eyes. Oh, God, he had Conner's eyes—crystal-blue and twinkling beneath thick, dark lashes. She also had blue eyes but they were merely ordinary blue eyes while Conner's (and Dylan's!) were more periwinkle and almost startling in their depth. Paul Newman eyes, her mother used to say. And this guy had them, too! Her parents must have had a love child they left on the church steps or something.

No. Wait. She knew him—the eyes, the name. It had been a long time ago, but she'd seen him before. Not in person, but on TV. On magazine covers. But then, surely it wasn't… Yes, the Hollywood bad boy. What had become of him since way back then?

"You can get back in if you want to," Dylan said. "Turn the heat up. I hope you don't have far to go."

"I'm almost there," she said.

Dylan put the cooler in, then the heaviest suitcase. He took a handkerchief out of his back pocket, wiped down his rain-slicked face and then began to wipe off his dirty hands. "You have a couple of stowaways," he said, glancing into the car.

She peeked into the SUV. A couple of identical sets of brown eyes peered over the backseat. "My boys," she said.

"You don't look old enough to have boys."

"I'm at least fifty now," she said. "Ever been on a road trip with five-year-old twins?"

"Can't say that I have."

Of course he hadn't, because he was some gorgeous godlike hunk who was as free as a bird and out either terrorizing or rescuing maidens in the forest. Wow.

"You're all set, miss," the big biker said as he came around the SUV, pulling on his leather gloves. Jeez, he had chains on those, too.

"Thanks for your help. The lugs get me every time."

"I'd never leave a lady in distress by the side of the road, my mother would kill me. And that's nothing to what my wife would say!"

"You have a wife?" she asked. And before she could stop herself, she added, "And a mother?"

Dylan burst out with a short laugh. He clapped a hand on the big guy's back and said, "There's a lot more to Walt than meets the eye, Miss… I didn't get a name…"

She put out an icy hand. "Katie Malone."

"I'm Dylan," he said, taking the hand. How in the world he had managed warm hands after changing a tire in the freezing rain, she would long wonder. "And of course, this is Walt, roadside good Samaritan." Then he addressed Walt. "I'll ride back and get Lang. We'll scoop up Stu on the way up the road."

"You should be just fine, Katie," Walt said. "Jump in, tell the little guys to buckle up, crank up the heater and watch the road."

"Right. Yes. Listen, can I pay you for your trouble? I'm sure it would've cost me at least a hundred bucks to have that tire changed."

"Don't be absurd," he said, startling her with his

choice of words. It just didn't seem like the vocabulary that would fit a big, scary biker dude. "You'd do the same for me if you could. Just be sure to replace that tire right away so you always have a spare."

"You always go out for a ride in the rain?" she asked.

"We were on the road already. But there are better days for it, that's for sure. If it had been coming down much harder, we'd have had to hole up under a tree or something. Don't want to slide off a mountain. Take care." Then he turned and tromped back to his Hog with the high handlebars.

Two

When Katie pulled up in front of the house in Virgin River, she saw her brother pacing back and forth on the front porch. He had told her that if she arrived before five the front door would be unlocked, yet there he was. She barely had the SUV in Park before the boys were out and tearing toward their uncle. He scooped them up, one in each arm, and just that sight alone caused all the tension she'd been feeling to float out of her, leaving her almost weak. Conner, like a great, faithful oak, always strong and steady.

She went up to the porch. "Why are you here?" she asked him.

"I wasn't really concentrating at work, so I came home to wait for you."

"Oh, Conner," she said softly, her voice quivering a little bit.

He frowned. "What's the matter, Katie?"

She opened her mouth to speak, but only shivered. Finally she croaked out, "I got caught in the rain."

"Let's get you inside. I'll get the bags. We can talk after the boys are occupied."

An hour later, with Katie fresh out of a hot, soothing shower and the boys crashed on the living room sectional in front of a movie, Conner poured her a cup of coffee. "Feel better?" he asked.

"Tons. I had a flat, that's how I got caught in the rain. Which, by the way, is freezing in the forest. A motorcycle gang stopped and changed it for me."

"Gang?"

"Motorcycle group?" she tried. "Not the Hells Angels, Conner. Just a bunch of bikers out riding in the rain, which begs the question… Never mind. I could've changed it, but I can never conquer those lugs. They were very nice men, apparently unable to listen to a weather report."

Conner sat opposite her at the small kitchen table. "What was it, Katie? You were talking about staying in Vermont. I didn't like that idea and I like this one lots better, but it was a sudden change of heart."

"Yeah, because I'm unstable, that's what. I had myself convinced I should find myself a guy like Keith, my old boss, even though the most passionate thing he said to me was, 'Great sea bass, Katie—you could open a restaurant'!" She shook her head. "That move to Vermont—it wasn't all bad. I made a few friends, the boys had fun at school, the neighbors were great. But I just didn't want to be alone anymore and I started thinking, I have to find a good man who could be a good father, and look what I almost did."

"What did you almost do?"

She took a sip of coffee. "Keith's an exceptional man and I bet there's no better father alive—he's gifted with kids. And right when my frustration level was about to peak because he still hadn't made a move, his sister Liz broke it to me. Keith is gay. It makes him nervous to think how his conservative community would treat a gay pediatric dentist, so he keeps it quiet. I saw myself getting desperate enough for companionship that I almost talked myself into a relationship with a man who had no physical attraction to me. None. Nada. Zip."

Conner sat back in his chair. "I thought he was a little on the gentle side, but I didn't see gay. Not that I'm any expert."

"Me, either. But to show you how off I was, I miss Liz more than Keith. And then..." She let that sentence trail off and glanced into her cup.

"Then?" he pushed.

"Then when I started sorting and packing, Andy asked if we had to move in the dark again and I knew—I have some work to do. On myself. On my family. The boys...they're so resilient that it's easy to miss the fact that they've been in a rocky place and they need stability."

Conner let go a low, resentful growl. "My fault," he muttered. "That goddamn trial..."

"I'm ignoring that comment. You weren't in charge and neither was I. We did well with what we had to manage. But, Conner, I have to make a change. Charlie was completely devoted to me, he was the most committed man I've ever known—to me, to the army, to his boys in Special Forces. And he wanted me in every sense of the word, and let me know it. I still miss that, Conner. I miss him enough that I almost made a mistake that would not only affect me, but the boys. I have to find a better way."

"You do great, Katie," he said, giving her hand a squeeze.

"Thanks, but I have to do great on *my own*. It's okay for the boys to depend on you, but I have to grow some independence. I want you for a brother, not the man I continually lean on. I'm going to lean on myself. Until I figure that out, I'm dangerous as a single woman on the hunt. Know what I mean?"

"Not really," he said.

"I know what you mean," a woman said.

Katie jumped in surprise, sloshing her coffee a little bit. There was a woman standing in the kitchen archway, a purse slung over her shoulder and some brown take-out bags in her hands.

"Hi, I'm Leslie," she said, smiling. She put the bags on the table.

"I didn't hear you come in, honey," Conner said, standing up to give her a kiss.

"There's a car parked out front, a movie playing to a couple of sleeping little boys in the living room, so I was extra quiet." She gave Katie a quick squeeze. "I know what you mean. I was in that exact place a year ago."

* * *

The open road or up in the air, rain or shine, were two of Dylan Childress's favorite places to think. In fact, that was how he met Walt, years ago. Walt had come through Payne, Montana, where Dylan and Lang operated their own small, fixed base operation and charter air service. They rode together for a day, Dylan introducing Walt to some of his favorite mountain trails and off-road routes with the best views. Dylan took Walt up in the Bonanza, a six-seater airplane for a different perspective on the views and Walt had loved that. And Walt, who had gone back to Sacramento to open a bunch of Harley franchises, had kept in touch, eager to return the favor someday.

The time had come. Living in Montana, there were only a few months of the year Dylan, Lang and the head of their maintenance operation, Stu, could enjoy their motorcycles. They took very few vacations or days off, so once a year in summer they treated themselves to a road trip. The Harleys were cheap to operate and they usually camped. Dylan had begun to worry this might be the last time the three of them might indulge their annual road trip because the business was struggling, so he got in touch with Walt and asked for some of his best California routes. Walt insisted on setting up a ride and joining them.

After arriving at the cabins Walt had reserved for them, all the riders wanted to do was warm up, dry off and have a stout meal. The first order of business was to check in, which amounted to meeting their landlord, shaking his hand and deciding who was staying with whom. There was a little grumbling about who would take the pull-out sofa beds because God knew, men couldn't share a mattress!

As far as Dylan was concerned, Luke Riordan's cabins by the river were a custom fit, and he was more than happy with the sofa. And not a little relieved that he wasn't camping on the wet forest floor.

When Dylan and one of his other pilots took a charter flight out of Payne or picked up passengers in Butte, Helena or some other city, they were frequently put up in nice hotels or lodges. A little luxury was granted the pilots since the kind of customers who could hire a jet could well afford it. But Dylan was a simple guy who preferred to relax in a more rustic setting. And this was definitely it.

The four men used two cabins. Dylan doubled up with Walt which left Lang to listen to Stu grumble about not having had a good date lately. Walt, being about the size of Goliath, got the bed.

Walt had found the Riordan cabins, operated by Luke, an ex-army Black Hawk pilot who owned his own Harley and had lots of tips about local, scenic, challenging rides. There were several things about this venue that Dylan looked forward to—maybe a little fishing in that river that ran by the cabin compound to see how it compared to some Montana rivers, the local bar and grill with the atmosphere and food Walt raved about, the challenge of the mountain roads around here, the remote location and, hopefully, some time with Luke, talking flying. Dylan would love to log a few hours in a Black Hawk.

When the men told Luke they were going to dry off, clean up and get back on the bikes to head for Virgin River for dinner, Luke said, "In this weather? Walt, take my truck, we're staying home tonight."

"That's awful neighborly, Luke," Walt said. "I'll treat her real nice."

"I know you will. The last time you were here you tweaked the engine for me and it's been purring like a kitten ever since. I appreciate it."

It took about thirty minutes to unload their packs into rooms, shower and pile in the truck, headed for town—enough bikes for one day. Walt took the wheel and talked the whole way about the cook who didn't provide a menu, cooked what he felt like, catered to the locals and visiting sportsmen and was real proud of his stuff. "I'm thinking on a wet day like today, a soup or stew—and it'll be something special."

Dylan and Lang had flown monied hunters to primo lodges all over the U.S. and Canada, but neither of them was prepared for Jack's. It was simple, but classy—well constructed and beautifully maintained. The interior was all dark, glossy wood, the animal trophies advertised for local wildlife and the ambiance was upscale in its own unaffected way. Even though there were a dozen empty tables in the place, the four of them sat up at the bar and the bartender immediately stretched out a hand to Walt.

"Hey! I've been wondering when you'd be back. This your crew?"

"My boys," Walt said. He indicated each one. "Dylan, Lang, Stu. We just got in about an hour ago, maybe less. Say hello, then tell me what's doing in the kitchen."

"I'm Jack," he said with a chuckle, introducing himself to each one. "And to the man with the appetite, you won't be disappointed. It might sound like just another day in Virgin River, but you'll be happy in the end. It's rainy—so it's soup. But you gotta trust Preacher—it's thick and creamy bean with ham soup, full of the best ham and onion and secret stuff. He likes to sprinkle a little cheddar on top—makes it stringy and rich. And he made the bread today—he's keeping it warm. He bakes when it rains, as predictable as my grandmother. And the pie of the day is apple from preserves he's had hanging around. For you tenderfoots who don't eat apple pie, there's a chocolate cake that will knock you out. Now, anyone want a beer or drink?"

"Bean soup?" Stu said under his breath.

"Didn't you hear the man? You gotta trust Preacher," Dylan said. Then he laughed. "My grandmother practically raised me on bean soup. Not the kind we're getting here, she could barely open a can. All she could do was scramble eggs, make toast, warm up soup and…" He laughed and shook his head. "She used to fry hot dogs, but she always bought all-beef so I'd have protein."

"You had a very strange childhood."

"You have no idea," he said.

When Dylan said his grandmother practically raised him on that soup, he wasn't talking about his early childhood, but much later, when she brought him to Montana to take over parenting him. She must have had nerves of steel to do that; he was a screwed up, spoiled, arrogant, defiant fifteen-year-old boy. Not just a challenging teenager, but a *star*. How she pulled him through to normalcy was one of the great mysteries of the universe.

Sometimes he felt like a Charles Dickens novel—*the best of times, the worst of times....* Being yanked out of his acting role and badass public life and carted off to some one-horse town in Montana, he thought he'd reached hell. On the other hand, someone finally cared about *him*. Focused on *him*. Worried about *him*. The first time Adele had given him bean soup, he spat it out, outraged. He'd been used to the very best; people had scrambled to keep him happy because if he was happy, they made money.

It had been years before he realized that Adele didn't exactly have a passion for bean soup or fried hot dogs, either. She'd been a megastar all her adult life and knew all about asshole child stars. And then he also realized she fed him bean soup every day until he finally *thanked* her for it.

"This is probably the best soup I've ever had," Dylan told Jack.

"I know. When someone around here caps a pig, or any other livestock for that matter, a lot of it goes to the clinic where my wife, the town midwife, works. We have a doc over there, too, but Mel, my wife, she usually brings her share to Preacher, since she can't cook worth crap and I feed my family here. It's usually a patient fee or an advance on a future patient fee—we have an interesting insurance system around here. People who need the doc and Mel—they make sure to share the wealth regularly. So Preacher, the second he sees something come into the bar, he starts thinking about how he can stretch it, what he can do with it. He has a lot of people he wants to take care of. He doesn't sleep at night until he has the best result imaginable. Mel might be the best thing that ever happened to me, but Preacher's gotta run a close second. He's the guy who makes this work."

"Is this your hometown?" Dylan asked.

"Nah, I'm a city boy, more or less. I needed something quiet after twenty in the Marines."

"You go to war?"

"Almost habitually," Jack said. "A few of the men I served with decided to settle here. You from Sacramento?"

Dylan shook his head. "Little town up north—Payne, Montana."

"How'd you hook up with Walt?" Jack wanted to know.

"Walt came through Montana and we met there. He was on some kind of solitary road trip, touring the U.S., and Montana is one of the most beautiful parts, so I took him into the mountains. We outran a moose once."

"Don't ever get the idea a moose is cute," Walt said. "That sucker didn't like me. Then Dylan took me into the air in his little plane," Walt said. "I've been promising to show 'em my state ever since."

"We were looking for someone to put together a road trip that would take us some interesting places we hadn't seen, and by interesting I mean, off the grid. With some views."

"Well, you got views, interesting and off the grid," Jack confirmed. "So, what does a man do in Payne, Montana?"

That brought an automatic smile as he remembered Adele on the phone to a Realtor when she was hauling his messed up fifteen-year-old ass to Payne. She said, "Find me something with built-in chores."

"Small charter flying business," Dylan answered. "Little, bitty airport."

Jack lifted an eyebrow. "Is there a big call for that sort of thing in Payne?"

"Some, but business is down like the rest of the world. When business is good we not only shuttle to larger airports, we pick up passengers all over the place and take them just about anywhere they want to go. We do a lot of corporate retreats, group trips, act like a real small regional sometimes, you name it. We've been known to fly hunters, rock bands and basketball teams. We're flexible."

"You're a pilot?"

"Among other things. Stu's head of maintenance, and Lang also flies and runs the instruction arm of the business—we give flying lessons, instrument instruction, et cetera. There are a few others attached to the company. Seems like we all have other things to do besides be on the road all the time."

"Sounds like it could be fun," Jack said. "If it makes a living."

"We live in Payne, Montana, man," Dylan said. "Population fifteen hundred. If we can pay for fuel for the planes, hay for the horses and oil for the furnaces in our houses, we don't need that much of a living."

"How do the wives feel about that?"

"Lang is the only married one and not only does his wife stay involved in the company, she tries to double up his schedule, keep him out of town more. Five kids, and she isn't interested in six."

Lang leaned forward on the bar and grinned. "What can I say? It just doesn't take much to keep me happy."

Dylan gave a chuckle. Not many people knew how much Dylan envied Lang's ability to do that, to make a happy home and have normal, civilized kids with a good, solid woman at his side. But, having come from a crazy, mismatched Hollywood family, he had long ago accepted that his genetic makeup probably prevented that possibility. Adele was the only sane and stable one. "Takes even less to make me happy," Dylan said.

"I'd think a single guy like yourself would be inclined toward some bigger town where there are more possibilities," Jack said.

"I get around. But I'll always live in Payne. Alone."

Jack gave the bar a wipe. "Yeah, I used to say that.

Look out. Tougher men than you have eaten those words."

"Like you, Jack?" Dylan asked. "You eat those words?"

"Boy howdy, as my wife would say."

Katie realized very quickly that coming to Virgin River was one of her better ideas. It took a day and that was all. Here she thought she'd been giving up, running home to Conner, but she found so much more. When she met her future sister-in-law, Leslie, she had found true family. Conner and Leslie weren't officially engaged, but the chemistry between them was obvious and they both admitted they'd been talking about marriage. Since both of them came from divorce experiences, they were taking it slow and easy.

While it continued to rain all through the evening, Katie and Leslie sat up late in the living room, wrapped in their robes, talking about anything and everything. The boys took the second bedroom and Katie would take the couch.

"Conner talks about how he missed so much time with the boys because he was working all the time. He wants to change that," Leslie said. "We're hoping you're not in a big hurry. It's been such a stressful spring for everyone—you both deserve a break."

"My idea exactly," Katie agreed. "I may have to get settled somewhere other than this little town for work and school for the boys, but I'm not going far. The boys need you and Conner in their lives. And I'll stick around, but I don't intend to live off you and Conner."

"Just take it slow. Conner wants to teach the boys to fish, take them camping, goof around with them, just enjoy them for a change."

"And what does he think I'm going to do while he goofs around?" Katie asked.

"Anything you want. We have a new school and before it opens for business in the fall, there's a summer program. It's real flexible, like a day camp—you don't have to commit to taking the boys every day, but it would give them playmates and give you a little freedom, something you haven't had much of since they were born."

"I wouldn't know what to do with myself."

"Well, wait till you see the darling little cabin Conner found for you—you'll think you're on vacation. Act like it!"

The next morning dawned bright and clear, the morning air crisp. She and Conner loaded up the luggage she'd pulled out the night before and she followed him out of town, down a long tree-lined road, then turned onto a drive at a mailbox. And there, sitting in the clearing with the sunlight streaking through the tree branches, sat the most adorable little A-frame cabin with a wide porch. There were hanging pots full of red geraniums and white Adirondack chairs on the porch.

She slowly got out of the SUV and approached it in wonder. There were flowering shrubs all around, lush ferns, a variety of tall pines, even a few sequoias. The boys were instantly out of the car, racing around the little cabin, while Katie stood transfixed. The A-frame seemed to be contained in a spotlight of sunshine. It looked like an enchanted cabin.

"Boys!" Conner shouted. "Do not go in the woods! Stay near the house! They're not going to listen, are they?"

"Conner," she said on a breath. "How did you find this place?"

"It's Jack's—he owns the bar in town. Now listen— see these shrubs that surround the place? Lilac and hydrangea and a bunch of stuff, but you also have blackberries, which you can pick and eat when they're ripe, according to Jack, but remember that bear also happen to like them…"

Her eyes widened. "Boys! Come here! Right now!"

"We'll go over the bear rules," Conner said. "You'll also have deer from time to time, and you want to learn those rules, too, because if you have bucks in rut, you really don't want to be involved. Does and fawns, not a big worry—they'll probably just run off if you happen upon them, but a mating buck might take the interference personally, if you get my drift."

"What man wouldn't?" she muttered. "How long do you give the boys before they're lost in the woods?"

"You're going to have to stay on top of that. Listen, if you don't feel comfortable out here…"

"So far, I love it. Can we check out the inside?"

"It's not locked. Help yourself. According to Jack,

this place has quite a history—his wife lived here before they got married and moved into a larger house. Their first child was born here. Then others lived here—the most recent being the town doctor. We just finished his house and got him moved. We barely put up fresh paint in here…"

She stopped and turned to look up at her brother before she reached the porch. "Conner, I love it. I love Leslie. I think I'm going to love the town—but you do understand, I have to find the boys something permanent with the right schools, sports, all that…"

"I know. I know. But can you just get your bearings? Take at least a few weeks to get to know the area?"

She could do that. After Disney World and a long coast-to-coast move, she was more than ready to take a break. She had to get her life in order, get the boys set up, find a job that she really saw herself staying in for a long time. The boys would be starting first grade in the fall. She'd love to be nested by then. Here? Nearby?

The inside of the cabin was as perfect for her as the outside had been—two bedrooms separated by a bath downstairs, a loft upstairs and the rest of the downstairs space was a living room/kitchen just the right size for a single mom and two little boys. "There seems to be one important item missing," she said to her brother. "Where's the TV?"

"I guess it went with the doc to his new house. But Jack said you have satellite out here, so we'll fix you up. We'll make a run to a bigger town on the weekend, get a TV."

"It's either that or take them off Xbox and Wii cold-turkey, and I might not be up to that."

"What did we have as kids?" Conner asked. "Did we have all this electronic stuff?"

"Atari and Nintendo," she told him. "And immediately following that, I think we went to work in the store. By the way, is there a hardware store around here?"

"On the coast, Fortuna and Eureka. And that has inspired some thought."

"Oh?"

"I've been thinking this place could use one. Maybe somewhere between here and the closer small towns, like Grace Valley, Clear River. Paul could use one—he's getting most of his stuff shipped in from a wholesaler. It wouldn't be like the last store—there aren't enough custom jobs around here to support it, but folks around here have to drive a long way for nails and paint."

She put her fingers on her temples. "Okay, don't give me too much to think about yet," she said. "Just help me get my stuff inside and go to work unpacking. I'll get settled and meet you in town for dinner."

While Conner brought in the boxes she had shipped, she wrangled the suitcases. She found someone had put staples in the refrigerator and cupboard—milk, cereal, bread, lunch meat, eggs. "Les," Conner said. "She thinks of everything."

Conner went over a few details—no food or garbage left outside to tempt bears, there was bear repellant in the high cupboard above the microwave and a fire extinguisher under the sink. If you leave a pie cooling in the window sill, don't count on it to be there later. And no wandering in the woods—it was way too easy to get lost if you didn't know your way.

"This bear thing sounds serious," Katie said.

"Jack said he heard Doc Michaels saw one bear, one time in two years. And Jack has seen more than that at his house. They're all over the place, and mostly run off at the sight of a human, but no point in taking chances. You'll have to talk to the boys about that, supervise if they're playing outside and get them inside if you see one."

"How many people have been attacked?" she asked.

"Jack said in the eight years he's been here, zero. But still, keep an eye out."

When you travel with only the essentials, it doesn't take long to settle in. Her keepsakes of Charlie's medals and their family pictures went in the trunk that served as a coffee table—the boys liked to look at them sometimes. Clothes went in drawers and closets and toys in the loft. The boys wanted Xbox hooked up immediately, though they seemed not to notice there was no TV until she pointed that out. So after lunch, the three of them threw a ball for a while in the clearing, then they kicked a soccer ball for a while, then the boys had a little quiet time with their videos and the portable DVD player.

And Katie had her own respite on the porch. It was miraculous, being surrounded by nothing but nature. The sounds of the forest—a variety of birds, rustling, the occasional caw or quack—lulled her and she let her eyes close. No growling, she observed.

Burlington had been so much quieter than Sacramento, but this—this was almost the wilderness. Having been raised in a city, Katie had no idea why the pristine and barely populated parts of the country held such appeal for her. She really hoped to take the boys to visit all those national wonders when they got a little older—Yellowstone, the Grand Canyon, Yosemite, Big Sur. Katie and Conner's parents had taken them to Yosemite when they were young and she never wanted to leave. Conner had looked up the face of El Capitan at the climbers and nearly passed out. He could barely stand on a ladder, heights made him so woozy, but Katie wouldn't mind learning rock climbing. The idea of scaling El Capitan had thrilled her. She had looked up that sheer rock at the climbers who spent the night in sleeping bags suspended from stakes pounded into the flat face of the rock and had envied them.

Even though she was a small girl, she was the athlete in the family and had planned a life of running a girls' gym in a school, that's what she'd studied. She had a degree in Phys Ed. Nothing could make her happier than going to work every day in a pair of shorts and sneakers with a whistle around her neck.

But she hadn't done any of these things. Instead she'd buried both parents, finished college, helped run the store, married a Green Beret and had twin boys—kind of a full plate.

By four o'clock, not only was her little cabin in the

woods in perfect order, her boys were in good moods because they'd had some downtime. She'd had some quiet herself and was giving serious thought to never buying a TV. Freshly showered and ready for dinner, she loaded the boys into the SUV and headed for her brother's. Leslie wasn't home from work yet, so Conner jumped in Katie's car and they drove the two blocks to Jack's. When she pulled up beside a neat little row of motorcycles she said, "Well, look at that, Conner. You're going to meet our motorcycle gang."

Three

It was a whole new scene at the bar now that Preacher knew Walt and his gang were in town. Walt planned on having every evening meal with Preacher and Preacher was clearly showing off. The cook was in the bar as opposed to the kitchen, which was not typical. "Tonight my best of show—stuffed trout. Trout's fresh—at least what you're getting is fresh. Me and Jack stood in the river this morning, reeling it in. Rice and corn-bread stuffing, squash, onion and pepper side from Jilly Farms... You probably don't know about Jilly Farms—she grows organic heirloom fruits and vegetables and her sister, a chef, cans a lot and makes up special sauces and bisques, which I'm willing to take off her hands—the flavor of these vegetables is beyond good."

"Bring it on!" Walt said, causing his pals to laugh. "Can't wait to hear about tomorrow night. What are the chances you'll have some of that seafood bouillabaisse again while I'm in town?"

"Aw, sorry man—not unless lobster tail and scallops

go on special at Costco. Otherwise it's just too high dollar for this camp."

"I'll get it," Walt said, with a fist on the bar. "How much do you need?"

Preacher looked startled. "If you're serious, it takes a lot to make it right. A case of each, fresh not frozen. And ask how long it's been on ice. Sniff it—I want you to smell the meat, not bottom of a boat or shipping crates. Can you do that?"

"I can do that," Walt said. "This is an exceptional nose. I'll make these old boys a map for their ride and head to Costco. If they don't have what I need…"

"If they don't have it fresh, go to the fish markets in Eureka—the closer to the marina the better."

"Done!" Walt said. "You boys won't mind too much, will you? You'll get payback when you eat."

"We're good," Dylan said with a laugh.

"How was today?" Jack asked. "You had sun."

"Awesome. There are some back roads along the cliffs right on the ocean. Good ride. There are a million logging trucks out there. They take up the whole road and then blast their horn at us."

"That's just a friendly hello. Don't you boys have loggers in Montana?"

"Our friends are mostly ranchers or loggers," Lang said. "Cutting back on the logging a little these days, and we were growing dude ranches like clover for a while there, but when money gets tight, girly stuff like that tends to be in a decline, though there are still quite a few."

"Easy," Dylan said. "I think I'm a dude with a ranch."

"You ranch, Dylan?" Jack asked.

"Depends on your perspective. I have chickens, some goats, a bull, six cows, two horses and a hand who's been watching that property for years. He was old twenty years ago, so now he's ancient. I don't exactly—" He was about to say, "earn money," but he was cut off when the door to the bar opened and a man, woman and set of five-year-old twins came in. He watched as she took them in, all smiles. Then she took the hand of the man she was with and led him to the bar, to Walt first.

"Conner, this is Walt, and he changed my tire the other day."

Whoa boy, Dylan thought. This little girl cleaned up nice. She had the look of a drowned Chihuahua when he met her, but here she was all fluffed and buffed and sexy as hell. He grinned stupidly.

Walt turned on his stool and grasped the man's hand. "Well, good to see you again. We met the last time I passed through. Yes, the miss here had herself an impressive flat. She was determined she was gonna change it if she could just get past the lugs."

Conner laughed and shook his hand. "Katie can change a tire—but the lugs always give her trouble. To tell the truth, they give me trouble."

"And, Conner," she said, moving to stand beside Dylan. "This is Dylan. He also helped. I didn't meet the others."

Conner shook his hand, thanked him, and then

Dylan introduced Lang and Stu. While Conner stood having conversation about the rides with Walt and the boys, Katie didn't move away. Of course he was at one end of their foursome while Walt was at the other, but still. She was right there beside him.

"The husband?" he asked rather quietly.

"No," she returned just as quietly, acting secretive, but she was mocking him. "The brother. Uncle Conner."

"Ah," he said. He took a drink of his beer. "Divorced?" he asked.

She leaned toward him. "No. Widowed."

That clearly surprised him. "I guess you need to be near your brother..." he speculated.

"Well, the boys do," she said. "Despite Conner's insistence to the contrary, I'm pretty self-sufficient. But you know big brothers..."

"Hmm," he said, as if he did. His big brother was in prison; his big sister was following in their mother's footsteps with lots of scandal and unsuccessful relationships.

And then Jack was there. Jack seemed to be everywhere. "How's that cabin working out for you, Katie?"

She lit up. Her eyes got so big, so bright. "Jack, it's wonderful! Conner told me some of the history—your wife lived there? Your son was born there?"

"It was provided to Mel for the first year of her service to the town as the midwife. We lived in the cabin while I was building our house and David showed up— kind of fast, during a thunderstorm. We bought the place, just to have a little extra space around here for… well, for things like this," he finished, with a smile.

"So, just how bad is the bear situation?" she wanted to know.

"Not significant, but they're there."

"If you say they're more afraid of me than I am of them…"

Jack laughed. "As long as you don't get between a mother and her cub, it's a true statement."

"So, you Virgin River people have sissy bears?"

"Scavenger sissy bears," Jack said. "Keep the garbage inside and drive it to the Dumpster in town. If you're scared…"

She scoffed. "I'm not scared. I love the cabin. It's perfect. I'm going to have to run into one of the bigger towns to buy a TV, however. My boys have an Xbox. But I love the loft—a perfect place for it. It's fantastic to put them up there with their noise."

"They won't make it without TV?" Dylan asked. And he was remembering when Adele refused to have a TV in the house, but of course her reasons were different. Dylan had been addicted to TV, to the news, celebrity gossip, sitcoms and series he'd been competing with. She was trying to get him off *all* his drugs.

"They might," she said with a laugh, "but will I? I need a whip and a chair for those two."

He glanced at the boys, already staking out a table, sitting on opposite sides and throwing packets of sugar at each other. "Gee. They look so well behaved…"

She just laughed and said, "Nice running into you, Dylan."

"Wait a sec," he said, catching the sleeve of her blouse to detain her. "So are you buried in the woods?"

"Sort of," she answered. "But I'm only about ten minutes out of town in this picture-perfect little clearing surrounded by flowers and blackberry bushes in a cute little cottage... It was way more than I hoped for. Excuse me, I'd better pick up the sugar packets..."

And she was gone across the room.

And wow, he thought. With her hair down and dry, she was such a fox. While he sat and watched, her brother introduced her to person after person. A woman came into the bar and sat with Katie and the boys; Jack took the newcomer a glass of wine without asking for her order. Dylan supposed it was like that around here, Jack knowing what everyone wanted. Then he spoke to Katie and fetched her one, as well.

Once their mother was sitting with them there was very little funny business from the twins because they didn't get away with anything—she seemed to have eight arms. She grabbed the packets, confiscated the ketchup bottle, removed the straws, pulled one back into his chair while she caught another by the wrist before he spilled his water. What she did even more easily was laugh with her friend. Sister-in-law? While Conner was BSing at the bar with men who came in and one by one introducing them to his sister, the girls were laughing and keeping the sugar packets in the container on the table.

"Where's Preacher? Get him out here!" Walt said. "This is unbelievable—this trout is amazing! The man is a genius!"

Dylan looked at his plate and saw that he'd been eating, but it hadn't even registered. "Excellent," he finally said. He took another bite. "Really excellent."

While the little boys had child-size hamburgers, Katie and her friend had the trout and made a very big deal about it with a lot of eyeball rolling, fanning their faces and letting their eyes fall closed as they hummed in ecstasy. Katie tried to coax a little fish into her son's mouth, but he shook his head and resisted, which made the women laugh.

She positively sparkled. But he wasn't interested in sparkle right now—he had too much on his mind. His business, his company, was in trouble and the only thing that mattered right now was coming up with a solution to their financial crisis. Besides, even though he was a world-class flirt, he was *not* attracted to young mothers. He was never tempted to get involved with a woman who had kids. He'd grown up around that— yours, mine and ours—and it might've worked in the movies, but it didn't work in real life.

But when Jack brought him a cup of coffee he asked, "How long are you renting that little cabin for?"

Jack gave a small smile. "At least a couple of weeks, but probably the whole summer. There's no waiting list. Why? You interested?"

"Maybe," Dylan said. "Like sometime in the future… if I get back down this way…"

"Really?" Jack asked. He shifted his eyes toward Katie and said, "I thought maybe you were interested right now."

With the enthusiasm Walt poured over Preacher's dinners, Dylan might've wondered if he had been more influenced by the food than their routes. But he had to admit, the riding around here was awesome. And it wasn't an original idea; they passed and followed a number of groups of riders while they were on the narrow mountain roads, the edgy cliff roads, beachfront, the dark paths through the redwood groves, the sunny hilltop ranch roads and the vineyards.

They stopped along the road to help bikers who had problems; Walt handed out a lot of business cards. None of his cards said President and CEO. They all said Harley-Davidson Sales and Maintenance. He drew attention away from himself. There really *was* a lot more to Walt than met the eye. Walt was an extremely successful businessman. Because of the look Walt presented, that of social outcast living hand to mouth, it was hard to imagine the amount of business acumen buried beneath that shaggy beard that would lead him to own five dealerships and build a small fortune. But he had.

"You have to remember, while the economy and fuel prices worked against you, they work in my favor," Walt told the Childress Aviation contingent. "Motorcycles— fuel efficient—and sold in a moderate climate where there are very few days of the year they can't be ridden."

"Yeah, we couldn't get away with that in Payne," Dylan said.

The four bikers sat on a ridge in Mendocino County that overlooked vineyards and the ocean. Their bikes were propped up on stands, and they were in various positions of repose with big submarine sandwiches and cans of cola.

"I get that," Walt said. "What's up with the company, Dylan? Last time we rode together, you couldn't shut up about it. This trip, you're not talking in a real obvious way."

Dylan took a long drink of his soda and lifted his head. "Sales are way down," he said. "In this economy, not only is fuel too expensive to run a cost-effective flying operation, but people don't hire charters as often. They fly their executives commercial. Coach. We're not profitable—we're barely above the red line."

It was quiet for a minute.

"Bummer," Walt said.

"We're probably going to have to downsize. We're going to have to give up the BBJ."

"Oh, no!" Stu wailed. "Not the BBJ!"

That made Dylan smile. As a mechanic, Stu so loved that BBJ.

"What's a BBJ?" Walt asked.

"A Boeing Business Jet—737 configured for luxury business travel. Instead of 120 passengers, more like 60.

Perfect for a sports team, a group of executives, a rock band. We've been leasing it."

"It's sweet," Stu said mournfully.

"We managed without her for a long time," Dylan said. "And we talked about this before—that's a damned expensive jet for a small company."

"I don't know if this'll help," Walt said. "My dad is real successful in lots of different businesses and one thing he taught me—always have an exit strategy. Just in case your current plan doesn't work, always know what your endgame is and where you're going next."

"What's your exit strategy?" Dylan asked.

"That's part B of the plan," Walt said. "My plan probably won't work for anyone but me—but I never put all my eggs in one basket. I invested outside my franchises as well as in them, so I'd have a little nest egg in a worst-case scenario. The idea of being a president and CEO doesn't mean anything to me—the only thing I've ever cared about are the people and the bikes. So with a little nest egg as a cushion, I can be real happy as a wrench. It's what I'm best at anyway." Walt took a long pull on his soda. "You just have to be clear about what drives you."

"I like to fly. I like living in Payne. I don't know what else there is."

"I'm a different animal, Dylan. As long as I have my little house, my bike, my parents in good health, my brothers on my nerves and Cassie in my bed, I have just about everything I need. I can always find work. It wouldn't be high dollar work, but it would be honest work." His cell phone twittered and he pulled it out of his vest pocket. "Speak of the devil," he said, grinning like a fourth grader. "Hey, baby…" Then he walked away from his group to have a private conversation.

And after all that baring of souls, all Stu had to say was, "God, I'd hate to lose that BBJ. She's *sweet!*"

The afternoon ride was not only beautiful, but silent. That part was typical as bikers didn't have conversations when they wound noisily around the mountain curves and broke single file for logging trucks. They ended their day as they had the three days before—at Jack's.

"Has Preacher got the bouillabaisse going?" Walt wanted to know, because he'd been to the marina and delivered the seafood components.

"I think you'll be satisfied," Jack said. "I've been helping and I'm satisfied."

"And how do you help?" Dylan asked.

"Every so often I wander back there, scoop out a little and let him know how he's doing."

They all laughed. Jack served up a couple of beers, a cup of coffee for Walt and a cola for Lang. By now, given the end of their fourth day in town, when people stopped by the bar, they wanted to know what the bikers had seen that day. And the men were more than happy to describe their ride, the views, the little towns they rode through, the other riders they ran into and sometimes rode with for a while.

They raved about the stew, had some coffee and dessert, and eventually said their goodbyes because they were heading out in the morning. There was a lot of handshaking all around. Preacher came out of the kitchen where he and Walt grasped fists and pulled each other shoulder to shoulder like brothers.

"You come back," Preacher said.

"Absolutely," Walt promised. "And you know how to reach me if you ever feel like a trip to the valley. I have some places I'd love to take you for dinner."

And then they retired to the cabins.

When they got there they found Luke was just stirring up a fire in a shallow pit in front of his porch and it was natural to wander down that way. Luke's wife, Shelby, sat in a chair on the porch and their handyman, Art, was beside her. Luke welcomed them all to join them and before long Walt had himself a chair by the fire while Lang, Stu and Dylan stood around with Luke. They talked about nothing in particular—weather, fishing, the long ride back to Montana. Little by little they broke up—Shelby went inside, Art retired to his cabin, Walt decided to turn in. And finally Luke indicated a bucket of sand.

"I'm calling it a day, boys. When you're done with the fire, bury it. We're coming up on fire season."

"You bet," Dylan said. "If we don't see you in the morning…"

"I'm up early," he said. "Knock before you go. It's been a real pleasure."

And then they were left, the Childress Aviation management, sitting on the porch steps in front of a small fire. A few moments of quiet passed before Lang asked, "So…this is really it for the company, huh?"

"Not necessarily. We're definitely gonna have to lose the BBJ," Dylan said, "but that should give us six months to figure out the next move. Either we find some charters for the Bonanzas and the Lear to keep us going or, the next step is, alternate work plans. We have a snowplow for the runway—maybe we start a little plowing business in the winter."

Lang laughed. "I've been using that plow on my road anyway."

"If you two can manage to find Montana on your own, I want to spend a little more time in California," Dylan said. "I'm going to check out the smaller airports around here, see if there's any work for our charters, any interest in a partnership. We have some things in common—charters into the mountains and isolated hunting and fishing locations. And also…" He paused. "I'm considering another idea. Sometimes over the years I'd hear from an old friend of mine, a producer, that he'd like to do a movie, if I had any interest. Jay Romney—he's one of the good guys. I should listen to his ideas. It could keep us in business."

"Make a movie?" Stu asked, suddenly interested.

Dylan lifted a corner of his mouth in a half smile. "I've made a couple of movies. And had that long-running sitcom as a kid."

"Yeah, but make a movie now?" Stu asked.

"I could," he said. "If the terms are right."

"Would actresses be involved?" Stu asked.

Dylan laughed and Lang gave Stu a wallop to the back of the head.

"Hey! I'm just saying…"

"There would undoubtedly be actresses, but I have no idea what he has in mind. Could be a totally ridiculous sitcom reunion show of some kind, or it could be something else. But if there's significant money, I should talk to him. Could buy Childress Aviation a couple of years and give the economy time to turn around."

"I hate to think of you doing anything you hate," Lang said. "Life's too short."

"What's the big deal?" Stu asked. "Make a lot of money, date actresses, have some fun… Tell him I'll do it."

Lang and Dylan had been best friends since college, so Lang knew everything there was to know about Dylan's childhood, but Stu didn't.

"My experience as a child actor wasn't good," he said. "I thought it was at the time because I was spoiled and could have anything I wanted as long as I did the job I was paid to do because a lot of other jobs depended on it. But I was an ass. Every kid on that set was an ass and we were pure trouble—I'm sure people hated to deal with us. By the time I was thirteen my best friend, Roman, and I were fooling with liquor, pot and girls when we could get away with it, which was often. We pulled pranks, we busted up property, made off with cars we weren't licensed to drive. I thought we were screwing around and having fun. We were cocky.

Immune to failure. I didn't really get that Roman was in over his head. He died of an overdose at the age of sixteen—he took a bunch of his mother's pills and washed 'em down with rum, looking for a high. He had been my closest friend for a long time. We weren't together the night he died. I was fifteen. The whole thing—it almost destroyed me."

Stu was younger than Dylan and Lang and hadn't been up to speed on the gossip surrounding Dylan's Hollywood career. Plus, being a guy, he had no fascination with another guy's antics. He merely whistled.

"My grandmother flew back to L.A. from London, took me to Roman's funeral and got me out of Hollywood. She put her own career on hold and raised me in Payne until I went to college. She probably saved my life. So, going back to that lifestyle…"

"Yeah, but you're not stupid anymore," Stu said. "You're older now."

Dylan opened his mouth to speak, to explain that it was more complicated than that, that he had an entire family there in various levels of fame and infamy, from his half sister's chronic problems with drugs to his half brother's long running habit of trashing hotel rooms in which porn stars or hookers always seemed to be present. One stepsister was in drug treatment and a stepbrother in jail for dealing. And that was not to mention his mother, who he considered the worst of all. But before he could say any more, Lang put a firm hand on his shoulder and, in the dark, gave his head the smallest shake.

Don't bother, he was saying. "All Stu wants is a girl to spend the night with. He's not going to understand any of this."

"Right," Dylan said. "So I'll get in touch with Jay and find out if this is just a lot of talk or if there's real interest with a contract and money attached. And if it's a way to keep us afloat a couple of years, I'll consider it."

Stu grinned hugely and stood up. "Call if you need backup on that movie or at some Hollywood parties!"

"You'll be the first," Dylan said drily.

And Stu ambled off to his cabin.

It was quiet around the fire for a minute before Lang said, "You probably should've told him you're not keeping the BBJ, even if you get an Oscar."

Dylan laughed.

"Don't do this unless it really feels right," Lang said. "Don't do it for me. I can always manage, you know that."

"Yeah? You have a wife and five kids."

"Five brilliant kids. I'll rent 'em out. Sell 'em to the circus."

Dylan laughed with a shaking of his head. Lang and Sue Ann were the most devoted and conscientious parents Dylan had ever known.

"Seriously."

"Yeah, trust me—I'm not stupid anymore," he said, echoing Stu. "I'm older now." And then with a touch of solemnity he said, "Trust me. I take this very seriously.

Jay Romney's a decent guy or I wouldn't even talk to him."

Lang stood up. "Do what you want, I've always got your back. But I'm with Walt—it doesn't take that much to keep me happy and working. I'd be happy to run that snowplow around town until Childress Aviation gets on its feet again. I'm better at driving a snowplow than running a company anyway."

Dylan stood and put out his hand. "Thanks, Lang. Can you manage without me while I stay behind?"

"You have to ask?"

"This is your chance to file a complaint with management."

Lang just gave a snort of laughter. "You going to bed?" Lang asked.

"I might sit here awhile."

"Kill the fire," Lang reminded him. "See you in the morning. I expect a good send-off."

Four

Katie laughed at what seemed like a perfect life shaping up. She'd had a great dinner with her brother last night—burgers on the grill with Leslie. She took her boys to the new Virgin River school, introduced them to Miss Timm, the teacher, and signed them up for the summer camp program. They needed at least one program to keep them busy, and to keep them from becoming bear food. She couldn't watch them every second. Then she went back to her enchanted cabin in the woods and installed the newly purchased TV in the loft, hooking it up to the satellite dish. Then she changed her oil.

How sexy, she thought. Well, after a major trip, that was a good idea, and these were the kinds of things it was always hard to find time for. When she'd finished and used a cone to pour the oil into an empty plastic milk container for discarding, she relaxed on her porch with a soda. She drank it out of the can and put her feet up on the porch rail. A small shaft of sunlight on the porch warmed her bare legs; it was nice to finally be in shorts again. Summer in the mountains would be so much more comfortable than the hot, steamy summers of Sacramento had been.

The hood of the SUV was still up, the jug of oil sitting next to the oil-coated pan on the ground and she thought, *I am seriously demented, because I consider this a flawless life.* Time for everything. No rush. Someone else watching the boys for a while. Isolated in the woods, surrounded by the beauty of nature. In fact, if it hadn't been marred by the growl of an engine, she would think she was in the Garden of Eden.

And then he drove his motorcycle right into her yard.

She didn't move a muscle, but took a drink of her cola as he, hidden behind the dark visor of his helmet, revved his engine a couple of times.

Then he shut down and got off the bike, dragging off the helmet. She gave herself a lot of credit for not sharply inhaling at the shock of his good looks. He swaggered toward her, peeling off his gloves. He had that swagger thing down; it was probably due to the constriction of the tight jeans around his hips. She took another slow slug of the soda. "Lost?" she finally asked.

"Just checking out the back roads," he answered. "Car trouble?"

"Nope. Everything's fine."

"You usually park with the hood up like that?"

"I just changed the oil," she informed him. "Lots of miles on that car in the last few months. I just moved here from Vermont."

He grinned at her and touched his cheek, indicating the oil on hers. "You might'a got a little on you, there."

"Yeah?" she asked, returning the grin. "I'll clean up later. I thought you left. I heard the gang pulled outta town."

"The boys left," he said, slapping his gloves into the palm of his hand and looking around her clearing. "I'm hanging out for a couple of days. Taking a closer look at this place. Interesting area."

"Don't you have a job?" she asked, unable to keep the sarcasm from her voice.

"Right now this is my job," he answered. "Don't you have a job?"

She gave him that one, laughing. "Besides mothering five-year-old boys? Not yet," she said, finally taking her feet off the rail and standing up. She tugged on her shorts; they'd been riding up. "Want a Coke?"

"Why not." He shrugged.

"Can okay?"

"I wouldn't have it any other way."

She disappeared into the cabin and was back in seconds with a cold can. She handed it to him and he studied it briefly. "Diet," he finally said.

"Well, if I sat on a vibrating machine all day, I probably wouldn't have to watch my weight, either. By the way, who pays you to do that? I might be interested in that job."

He came up on the porch and casually took the second chair, propping his feet up on the rail as hers had been. He wore leather pointy-toed cowboy boots;

she wore old beat-up tennis shoes with a little oil on them.

"I probably wasn't clear. The bike was recreation while I was riding with my friends but it's now transportation—I'm here on business." He popped the top on the can and took a drink. He made a face.

She returned to her seat, put her feet back on the rail. "What kind of business?"

"Well…my friends and I have a small air charter operation in Montana. Very small. A little airport in the middle of a bunch of national parks, great hunting grounds and dude ranches that aren't doing such a great business right now. People are a little too hard up for fancy vacations. So I'm checking out the area fixed base operations to see if there's any opportunity around here."

She sat up a little. "Really? You fly?"

He gave a nod. "I fly. Our airport is a long way from the big airports, so, sometimes people need a puddle jumper. Or a charter to a lodge or something."

Genuinely interested, she turned and faced him. "Fun," she said, smiling. "I'd love to do that. Fly planes. Or jump out of them. Fun."

"Why don't you?" he asked. Because it never occurred to Dylan that you didn't pursue any old thing that came to mind.

She laughed indulgently. "Oh, gosh, a little busy, I guess. And my line of work never left a lot of disposable income for extras, like learning to fly or skydive or mountain climbing or…or a lot of things."

"What line of work is that?" he asked, completely interested.

"Hmm," she said, taking a drink of her soda. "Well, my dad owned a hardware store, in which I was working on Saturdays by the time I was eleven. By the time I was twenty and had a couple of years of college under my belt, both my parents were gone, and Conner and I were struggling to run the store. He made sure I stayed in school, but I worked as hard in that store as he did until I got married and moved away."

"In a hardware store?" he asked. Then he gave a little laugh. "She changes tires and changes oil…"

"I do a lot of things. When the boys came along, Conner stuck me with paperwork. I was happier in the store, building things, helping customers learn how to build and repair things, but you know—a person can only do so much." She whistled and shook her head. "Twins. Couldn't be twin girls, right? I'm probably better off with boys, given that I enjoy team sports a lot more than things like ballet and origami."

He looked into her eyes. "You were kind of busy, I guess."

"I lost Charlie right before they were born," she said. "If not for Conner, I don't know what I would've done, so when he gets all big brother on me, I let it go. But from twenty-one to twenty-six I worked full-time in that store. I worked as hard as Conner and I did as much, too. I wasn't some girlie girl who could only do the books. I trained to be a phys ed teacher, but we had a commitment to the store."

Now, this business about losing Charlie, this brought Dylan upright. His feet came off the rail; he turned toward her, leaning his elbows on his knees and said, "If you don't mind my asking about Charlie…"

"He was army. He was deployed, I was pregnant, he was killed on a mission, the details of which I'll never know, and the boys never knew him. But I have medals and pictures and I try to be sure they know about their dad. He was a great guy. He was a hero. When they're older, they'll be proud of him."

Dylan nearly blanched. The closest he would ever come to being that kind of hero would be playing one in a movie. "Army widow," he said for lack of anything intelligent.

"Army widow."

He cleared his throat. "And you can do all the guy chores because…"

She looked at him with dead seriousness. "My dad taught Conner and I all the mechanical and maintenance stuff. He was so proud of that—that he didn't cut me out of the loop. That store was to be in the family for as long as we wanted it to be. And it was to be as much mine as Conner's. You don't get a bigger cut for being a boy." Then she laughed and said, "My mother did none of that stuff, by the way. She was old-fashioned and not very stylish. She cooked and cleaned and tended kids. She could never have been a soccer or softball coach and I might've been such a disappointment to her—I pitched girl's softball rather than sewing or learning to bake. But when I was fourteen she said,

'Katie, never underestimate the power of red lipstick.' From that point on I knew when their anniversary was because they went out to dinner *alone* and she put on the *red* lipstick." And she laughed. "My parents were pretty boring," she added. "But they were in love in their own way. I mean, come on," she said with a lift of a brow. "Red lipstick! Priceless, right?"

Dylan was transfixed by the smile, the laughter. How did she do that? Talk about dead people, people who had ultimately let her down, even though not by choice, and laugh with such beauty? He wanted that mouth....

"What?" she asked, studying his expression.

"That must have been hard. Losing your parents when you were young."

She sat forward and her expression became serious. "Everyone I lost, I lost young," she said.

He was quiet for a minute and then said, "We have that in common."

She relaxed back in her chair, waiting.

"My dad died in a car crash when I was twelve. My best friend when I was fifteen."

"Wow. I'm sorry. I should've known there was something that linked us. We kind of connected the first time we looked at each other."

Suddenly his grin was enormous and his eyes twinkled and she remembered the wet T-shirt display when his eyes dipped to her chest, which was such an ordinary chest.

"You're a dog," she said.

"I am a dog," he admitted, smiling. "So, your husband was lost five years ago or so, yet you didn't get married again? It wouldn't have taken my mom that long."

She shrugged and studied her cola can.

"Oh-oh," he said. "I smell a broken heart."

She looked up suddenly. "Me? Oh, God, no. A slightly disappointed heart, maybe. I haven't even dated much since Charlie died. I was just starting to get interested again when…I guess I just lost that old knack for knowing what to look for in a guy. Besides, I'm happy with my life—my family."

Dylan was quiet for a second. "My grandmother said I made my dad more perfect every day after he was gone. Did you—?"

She shook her head. "I don't do that. I remember every one of his faults even though I loved him like mad. But the last guy I was optimistic about was talking about marriage and family, and he never even kissed me." She briefly considered the details of that experience and decided not to share too much. "That should've tipped me off, right? Think maybe he forgot? That's when I decided to count my blessings. I'll stick with the men I have in my life and call it a day." When he looked a little confused she added, "The boys and Uncle Conner."

Dylan cocked his head. "Is that right? Dated you and didn't kiss you? What did he date you *for?*"

"Well, I'm a very good cook, even though that never interested me as a girl. And I can keep small appliances running…"

"Wow," he said facetiously. "Every man's dream."

She smiled at him and asked, "Are you married?"

"No," he said on a laugh. "*No-ho-ho.* I am not the marrying kind, trust me."

"Oh? And why is that?"

"Very simple. I come from a family that has a very bad track record."

"But your father died," she said.

"Oh, my parents had both been divorced and remarried by then. More than once."

"Oh. Gee, that's too bad. My brother, Conner, and I have each had one marriage on the record—he's divorced. But we don't have commitment issues. Just the opposite. And Charlie…Charlie was a soldier and his commitment was his life. His commitment to me was…" She stopped and slanted a look at Dylan. "This is surreal," she said. "Sitting here talking to a perfect stranger about love and marriage and commitment issues. You haven't even told me your last name."

"Childress," he said, watching her for a reaction. There wasn't one. He drained his cola and tapped the empty can. "Where should I pitch this?"

"Just leave it," she said. "I'll take it inside."

He put the can down beside his chair and stood. "Thanks for the soda, Katie Malone. I'd better get back to work."

She laughed at him. "By all means. And if that job has any openings…"

Katie stayed in her chair, feet propped, watching him don gloves and helmet, mount, wrangle that big bike off the stand, rev the engine and turn out of the clearing. She had to smile to herself as she heard him rumble away, the engine noise diminishing as his distance grew. How had he managed to stumble on her little hideaway?

Then she heard another motorcycle coming down the road, getting closer and closer until—

He turned back into the clearing and drove his bike right up to the porch. Then he turned off the motor and used his long legs on either side of the bike to prop it up on the stand. He slowly dismounted, removing his helmet and gloves, leaving them on the bike seat.

"So? Back for another soda? More conversation?" she asked.

He had an odd look on his face as he approached her, smiling a little as he took those two steps up to the porch. It was the strange look that brought her to her feet.

He slipped his arm around her waist so stealthily, she never saw it coming. Then he didn't so much draw her against him as *snapped* her against him with that one arm, which put their faces close enough to feel each other's warm breath. And his, she noted, was a little rapid. She felt his pounding heart against her breast.

His eyes were close enough so that the startling blue appeared in mere glittering slits, buried beneath the thick lashes. Her eyes were wide, on the other hand. Her mouth open, startled. "I just wanted to be clear," he said in a hoarse, whisper. "I wouldn't have forgotten."

And then he crashed down on her mouth.

Katie was startled somewhere between pain and a pleasure so remarkable, she wasn't sure how to respond. There was a taste in him that verged on desperate, something that felt so much more welcome than nice-but-dull. Her inner voice said, *This will probably be the only kiss you ever get from him.* And with that thought, her hands slid slowly up his arms to his shoulders, shoulders so hard and inviting. But it was the mouth that sent her reeling, his soft lips, his tongue, tentative and cautious before becoming demanding. She joined the tongue play, trying to remember when she'd participated in a kiss like this, and failing.

And thank God it wasn't quick. No, this guy wasn't a tease, he was the real deal. He threaded his fingers up the back of her neck and into her hair until he palmed her head. He tilted her right, then left, changing their slant and deepening the kiss. And she found her own fingers on the back of his neck, in his long hair, pulling him closer, bringing him harder against her. If his mouth wasn't intoxicating enough, that long, hard body against hers was certainly brain-numbing. Her senses became so sharp while her thinking was dull and all she wanted was to do this for a long, long time. She was tasting him, hearing his raspy and rapid breathing, inhaling that musk that contained some unidentifiable component she wasn't familiar with… Was that motor oil? Nature? Pheromones? *Lust?*

He pulled away from her lips, continuing to hold her close. "Well, that opened your eyes, Katie Malone."

"It usually does," she said weakly.

"I thought I heard you complain about being forgotten in the kiss department," he said. "I felt a little sorry for you. Wanted to be sure that was taken care of."

"Oh, I get it. I'm supposed to thank you now," she said.

He just chuckled and released her, jumping off the porch and heading for his bike, which was only two feet away.

"You're kind of an arrogant ass, aren't you?" she asked.

"Depends on who you ask," he said with a devilish grin, mounting the bike and getting the hell out of there. Fast. In fact, he popped a wheelie. Show-off stud.

When he was riding down the drive, she collapsed into the chair. "Well, if you ask me," she muttered to herself. And then she thought, *I just Frenched a movie star.*

Dylan rode hard and in some discomfort as he realized, well that was stupid. He'd acted on some lame instinct and now the only thing to do was get the hell out of her range as quickly as possible. He should never have tasted her.

Of course he'd been attracted to women before—many times. But he always calculated his moves and he never messed with young mothers. When Dylan felt a spark of interest in a female, he thought it through very carefully before he approached, touched, tempted, became tempted. One of the first things he considered was the window of opportunity, because he wasn't interested in the long-term. There had to be an understanding and it had to be consensual. He restricted himself from Payne, Montana, residents, much to the disappointment of some. He hadn't dated a girl from Payne since the high school prom; small towns could be harsh toward men who played the field with their women. And the closest he'd come to setting foot back in Hollywood was picking up a touring rock band in the BBJ.

He blamed Katie Malone's boobs, large, luminous eyes and easy laughter. The boobs weren't extraordinary. In fact they were kind of small, but they certainly spoke to him. Unforgettable, when you got right down to it. What was really strange was, Dylan saw pretty breasts everywhere, but his hands didn't usually ache to touch. And how about the laugh—so natural and filled with fun. Then there was the fact that he hadn't really impressed her that much—that turned him on. Then there was that petite figure with a nice little…

He forced himself to block any further thoughts of her body.

He couldn't figure out what had turned him around on a back road and sent him hurtling like a rocket back to her front porch to kiss her. He didn't understand why she responded to the kiss—hadn't she more or less said she was done with all that? Concentrating on her family? And he was turned on beyond his own comprehension. He'd been turned on a hundred times, but not like this. He felt as if he'd better get a lot of miles between him and Katie Malone or face dire consequences. And he had no one to talk to about this. So he rode hard for the rest of the day, stopping off to visit a couple of small airports as he went.

That was one thing Hollywood would have to recommend it—girls. There were plenty of the kind who would put their careers ahead of any relationship, but they still liked to have a man around from time to time. Brief, impersonal, nonrisky hookups.

The thought left him feeling just as empty inside as ever.

He remembered when Lang found Sue Ann, a Prescott, Arizona, girl. They'd been in college there and Lang, being a good-looking guy, was a great one to go running with; he always attracted women. But then he met this girl, this pretty but not flashy girl who was full of confidence and just wouldn't be played. And good old Lang took a dive. He glazed over, saw no one but Sue Ann and his days of running with Dylan were over.

And Dylan was grateful that hadn't happened to him, because he was convinced he wasn't good for the long haul. Not that he wanted it to be that way. It just was.

Dylan stopped off in a small town near the coast where there was a little fixed base operation. He went inside, introduced himself to the airport manager and asked if they had a charter operation or any aviation instruction. The story seemed to be the same everywhere—people were chartering less often, this particular airport was sending people interested in pilot instruction to other airports. Dylan learned there had once been a couple of instructors there as well as a charter pilot who operated a six-seater and had done a respectable business, until fuel prices soared and he moved on to other work. Now that airport offered storage, maintenance and fueling for a few private plane owners and the occasional inbound flight.

He had a lot more looking around to do, but that was enough for one day. Since he was in a good area, he took the opportunity to phone Jay Romney. He was a little surprised to find that Jay took his call even though his assistant warned Dylan that Jay was in the middle of a meeting.

"Dylan!" he boomed. "If you're calling me, I'm optimistic! How can I help you?"

"You can tell me if you have any acting work that I qualify for."

"What? You're coming back?"

"Not exactly, but I'd consider taking a leave from my business in Montana for the right project. And let me save you some time—no silly TV reunions or game shows or commercials."

"Can you tell me what you *are* looking for?" Jay asked. "Because there are a lot of projects under option."

"I can't," he said, inwardly shrugging. "A movie. Something that resembles what I've done in the past, even though it's been over twenty years. And above all, I want a good experience."

Dylan still had a lot of family in Hollywood and, Dylan was all too aware, Jay wouldn't have interrupted a meeting for any of them. "Maybe you have something you're interested in that will make a break from aviation seem worthwhile," Dylan told Jay.

"And why the break?" Jay asked.

"The charter business is down, given the economy," he said honestly. "A little movie pocket change can help me making a living and suck up some of the boredom of waiting for things to turn around. That is, if you have anything. I'm not looking for a favor—I'm only looking for honest work."

Jay Romney laughed. "I'd be happy to do you a favor, Dylan, but I won't have to. You're still a big name around here. I'll be in touch soon."

"I'm spending a little time in the mountains, Jay. My cell reception is spotty. Leave a message and I'll get back to you."

"Good enough. And hey, nice talking to you. Give my regards to Adele."

"Absolutely."

As a kid, Dylan had been cast in an incredibly successful sitcom from the ages of eight to fifteen. He'd also done a couple of big movies, Disney features. His father had been a famous actor before his death when Dylan was twelve and his grandmother, Adele Childress, was still very much alive and working at the age

of seventy-six. He was Adele's only biological grand-
child.

Back in Payne, once Dylan accepted there was no
way out but to try it Adele's way, he settled in. He first
learned to ride a horse. Then he went camping with the
old guy who managed the ranch and was still on their
small property to this day. As time went on, Dylan took
to driving to Helena and hung out at a small private airport, just watching the planes and gliders take off and
land for hours. He talked someone into a ride in a little
Cherokee and fell in love. He'd been looking for freedom for years and found it in the sky. He chewed the
fat in the little tower and in the airport office and found
out how the pilots there got in the business. And finally
he screwed up the courage and told his grandmother he
wanted to learn to fly, get his pilot's license.

She said, "Talk to me when you bring home straight
A's and I like your chances."

He'd never worked so hard, and that was the beginning of his new life. After high school he went to
Embry-Riddle Aeronautical University in the mountains of Prescott, Arizona, and while logging flying
and instructor hours, got himself a degree in aviation
management. And that's where he met Lang.

When he learned to fly, life really turned around for
him. And here he was, considering going back to that
insane movie life. But, at least this time he had a good
reason.

There were more airports to visit and Jay would need
at least a few days to come up with an idea that might

put Dylan to work. And during those few days, Dylan thought he might have to see what could happen if he ran into Katie Malone again.

Five

Dylan hadn't timed it, but he wasn't entirely amazed by the coincidence. There seemed to be some invisible and unconscious forces drawing him to Katie Malone and when he got back to Virgin River, she was just coming out of the little prefab schoolhouse at the end of the street, a child on each side of her. She was walking toward her SUV when Dylan pulled right up to her. He cut the engine on the bike, though he stayed astride.

"I'm running into you all over the place," he said to her.

"I'm not so sure you're running into me," she said. Then she pushed her boys off in the direction of her car, telling them to get in and buckle up.

"Totally by chance," he said. "But I'm glad I did because I wanted to ask you something. Should I apologize for…you know…earlier?"

"Oh, please don't," she said, giving her head a shake. "That would make it seem like you regretted it. We are thinking of the same thing, right? The kiss on my porch?"

He nodded his head. "Oh, man, you're going to get me in so much trouble…"

"Why?" she asked, stepping toward him. "You said you weren't married. Oh, no, is there a girlfriend? A fiancée?"

"No…"

She grabbed a piece of his shirtsleeve and, lowering her voice slightly, asked, "Are you gay?"

"No! Jesus, did I *seem* gay?"

"I'm no judge of that," she said.

"There's no one," he said, shaking his head. "It's just that…" He straightened and tightened his hands on the bike grips. It made him very nervous to pretend to be normal. "Listen, how'd you like to go out for ice cream?"

"I can't," she said. "I have the boys."

"We'll take them."

"What are you going to do? Put me on the back of the bike with one under each arm?" she asked.

"Sounds like fun, but maybe we should just drive. You have a car."

"Where?" she asked.

"I don't know," he said with a shrug. "Fortuna? It's an adventure. What about it? You don't have to recalibrate an engine or anything, do you?"

She made a face; it wasn't unusual for people to tease her about her mechanical skills, especially men. "I suppose we could meet somewhere, if you had any idea where you wanted to go," she said.

"How about if we really get crazy and go in one car?" he returned.

She looked at her watch. "I don't know, Dylan. It might be a little too close to dinner to give them ice cream. I try to get a couple of nutrients in them before they pack on the sugar."

He was stumped about what to do for a minute, looking at his own watch. "Well, how about pizza or burgers and *then* ice cream...?"

She frowned. "Are you sure you want to do that?"

"Katie! Stop making me work so hard!"

She laughed at him. "All right, park the bike and come with me."

"I'll drive," he said, running his bike up alongside the school, turning it off and following her. And didn't she get right in the driver's side. He held the door for her and tried again, saying, "Come on, I'll drive."

"No, thank you," she sweetly answered. And in a whisper, she added, "My car."

He gritted his teeth into a smile and said, "I'm a pilot, let me drive."

"No. Boys, this is Dylan. Do you remember Dylan? I don't think you met him, but he helped change the flat tire. Dylan, jump in the car." She smiled again. "Go ahead."

With a *grrrr* under his breath, Dylan walked around the front of the car and got in the passenger side.

Katie twisted around and peered into the backseat.

"This is Andy," she said, pointing left, "and that's Mitch behind you. Dylan suggested we go out for burgers or something and if you eat a nice dinner, there will be dessert."

Dylan looked between the boys and Katie a couple of times. Without being asked she said, "You'll figure it out."

Dylan could not tell them apart. "There's not even a stray freckle," he said. "Seriously!"

"It's subtle," she said, putting the big SUV in Drive. Then she looked over at Dylan and said, "Seat belt."

He did as he was told.

Even though Dylan had spent many hours with Lang and his family, often with kids aged two to ten climbing all over him, he still marveled at Katie's ability to multitask. She drove that big SUV down the mountain with its winding roads while keeping her boys relatively manageable and trying to carry on a conversation with Dylan. It went something like this:

"Andy, seat belt stays *on* or I stop the car. So, Dylan, this is how you want to spend your time—by yourself in a town of six hundred, just riding around on your motorcycle? Mitch, window up, please. Huh, Dylan?"

It was kind of hard to know when to jump in with an answer. He gave the short one. "We don't have any charters right now, so I thought I'd spend the time visiting local airports."

"That must be a little uncertain on the pocketbook," she said. And then she peered into the backseat and added, "Andy, if you don't stop bouncing around, you won't get ice cream. No, Mitch, I didn't bring movies. Well, Dylan?"

"Sheesh," he said, running a hand over his head. "We should've put harnesses on 'em and run 'em behind the car." He turned to face into the backseat. "What did you do at school all day? Color? Nap?"

"It's not school," Mitch informed him.

"It's summer *program*," Andy explained. "So we don't have to be really quiet or spell things."

"It's like babysitting," Mitch said.

"And there's some little kids who are like two!" Andy added with some disgust. "One of 'em bit another one today and everybody freaked out."

"We definitely need a little more running and jumping in that program," Katie muttered. "Well, Dylan? You didn't answer me."

He looked at her and, shaking his head, said, "I don't remember the question!"

And she shot him a grin just as she reached one hand over the seat to snatch a plastic gun that made a very annoying racket out of Andy's hand while she was maneuvering a curve in the road. "We're not having that right now," she said, bringing the weapon to the front seat and cradling it in her lap.

Dylan closed his eyes.

When they got to Fortuna, she was leaning over the steering wheel to look around as she drove and finally she said, "Aha! McDonald's! You'll thank me later."

Dylan had no idea what she meant. They wandered in like a family of four, except that Katie took the lead

Robyn Carr

and did the ordering for the three of them, getting her opened wallet in her hand. She looked over her shoulder and said, "Dylan? What would you like?"

He wasn't having it. He nudged her aside with a hip, closed his hand over her open wallet to prevent her from pulling out her money, placed his order and paid the bill. "Thank you," she said. "You didn't have to do that."

"I invited you," he reminded her.

"Yeah, but I get the impression you had no idea what you were getting yourself into."

It was pretty close to what he expected, but he didn't share that. He'd had the McDonald's experience a number of times, but they were his best friend's kids. Never the kids of some woman who had him doing crazy things!

When their food came, Katie sat on one side of the booth, sandwiched between her boys while Dylan sat on the other side alone. While Dylan worked on his Big Mac and fries he watched with admiration as Katie managed her boys. When Andy laid out and aimed a ketchup packet toward Mitch, raising his fist high to bring it slamming down to fire on his brother, she caught his arm in midair while she was telling Mitch he had to eat at least half of his McNuggets to get dessert. When Mitch pulled a fistful of straws out of his pocket and began firing the paper covers into the air like rockets, she confiscated them while disarming Andy of more concealed ketchup packets. As she did these things, she kept them from blowing bubbles in their drinks, made sure they were eating and explained to Dylan how the town put together and assembled the schoolhouse—men taking time off from work and volunteering their services. And then...

"I have to pee."

"Me, too."

"Okay," Katie said. "Let's go."

"Aww, I don't wanna go in the girls'!"

"Please, I don't wanna go in the girls', either!"

"In public places, you cannot use restrooms without an adult you know with you," Katie said calmly. "It's a rule and it's for safety."

"So no one *gets* us," Andy blurted, far too loudly.

"Well, if they'd had dinner with you, they wouldn't *want* you, but still..."

"I'll go," Dylan said. He shrugged. "I need the restroom anyway. And I used to hate going in the girls'."

"Sucks, huh?" Mitch asked.

"Anything special I should know?" he asked as he was sliding out of the booth. "Like, should I watch for cherry bombs in toilets?"

"Just watch for water sports," she said. "Of all kinds."

"Gotcha," he said. "Come on."

But they weren't coming with him, they were *way* ahead of him, running through McDonald's to the men's room, slamming into said facility, so that he had to pick it up a notch to keep up with them. When he got into the bathroom, they were standing there, waiting. He just stared at them for a second. "I thought we had to pee," he said. "Let's do it." And he held open a stall door because these guys were big for five-year-olds, but not quite tall enough for the urinals. "Seats up, please."

And, being twins, they gathered around the same bowl together rather than taking separate stalls. He just shook his head and laughed.

Andy looked over his shoulder at Dylan. "You gonna watch?"

"S'cuse me," Dylan said. He made his way to the urinal and prepared. In just seconds the toilet in the stall flushed and there were two little boys, one on each side of him, which went a long way to creating an embarrassed bladder. He lifted a brow and peered at them. "Are you? Gonna watch?"

And they nodded.

Dylan leaned a hand against the wall and kept his groan inside. He sought composure. Finally he peered at the one he thought was Andy. "Could I have a little space, please?"

Though he'd only spoken to one, they stepped back as they both got the message. Then turning as one, they bolted out of the lavatory. "Hey!" And there he was, stuck with his dick in his hand, doing absolutely nothing. "Crap," he muttered, zipping up.

When he got back to their booth, there was only Katie. "Everything go all right?" she asked.

"Curious little buggers, aren't they?"

"Oh, no," she said, color rising to her cheeks on a laugh.

"No biggie," Dylan said. "Aren't you hungry?" he asked, indicating her half of a Big Mac.

"Hmm," she said, lifting it and taking a small bite. After she chewed and swallowed, she said, "My meal usually waits until they're done with theirs. I was a little busy."

"Where are they? Were they taken into custody?"

"Playground." She leaned to the left to look past Dylan. "My secret weapon. I can keep an eye on them from here. I try to choose restaurants for their distraction devices. They're like littermates—they listen to each other more than me, sometimes. A place to burn off some energy works to my advantage." She popped a French fry. "Are you a little uncomfortable around kids, Dylan?"

"Me? Not at all. I like kids."

"And yet, you'll never marry?"

He tilted his head, looking at her, and made a snap decision. No reason they shouldn't have cards on the table. He had kissed her, after all, even if it was a completely impetuous and probably foolish move. That he'd never, ever done this with a woman before didn't cross his mind. He followed another one of those instincts that were beginning to take over his life. "Well, I come from a broken home," he said. "A very broken one. Many failed marriages among my immediate and extended family."

She lifted a curious brow and took a small bite of her burger.

"My mother has been married four times, my father

was married three times before his death, which was premature. That gives me lots of half brothers and sisters and stepbrothers and -sisters, many of whom have been married a couple of times or more. It probably has us all screwed up, but the thing that really works on me is what it does to kids—it can make kids feel so bad about themselves. I totally understand there are times it just can't be avoided and the separated parents have to work really hard to be sure their kids get through the rough patch of divorce, but my parents weren't real concerned about the kids. They were always worried about who they'd end up with next. And we always wondered, too. There's just no reason to put kids through that."

She leaned left to check the boys on the play stuff, then leaned back and tilted her head at him, listening. He took that to mean he should continue.

"I was my mother's third child by her third husband, my dad's first and only child by his second wife. Do the math, by the time I came along my folks had five marriages between them. If they can't hold a marriage together, make relationships work, I can't figure out why they kept having kids, but they did. Or maybe they could have concentrated on parenting the ones they already had before moving on, be sure they're not completely traumatized? Makes sense to me…because it wasn't just new stepmothers and stepfathers, but also quite a few potential stepmothers and stepfathers who lived with us, then disappeared.

"Now my best friend, Lang, he's been married eleven years and has five kids and you can tell when

you look at those kids that he and Sue Ann have it together, that they have a solid marriage and the kids feel
safe. The kids are normal—smart, happy, fun kids."

She took another bite. A sip of her drink.

"What I think is behind that is that they know their
strengths and weaknesses, and if I come from a family
with relationship and commitment problems, long-
term problems, and if I know how much it can poten-
tially upset the kids, I shouldn't walk that path. I'm
crazy about kids, but this might be some DNA thing in
our family—maybe we just can't help it. Maybe it's a
curse—like eons ago some Childress pissed off a witch.
Who knows why? My buddy Lang reminded me that I
told him a long time ago, when we were in college, that
most of the people in my family were so self-centered
and short-sighted that when they get a little hungry they
buy a restaurant."

She took another sip.

He chuckled. "It's only in the marriage and family
arena where I think I might have the curse. I have good
work and business relationships. Lang has been my
best friend for over fifteen years. But the kind of background I have—it just doesn't seem worth the risk to
attempt the marriage and family thing. So, you should
understand, Katie—that's why I *never* date women with
children."

She lifted her chin and both brows, as if surprised
to hear that. She took a small bite and retired the last
quarter of her Big Mac, apparently thinking of all he
had said while she chewed and swallowed. And then

she leaned toward him, looked him in the eye and said, "You call this a *date?*"

And Dylan laughed so suddenly, he almost choked on his cola.

When Katie pulled up to the school where Dylan's bike waited, she recognized her brother's truck. He was with his boss, Paul, unloading what looked like logs. "Huh, wonder what he's doing."

"You going to ask?" Dylan wondered.

"Nah. I'll call him later. Jump out so I can get these heathens home and in the shower."

"Done," he said, opening the door.

"Tell Dylan thank you, boys!"

"We'll do it again sometime," Dylan said, leaping out of her big SUV. She hadn't even let him drive *back* to Virgin River. He chuckled. She might have some control issues. It reminded him of Sue Ann…

After he'd watched Katie's SUV disappear out of town, he turned to see that Paul and Conner were standing there, staring at him. "Hey," Dylan said by way of greeting. "What's doing?"

"Play set," Paul said, dropping a post onto a pile of wood. "Bars, swing, slide, jungle gym, that sort of stuff. We went over to Eureka to pick it up, but we're going to be out of daylight soon so we'll assemble it in the morning, before work. Early."

"What's early?" Dylan asked.

"Five or so. We like to get to the real job by seven, if possible."

"I can help with that," Dylan said.

"That's nice, but we understand, you have no stake in it," Paul said.

"I also have nothing more important to do. I'm not on the clock right now. Besides, that's the way things work in my town, too. You know."

Paul dragged off his hat, one of his gloves, and ran a hand over the top of his head. "What kind of work do you do, Dylan?" After Dylan explained, Paul said, "Too bad. I have some part-time work available in building. But experience is required."

"I built my grandmother a coffee table in high school," Dylan said. "A really ugly coffee table," he added with a laugh. "But I'm great with an engine. I'll show up here early and you can check out my building ability. You'll probably be sorry I offered to help."

It didn't escape Dylan's notice that Conner hadn't said a word. He scowled a little and seemed to study Dylan. Finally he asked, "You dating my sister?"

He couldn't help it, it made him laugh outright. "Not according to her," he said. Then he went for his bike. He'd let Conner ask his sister that question when she checked in with him later. He kind of wished he could hear her answer, though he suspected it would be unflattering. Women were usually kind of jazzed to date him. Not this one, apparently.

As he drove back to his little cabin, he thought hard about the fact that this was an entirely new experience for him—Katie Malone could take him or leave him. Even though Dylan never played the movie star card, he was accustomed to the women being a little more… motivated.

Back at the Riordan cabins at dusk, Luke was starting a fire in the pit. After parking the bike, Dylan walked down to the fire. "Is this a nightly tradition?"

"Only on cool nights when Shelby isn't working," Luke said. "She's getting the baby settled. How about a beer?"

"I could be talked into that. What I'd really like is to hear about the Black Hawk—your training and some of the stuff you did."

Luke grinned. "I did some war, buddy. Including Mogadishu." And then he went for the beer.

Luke knew what Dylan and his buddies did for a living, but he didn't know the details. Nor did he know the company was Dylan's and it was struggling. He was more than happy to swap stories over a couple of beers. While Dylan wanted to know all about a career in a war chopper, to his surprise Luke was very interested in flying charters and impressed to learn that Dylan had type ratings in several aircraft. They talked through a couple of beers before they killed the fire.

He set his phone alarm for 4:30 a.m., which would give him plenty of time to brew a little coffee before heading to town, but he was wide-awake at four. That put him in Virgin River just after four-thirty. He took a look at the stack of play-set parts. There were no plans, of course. Likely Paul would bring them later, but it seemed pretty straightforward—four A-frames that would be joined by top bars, to which ladders, slides, rings and other stuff could be added. So he got to work on that.

It wasn't until Conner pulled up in his truck that Dylan realized he'd made it to the school early deliberately. He might not have planned it, but he woke up ahead of the alarm, ready to go, anxious to get there ahead of the other men.

He stood from the crouch where he was piecing together the A-frames to greet Conner, who was wearing the same grumpy face. "Good morning," Dylan tried. Conner merely nodded. "I didn't have any plans, but I think it's pretty obvious how this fits together so I got started." Conner just went to the tool chest in his truck bed and pulled out a smaller, more portable tool chest and carried it to where Dylan had been working. "I said good morning," Dylan repeated.

Conner glowered at him. "And I said—" He dropped his chin in a nod.

Something from his childhood came back and he said, "I hope your face doesn't freeze that way." When that made Conner's expression slightly more fierce, Dylan couldn't help but laugh. "Come on, man. Relax. I took them to McDonald's. And I'm only going to be around a couple more days."

"Why *are* you around?" Conner asked.

"I'm checking out the area and waiting for a call from L.A. about a possible job. After that, I'm headed home. Of all the people I've met around here, you're the only one who's been unfriendly!"

"I'm probably the only one with a little sister," he

said. Conner pulled out a battery-operated screwdriver, the baby version of a torque. "Tighten up those screws with this," he said, handing it to Dylan.

"You mean I got this right?" he asked, accepting the screwdriver.

"Not exactly brain surgery," Conner said.

"You know, I'd be a lot nicer to you if you were trying to learn to fly."

"You teach flying?" Conner asked.

"I'm a flight instructor, yeah. Among other things aviation. It's what I do."

"In Montana," Conner seemed to want to confirm.

"You can start timing me," Dylan said. "I should be a memory in a couple of days because I do have things to do."

"Okay, sorry," Conner said, but he didn't look all that sorry. "I'm Katie's only family and I worry about her sometimes."

"Well, from what I saw, she can take care of herself." And then he turned and proceeded to tighten the screws.

It was only moments before some others showed up. Jack had a big thermos of coffee and a box of doughnuts in the back of his truck. "Hey," he said, all grins as he stuck his hand out to Dylan. Paul was right behind him and then, to his surprise, Luke followed. They all stood around the back of Jack's truck with coffee and doughnuts for about fifteen minutes and it was confirmed—the only grump in the crowd turned out to be Conner, who kept looking at him suspiciously. As if he was going to kidnap Katie.

Dylan tried to imagine what Conner was so worried about. That Dylan would hurt Katie? Oh, he hoped not. If he just spent a couple more days here, that shouldn't happen. Not unless Katie was one of those weepy, wimpy, clingy girls who got all in after a trip to McDonald's. The Katie he'd experienced was not that girl. If he got a few more kisses out of her before he left, that shouldn't do any harm and he wouldn't complain.

The men nearly finished the work on the jungle gym and swing set by seven-thirty. It was time for Paul and Conner to head for work. Jack had to get back to the bar to serve breakfast. Dylan volunteered to hang all the equipment—swings, rings, et cetera—and rope off the play set so that it wouldn't be used this first day. They had anchored it in quick drying cement around the posts and while it would probably hold just fine if a bunch of little ankle biters started wiggling it, it was guaranteed to hold if they gave it another twenty-four hours.

His good deed paid off. Right around 9:00 a.m. Katie showed up with the twins. She seemed completely surprised to see him there and while the boys rushed into the building, she went to Dylan.

"What are you doing here?"

He indicated the play set. "I offered to help with that and they took me up on it."

"That's pretty nice of you," she said. "For a guy who is just passing through."

"I'm pretty nice," he confirmed. "What's on your agenda today?"

"Not sure," she said. "I thought about going into Fortuna and looking around while the boys are held hostage. I could go as far as Eureka," she added with a grin.

"Ever been on a motorcycle?" he asked.

"Of *course* I've been on a motorcycle. I secretly dated a boy with a bike in high school."

"Secretly?"

"I was not allowed on the back of a motorcycle or in the bed of a pickup truck. I beat the odds." Then she grinned again.

That grin of hers was completely irresistible. It made him want to grab her right here in front of the new elementary school. "If I were going to be around when the boys were sixteen, I'd tell."

"I'm not worried," she said confidently. He'd be gone before they were five and a half. "You won't be."

He didn't like the way she said that, but he shook it off. Ignored it. After all, he had already said he was hanging out for a few days and then would have to get going, so it was hardly a psychic prediction. "I have an idea. I have a rider's helmet at the cabin where I'm staying. Follow me out there. You can leave the car and I'll take you to breakfast, then for a ride."

"I don't know…. Think that's a good idea?"

"Nervous?" he asked with a lift of his eyebrow and a sly smile.

"The roads around here are kind of freaky," she said.

"But worried about you?" She shook her head. "You don't scare me. I think I scare you!"

"You shouldn't do that, Katie. Set up a challenge like that." He stepped back. "Follow me."

"Okay," she said. "I don't have anything better to do."

Six

This is okay, Katie told herself. *This isn't going any-where*—it was just for fun. She might be a little vul-nerable in the man department, but she was *smart*. No way was she getting involved with a guy like Dylan Childress. She remembered him all too well from her youth—she had watched his show every week when she was a girl, adored him, and lapped up every story printed about him in the gossip rags and teen maga-zines. He had a bad, bad reputation, which had thrilled her when she was about twelve. He had seemed very exciting and dangerous back then. But she was a grown woman now, a mother, a widow for God's sake. Fan-tasies like Dylan Childress were fun brain candy, but not her weakness.

Still, she could take one lick of this ice cream cone without selling her soul.

They took off away from the Riordan cabins on his bike and headed down the mountain to Fortuna, where he parked in front of a little café between a tattoo parlor and a liquor store. While they ate omelets, he asked her a lot of questions about herself, her brother, her life before Virgin River. Clever, she thought. Directing the conversation away from himself the way he did.

She told him everything, but not the long version. Her life the past year had become very interesting. She explained about Conner's ordeal as a witness, how they'd gone into protective custody—separately. That accounted for him coming to Virgin River and Katie going to the other side of the U.S. to Vermont. And now they were ready to start over. As a family.

"In Virgin River?" he asked.

"Well, that's an accident. Conner came here to lay low and he met Leslie. They fell in love. We've agreed, Conner and I, that we don't want to live in Sacramento again after what went on. Sacramento is a very good place, but our recent experience is a bit too jarring. It's time for a change. And now that I've experienced a couple of smaller communities—Burlington and Virgin River—I think it might be a good idea to raise the boys in a different kind of place. And they should be close to Uncle Conner—Conner has been like a father to them since they were born. They need that kind of consistency. It's the least I can do for them."

"That sounds like you aren't completely sold on Virgin River," he suggested.

"Not quite yet," she answered with a shrug of one shoulder. "But that's because I haven't looked around too much yet. No matter what, I'll make sure the boys are close to Conner so they can spend time together.

Why wouldn't I do that for them? They need stability. They need family. Most of all, they need a strong masculine influence."

"Well, then," Dylan said, wiping off his mouth and putting down his napkin. "Why don't we look around? See if there's anything around here you like."

And they jumped on the bike, heading south first.

She hung on around his waist and thought, *It's so funny that he thinks he's anonymous.* Maybe to her brother or to Jack Sheridan he would be, but to a girl who was in love with him from eight to twelve years old? Hah! Could he really be oblivious to the number of eight-year-old girls who'd loved him with their entire hearts? And grieved for him when he dropped out of sight? Well, at least until Jason Priestley and the Backstreet Boys came along.

Of course, when she was eight, nine, ten years old, she believed that Dylan lived in that family she watched on TV every week. If not specifically that family, then one very much like it. The show was called *Rough Housing* and it was a comedy about a dad who went to work every morning with a lunch pail, a mom who cooked and cleaned and tore her hair out because she had three sons who were constantly in some crisis that could be completely resolved in thirty minutes. They were that classic middle-America family who stayed in love and positive and devoted and wise despite their struggle with the bills, the work pressures, the challenges of family life. Dylan played the handsome middle child and was clearly the most popular of all. His additional movies that had nothing to do with *Rough Housing* were also successful and his popularity soared; the other boys in the series didn't score big movies.

Over time, as she got a little older and threw him over for other teenage stars, she recognized that he was not a good boy, that all the gossip must be true. He came from a world she didn't understand, a Hollywood family that bore no resemblance to hers.

She wasn't going to tell him she knew. Or maybe she would when they said goodbye in a couple of days, if they actually said goodbye, just to see the look on his face. But was he used to this? she wondered. Women who'd had girlhood crushes on him gasping with awe and star worship when they recognized him? Because Katie had been that way at twelve, but not now. Hell, at thirteen she might've thrown her panties at him, but now she had some class. Or stubbornness. Or just plain old experience.

But there was no denying his sex appeal. Within ten miles of their twisty-turny travels she was leaning with him and the bike and loved the tight curves, scary tilting and high speed.

He took them through a small Victorian town, around a road that seemed to go into the hills but popped out on top of a small mountain high above the ocean and she squealed with delight. The descent was exciting, exhilarating. Then along the oceanfront, through a couple of towns that hardly qualified as towns. He braked for crossing deer, slowed to pass what appeared to be a bull ranch, through a dark, dense, overpowering redwood grove, into a vineyard. She was pretty sure they were trespassing in the vineyard, but she didn't care. In fact, that made it more thrilling.

She had no idea how long they'd been riding when he took them along a winding road that went up into the trees. It felt like the spiral ascent inside a parking garage and her ears popped. When they finally broke through, they were on top of the world and in front of her the ocean spread out again. This was where he stopped the bike, turned it off and raised it onto the stand using his long, strong legs. She got off and removed her helmet and he did the same. Then he flopped down on the soft grass, flat on his back. He moaned.

"Are we quitting?" she asked.

He lifted his head. "We're taking a break."

"Why?"

"We've been riding for two hours! It's time for a break!"

She sat down beside him, circling her raised knees with her arms. "Do you tire easily, Dylan?"

"I was driving," he said. "You were riding."

"Can I drive?"

"No." He raised up, bracing on his elbows. "Did you talk to your brother last night?"

"I did."

"Did he ask you if we were dating?"

"He did."

"And what did you say?"

She reclined on her side, holding her head up by

bracing on one elbow. "I could have just said no, but I said he should mind his own goddamn business. I have to keep an eye on Conner. When he steps up to help me or be there for the boys, it warms my heart, it really does. Getting in my personal life, that annoys me."

"Has he been doing that for a long time?" Dylan asked.

She made a face. "When I was six, he walked me to school. I wanted my mother to walk me and he could have raced off with his friends, but the truth is— Conner took me on at an early age. Which is sweet, don't get me wrong. And I love him. But I want to pick my own boyfriends."

Dylan grinned. "Am I your boyfriend?"

"Oh, please!" She laughed at him. "A kiss just to show off and a trip to McDonald's and a promise to be gone in a couple of days? I can do way better than you."

He sat up. "Wait a minute. I took you to breakfast and on a fantastic bike ride!"

"That's on the cusp," she said. "Close, but no cigar."

"Jesus," he said, running a hand over his head. "You're tough! What's a date to you, anyway? It's not like there are fancy places to go dancing around here."

She was shaking her head. "I can't remember when I last danced anyway."

"What is it you're looking for? Want to cut me in on the secret?"

She shrugged. "I'll know it when I see it."

He stared at her for a moment. He liked that smile; he liked that she was an uppity, self-confident little witch. One corner of his mouth lifted, then he slid his hand around the back of her neck and deftly lowered her to the ground. He hovered over her and concentrated on those large eyes for a second before he leaned in to her plump, delicious mouth. He teased, a little kiss, a little nibble, a lick, waiting for her to let him know she was interested in more. And it didn't take long, either. She slipped her hands around his neck and pulled his lips down to hers, lowering her lids and opening her mouth for him immediately.

She made a low sound in her throat and he groaned. Their tongues tangled together; he threaded his fingers into her wild hair. He was drowning in her and let his lips slip from hers to her neck with a whispered exclamation. "God, you taste good." And he kissed her neck, her collarbone, her jaw, her ear, then went back to her mouth for more, licking her open and devouring her. He hadn't planned this part, but it came to him that he needed her and he was glad it had. Of the hundred or so women he'd kissed, this one was somehow different. As he moved over her mouth, he thought of her as belonging to him. This kind of thought had never happened before; he'd always focused on "this is for now."

He didn't want to let her go.

And she didn't want him to, that was obvious. As he fell onto his side, pulling her against him, she embraced him and stroked his back, his neck, his arms, holding him close. He kissed her for a minute, two minutes, three minutes. He broke from her mouth, but didn't let her go. "Whoa," he whispered. He went back for more.

It had to happen. He was aroused and wanted a lot more from her, but resisted the temptation. He did consider how sweet it could be, in the soft grass, under the warm sun… If being inside her mouth felt this good, he couldn't imagine the thrill of getting inside her body.

She tilted her pelvis against him; now she knew. She didn't seem to mind, either. He ran a hand down her spine to her little butt and fanned his fingers, pulling her more firmly against him, pressing into her. Yeah. Bliss. He could start with the buttons on her blouse and in less than ten minutes, which was a very unhurried projection, he could turn bliss into rapture.

He lifted his head. "Is this a date?"

She shook her head. "This is making out," she whispered back. "Very good making out, I admit."

"How much food do I have to buy you to qualify for a date?" he asked. And she only giggled and pulled his mouth back to hers.

After a few more minutes of awesome kissing, he relaxed the hand against her perfect ass and pulled reluctantly away from her mouth. "Let's get undressed. A little undressed, at least. Enough undressed…"

"Enough undressed for what?" she asked him, aiming her lips toward his for more.

"I want you," he said. "Really, really want you. I promise, I'll make it worth your while…"

"Hmm. While that just sweeps me away, I'm not prepared."

"I'm prepared. I have protection," he said.

"No, Dylan—I'm not prepared to get that involved with you."

"Why not?"

"Besides the fact that you're leaving in two days?" she asked him.

"Okay. I'll stay the rest of the week…"

She laughed lightly. "If it matters, it is very hard to say no to you. You have fantastic lips…and stuff."

He groaned in misery. "Katie, I'm hard as a hammer here…"

"I know," she said. "It's very nice. I'm sure if I were ready, it would do the trick."

He rolled onto his back, lacing his fingers behind his head. He closed his eyes and said nothing, but his lips were tight.

"Maybe we should just go," she suggested.

"I can't go yet," he muttered, not opening his eyes.

"Because…?"

"Because I'm sporting a rod," he said.

She shook her head and tsked. "Wow, you remind me more of Charlie all the time. But don't misunderstand, that's not why I like you." She flopped down beside him, lying on her back. "We'll wait till you're ready."

"I'd like it better if we could get *you* ready," he grumbled.

"Remind me to hold back on the making out next time. I think it makes you a little cranky."

"Seriously," he admitted. "Give me a little time. I'll be fine."

So she lay quietly beside him.

It wasn't hard to relax, even though she had as much frustration as he. But the day was so perfect—the sun was warm, the grass soft beneath her, the cooling breeze just right. It was a perfect time to think about a few things—like was she among the first to tell the once famous Dylan Childress no? The fact was, "yes" had been on her lips. Oh, she wanted him right back. She hadn't wanted that much or been that ready in more than five years. But she'd been through a lot and didn't feel like piling regret on top of it all. She didn't feel like being the girl he could turn and walk away from without a thought.

It wasn't as though Katie had unrealistic expectations. All that she'd been through had also taught her that. She could make love to a wonderful, thrilling man without a marriage proposal in the works. She could have a fling, of course she could. But really, the idea that he could take his pleasure and move on easily, without looking back, without longing, without wanting, without even missing her a little bit, that would be very hard to take. And she knew this guy—he was a playboy born and bred. He would go and he wouldn't lose any sleep over her.

All she wanted was to matter. To be more than an opportunity. That's all. She didn't expect to be the love of his life or even one of the memorable ones. But she had to be more than a day on a hilltop in the sun...

"You about ready?" he asked.

She opened her eyes and saw that he was sitting up, looking down at her. "Are *you?*" she asked.

"Ready when you are."

"Are you feeling all right?" she asked.

"Much better. I needed a little meditation, so to speak." He leaned over and put a little kiss on her forehead. "We should go north now. There's a lot to see."

She sat up. "Are you going to be grumpy?"

"No, of course not. Look, I know you understand this… A guy needs a little time to relax the parts, as we say. I didn't mean to pressure you. I won't walk us into that trap again."

"Of course not," she said. But she didn't quite believe him. He seemed more the type to try that again. Because he was leaving soon. And if she was right about him, he was in for a few surprises.

She jumped on the back of the cycle and rode behind him. They stopped in Ferndale for an outstanding burger in an old hotel restaurant, laughed about the difference between a meal out with the boys and alone, then rode another three hours before heading back to Virgin River. Katie had kids to pick up.

When they got to the cabins so she could pick up her SUV, he slipped an arm around her waist and treated her to a delicious kiss. Not a ten-minute kiss, but a very tempting one. And he said, "Thanks for going with me. It was a good day. See you around."

"Um, listen… Before you leave the area… Would you…" She stopped and chewed on her lip for a second. "If you have time, you might swing by and say goodbye."

"You bet," he said. "But instead of saying goodbye,

I think I'll pick you up at your place day after tomorrow at about eleven, take you for a ride, maybe lunch. If you have nothing better to do."

"I'm free," she said.

"Good. See you then." And he gave her a pop on the fanny.

Dylan took Katie out on the bike three times in a week, a couple of hours of riding, thirty minutes or so of kissing, a little something to eat. "Have I dated you yet?" he asked.

"You're definitely getting closer."

"I have to work tomorrow and the next day," he said. "I have a couple of meetings—airport stuff. But I'll be in touch."

And then he seriously considered moving on. He'd been in Virgin River over two weeks. Four days later, four days away from Katie, after having spent considerable time visiting small airports all over Humboldt, Trinity and Mendocino Counties, Dylan found himself back on that memorable hilltop, looking out over the ocean. The hilltop where he'd seduced Katie, a memory so delicious he just couldn't shake it. His bike was propped up and he leaned back, legs extended over the handlebars.

He had good cell reception so he called Lang. "What's shakin'?" he asked.

"Same old, same old. Mostly just what we expected," Lang said. "But there have been a couple of developments. We lost two crew members—one of the BBJ cabin crew and a pilot. Both moved on to more secure jobs, which is a gift. They probably saw the handwriting on the wall—it's not a secret business is down. Frankly, I'm relieved we won't have to let them go when we give up the BBJ. And we picked up a charter, but I had to bid it so low, it's not a moneymaker."

Dylan whistled. "What's next?"

"I'm working on the paperwork to let go of the BBJ. The second I tell the leasing company we can't make the payments, they're going to be in here to pick her up. I just hope they don't try to hold us to the full term of the lease, try to make us pay something for the months we're defaulting on. If that happens, we might have to file for bankruptcy protection. And before you panic at the thought—it's not the end of the world if that happens."

"Can we hang tough through summer?" Dylan asked.

"I think so. Then we'll have to downsize some more. If crew keeps moving out on their own, it might not be necessary to let them go."

Terminate employees. They didn't have that many, but it hit Dylan in the gut. He was a conscientious employer and every single one mattered to him. "I've talked to Jay, the producer. He has some ideas, but nothing concrete yet. He's optimistic—I think something will come together."

"And you're still hanging out in Virgin River?" Lang asked.

"Same cabin at the Riordans'. I think I've dropped

in on ten small airports in the area. This won't surprise you—everyone is experiencing the same problems we are… At least I have an option. I hope."

"Okay, listen. I can't say what I'd do if someone wanted to give me a shitpot full of money just to stand in front of a camera and look pretty, but you don't have to do it for us. You should only do it for you. Because we might have to make some painful adjustments around here, but we can keep coffee in the pot with a skeleton crew for a long time. A long time, Dylan. Just on our instrument instruction, aircraft storage and maintenance, occasional flight instruction and the odd charter…"

Dylan ground his teeth. "Might be a little more to it than looking pretty…"

"Yeah, yeah… What have you been doing since Stu and I left?"

"Nothing much…"

"But what?"

Dylan didn't answer.

"Had someone on the back of your bike, did you?" Lang asked, laughter in his voice.

Dylan sighed. "I think I'll probably head out tomorrow. I'll let you know if I'm coming back to Payne or going straight to L.A.…"

"Stay awhile, D," he said. "Stay until that doubt is gone from your voice."

"She's got a couple of kids, man…"

"You're great with kids," Lang said. "And even though you've been whistling that old 'I'm a bad relationship risk' tune for years, I've never seen any evidence of it. You haven't tripped over the right girl to lock down with, maybe, but your relationships are solid. In fact, if I die, you have permission to marry Sue Ann."

He laughed in spite of himself. "She wouldn't have me."

"There's nothing for you to hurry back here for, D. You've carried this company on your shoulders for a long time and it's all about to change. Time to chill. Think about the future."

"I'll check in when I'm on the road," he said. "Thanks for holding down the fort."

"Hey, no problem, buddy. My fort and all my little Indians are here."

His fort and all his little Indians... Fortunately, Lang knew exactly how lucky he was, so there was no re-crimination there. Envy, yes. Since Dylan was a little kid and had that pretend television family, he'd longed for those kinds of ties. And ever since he was a teen-ager he had known it wasn't likely to ever happen that way.

But, he wanted to be in only one place—right beside Katie, in her arms. Fearing that, fearing how much he wanted that, he avoided her. The hardest thing right now was knowing he had promised to say goodbye. He wasn't sure he could get through that. He thought it was probably far safer to run.

He scrolled through his emails on his phone while he was still up high and had service. Several were from

Jay, and they all said approximately the same thing. Still talking to people and lining up details for a potential deal—don't give up on me. I'm getting closer. I'm determined to make this work.

No surprise there—Jay Romney had been in touch with him at least once a year for the past ten years.

He responded to the email. I'm standing by. D.

And then there was an email from his grandmother. She didn't usually bother with emails. It was short and to the point. I'm tired of being sent to voice mail. Lang finally answered the company phone and while he pretended not to know where you are, he indicated it could be about a girl. If you don't want me to hunt you down, call me. A.

Okay, now this created a problem. It wasn't like him to not talk to his grandmother and he hadn't realized she'd left a lot of voice mails. And he hadn't discussed a potential movie deal with her for a very good reason—she'd want to give him whatever money he needed. True, if she thought he wanted a film career, she might even encourage him, but she was far too intuitive. If she knew he was too proud to take her money and a movie was the only thing he could think of, she'd push.

But he was without choice. So he called her.

"Gran…"

"Well, finally! So, Lang said you were riding through this little town and you met a girl and you stayed on for a while."

Dylan was going to kill him. "I stayed to check out

the small flying operations in the area. I want to know how they're holding it together in a down economy with these high fuel costs and I'm throwing out the net for charter contracts. It's business, Gran."

"Is she a nice girl?"

He groaned. "I met a girl, that's accurate. I took her and her children to McDonald's, took her on a few bike rides, bought her a couple of hamburgers—not a real big deal. There is something else I meant to mention, but since nothing is firm…"

"What?"

"I've had a conversation with Jay Romney about work. If it's the right project and the right terms…"

"Now that stuns me," she said. There was silence, which was very strange for Adele. "I guess you've thought it through…"

"Jay has been in touch now and then over the years, always throwing out the invitation. And now, while business is down and Lang can handle things, it's not a bad way to earn a little money."

"The good news is, I think you can trust Jay," Adele said. "But you haven't shown an interest in acting since you started flying."

"I'm motivated," he said. "Business being what it is, and all."

"Hmm. Listen, remember what we've always talked about…change can be good. What feels like a disaster can be your new opportunity. That's how you got into flying in the first place—crisis pushed you. Stay positive. There's a light at the end of the tunnel."

"It's probably the train," he muttered.

She laughed at him. "Sometimes you're older than I am. Call me tomorrow. I want to talk to you and if you don't call me, I'll send out a search party. Or, I'll just fly to Montana and camp out until you get there."

"I'll call," he said, somewhat surprised that the offer of an easy way out hadn't come.

"Incidentally, I'm fine," she said curtly.

He moaned. He could be such a self-absorbed asshole. "I'm sorry, Gran. I've had so much on my mind. Are you really? Fine?"

"Never better, Dylan. Talk to you tomorrow."

She disconnected.

He sat on top of that hill for a long time, staring out at the ocean. It was a while before he accepted the only conclusion he could have come to. He wasn't going to be able to sleep at night unless he saw her one more time. He had to keep his word and say a proper goodbye to Katie. And if he was going to do that, he was going to make it memorable.

Seven

Conner had taken the boys to the river to try a little fishing on Sunday, leaving Katie to sit on the front porch with Leslie and a couple of glasses of iced tea. "You can talk about it if you want to," Leslie said.

"Oh, it was just a little crush," she said. "I'll get over it."

"You're so quiet," Leslie said. "It must have been more than a little crush. At least a medium-size crush."

Katie shrugged. "I first laid eyes on him just over two weeks ago, so no more than medium. For sure," she said. But she didn't sound convincing even to herself. "It's all a fantasy, Leslie. There wasn't anything real about it. But you want to know what bothers me? It's so silly—I asked him to say goodbye before leaving the area. He said he would, but I guess he didn't."

"Damn, I wish I'd been paying attention when we were all in the bar! I can't figure out which one he was."

One corner of Katie's mouth lifted. "He was the cute, dark-haired one with the outstanding butt."

"I'm having an even harder time now," Leslie said. "Since Conner came into my life, I haven't noticed any other outstanding butts. Tell me the first thing that happened to make you think you had a little crush…"

"The second I saw him I couldn't breathe for a minute, like a full minute. Then when I saw him at Jack's it made me feel all tickly inside, but it was just one of those things. Seeing a cute, sexy guy and thinking, *wow*. I didn't expect to ever see him again, but his friends all left, he stayed behind, he found the cabin and we talked. We went on a few bike rides. More talking. He kissed me. But boy…"

"He stayed? He found you? He kissed you?"

"Uh-huh. It kind of started when he happened to be in town one day when I picked up the boys from summer program and he took us to McDonald's for dinner. Nothing much happened, except the boys were a little wilder than usual. And…well…" Her voice trailed off.

"And? Well? That's when he kissed you?"

"No, not in front of the boys. One day when I dropped the boys off at summer program, he took me out on his bike—all day. He bought breakfast and lunch, drove us all over the place on some of the craziest roads—God, was that fun! I hadn't been on a motorcycle in a long time. We did that again and again. I hadn't held on to a cute, dangerous guy for several hours in such a long time. Charlie might've been my last cute, dangerous guy."

"No kidding?" Leslie asked. "In over five years?"

"Pathetic, huh? I've been out on some dates, but no bells."

"We don't know that it's all over already. He might find your little cabin again."

"That's probably not a great idea," Katie said. "See, he's thirty-five, has never married, likes to play the field, has no intention of ever settling down, likes kids fine but doesn't want any, and— Okay, the bottom line here is—he's ready Freddy and I am not a one-night stand. So I hope he's gone. I do. Because I don't know if I can say no to him again."

Leslie sat up straighter. "Again? Did you leave out some parts here? Because a few bike rides, hamburgers and chitchat is all real nice, but…"

"We made out like a couple of teenagers on prom night. I nearly got nailed in broad daylight on a hilltop. It was awesome. And I'm not sure if I'm glad I held off or if I totally regret it."

"Wow!" Leslie said. She fanned her face. "That's what you left out. And that was it? He said goodbye and went back to wherever he came from and you'll never see him again?"

"Sort of. But you know what? I had some fun, I have to remember that. He's fun. Why are the bad boys always the fun ones, huh? I made him laugh even when he was trying to be serious, so he had fun, too. I have to remember that it was a good experience, didn't get out of hand and it was about time there was a little something going on with a guy. But the hard part is that there was no goodbye. No closure. The one thing I didn't want to be was completely forgettable."

Leslie thought about this a second. "Maybe he's still around?"

"Hmm. With some other girl, a little more willing than me, up on that hilltop? He said he'd be in touch. It's been four days."

"Does he seem like that kind of guy? A guy who would strike out with you and just find himself an easier target?"

"I don't know, Les," she said. "I can't say I really know him. I got a strong sense of him, but that doesn't mean I know him. The only thing he was really firm about is that he'll never marry and have kids." She gave a little shrug. "Anyone I get involved with has to take us all on."

"Whoops. I guess you eliminated him first."

"I told him he hadn't done anything for me that qualified as a date yet."

And Leslie spewed her tea as she burst out laughing. Katie couldn't help but join her. "Well, at least he'll have something to think about on his way out of town."

"Totally," Katie agreed.

And then there was the slow rumble of a motorcycle. They exchanged looks and they both went completely still. It seemed to growl through the town without ever accelerating or stopping. Neither of them could move. And then it came down Leslie's street, stopping behind Katie's SUV.

He casually braked, stabilized and dismounted,

walking slowly toward the porch with his helmet in the crook of his arm, grinning pleasantly. "I thought that might be your car," he said. "I checked at your place, but you weren't there. Because you're here, I guess." He approached the porch and put one booted foot on the step. Katie *loved* those pointy-toed cowboy boots.

"Lost?" she asked.

"I was looking for you," he said. He glanced at Leslie, whose mouth was hanging open. "Hi. I'm Dylan."

"Hi," she said in a whisper. Then she cleared her throat and said, "Hi."

"This is Leslie," Katie said. "My future sister-in-law. Les, this is Dylan."

"Hi," she said again.

Dylan chuckled. "I don't see the twins. What are the chances they're in jail?"

"They're fishing with Uncle Conner." She glanced at her watch. "I guess they'll be back in an hour or so."

"I was hoping you'd have a little more than an hour. I wanted to take you somewhere. And it's a grown-up thing."

"Where?" she wanted to know.

"It's a surprise, but I'm convinced you'll like it."

"She's covered," Leslie shot in. "The boys are… um…they're staying overnight. They want to…camp out in the backyard with Uncle Conner. Or something."

Dylan lifted one curious brow. Suspicious.

"Can I talk to you for one second before you go?" Leslie asked Katie. "Inside?"

"Sure," she said. "Be right back." And she followed Leslie into the house.

They were barely inside when Leslie grabbed Katie and shoved her up against the wall. Her eyes were a little wild, which came close to frightening Katie. "Do you know who that *is?*" she whispered.

"That's Dylan."

"Dylan *Childress,*" Leslie informed her, letting go.

Katie chuckled. "I forgot, we're the same age. The guys around here would never notice."

"But you knew, right?"

She gave a short nod. "But I haven't mentioned it and neither has he. And even though I was in love with him for a good five years when I was a kid, that has nothing to do with the guy I know now. I swear to heaven."

"He thinks you don't know?" Leslie asked.

She shrugged. "I'm not sure. I'm not squealing, screaming and throwing my underwear at him. I'm making him work for attention, like a regular guy." Then she grabbed Leslie's arms. "I'm not playing hard to get, Les. I'm just not laying down because twenty years ago he was a twelve-year-old's heartthrob."

"But…you're *glowing,*" Leslie said. "Oh, my God, you're *glowing!*"

"Pah," she said. "I can't imagine why—of all the Hollywood boys during our adolescence, didn't he have almost the worst reputation? He acts like a regular guy, but I honestly have no way of knowing if he's overcome all that naughtiness."

"Oh, I hope not…I mean *so,* I hope *so,*" Leslie said. "You look pretty happy."

"I might be pleased that he came looking for me, but I am not going to be fooled by a little showmanship. I'm a little warm, however." She fanned her face. "Besides, he's just going to say goodbye. Which is admirable, when you think about it. He could've just left and it's not like I could chase him down and reprimand him." Then she swallowed and said, "I should have a drink of water."

"I'll keep the boys overnight. We'll grill hot dogs. Watch a movie. I'll bring them home on my way to work in the morning. You can get them into fresh clothes for summer program. And after work? I'll be wanting every detail! Every single detail!"

"I don't do that to you, do I?"

"Totally different!" Leslie said. "Conner is your brother. And Dylan was my secret boyfriend for *years.*"

Katie laughed at her; half the female population in this age group probably felt the same way. "Can we go out there now? Find out what he has in mind?"

Leslie ran her hands over her hips to dry her palms. "By all means. Try to look calm."

"I think you're the one who should take a few deep breaths."

Dylan was waiting, his foot still on the porch step.

"So," Katie said. She lifted one brow.

"I want to show you something very cool."

"Want me to follow you?"

"I want to take the bike. You like the bike and it's

a lot easier. But you have to change into jeans. You know—bike rules." He looked her over with a smile. She was wearing a pretty, lightweight summer dress. "That's sexy as hell, but it could end up over your head on the freeway and you could cause accidents. We need jeans. Want to go change? And I'll follow you?"

"Okay," she said with a laugh. Then she turned to Leslie and asked, "Are you absolutely sure?"

"Of course. Conner will be thrilled."

I'm not so sure about that, Katie thought.

When they arrived at the cabin, Katie parked and gave him a wave as she went inside. To her surprise, he was tailing her and the second she was in the door, he grabbed her hand, whirled her around and planted a deep, wet kiss on her. His voice was hoarse when he broke from the kiss and spoke. "I wish I'd thought this through better," he said. "A dress. I never thought you'd be in a dress. I bet I could get under that dress without as much fight out of you."

She laughed at him. She couldn't help it—she was so happy to see him, she stroked his face. "Do you get a big kick out of being a bad boy?"

"I was planning to be very good," he said, diving for her throat. Then he groaned and said, "Go on. Change. I have a reservation."

"A reservation? Are we going out for dinner?"

"Just change."

"Because I want to dress right…"

He looked down at himself. Boots, jeans torn in strategic places, long-sleeved, faded shirt. "You're bound to look better than this no matter what you do. And grab a jacket."

"You sure you don't want to take the car?" she asked.

"Oh, hell no," he said with a laugh. "The bike turns you on." He touched her nose. "I know it does."

"I think that bike is just one big, expensive sex toy, vibrating all our secret parts and making us vulnerable. We should probably drive."

"Jeans," he said. "Jacket."

She sighed. "If you insist." When she got to her bedroom, she smiled, very glad he insisted on the bike. And although she was a little afraid he might notice that she went to some trouble, she dabbed on a little makeup—some gloss, some blush, some mascara. And while it was completely futile, she ran a brush through her hair. Then remembering the havoc a bike can wreak on hair, she filled a purse with brush, comb, gloss and hair clips.

"Ready," she said.

"Let's do it," he said, holding the door.

Katie hopped on behind him and they took off down the mountain toward the freeway north to Arcata. Every time they passed a road that led to the beach or up into the mountains, she wondered if that was where he was taking her. Yet it all made sense when he finally pulled into a small, isolated, private airport. Her eyes grew large.

"We're here," he said while she just sat there. "Come on, Katie."

"Is your plane here?" she asked.

He shook his head. "I rented a little Cherokee. Two seater. I'm going to take you up. Ever been in a small plane?"

She shook her head. "Never," she said in a whisper.

"You said you'd love to learn to fly. I thought you should start with a ride."

"Oh. Dylan." She sighed. Tears sparked in her eyes. "You were listening," she said softly. Oh, God, her heart was going to be broken. "I can't believe it."

He was frowning. "Can't believe what?"

"Tell the truth, Dylan. Are you just trying to get laid? Or did you really do this for me?"

He ran a finger along her jaw. "I thought it was pretty clear, I'm into you. But I did this because I want to show off and I thought it would be fun for you. Wanna go up?"

"I so wanna go up. Can I take my purse?"

He laughed at her. "Yeah, of course. And your jacket. Come on, I have a little paperwork to finish."

While Dylan shot the breeze with the guy behind the counter and signed off on some paperwork, she sat taking it all in. "She's all ready for you," the man said. "Little bumpy out there over the ocean, Dylan."

He grinned. "That's the fun part." Then he turned, and said, "Come on, Katie."

The Cherokee was lemon-yellow and just adorable. He put her inside while he looked over the airplane on the outside, giving it a preflight inspection. Then he jumped in, checked some of the instruments, cranked it up and taxied out. She let go an excited squeal as they lifted off the ground and he laughed.

Katie certainly wasn't the first girl he'd taken up for a ride in a small plane, but this ride felt like the first time. Her eyes shone and her grin was infectious. When he turned up the coastline, she was all but hanging out the window, looking at the shoreline, the fishing boats, the rocky coast. He took her inland over the trees and told her to look for marijuana patches or deer.

"How would I know a marijuana patch?"

"Bright, bright green, greener than any green you've ever seen. Deer? Self-explanatory. Wanna have some fun?"

"What kind of fun?" she asked suspiciously.

"Want to see the map float?"

Oh, that grin! "Yes!" she said. It was just like the bike—she really liked the sharp turns, the speed.

He took it to a higher altitude, then dropped the plane into a rapid descent and the map floated for a moment, making her giggle. So he made a sharp turn and pulled back on the yoke, loading some G's on them and she laughed as if he was holding her down and tickling her.

An epiphany was coming into focus. Everyone he dated, briefly dated, was so easy to please. They thought he was the catch of the century—he picked the best restaurants, was the best date ever, sharpest dresser (even covered with motor oil from some airplane engine), and they'd sure been willing to give it up right away. He just realized it hadn't felt real. They always knew him as the owner of a small aircraft operation or an actor. Celebrity.

Katie was tougher and yet, completely authentic. She had fun on the bike; the flying thrilled her. But she didn't give in to him. She had rules and held to them.

"Can I try?" she asked.

"Gently," he said. "Pull back, the plane goes up. Push forward, down. Let's not turn."

"Oh, thank you," she said, and she gave it a try. At first she was careful, gently moving the yoke. But then she got a little more aggressive, laughing as she pulled back, pushed forward.

"Okay, okay, you don't want to put us into a stall."

"A stall?"

"As in no engine."

She let go at once. "You fly. I'll ride."

"Good idea," he said with a laugh. "Let's look at some boats, look for some dolphins." And he turned out to sea. They saw birds flying under the airplane, a bunch of dolphins jumping, a few fishing boats and a big yacht. And then the plane started to bounce.

"What's that?"

"Just a little choppy out here, that's all," he said.

She was unusually quiet for a moment and Dylan didn't really notice anything; he was used to turbulence. It was usually especially bad over the Montana mountains. But then he heard that telltale sound from his passenger. "Whoa," she said. Then, "Ew."

He glanced over at Katie. She was white as a sheet.

He didn't waste a second. "Katie! Bag!" He pointed to the side pocket. "Bag, bag, bag!"

She turned to look at him, glassy-eyed, confused. He reached across her and pointed closer to the side pocket. "There's a bag in there if you don't feel right!"

Weakly, she slipped her hand into the side pocket and pulled out a sick sack. She just held it, like that was the last thing she wanted to think about. And Dylan turned back toward the airport.

He didn't make it far before she was holding the bag up to her face, retching.

"That a girl," he said approvingly. "You'll be fine when we're on the ground. Ten minutes, tops."

And she retched again.

Poor kid, he thought. She liked speed and tight turns, but apparently her inner ear wasn't crazy about turbulence. Now that he considered it, that probably was a little more than she'd have been used to. Certainly not the first candidate for Dramamine....

"Ew," she said again. "Oh, God." Then she reached into her purse with a trembling hand for a tissue. While she wiped her mouth, he was on final approach.

He landed smoothly, taxied in and checked his passenger frequently, noting that her color was slowly coming back. He parked the little plane, jumped out and went around to her side to help her.

She held on to that sack protectively, embarrassed. Her head was down, her hair falling in a canopy, hiding her face.

"It'll be okay, babe," he said gently. "Happens sometimes. Even to big tough guys."

Finally she looked up at him, her eyes watering, her face pale. "Now *that,*" she said, "was a date."

After a little time in the restroom, splashing her face, braiding her hair and generally putting herself back together, Katie made a miraculous recovery. When she walked outside, she found Dylan leaning against his bike.

"You look a lot better," he said with a smile.

"It seems to have left me as fast as it arrived. Whew, that was perfectly awful. I'm so sorry. Probably not what you were expecting, huh?"

"It happens," he said. "Jump on."

And away they went. He took a side trip through Arcata and stopped first at a drugstore. He left her on the bike and promised to return quickly. When he came back he handed her a small bag. Inside was a toothbrush, paste, mouthwash, disposable wipes and antiseptic hand wash. "I couldn't think of another thing you might need," he said. "I'm taking you to a restaurant—we'll get you some tea and something mild, like mac and cheese."

"You act like a man who has had a lot of experience with this," she said.

"You're my first," he said. "Not the first passenger or student to get sick, but the first time a girl I was trying to impress... Well, I wanted it to be memorable."

"It was," she said. "A lot like morning sickness. One

minute you're going to die, then it's over and you feel like you could eat a side of beef."

"Tea and noodles," he said. "And if it was morning sickness, it had nothing to do with me."

"Oh, stop complaining."

He looked over his shoulder at her. "At least you pronounced it a date."

Dylan took her to a quaint bar; they had to walk up a flight of stairs to the second floor and, given it was still afternoon, they were among just a few diners. The view was of the marshy headlands; the birds were flying low over the tall grasses, the Pacific shining beyond. It was beautiful and so serene. "It looks so harmless out there, doesn't it?" Katie said. "Some of us know it can really pack a punch. What got you into flying?"

"My grandmother moved us to Montana, where I had no friends or connections and, long story short, out of boredom I was hanging out at the nearest small airport. I started driving my little truck out there and did my homework while watching planes take off and land. Pretty soon I got the courage to wander into the building and asked them how much a ride would cost and they said, 'Ride in what?' I wanted to go up in their Lear, but I could afford thirty minutes in a little Cherokee." He gave a shrug. "I fell in love."

"I guess you didn't get sick…"

He shook his head. "Never. I love to do loops and spins and all kinds of crazy stuff. I think I could rock as a test pilot. I was about sixteen when I told my grandmother I wanted to take lessons, get my pilot license, and she said she'd be on board with that if I brought home straight A's. And did my chores—a lot of which were really crappy chores, pun intended. She bought a place on a lot of land with a barn, a couple of horses, a chicken coop, a couple of cows. Most of my chores involved a shovel and a lot of shit. By the time I was seventeen, I had my license and was instrument qualified. And then I went to Embry-Riddle and majored in aviation."

"And started a company?" she asked,

"Does that seem ambitious?" he asked her. "It wasn't. We couldn't get hired by the major airlines— not enough hours in the cockpit and no hours in a heavy jet. We couldn't even get on at the smaller regionals. Lots of training in all things aviation, but without the hours…"

"We?"

"My friend Lang and I. He was with me when we rode through Virgin River. We went to college together and he came back to Montana with me. We started real small and grew, but now…" He shook his head.

"Now?"

"The economy is kicking our ass."

"Oh, no," she said. "What will you do?"

"We'll make changes, probably drastic changes. One of the things I'm supposed to be doing while I'm taking this break in the action is having meetings with airport managers, picking their brains about survival skills. And if possible, picking up charter work. Meanwhile, Lang is running things, beginning to downsize the op-

eration, scheduling and probably operating any charters that come our way. We have to think out of the box
now—might be time to consider other work options."
He shook his head. "I'm not sure. I have other ways of
earning money, but—"

"Other ways?" she asked.

"We have a snowplow," he said with a grin. "To keep
the runway clear. Maybe we can start plowing roads
and driveways in Payne. There are flying jobs all over
the place…not always convenient ones, but they're out
there. Contract labor—all over the world. That would
be hard on Lang—he's married and has five kids and
usually international jobs take you away for a month
or more at a time, at least. He's pretty committed to
Montana—sees it as a good place to bring up the kids.
Last year one of our pilots left for Nigeria—it was a
one-year contract and it was good money. But it was
a long way from home. And we like that little airport.
We built it."

She leaned her chin on her hand. "This must be very
tough for you."

"It's a challenge, that's for sure. Pretty soon we're
going to have to let people go. I hate to do that. They're
all good, loyal people. In most cases, my neighbors."

She smiled at him. "There's a lot more to you than
meets the eye," she said.

He also leaned his chin on his hand. "And what
meets the eye, Katie Malone?"

"Hoodlum," she said. "Biker bum. Ne'er do well.
Notorious flirt. Opportunist…"

"Hey! I'm only an opportunist in the best possible way—the kind who will start a company that puts a few people to work."

Her expression softened and grew serious. "I do know how it is to have your own company and to have it mean the world. I had a hardware store with my brother, remember. It was doing well when some jackass burned it down and sent us into hiding. Conner talks about maybe rebuilding. Maybe around Virgin River. But..."

"But...?" he prompted.

"But it took the store burning down for him to see that he needed a little more balance in his life, that he'd been working too hard and wanted more time to relax, more time with the boys and with his woman." She shook her head. "I've never really seen Conner like this. He's mellowed out a lot."

"Couldn't prove it by me," Dylan said. "He pretty much snarls when he sees me, which fortunately isn't too often."

She giggled. "I told you—he'd like to pick my boyfriends."

"Am I your boyfriend now? After the plane ride, even considering...?"

She ignored him and asked, "Tell me more about your company. Your airplanes, your barn, your best friend, your town, your grandmother..."

Dylan tried to remember how many times he'd been asked questions like these by lovely young women. The answer was never. Oh, he'd been asked about his famous grandmother, about his days in Hollywood, about how big his company was and how many planes he had and they stopped just short of asking what his bank balance was. But about his best friend? His barn? His town? Was it like this just because Katie Malone didn't really know a thing about him?

He found himself talking and talking. He loved telling about how his grandmother took charge and found a place off the grid for them to live while he struggled to enter adulthood; about Lang and Sue Ann; about going to high school in Payne, college in the Prescott mountains. He told her about the girl he took to the senior prom, and had her laughing when he told the story of Lang falling for Mrs. Lang and how Sue Ann pinned his ears back and just wouldn't take any of his big-city, playboy crap.

Then he asked her all about growing up in a hardware store, asked what kind of high school experience she had. "I'd like to teach while my kids are in school. It would be perfect for me. I'm sorry about the store, of course, but teaching and coaching girls' athletics— that's more me." Then she grinned and said, "As long as I stay on the ground, I guess."

Even though they lingered a long time over their dinner, it was still early evening when they headed for Virgin River. He took her off the road just long enough to view the sunset over the Pacific, then on to the little town, to her cabin.

He'd never felt closer to a woman in his adult life.

And then they were standing there, in front of that

little cabin. All around them in the darkness were the noises of the forest, the crickets and squawks and occasional rustling sounds, but Katie just stood on the first step of the porch, looking into his burning blue eyes. He gently touched her cheek and the line of her jaw. He kissed the left corner of her mouth, then the right.

"This is going to be goodbye, I guess," she said.

"That would probably be for the best," he said. "You don't want to get mixed up with me. You don't want to put your boys through that…"

"Dylan, understand something—I will *always* take care of my kids first. *Always.* If I thought being around you was bad for them in any way… They're first, that's all. I could love you more than life itself and they would still be first. It's a commitment a mother makes when she has children. And besides, I'm not so sure you're bad for them. You're a very nice guy."

"But I should probably get out of here…" And he touched her lips again, more seriously. He covered her mouth in a hot, demanding kiss that robbed her of breath. "Unless…" And he kissed her some more.

"Unless…?" she asked weakly.

"Unless you want me to stay for a couple of hours… and make sure you never forget me."

"Hmm," she said, leaning toward him for more of his mouth. "Tempting. But unnecessary. I'll never forget you, Dylan. I've had a very fun couple of weeks. Thank you."

"Katie, Katie…I hate to leave you…"

"I understand, Dylan. You have things to take care

of. And besides, I don't want to have the best sex of my life with a guy who's on his way out of town... Just kiss me some more and then tonight I'll imagine it."

"When you imagine it, multiply it times ten..." He went after her lips again. He pulled her hard against him and slid a hand up her side to briefly cover her breast. He feasted on her neck, jaw, ear, temple, mouth, then just held her still and close.

"Times a hundred," she whispered.

They were locked on each other for another five minutes and she was the one to pull back. "I could do this forever, but I don't want to make a fool of myself and cry. If you're going, you should go while I still have some dignity."

Dignity he understood. He backed off a bit and gave a nod. "I'll think of you as the best part of my summer, Katie," he said.

"I hope you can save the company," she said. "And thank you for making me feel so special."

He gave her waist a squeeze. "You *are* special. Don't you ever forget that."

And he turned from her, going to his bike.

Eight

She hurried into the cabin because her breath had started coming in little gasps and in a second she knew she was going to fall apart. Inside, she paced in the small space, plunging her hand into her hair and making small whimpering sounds. Why, why, why couldn't things be different? she asked herself.

Oh, she was going to cry all night, she knew it. She was flat-ass bonkers over him and did not feel better off this way. But he was probably right—if it was only going to end suddenly, leaving her grasping for something that just wasn't there, it was better that he was gone.

Better? she asked herself. Wouldn't it be easier to adjust to his leaving after a couple of drop-dead orgasms than never knowing? Why was she always so careful? What did she have to lose, really?

Screw it, she thought. She might have sent him off but she knew where that little Riordan cabin was and could still have her unforgettable couple of hours. After all, the boys were tucked in at Uncle Conner's house and Leslie, so optimistic, would *never* let them come home before morning.

She grabbed her purse and shot out the door.

And there he was, sitting on the motorcycle.

She skidded to a stop on the porch. "Ah…before you leave…"

"Yeah?" he said, sitting up straighter.

"I've been thinking…about a couple of hours…"

"Yeah?"

She shook her head. "Don't go yet, Dylan."

His leg came over the bike and he vaulted off, eating up the space between them in three long strides, leaping up the porch steps and pulling her into his arms, covering her mouth in a searing kiss that demanded every emotion she had. His hands were all over her, running up and down her back and pulling her against him, up her sides and covering her breasts, tangled in her hair, pulling her face onto his. He was murmuring her name and she was clutching him close so he wouldn't fly away.

Dylan walked her backward into the cabin and kicked the door closed when they were inside, but they didn't get far. Standing there, just inside the door, he pulled her shirt over her head, pulled his over his head, and he began kissing her breasts through the lace of her skimpy bra. Before she could see what happened, that undergarment was gone and he was attending to her erect nipples—a lick, a kiss, a suck. It brought the deepest of sounds from her, her fingers in his hair.

He began kissing his way down her belly while his fingers deftly worked the button on her jeans and kissed his way below her waist just as he slid them over her hips and down, down, down. With the jeans went the tiniest thong. He fell to one knee before her and pulled off her right shoe, then the right leg of her jeans, and his lips were teasing her lower belly, upper thigh, his fingers moving deeper. With his hands on her hips, he drew her toward him. As she cried out, he lifted that bare leg and pulled it over his shoulder and all of a sudden, he had his mouth on her softest parts. "Dylan!" she cried out, knotting her hands in his hair. He devoured her hungrily, like a starving man, licking the deepest part of her. A minute inside the door and she was exploding!

"God," he cried, going in for more. "Sweet heaven…"

Her knees gave out with pleasure so electrifying she could no longer stand, but he caught her and gently lowered her to the floor. His fingers replaced his mouth and he found her lips with his. "You are the best thing I've ever…" He kissed her deeply. "Katie, I'm not sure I'll be able to get enough…." But while he murmured against her lips, he freed her from the left shoe and the rest of her jeans. His belt came open and disappeared and she reached down to open his jeans.

And she had him in her hand. He groaned in beautiful agony. He instinctively moved toward her, probing gently, wanting all of her. He was slipping inside and he wasn't going to last long. He was so right, the sensation of being inside her was the most intoxicating thing he'd ever felt. He went into a trance at once.

"Please," she whispered. "Dylan. Please find that condom so we can…"

"Condom," he said. "On it." And he sat back just long enough to get rid of the rest of his clothing and get that protection from his back pocket.

And then he went still for a second. He lowered himself over her gently, touching her lips. "I know this is going too fast, baby, but we'll take our time a little later. I know I sound like a madman, but I need to be inside you."

She nodded, her eyes glassy and wide. "I need that, too."

"I'll go easy…"

"Don't go easy…"

He gave it his best effort, moving into her slowly, but she grabbed his butt and pulled him into her and he lost his mind. His hips began to move, hers moved in concert and they were slamming against each other in a magnificent rhythm that took about ten strokes to make her freeze and hold him, cry out his name and squeeze down on him with all her internal muscles.

"Holy…" He couldn't speak any further. All that escaped him was a powerful groan as he held himself for a moment, then pumped his hips and joined her. He pinched his eyes closed and held her hips. As the pleasure slowly let him breathe again, he kissed her everywhere—her eyelids, her lips, her cheeks, her neck, her breasts…

And he held her, stroking her hair, her neck, touching her beautiful face. "Are you okay, honey?" he whispered.

"Hmm," she said, giving a little nod, her eyes closed. "Possible rug burns…."

"My God, Katie…I wanted you so bad, I didn't even get you to the couch. I think I went insane."

She giggled. "When a girl says yes to you, she better stand back, huh?"

"Come on, sweetheart, let me get you to bed…"

"Just a minute, Dylan," she whispered. "I'm trying to grow the bones back in my legs… Can't we be still for just a minute more?"

"Yes," he said, placing gentle kisses everywhere he could reach without separating them. "My God, I'm having aftershocks."

"I'm weak," she said softly. "Pleased, but totally limp…"

After a minute passed, he carefully lifted her and she looped her arms around his neck. "Don't worry about growing your bones back. You're not going to have to walk for a while," he whispered. He carried her to the bed with his lips locked on hers. He put her down and climbed on beside her, pulling her into his arms. "Yeah, this is going to work better. Yeah, I like this," he said, settling his lips against her neck and his hand over her breast. "Now we start over. Nice and slow."

Dylan felt Katie stir against him and he instinctively pulled her closer. He wanted her again.

"Best sex of your life?" he asked in a whisper.

"I'm not ready to commit," she whispered back.

He chuckled. "Was for me," he said.

"But…"

"Seriously," he said. "And it was for you, too."

"Don't go getting a big head, just because I had a couple of orgasms—"

"Four," he said. "I gave you four and helped myself to two."

"You're counting?" she asked, rising up and looking down at him.

"I'm going to keep counting, too. I think you can reach your personal best." He grinned at her.

"Aren't you tired?"

"I was sleeping, until you started wiggling around…" He nuzzled her neck. "I can do better. Just trust me…"

"We made love on the floor," she murmured. "Ten feet from the bed…"

"Hmm. I think I lost my mind a little bit. Are there rug burns?" he asked, trying to roll her over. "I'll give them a little kiss…" He found a couple of pink patches on her rump and did kiss them sweetly. Then he rolled her back and his hands and lips began to move over her body again.

"Boy, am I glad the rumors weren't true."

"What rumors?" he asked, his voice muffled.

"There were lots of them. I think the worst one had you in a drug-induced coma in an institution in New Zealand…"

He lifted his head from her breast. That one had appeared in *The Star* twenty years ago, shortly after Adele took him out of Los Angeles. "You know," he said. She nodded. "How long have you known?"

"Well, I strongly suspected at the flat tire, then at the bar I was more sure, then when you told me your last name and a little about yourself, right before you kissed me, I was positive."

"And you didn't say anything?"

She shrugged. "It appeared you didn't want to talk about that Dylan Childress. If you'd brought up your Hollywood career, I would've said something. I admit to being curious about which parts are true, which aren't. The press and rumors were pretty horrible. Liquor and drugs, an unbelievable number of girlfriends, crazy behavior, vandalism and general delinquency…"

"I was just a stupid kid…"

"I always wondered which parts of that were true…"

"Probably too much of what you read was true…"

"I read about the terrible incident that seemed like the end of it all—Roman's drug overdose."

"An accident," he said. "I'm sure it was Roman being stupid, trying to get high, not get out."

"And that's when you kind of disappeared," she said.

"My grandmother got me out of there, away from the insanity. She didn't know what else to do, I think. She thought I needed to rehab, to put it simply. How many people around here know?"

"Les knows, but she won't out you. I bet the number of Virgin River women who were in love with you when they were twelve is pretty limited. You probably don't have to worry."

He smiled at her. "You? Were you in love with me?"

"Oh, God, wildly. Madly. I sincerely believed we would meet somehow and you would marry me. But you went away and I threw you over for Jason Priestley. Later I threw him over for the Backstreet Boys. Then I got interested in boys my own age who were real. I had to finally accept the fact that Jason Priestley would never take me to the prom."

"The Backstreet Boys," he muttered. "Priestley— I can live with that. But the Backstreet Boys? Jesus, Katie."

"It was a rough time…"

"So now will you tell everyone you can think of that you had sex with Dylan Childress? The ex-star?"

"Is that what you're used to?" she asked, knowing the answer.

"It's happened. That's why there haven't been that many…"

"Like who?" she asked. "Who does a guy like you hook up with?"

He gave a little shrug. "Women who didn't want a boyfriend. Never local girls—they want to get married. Almost strangers, but not total strangers. Sometimes I'd meet someone when we flew charters—there was an expiration date on those relationships. I was kind of hit and run…involved with people I probably wouldn't see again…"

"How original, for a playboy," she said. "Well, this

may come as a shock, but I haven't ever let myself get involved with someone like you before, someone who absolutely swears he can't be committed. In fact, I don't think I can build much self-esteem by bragging that I nailed an actor—especially one who promises to ditch me as quickly as possible. That really undermines my self-image, which I'd rather bolster." She thought for a second. "I might get some interesting press out of the fact that I threw up in your plane... I think, since I'm awake, I'll have a quick shower. That way if you're still here when I'm done, I'll be all fresh and sweet and you can resume counting." She lifted an eyebrow and slid away from him, stalking across the bedroom stark naked. Head held high.

Damn, he thought. *Look at her.* She gave her long hair a toss and gathered it on top of her head before entering the bathroom. And he was hard again. She was way under his skin.

He rolled onto his back and stared up at the ceiling. Well, there was an upside, he thought. Now that it was all out in the open, she would understand where he was coming from, why he was a bad relationship risk and was doing her a favor by not getting involved with her or her kids. She would know all the names in his familial periphery—all those Hollywood losers who couldn't stay out of trouble or make a normal family life work. And obviously she'd heard all the rumors about how much trouble he'd been in, how unreliable he was....

If you're still here when I'm done...

He could spend a little time with her, as long as it

didn't get too serious. As long as he explained, with consideration for her feelings, why he'd have to move on. And she'd be fine with that because she was no longer a twelve-year-old fan girl.

And he leaped out of bed and went to the bathroom. The shower was running and he stepped inside. "You're not going to get away with this," he said.

"What?"

"Showering alone while I'm still counting." And he took her lips just as he took the soap out of her hands.

Katie was making coffee in the kitchen when the door to the cabin opened and the boys came in. "Shh," she said. "Be very quiet. You can go to your bedroom and change clothes for summer program if you're very quiet."

Right behind them, Conner stepped into the cabin.

"Well, you're not Leslie, now are you?"

"There's a motorcycle outside your cabin."

"Yes, Conner, I know this," she whispered. "Please don't wake him."

"Why? Did he have a rough night?"

"Don't go there unless you really want to know, because if it will back you off just to give you the grim details, I'll do it," she said.

"Don't," he said, closing his eyes. "I don't want my ears bleeding… Do you know what you're getting yourself into?"

Unlikely, she thought. But she said, "I'm a grown-up."

In the bedroom, Dylan felt the sunlight on the back

of his lids and thought, whoa, that last session they'd had had really knocked him out. God, she was going to kill him, she was that good. He slept like the dead. And in the distance, he heard soft talking. Phone call to a girlfriend? He smiled to himself—guys always got the bad rap for locker-room talk when really, the girls were worse. They couldn't wait to get their friends on the phone and describe every detail.

He felt eyes on him. He opened one blue eye and met with four brown ones.

"Did you have a sleepover, too, Dylan?" one asked.

"Did you forget about your pajamas, too? Because we had to sleep in our unders because we forgot about them."

"Did you have to sleep in your unders?"

He lifted his head. "Katie!" he yelled.

She darted into the bedroom and when she saw her sons, she put her hands on her hips. "Is this where you keep your school clothes?" she asked. "Go change, right now."

"Mom, did Dylan have to sleep in his unders?"

"Did he forget his pajamas?"

Her lips twitched as she struggled to keep from laughing. "Well, for heaven's sake, will you look at that. He must have. I wouldn't have noticed, since I'm more polite than you—I gave him privacy and slept in the other room, since he's a guest." She shuttled them out of the room. "Get changed now—you don't want to be late." Then she looked at Dylan and covered her laughing mouth with a hand.

"Not funny," he said grumpily.

"Funny," she insisted. "You can have the cabin to yourself—get up, go back to sleep, whatever. I'll be gone about a half hour. Coffee's on. I'll bring back breakfast from Jack's."

"Then I have to go," he said.

"Of course," she said with a smile. "I understand completely."

My God, he thought. Did she take nothing seriously? Here they'd romped the night away in complete carnal pleasure and at first light he's caught naked in her bed by her *children!* They'd be in therapy until they were twenty.

But of course they hadn't seen anything... He was covered, Katie claimed to have slept in the other room and the clothes he'd left on the living room floor the evening before were neatly folded on the top of the chest of drawers, his boots standing politely on the floor. Even the dresser drawer where she kept all the extra condoms was closed; no wrappers on the night side table. Katie had tidied up and taken a shower; the ends of her hair were still damp and she wore jeans and a sweatshirt.

But they knew he'd been there. Was that a bad thing?

He took a shower and while the spray ran over him he closed his eyes and remembered the last shower here, in the middle of the night, with Katie. And with the help of a little soap and shower gel, he had her up to seven while he lingered around four because she couldn't keep her soapy hands off him and he didn't have a condom in the shower and he lost his mind and *damn!* She really was going to kill him. And he was going to die with a smile on his face.

But how did she do that? Show him the sex goddess when they were alone and that primly amused young mother in the light of day? She was like two completely separate women in one skin. He was going to have to get out of here before it became any more obvious he couldn't be without her in his life. Over breakfast they would talk, he would thank her for being the best sex of his life, tell her truthfully that he'd never forget their "date" and then he'd head for L.A. or Montana.

When she walked in with a brown paper bag, she was smiling. "Preacher's omelets are so huge, we can split one…"

"Okay," he said weakly.

"What's the matter?"

"Nothing." *Everything.*

"You have a very strange look on your face."

"Crap," he said. He took the bag from her hands, put it on the counter and threw her over his shoulder, her laughter pealing out through the little cabin as he carried her back to the bedroom. Once there he pulled off her clothes, put his hands and lips on every inch of her body and took her to eight. And nine.

"My God," she said, breathless and glistening. "This has to stop! At least long enough for nourishment!"

He laughed at her and said, "That omelet's cold anyway. It'll keep ten more minutes. I have to ask you something."

"Shoot."

"How screwed up are your kids going to be about finding me in your bed?"

"They didn't even mention it, Dylan. I suspect they thought nothing of it."

"But we're not married or anything…"

"Neither are Conner and Leslie, where they spent the night last night, although they are an established couple who live together. But the boys are very curious—if they'd had questions, they would've asked. It was a first for them, however."

"A first?"

"You're my first sleepover since they were born. They never even witnessed their own dad in my bed."

"Oh," he said. "You got your guys out the door before the boys were up?"

She laughed softly. "You're my first since Charlie. I was open to the idea, but never met anyone who qualified. I hope that's not too much pressure…"

He leaned toward her until his forehead was resting against hers. "Nine," he said.

"I was faking seven and eight," she said.

He smiled at her. "Good fake. Your whole body shook. So, can you talk about him? Can you explain about your marriage? Even though we're…" He ran a hand down her naked body.

"Of course. I'm not cheating on him. What would you like to know?"

"How was marriage? Romantic?"

She laughed. "Sometimes, but not always. See, Charlie was a soldier, and not just any soldier, but Special Forces. Highly disciplined, expertly trained and dangerous in many settings. To say he was rough around the edges would be an understatement. He was a man with a very special commitment. It took remarkable strength and conviction for him to do his work. And, it took a unique kind of commitment to be married to him. For example, one night at a bar a young soldier saw pregnant me and said something off-color—I think it was, 'Holy fuck, mama.' And Charlie slapped him around. Almost knocked him out without leaving a mark—Green Beret. He knew how to do scary things like that, but with me he was so gentle, so wonderful. He was upset that the man used that language in front of me. Yet just a few hours later he yelled, 'Katie! Where's the fucking towel!'" She shook her head and laughed. "His language—the worst. I'm afraid if Charlie was still alive my boys might be saying things like, 'I can't fucking tie my shoe.' But there was never any question about how he felt about me."

"Do you think you'd still be married today if he was alive?"

She took a moment to think. "Some groups like Green Berets, Rangers, SEALs, that sort of thing— they do have trouble in marriages—they were gone a lot, had a lot of combat issues, some of them had trouble with that line between rough and gentle with their families. Not Charlie, though. I never doubted how much he valued me, loved me. I think I felt more respect from Charlie than I had before in my life. And I always felt safe with him. Yes, I'd like to think we'd have lasted. Forever."

"He sounds perfect..."

That made her laugh. "I'm well aware of his flaws, believe me. He could be a slob, unless he was standing inspection, and then he was meticulous—pressed and shiny and buttoned down, while I'd have to follow him around and pick up his towel and underwear. He could get silent on me—deep and quiet and hard to draw out. Who knew if he was thinking about some dark combat experience or his breakfast cereal. If I cried, he had no idea what to do—he was not a natural at handling a woman's emotions. Sometimes he laughed at the most inappropriate times and he was one of those alpha idiots who always had to ask if I had my period when I got upset with him. He could get jealous and possessive, but he completely forgot my birthday. And no one had ever made me feel more cherished on a daily basis than Charlie. He was full of flaws—and I'd marry him all over again. I trusted him with my life—that's hard to find."

It was Dylan's turn to be quiet. He'd never heard a testimony like that before, not even from Lang, who nearly worshipped Sue Ann. "Do you still miss him sometimes?" Dylan asked.

And she decided on honesty. Actually, she had decided over five years ago, she would never lie about something like that. "Yes. Whenever I look at his boys. But missing him isn't the same as longing for him. As long as I can do right by our sons... That's my job,

Dylan." She gave his arm a stroke. "Don't worry about screwing them up by being around them, Dylan. I'm always going to protect my boys."

"Losing him must have been horrendous."

She gave a rueful laugh. "Eight months pregnant with twins? Alone and afraid with a widow's benefit that would barely allow us to live in our car? *Horrendous* would describe it."

"Did you ever regret any of it?"

She smiled with such patience and understanding it almost broke his heart. "It made me grateful for every second."

He looked into her eyes for a long time. He ran a hand over her hair. Then he said, "Let's warm up the omelet."

Over breakfast he told her about Jay and the possibility of a movie deal.

"That would mean living and working in Hollywood again, wouldn't it?" she asked.

"For probably six months, more or less," he said.

"And that's what you want to do, I guess?" she asked.

"I think I'm pretty lucky to have the opportunity. I've visited about a dozen small airports and charter companies around here and I haven't run into any owners or managers that can get their companies out of trouble by signing on for a movie deal."

"Wow. That's a life I can only imagine. It must be crazy."

"A lot of work, really," he said. "I'd rather not need to, but it is what it is."

"I think all those little girls who are now young mothers will be so happy to see your face again," she said.

When they were finished with breakfast and standing on her porch, she said, "It's been wonderful, Dylan. Thank you for everything. And be safe."

He smirked slightly. "I'm going to hang around a couple of days," he said. "But you're going to have to put out."

And she burst out laughing.

Nine

"We have a slight issue," Luke Riordan told Dylan a few days later. "I have reservations on all these cabins—summer people. But I have a solution, if it's not too rough for you. I parked my fifth-wheel trailer on the RV slab behind the cabins and hooked her up— water, sewer and electric. It's yours as long as you want it."

"I'm just thinking about a couple more days," Dylan said.

"Right," Luke said with a crafty grin. He wasn't saying it, that Dylan's "couple of days" had stretched out, edging over three weeks. "Like I said, as long as you want it. It's for special cases like this—when we have one more than we planned on. And I'll give it to you cheaper than the cabin, but don't worry, it's comfortable. Your legs'll hang off the bed, but you get used to that. You'll have everything you need, except the washer and dryer, but you're welcome to borrow ours anytime. And the shower is smaller. If you drop the soap, you're in trouble. You'll have to step out to pick it up."

Dylan laughed, but what really tickled his good humor was the fact that he'd been getting most of his showers at a little cabin in the woods the past week.

Any other woman would have extracted some kind of statement from him, some sort of lame commitment or expression of affection. But not Katie. He'd been in Virgin River for almost a month, the first four days of it having been with his boys on a ride. And it wasn't easy dating a woman with kids. She called the shots. She saw him during the day while the boys were at their summer program, and if she saw him evenings or on weekends, they were busy doing things with the family. He'd been to an animated kids' movie, the kind where you get a red Slurpee spilled right in your lap, popcorn down your shirt and gum in your hair, not to mention the headache that follows. They had dinner at her cabin, dinner at McDonald's, and burgers on the grill at her brother's house. He'd played catch, did a little fishing without catching and had learned video games. All this so he could get laid when the kids weren't home. He had never, not even as a teenager, traded so much of his soul for the affection of a woman.

Katie's brother had stopped scowling so much and was working on getting to know him.

"What will you do if the charter business goes under?" Conner asked.

"There's more to a fixed base operation than charters, but that was the big moneymaker, and that's the part of the business that's suffering the most. We still have aircraft storage, maintenance, instruction, et cetera. My partner is managing all that while I hang out here trying to—"

"Trying to decide how much you like my sister?" he asked.

"Aw, it's not really like that, Conner. There's no question about how much I like your sister. It's just that…we're good friends. And don't worry about Katie or the boys—we're very responsible. Nothing inappropriate going on there—when we're all under the same roof, it's all good and proper."

"So she says…"

"I have a potential job in Los Angeles. I'm waiting to hear more about that, then I'll have to go down there. I'd rather live and work in Montana, but through no fault of anyone's, that might be out of reach at the moment." He laughed lightly. "Lang, my partner, is expecting a slow exodus of our employees from the company—pilots, instructors, maintenance—until we're down to just a few. So I should think about getting a paycheck. But I hate the city."

"I can relate," he said.

"But you always lived in the city, worked in the city," Dylan said.

"And was mad as hell at the circumstances that moved me to this little town…till I got to know this little town. Over the course of a couple of months I realized I didn't just want a different location, I wanted a different kind of life. A slower, simpler, more balanced kind of life. So how do you know you won't enjoy flying out of Los Angeles? Maybe it'll work out."

Of course, Conner assumed it was a flying job. The only thing Dylan had told him about himself was that he was a pilot and instructor. To his amazement, Leslie must not have said anything. Girls usually liked to brag about a Dylan sighting… "I'm sure it'll work out one way or another and as much as I like kicking back here, I'm going to have to go check it out. But there is something I'd kind of like to do before I go— I've been thinking about that jungle gym we put up for the school…why don't we drive over to Eureka and get a smaller version of that for Katie's yard. The front yard, where there's room and she can see them from the porch. Interested?"

Conner tilted his head and lifted a brow. "Are you thinking with a jungle gym in the yard you might be able to sneak Katie into the house for a little nookie?"

"Now, why would I think something like that?" Dylan asked, affronted.

Conner shrugged. "Probably what I would be thinking if Les had a couple of kids. But don't do that. Really, don't. And I'll ask Jack if he minds."

"I'll split the cost," Dylan said. "Might keep her around longer."

"You're a peculiar guy, Dylan," he said. "You're looking at two possibilities for yourself—L.A. or Montana. Yet you want to help me keep her here? Is that to take the heat off? So you can leave her here without feeling guilty?"

"Not that, Conner. I'm on your team. Katie should have someone in her camp she can depend on and the boys need their uncle. I wish I was a better bet," he said. "With the kind of work I do, you never know where I'll end up."

And yet, Dylan was still here. Unable to leave. He could just as easily go back to Payne to await that phone call from Jay Romney, but he hadn't.

Dylan and Conner went to Eureka together on a Tuesday afternoon to pick up that play set for the cabin. Katie was surprised and so delighted she could hardly contain herself. The boys were immediately crawling all over the pieces until their mother yelled at them not to get the parts all mixed up.

"I think I can get this together," Dylan said to Conner. "Why don't you swing by tomorrow after work and see if I put it together to your satisfaction."

"If you have Katie to help, it'll be done right."

"You sound like you trained her yourself."

"Nope," Conner said. "But the same guy who trained me, trained her."

"That's good enough for me."

"Don't get the idea we're bonded here," Conner said. "I'm still pretty concerned about what's going on with you and my sister."

Dylan shook his head in a silent chuckle. "Probably a good thing you ended up here, Conner. I think you're perfect for this place."

Conner narrowed his eyes. "Why do I get the impression that's not a compliment?"

"That kind of thinking is why I haven't dated a female in Payne, Montana, since the senior prom. Not everyone who likes each other ends up married for fifty years. And Katie can think for herself, believe me."

"That's what she keeps telling me, but I still look out for her."

Dylan slapped a hand on Conner's shoulder. "You're a good man, Conner."

"We're not bonded..."

"Right," Dylan said. "Got it."

Dylan passed Katie on the road—she was taking the boys to summer program while he was en route to her cabin to work on erecting the play set. He was still studying the plans when she returned. He suspected she was speeding to get there.

"Let me see," she said, taking the instructions out of his hands. She glanced at them for less than one full minute. "Okay. Good," she said. And then she went to the back of her SUV, lifted the hatch and the floor and pulled out tools and—his eyes almost popped out—a pink tool belt.

"Whoa," he said as she buckled it around her hips. "Katie, baby, I'm not going to be able to concentrate on the joints and trusses if you wear that thing around your hips."

She laughed as she secured her belt, then reached back into the SUV for her toolbox. "We'll have this thing together in no time. I'll do some measuring and you can dig the holes to secure it." She pulled on gloves, grinning at him. "Wanna get going here?"

"You don't know what I want to do," he said.

"Get the post digger. The one Conner left. And get ready to work."

They started at nine-thirty in the morning. At two in the afternoon they stood looking at the finished product, the posts still settling in fast-drying cement. Given there would only be two rambunctious little boys at a time on the jungle gym, there was no concern about it not being quite dry when they were home from their summer school.

"Perfect," she said. "Want a quick shower?"

"After a quick something else…"

"I'm all sweaty…"

He got an evil grin on his face. His eyes were glowing. "I know."

"Are you ninety-nine-percent testosterone?"

"I want you. I've been fighting it all day. That tool belt…"

"Want to sing a round of 'YMCA'?" she asked with amusement and a lift of her eyebrow.

He approached her looking lethal, grabbing her around the waist. "Sadly, the tool belt will have to go…"

"What if Conner comes early…"

"Won't he be surprised," Dylan said, undoing the tool belt. "You and me. Now."

She sighed and took him by the hand. "Come on,

Dylan. You know, I think I give in to you way too much."

"If you're suffering, I'll back off," he said, but he said it with his usual naughty smile.

"You take very good care of me," she said. "But I'm not sure how you survive in Montana if you don't get involved with the local talent. For someone so determined to never marry, I've never met a man who needs a good wife more than you."

Katie's words really hit home with him. Not so much because she was right, which he realized she was, but because he'd never been in a relationship like this. Thirty-five years old and she was his first steady girl since high school. Never mind all his determination to remain single and childless, he'd never met a woman who was so hard to leave. A woman whose special scent and the perfume of her hair and skin made him love drunk. Her body beneath his hands put a fire in him; her voice lulled him and brought him ease. Her laugh lifted his spirits and her self-confidence somehow made him more sure of himself.

Katie might be the one woman in the universe he wanted to touch, to caress and possess, but she was hardly the first person to make this observation about him—that he needed a good, one-man woman in his life. Lang and Adele had made similar comments, though not based on any knowledge of his sexual needs, needs he'd never before been so aware of. Satisfaction usually set him free; sex with Katie only left him wanting more.

Adele had witnessed, while Dylan was growing up, how much he had longed for a safe and nurturing family unit and would often remind him, "Remember that TV family is make-believe, Dylan. Don't depend on it for love." And his best friend would see him around his own family, around Sue Ann and all the kids, and often remark that Dylan had himself all wrong—he was probably the most marriageable man around. "It's obvious you take to it," Lang often said. "You're calmer hanging out around all these little hoodlums than I am."

It was true. The one thing he had long been avoiding was a connection like the one he had with Katie. He feared it more than anything else. He wasn't sure where she found her strength, but he wasn't made of the same stuff. Having her and losing her, by any means—death, divorce, even malignant discord, it would kill him.

The boys were wild about their play set. Dylan and Katie sat on the porch and watched them risk life and limb testing the limits of the jungle gym. Katie interjected commands like, "Not upside down, please," "That's too high!" and "Don't do that!"

And once Dylan said, "Andy! It's Mitch's turn!"

And they all stopped dead still and stared at him.

"What?" he asked.

"You can tell them apart," Katie said softly.

Could he? Well, maybe he did that once. It must have been subconscious. It was definitely spontaneous.

"Well, I've been around a while now."

"A little over a month," she said, smiling at him. "But you're leaving in a couple of days, right?"

He turned to look at her. "Have I stayed too long?" he asked her. "So long that when I leave now, because I *will* have to go, will it hurt you so much that you hate me?"

She looked at him, patiently shaking her head. "Dylan, did I say or do anything that made you think I was involved with you against my will?"

"Of course you didn't…"

"I'm not offended that you have so little faith in me. You haven't known me long enough to judge that fairly. But sometimes it hurts me how little faith you have in yourself." She gave his cheek a stroke. "Do what you have to do. You've had so many successes in your life, stop being so afraid of failure. You're not going to fail."

Those eyes of hers put him in a trance. He could drown in those eyes. He found himself leaning toward her and she turned in her chair to lean into him. And their lips met. He threaded his hand around her neck, his fingers stretching into her hair and he moved over her mouth with longing.

And there was a shriek and a shout from the yard, breaking them apart. "Ew, *Mom,* gross," Andy cried. And Mitch pulled Andy to him and made wild smacking noises. They hugged like little bears and fell to the ground, rolling around in the dirt as they made kissing noises and laughed themselves stupid.

"Silly asses," Dylan muttered to Katie's laughter.

* * *

Almost daily, Dylan rode to the top of that hill where his view was sensational and his iPhone reception was excellent. It was a Thursday afternoon; he'd spent some time with Katie in the morning and now was attending to his business. His first call was always to Childress Aviation. And the news was not getting any better.

"Dylan, buddy, we've had charter cancellations, the BBJ leasing company came for their jet and they're talking about holding us to the lease. That would definitely wipe out petty cash."

"We had petty cash?" Dylan asked.

"By September we're going to have to shut down the training center—not enough instructors or students to run it. I thought we could limp along for six months, but it doesn't look like it. By fall we'll be down to just the fixed base operation—storage, maintenance, fueling and landing facilities. I'm sorry, buddy. We'll be joining the ranks of many other small airports in this country, gasping for breath."

"I'll be on the road in a couple of hours," he said when he could find his voice.

"There's no hurry, man. There's nothing you can do here. Come home when you feel like it. I'm sending out résumés—just looking, just in case something pops up. If I get a job offer, I'm going to take it."

"Flying job?" Dylan asked.

"I've heard some shipping companies are hiring pilots for freight transport. Multiengine heavies, which, thanks to you and your fancy BBJ, I'm qualified to fly.

I might as well throw out my net. It wouldn't have to be forever, just until we get back on our feet."

It was on Dylan's lips to shout *Don't do it!* He knew Lang wanted to live and work in Payne; wanted to raise his family there. So he said, "I know you have your reasons…"

"Five of 'em," Lang said.

"I understand. But you want to live in Montana…"

"I'm just looking around, D. You can't carry us all forever, not on just a little airport that gets minimal use. I'll let you know if I get any promising news."

Dylan pressed his thumb and finger into his eyes, trying to ease the ache there. If Lang got a job offer, he'd probably have to move to a larger city, a larger base of operations. He felt like shouting, *You're my only family! You can't move away!* He said, "We probably should have done this a long time ago, when we could have found flying jobs at the same company…"

"Nah, we had us some good years here and I don't regret a day of it. With any luck, and we're due some, you can operate this company on your own. You can still instruct—you'll get the occasional student. With Stu on maintenance, you'll have yourself a two-man show. It's your land, after all."

"Only sort of," he said. It was Adele's land. They'd paid back what they owed her for the runway and buildings, but she wouldn't take lease payments on the house or land. And he was her only heir.

"Your gran will be fine with it, Dylan. Listen, try not to take this personally—it's a shitty time for businesses like ours. Can't make a living if you can't gas up the planes."

"I feel responsible. I feel like—"

"Bugger off," Lang said. "We knew what we were doing. We did what we wanted to do. We could've gone to work for a commercial carrier and been furloughed ten times by now. We had it good, we just didn't have it forever. I'm not divorcing you, I'm just going to try to get another job."

"Carry your cell," Dylan said unnecessarily. Of course he'd have his cell with him.

"I'll talk to you in the next couple of days. Don't let this gut you, D. It's just change, it's not the end of the world. We do what we have to do."

"Right," he said. "Good luck, man."

The truth was, Dylan could manage his livelihood just as Lang described, though it would be reasonably modest. But then Dylan, alone, didn't need much. He just hated cutting all those other people—Lang, instructors, charter pilots—out of the loop because the company fell on hard times. And since he had a chance to try to save it, he had to at least give it a shot. But he was running low on time and Hollywood had a reputation for moving with all the speed of bureaucracy. If Jay didn't have anything soon, Dylan would have to get back to Montana and try to drum up something to pay the bills. He was open to anything from crop dusting to renting a big truck and turning his airline into a moving company.

When they signed off, he called Jay Romney. "I hope

you have something encouraging to tell me," Dylan said. "If you don't, I'm going to have to—"

"I have excellent news, and thanks for your patience. I have an interested director and a script I optioned last year that I think you'll love," he said. "The director is Sean Adams—big name with a lot of juice. He'd like a meeting. Can you meet us at my office on Monday at noon? I'll have lunch catered in."

"I'll be there," Dylan said. "And, Jay, until we have something nailed down, not a word to anyone."

"Absolutely. Tell me your nearest airport, son," Jay said. "I'll have a chartered jet bring you in."

Dylan burst out laughing. "Is that right?" Dylan could've brokered that deal if he'd been at home. "I'll get there. I'll give you my ticket stub and you can reimburse me."

How funny was that—apparently there were some business entities that still made use of charters.

Dylan would fly down. He'd try to make a deal. Because his best friend might be right, it might be time for a change. But just in case Lang didn't get a flying job right away, Dylan was going to find a way to keep Lang and other employees who were left behind in paychecks. He could sacrifice a few months on a set to get that done.

He'd have to give himself at least one extra day in L.A. before meeting with Romney and Adams—a day to buy some "meeting clothes" since all he had with him were jeans and boots—pretty roughed-up clothes at that.

He dialed again. "Gran, hi," he said. "I'm headed to L.A. to meet with Jay Romney. Are you going to be in L.A.? I'd like to see you."

"I'm here for another month, at least," she said. "Will you stay here?"

He hesitated. He had a feeling he was going to crave a little time alone. "I…ah…I think I'm going to take a rain check on that, Gran. I'll get a hotel room. But I definitely want to get together. I'll call you when I have some kind of schedule. It'll be easier to plan once I know what Jay has to say and whether he needs more of my time. I'll be sure to fill you in."

"Dylan," she began. "Are you coming alone?"

The question almost paralyzed him. The impact of what he was doing hadn't quite hit him until his grandmother asked. "Yes," he said. "Of course."

"I see," she said. "Well, call when you get here. I think we'll have plenty to talk about."

For now he had plenty to *think* about. He really was leaving this time, and once he left he couldn't imagine being able to come back. He had a home in another place and no work in this little mountain town. All he had here was the most awesome woman he'd ever met, and no way to stay with her. He wasn't sure how to tell her that and even considered just running for his life, something he hadn't hesitated to do when involved with other women.

He wouldn't do that to Katie. He'd face her and tell her the truth.

* * *

Early Friday morning he packed up his duffel and settled up with Luke Riordan. Katie usually dropped her boys off at nine so he went to the bar for breakfast. Once she was alone, they'd have their talk. He wasn't sure whether that would happen on her front porch, on their favorite hilltop or wrapped in each other's arms in bed. But it was happening this morning.

"Kind of moody," Jack observed, refilling his coffee cup.

"You?"

"No." Jack laughed. "You."

Dylan thought about it only briefly before he said, "I'm heading out of town this morning."

"I know," Jack said. "Talked to Luke about ten minutes ago."

Dylan put down his cup. "Could news travel any faster around here?"

"Maybe," Jack said. "If you had two bartenders." Then he grinned.

"Well, tuck it under, will you? I just found out I have potential work south of here and haven't told Katie yet. I mean, we're not serious or anything, but—"

The phone rang and on his way to answer it, Jack said, "But you'd like to be a gentleman about this?"

"Exactly," he confirmed.

"I bet we'll see you again," Jack said.

"Don't bet a lot," Dylan muttered.

Jack lifted the cordless that sat beside the cash register. "Jack's," he said. "Yeah? Is that a fact? Oh, yeah, trust me, she's close. Well, stay inside, I'll come right out." He hung up and looked at Dylan. "Katie says she's got three bear cubs playing on the new jungle gym and she can't get the boys to the car." Dylan shot to his feet. "She can't see the mother, but I guaran-damn-tee you she's nearby. Real nearby."

And Dylan shot for the door.

"Whoa, whoa, whoa! What are you thinking, man? We'll go in the truck, you don't want to be riding out there to chat with Mama Bear on a motorcycle. Let me grab my rifle and tell Preacher to mind the store." And then he turned and walked through the kitchen, leaving Dylan to follow.

Dylan just stood there for a moment. Then he shot outside and got on his Harley, but he rode it around to the back of the bar and caught Jack just as he was getting into his truck. "I'll follow you. I can outrun a Mama Bear on this if I have to."

"Your funeral," Jack said.

"We have bear in Montana, you know. And not these candy-ass bears—we have grizzlies."

"I realize that," Jack said. "I bet you also have a rifle in Montana."

"I'm a little under-armed this trip. But I'd rather face a bear than a moose."

"I hear bad things about moose."

"Who do you think chases them off the runway? Could we move it? Or you'll be following me."

"Don't worry—I told her to stay inside." And with that, Jack got in the truck and led the way.

Ah, just as I thought, Dylan observed silently. He spotted Mama in the bushes, scavenging. And sure enough, three fat cubs were enjoying the jungle gym. When Jack entered the clearing, her back had been to her cubs, digging around in the bushes, maybe for berries. But she turned and stood to her full and intimidating height; she was an enormous black bear. Jack tooted the horn while Dylan positioned his bike to make a run for it. Mama puffed up and made annoyed noises while her triplets ran for the cover of her skirts. Dylan saw Jack pull the rifle out of the rack.

Jack pressed down on the horn again and both men watched as Mama Bear, not real happy with the situation, disappeared into the brush, her triplets behind her. The men watched as they ambled off as if bored and perturbed. Typical black bear, she was passive and really didn't want to tango with humans as long as the kids were safe.

Jack gave the horn a couple more blasts, waiting a full minute and then opened the door, rifle in hand. Dylan moved his bike up beside Jack, but kept it running.

"She could be two feet on the other side of the big blackberry bushes, but I kind of doubt it. If she felt threatened, she'd get the triplets to a safer playground. I had to shoot a bear once—same deal. She was scavenging while her cub was curious about the building I was doing at the bar. Next thing you know, I'm in a situation…"

"Those lessons come hard when you're not raised

around 'em," Dylan said, turning off the bike and raising it on the stand. When he'd been transplanted from the city to the near-wilderness, he knew nothing. Ham, short for Hammond Pierce, the daytime hand, had been a grumpy old coot twenty years ago. He took Dylan under his wing as a matter of survival—if Dylan stupidly got himself killed around the horses, cows or wildlife, Ham would be out of work. Now he was even older, more weathered, crankier, and yet did even more work around the place than he'd done twenty years before.

Dylan ran up on the porch just as the cabin door opened. Katie looked scared. He'd never seen her with that look.

"Maybe I've been kidding myself about wanting adventure," she said. "I threw up in the airplane, the bear scared me to death and I bet if I ever got a chance to learn to rock climb, I'd probably fall off and break my neck. Maybe I'm just a city girl who should stick to books and movies for my adventure fix."

Ten

"First of all," Dylan told Katie and the boys, "you don't want to run away from a bear—they'll probably chase you and they're very fast. If you're farther away like you were, you can make a lot of noise, like Jack did with the horn. If you're closer, back away slowly. Bears like this one are usually kind of shy—"

"She didn't look shy," Katie said.

"That's because she had to protect her children—you know how that is. But if you don't threaten the children, she'll probably go away quietly. The one thing you never want to do is get between the mother and her cubs. And if you find yourself in a really scary situation with a bear, lay facedown on the ground, cover your head and neck with your hands and play dead."

Dylan crouched in front of Mitch. "Mitch, if you come face-to-face with a bear, what are you going to do?"

"Back away slowly."

He swiveled. "Andy, if you find yourself between

a bear and her cubs and the mama seems angry, what should you do?"

"Make noise?"

"That's if you're not too close—if you're kind of close and she seems angry, you lay down—"

"And play dead!"

"Right. On your stomach, facedown, cover your head, like this," he said, demonstrating by lacing his fingers together behind his head. "Now here's an easy one—if you're about to go outside but there's a bear in the yard…?"

"Stay in," they answered in unison.

"Excellent." He rose to his full height. "And if there's a bear in your yard but you're safe in the house…?" he asked, looking at Katie.

"Noise?"

"That could work. Not like screaming, like maybe banging a spoon on a tin pan. Something to alert the bear there's a person around so they just leave. And you have that mace, in case you get right down to it."

"They don't actually like that too much," Jack said. "I've heard of bears getting very angry about that, but if it's your only option…."

"Katie, since you've had this bear family in the yard, can you remember to go over bear safety rules with the boys often?" Dylan asked. "You'll probably never see them again, but… Rules for safety. Every day isn't too often."

She got a very queer look on her face before she said,

"Of course." She blinked a couple of times. "Ready to get to summer school, guys?"

"Let me drop them off," Jack offered. "I'm headed back to town anyway. I'll make sure they get checked in. Miss Timm is a bear about that." Then he laughed at his own joke.

"Thanks, Jack. Get your backpacks, guys," she said.

In less than two minutes the twins were in the truck and Jack was backing out of the clearing. Dylan and Katie were still standing on the porch. When the truck was out of sight, she faced him.

"So. You're leaving."

"How would you know that?" he asked.

"Your duffel is on the back of the bike and you have a confused look on your face, like you don't know the way out."

He shook his head. "I can take that duffel off the bike and put you there for one more ride. Anywhere you'd like to go."

"Tell me what you came here to tell me," she said.

He gently grasped her upper arms to pull her closer. He kneaded her arms and looked into her eyes. "Here's what's happening, Katie. I talked to Lang—a couple of our employees have left the company, hopefully for greener pastures because they know we're in trouble. Our big plane is gone. Lang is going to send out his résumé—he has a family to think about. I have a company circling the drain and a producer in L.A. who wants to sign me for a movie if he can, a chance for me to bankroll that little Montana airport. I'd rather fly than act, but I'm a businessman—I'll do what I have to do."

"I think that's admirable," she said.

"Movies—they're not exactly forty-hour weeks," he said. "It's a major commitment, for months. It won't be quick. There won't be time off. And for me, who has been out of the business for twenty years…well, I have a lot of catching up to do if I'm going to do a decent job."

"I'm sure."

"I don't know when I'll see you again, Katie."

"I told you—I don't have any expectations."

"I have work there and in Montana," he said. "I don't have any real reason—"

"I know, Dylan. It was a fling, I know. Not something I've ever done before, but I knew going in that you were… How did you describe yourself? Kind of hit and run?"

"You're probably better off," he said.

"Sure. Right. You told me—you have bad-relationship DNA. Listen, don't drag this out. This is no big surprise… Actually, I knew before my tire went flat, and it has nothing to do with your DNA. Our lives just don't match."

"I'd like to ask you to come with me, but I have no idea what I'd be asking you to do. I have no idea what the next months would—"

She was shaking her head. "Nah. Tempting though you are, I have commitments here. I have kids to raise and I promised them a stable and steady father figure.

Plus, I think I like it here, bears and all. People step up for each other. There's a real dearth of handsome movie stars, but…"

"I haven't been a movie star since I was about four-teen. You do get that, right?"

She nodded. "Sure. But listen—my life has finally leveled out after a rocky year and I'm not in a position to take risks. Not with my boys. They're so good, so re-silient, I sometimes take them for granted. But now and then one of them will say something that reminds me they're only little boys—they're tender and they need security. Just a few weeks ago Mitch asked if I thought his dad would like him." Her eyes misted. "My first commitment is to them. I'm not for taking chances. Do you get *that,* Dylan?"

He gave a slow, solemn nod. "You don't have any regrets about us, do you?"

She shook her head and tried a smile, though it was tremulous. "You're the best four-week boyfriend I've ever had. The only one."

He swallowed hard. "Will you tell them goodbye? Will you tell them I couldn't wait to see them again and I said goodbye?"

"Sure."

"I could wait, but—"

"If it's all the same to you, I can't do this all day. So I might've regressed to my childhood and had a little crush…"

He leaned toward her and touched her lips gently. "Little?" he asked softly.

"Come on, think about this," Katie said. "You don't really want a lot of blubbering and sniveling and someone clinging to your ankles as you try to get away. You have business to get to and I..." She lifted her chin. "I have a life to get on with."

He smiled at her. "You were the best time I've ever had, Katie."

"You weren't bad. I'll think about you sometimes."

"Our timing might've been off," Dylan said. "If we'd met at another time, in another way..."

"There's a small danger there, too," she said. "You don't want to get between me and the cubs. If you think that bear was scary..."

"If it matters, I've never had this much trouble saying goodbye before."

She swallowed and her nose got a little pink. "Thanks for saying that. Now please, get going. Are you driving the motorcycle all the way to L.A.?"

"I rode it all the way here from Montana—not a quick trip. But I'm in kind of a hurry now. I should... Katie, I'm sorry. I don't think I'm going to see you again because... I let you down." He was quiet for a second. Then in a hoarse voice he said, "I hope you get on with your life in exactly the way you want to."

He leaned toward her, kissed her forehead and turned to go. Halfway to his motorcycle, he turned back, closed the distance between them in two giant strides and took her roughly into his arms. He covered her mouth in a powerful kiss, licking open her lips and taking possession of her. She let out a small whimper, holding him tightly, answering his kiss with her acqui-escence. A tear slid down her cheek.

When he pulled away, he touched her cheek gently with his thumb.

"Yeah," she said. "You just weren't going to be happy till you made that happen. Now get outta here. I'm really done saying goodbye."

A little peck on the lips and he left.

He popped a wheelie on the way out of the clearing.

Katie stood there for a while after the sound of that motorcycle was little more than a distant purr. Then she sniffed, wiped her cheeks and muttered, "What was I thinking? I should've known better. Those Hollywood bad boys never change."

Dylan had been on his bike for over four weeks and he was in no mood to ride all the way to L.A. His brain was sluggish and he was distracted. *This is exactly what happens,* he told himself, *when you let yourself get too comfortable.* He'd had plenty of girlfriends in the past but had never had the kind of routine he'd had with Katie. He'd let himself get lured into a false sense of security and now, headed for the job he dreaded but had to do, he was feeling a profound sense of loss.

And he had to get over it. Fast. She was moving on. A kind man would not do anything to hold her back.

He drove to that small airport in Arcata, talked the manager into storing his bike in a hangar and hitched a flight to Santa Rosa where he'd pick up a nonstop to Los Angeles. A month ago he'd packed for a seven-day ride with his friends and everything was getting pretty worn out even though he'd done laundry; he intended to spruce up his scant wardrobe. He wasn't going to try to impress anyone, but he would have the courtesy to look civilized for business meetings.

Dylan was completely miserable about setting Katie free, but kept telling himself it was necessary. She might be disappointed in him for a while, then maybe a little angry, but ultimately he believed she'd be glad she didn't have to worry about how her future would turn out with someone like him, some actor with a bad track record. A fling, she'd said. And as she'd said from the beginning, she could do a lot better.

There was one significant problem—he'd never met a woman like her before and probably never would again. Better? He wouldn't. Not a chance.

"Okay, so I want Katie," he muttered. So what? he asked himself. He'd get over it. He'd gotten over other things he wanted but couldn't have.

The minute he got on the ground in Santa Rosa and turned on his phone, it came alive. There were voice mails and missed calls. He checked the call log while he waited for his flight to L.A. to depart. His mother? His *MOTHER?* And his half brother, Bryce? His stepsister, Blaine? There must have been twenty calls and he'd never given anyone this phone number. Lang, knowing his family history, would never have shared his cell number. He'd had a few calls from family members over the years, either at Childress Aviation or the Montana house, but they always wanted something from him, not looking for ways to reach out in friendship or, God forbid, affection.

He couldn't resist and listened to the first message. And he thought, *This is exactly how you get reeled in, by letting them in your ear, your head.* Even though he hated his mother, he loved her and had always wanted her to act like a mother.

"Dylan, darling, I heard you're going to be in town to talk about a movie and I have to talk to you first, because, well, the business hasn't been real nice to me in the past few years and I'd like to…"

He clicked off. He didn't even want to know what Cherise would like—a part? A job? A loan from his grandmother? A contact? She had a script he should read? A little party at which she would like him to appear to show the public they were still family? The possibilities were endless.

He called Jay Romney. "It's been twenty-four hours since I made an appointment with you and I have twenty messages on my phone from family members. I never gave them this number. I thought we agreed— no one would be told about the potential for a movie."

"Are you fucking kidding me?" Jay asked, genuinely shocked. "It just figures. Listen, kid, with all due respect, your family has a lot of friends in low places and your call came into my office. Delete them. I can't control everything."

"You're saying you had nothing to do with this?" he asked.

"Absolutely not! Why would I? I want you for a

movie! You think I'd screw that by handing out your personal cell number? Here's mine, log it. You call me on my cell only. And if you want to reschedule to avoid these people, I'll do it. Just say the word."

He keyed in the cell number and then, after a moment of silence, he asked, "No one's dying, are they? Because I didn't listen to the messages."

"No one's dying that I know of. But in your family…"

"I listened to my mother's voice mail—she said she heard I'd be in town about a movie and the business hasn't been kind to her the last few years…and that's about where I deleted," he said.

"You're a sweet kid, Dylan, but you can cut 'em loose. You're on your own here. I'm not dealing with anyone but you."

"If any of them are involved in this…"

"I'm not dealing with anyone but you, Dylan. That's it. On my word."

His word was probably worth a cup of coffee and little more, but of all the people he had worked with in Hollywood, Jay was probably the most honest and trustworthy. He said, "I'll see what happens. If this gets out of hand, obviously there won't be a movie with me in it."

And then he traveled the rest of the way, with his phone off. He made it to L.A. in the late afternoon, rented a car, found himself a nondescript hotel and watched TV, something he did rarely. He spent Saturday at a mall, buying more appropriate clothes and shoes. He checked his call log and messages, looking for one in particular, but the only one that mattered to him wasn't there. And of course it shouldn't be—they'd said goodbye.

Sunday night he drank a little more than usual and when he slept he dreamt of Katie, her warm body against him. Not a sex dream… It was much worse than that—it was more intimate than sex. It was the kind of closeness he had with her. She was there, soft and sweet and laughing, saying smart-ass things, holding him against his worst childhood fears of loss and abandonment.

On Monday when he went to Jay Romney's office, standing in front of the door, waiting on the street, was Cherise. His mother.

"Dylan," she said, a bit breathless. *"Sweetheart!"*

"Why does anything ever surprise me," he muttered.

Cherise straightened herself. She would be sixty-three by now, older than his father would be had he lived, but she didn't look a day over forty, though her skin was a little tight across her face. She was too thin, but that would not be too thin for Cherise's tastes; she worked hard at thin.

"Is that all you have to say to your mother after all these years?"

She hadn't called him once in twenty years to ask how he was getting along. Never just to talk. She always had an agenda that revolved around him helping her out in some way. For reasons he would never be able to explain, he had achieved the kind of enduring popularity and success his extended family found enviable and it was that for which they reached out to him, the rare times they had. "Pretty much," he said. "I didn't listen to all the messages."

She stiffened as if affronted. "I only said I'd like to see you while you're in town…"

"There were calls from Bryce and Blaine," he said. "Why are you circling the wagons? What is it you think I can do for you?"

"Can we have a late lunch? Talk things over?"

"How did you find out I'd be here?" he asked. "How did you get my number?"

"I can't actually remember… Can we just have a meal? A drink? Dessert later on?"

He laughed. "You don't eat dessert, Cherise."

"Please, can't you call me Mother?"

"No, I can't. That train left the station a long time ago," he said.

She straightened her spine. "Are you staying at your grandmother's house?" she asked.

He briefly wondered what that had to do with anything and then as quickly he realized family would start showing up wherever he was housed. He employed his considerable acting talents to behave as if bored. He looked at his watch and said, "You have sixty seconds to spit it out—tell me what you want from me. Otherwise, there is no conversation between us. I'm here on business."

"I want a job in your film."

"Well," he said, smiling. "There's a big surprise. And jobs for Blaine and Bryce, as well?"

"I'm not in the business of finding them work—we're not in touch. I just want something to do, quite honestly. And if I could do it with my son…"

He took a step toward her. "You're not in touch with them, yet they also had my cell number?"

"I can't explain that. I have nothing to do with that."

He whistled. "Amazing," he said. "Sorry, Cherise, but we're not going to work together. It would be a very bad mix. Have a nice day." And he stepped past her into the office building. But his heart squeezed. That was his mother, and she was still not above using him. No wonder he was so fucked up.

When he stepped into Jay's office, Sean Adams was already there and rose to shake his hand. The first thing Dylan said to Jay was, "Your office is now off-limits. Cherise Fontaine met me at the front door, looking for work in a movie I haven't even agreed to do. I think we'd better move this meeting to a more secure location or you might have every one of my extended family in the lobby. You have a leak."

"Well, shit," Jay said. "Come with me."

"I hope there's a back door," Dylan said.

Katie had been cautious about how much time Dylan spent around her cabin while the boys were home so they didn't start to think of him as a member of the family. If he was around for dinner or the evening, she shuffled him out the door by the time she was getting the boys ready for bed. But it didn't take Andy and Mitch any time at all to notice Dylan was missing. They asked if he was coming over five minutes after they got home from summer program on Friday afternoon. Katie had talked to herself all day long about sucking it up; she did not want her boys to grieve his departure. "Well, funny you should ask," she said with fake non-chalance. "Dylan had to leave town—he has to work."

"When is he coming back?" Mitch asked.

"I'm not sure," she said. "I'll be sure to ask him that if he calls. But, honey, if he's out of town working, he's very busy."

"I don't want to miss him," Andy said. "When is he calling us?"

Oh, God, that shot her through the heart. He was not likely to call. All part of goodbye was admitting their relationship, such as it was, was over. He had to go where work led him and she had to get on with her life. That was a roundabout way of saying they'd go for the clean break.

But what she said was, "I'm not sure, sweetheart. But if he does, I promise to ask him if he's coming back to visit."

That brief exchange had prompted her to reach out to her brother. "I need a little backup," she said. "If you have a little time this weekend, could you spend some with the boys? Anything that comes to mind."

"Sure," he said. "You and Dylan have some plans?"

"Well, that's the thing—Dylan had to go to L.A. to

work. Of course I knew this was going to happen soon. L.A. or Montana. The man has to earn a living."

"Are the kids upset about that?"

"No, I wouldn't say so, but they did have fun with him when he was here and they asked about him. I think it might be best to distract them. Do you mind?"

Conner, oblivious to what might be under the surface of Katie's request, simply answered, "Be glad to. I love hanging with the guys. Think they'd like to go fishing?"

Katie let go a sigh of gratitude. "Sunday?"

"Sunday it is. You want to go?"

"I think I'd like to spend a little time with Les. Thank you for her, by the way."

Conner chuckled. "My pleasure, but I didn't exactly get her for you."

Just what the doctor ordered, Katie thought. The boys were distracted by fishing with Uncle Conner and Katie had some girl time with Leslie. When Leslie suggested the front porch, Katie asked for the back porch, away from the curious eyes of neighbors who might pass by.

"Have you heard from Dylan?" Leslie asked right away.

Katie shook her head. "I'm sure that's my doing. I suggested he had to do his thing and I should get on with my life. Les, I don't fit into his life and he doesn't really fit into mine."

"Are you sure about that?" Leslie asked.

"From the first second I saw him, I knew we came

from opposite worlds. He might be living in Montana and running a small airport, but he's a movie star. All he had to do was pick up the phone and bam! Hollywood wants him back."

Leslie was shaking her head. "He doesn't seem like that kind of guy…"

"But he is, that's the fact. He's never going to be a regular guy who does ordinary work—he's always going to be that guy that everyone wants, the guy with one foot out the door. And surrounded by a lot of irresistible women, I'm sure."

Leslie straightened and leaned toward Katie. "Your feelings are hurt," she said. "I don't blame you, but I think you're dreaming up roadblocks instead of bridges."

"He told me he didn't know when he'd see me again. And that I was the best time he'd ever had."

"Well, that was dumb of him. I think he missed his cue to say he loved you."

"Because that's not in the script, Les."

"I don't usually do this, but… Call him, Katie. Call him and ask him how he is—tell him you miss him."

"I can't," she said.

"Why not?"

"Because right now my heart hurts. If I call him and he doesn't answer or return the call, my heart will be in tiny pieces." She shook her head. "I'm so naive—I didn't think after just a few weeks, I'd be in this kind of shape." Then with glistening eyes she said, "Please don't tell Conner. Dylan didn't do anything wrong—

it's not his fault I let myself fall in love. He told me he was only staying a little while, waiting to hear about a potential job in L.A.—I knew that from the start. Honestly, I sent him away. He's not the kind of man to put down roots."

"He had roots in Montana... I'm just saying, maybe he didn't really want to be sent away."

"If he didn't, I'll hear from him," Katie said. "But I haven't yet. Not even a call to say he arrived safely."

Katie didn't like how much she thought about her time with Dylan, but she was determined to move forward. On Wednesday after summer program, she took the boys to McDonald's. She told herself it was just a treat for them, not a walk into the past for her. But when they wanted to go to the bathroom and she said she'd take them, Andy said, "If Dylan was here, we could go in the boys'!" And she almost burst into tears.

Man, she'd really been living in a fantasy land. She had briefly thought both their lives were about to change based on a chance meeting. What a little girl she'd been!

One thing she could hold close to her heart—he had been very good to her. Generous, tender, funny and considerate. He didn't act like the kind of guy who was using someone for sex, not that she had any experience with that. And when she could stop feeling sorry for herself long enough to be honest with herself, she had to admit, he never misled her. Never. She was determined to be a grown-up about this. It was brief, it was awesome, it was over.

If you love THIS book...

We'll send you 2 FREE BOOKS from the same collection right to your door when you return the attached card.

No purchase required. This is a fast, fun way for you to try the convenience of the Reader Service without risking a penny. Keep your free gifts with our compliments, whether or not you continue.

4 Mail card for **FREE GIFTS!**

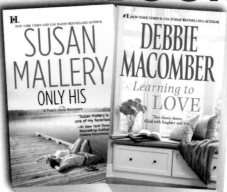

How do you spell

EASY?

E for "**enjoy** the convenience of home delivery!"

A for "**absolutely** no commitment." (Try it risk-free!)

S for "**savings** on every book, every time!"

Y for "**YES!** Send me 4 FREE GIFTS worth over $25.00!"

We'll send the best new books in this collection *right to your door*— starting with **2 FREE BOOKS** and **2 MYSTERY GIFTS**, and no obligation to purchase anything. See details on back of this card.

194/394 MDL FMR6

FIRST NAME   LAST NAME

ADDRESS

APT #   CITY

Visit us online at
www.ReaderService.com

STATE/PROV.   ZIP/POSTAL CODE

▶ DETACH AND MAIL CARD TODAY!

RSA-ROM-12

The Reader Service - Here's How It Works:

Accepting your 2 free books and 2 free mystery gifts (gifts valued at approximately $10.00) places you under no obligation to buy anything. You may keep the books and gifts and return the shipping statement marked "cancel". If you do not cancel, about a month later we'll send you 4 additional books and bill you just $5.99 each in the U.S. or $6.49 each in Canada. That is a savings of at least 25% off the cover price. It's quite a bargain! Shipping and handling is just 50¢ per book in the U.S. and 75¢ per book in Canada.* You may cancel at any time, but if you choose to continue, every month we'll send you 4 more books, which you may either purchase at the discount price or return to us and cancel your subscription.

*Terms and prices subject to change without notice. Prices do not include applicable taxes. Sales tax applicable in N.Y. Canadian residents will be charged applicable taxes. Offer not valid in Quebec. All orders subject to credit approval. Credit or debit balances in a customer's account(s) may be offset by any other outstanding balance owed by or to the customer. Please allow 4 to 6 weeks for delivery. Books received may not be as shown. Offer available while quantities last.

And after that trip to McDonald's, the boys stopped asking when he would call or come back.

The following weekend brought the Fourth of July and a town picnic, an event she hoped would help take her mind off Dylan. She met even more neighbors, got to know quite a few of the young mothers who took their kids to the summer program and relaxed in the shade of a big tree while her kids ran around with their new friends. But she couldn't help wondering how Dylan was spending the holiday.

A couple of days later she drove to the grocery store while the boys were in school. She loaded up on basics—milk, cereal, bread and eggs. Standing in the magazine aisle, she glanced at the gossip rags. And there, looking back at her, was Dylan Childress, those bedroom eyes and sexy smile grasping at her. On one paper there was a headline that read Guess Who's Back in Town? The next had a picture of him laughing, holding a drink, his arm about the shoulders of an older man described as his producer. Apparently there would be a movie after all. And the third front page picture was Dylan pressing his lips into the neck of a beautiful blonde, an actress who had briefly played his girlfriend in the old sitcom, *Rough Housing,* when they were both about fourteen. The caption was Old Flames Reunited?

Well. He'd moved on. She had been having trouble up to that very moment, but the sight of those pictures provided a terrific kick in the ass.

She left her grocery cart standing abandoned in the aisle and bought all three papers. So…he managed to slip back into his former lifestyle with ease. He'd gone to Hollywood to make a movie, to party, to hook up.

No wonder he hadn't called. He'd been quite busy.

Eleven

After reading a script and having a few meetings with Jay and Sean about potential costars, Dylan put the contract negotiations in the capable hands of his grandmother's current agent, Lee Drake. From this point on his conversations with Jay or Sean would not involve details of the terms of the contract.

They did have conversations about the script, about rewrites and wholesale changes to the story, other actors being considered. Although the agents were still talking, Dylan was aware of a ridiculous amount of money for his role as a badass biker dude who ends up being the good guy. "That's my favorite part," he told Adele. "I've been trying to end up the good guy for a long time now."

"I don't think you see yourself clearly," she replied. "Not in terms of the script, but in life."

It should not have surprised him that he continued to show missed calls on his phone log from Cherise, Bryce and Blaine after a week of ignoring them. He was nearly to the point of returning at least one of those calls if only to make the point that he was not taking their calls. But that choice was taken away from him while he was standing at the Starbucks counter waiting for his coffee.

"Dylan?"

Even though it had been many years, he recognized his stepsister's voice. He turned and said, "Hello, Blaine. What a coincidence, running into you here."

She shook her head and her pretty blond hair swished over her shoulders. "It's not a coincidence. I've been looking for you."

He figured as much. She must have followed him. But from where? He hadn't been going to Jay's office since that first day. They'd met in restaurants, lobbies, Jay's or Sean's homes, various venues not advertised or even recorded in appointment books or on Black-Berries.

"Do you have a minute?" she asked.

She was a beautiful woman and he remembered when he was just a boy that he had a terrific crush on her. She was his third stepfather's daughter and spent lots of time at his home. Thank God she'd never given him the time of day; he'd been far too young to know how complicated she was. Now, at about forty, she was still stunning, difficult to comprehend given the problems she'd had since her teen years—prescription drug issues, some alcohol abuse, a few stints in rehab. He'd lost track of her marriages, or maybe he'd ignored them.

"Let's get this over with. Can I buy you a coffee?" he offered.

"Skinny latte," she answered.

When he handed her the latte, she tilted her head and said, "Patio?"

"After you."

She led the way outside and sitting on the far side of the patio at a table, under the protection of an umbrella, was Bryce. Of course.

Bryce, only thirty-two, wasn't holding up nearly as well. He looked bloated and bleary-eyed and Dylan was having trouble even remembering what his issues were. And in a flash of pity he recalled that Bryce had been only twelve when Adele took Dylan away. Blaine had been twenty and had already had many acting jobs, including a brief guest appearance on Dylan's sitcom. But ages aside, these two and a few others from his family had been left to the dysfunction of Cherise and her ex-husbands, not to mention the instability of their peer group. They probably had no idea what a functional family looked like.

Dylan had a moment of feeling like the most emotionally stable member of the family and that was a first. He usually felt impossibly screwed up.

Bryce stood from the table and, with hands in his pockets, gave a solemn nod, eyes at half mast. And Dylan remembered—depression was his half brother's shtick. Medication might account for his dazed appearance. "Sit down, Bryce. Take a load off," he said, gesturing with his cup. "All right, you two. What's this about?"

"We heard you were back for a movie," Blaine said. "Good luck with that. We have an idea."

"First of all—how'd you know I was here? And how'd you get my number?"

"Someone saw your name and number on an appointment book and copied it. It happens all the time, you know that."

He shook his head in wry amusement. "I've been away a long time. Why don't we cut to the chase here—save us all some time. What are you looking for?"

"Like I said, an idea," she repeated. Bryce merely nodded. "A reality show—a reunion of the Childress family. We could bring the family together, the ones who are available, and get some of our relationship issues resolved. *Big Brother* meets *Kate Plus 8*. Brothers and sisters reuniting."

It took great effort to keep his mouth from dropping open. "Get outta here!" he said, astonished.

"Mom would produce."

Dylan leaned toward Blaine. "First of all, Cherise isn't your mom, second, I'm the only Childress besides Adele and third, if you think I'd even consider trying to resolve our relationship issues at all, much less on camera, your last link to reality has slipped." He leaned back. "Besides, I already ran into Cherise. She wanted me to get her a part in a movie, which by the way hasn't been signed yet."

Bryce and Blaine exchanged surprised looks. "You saw her?" Blaine asked.

"I did. I told her the same thing I'm telling you—this isn't going to happen. If by some miracle you managed to convince anyone on this movie to put either of you on the roster, that would be my cue to move on. And no—I would never air our dirty laundry in public. God, what a thought."

"Dylan, she didn't say she'd talked to you," Blaine said.

"She said you're not in touch," Dylan pointed out.

"It was her idea," Bryce said.

Dylan looked at Bryce. "Oh, you do speak?" he asked.

And Bryce nodded. "Mom came up with this. I didn't like it too much, but—"

"It would be therapeutic," Blaine said. "Honesty and accountability and amends. It could help people. We could get a really good therapist on the show."

Dylan was surprised he didn't run screaming from Starbucks. He was almost sympathetic. Obviously Cherise was going to try to stack the deck by getting herself a part in Dylan's film first, then push for the reality show. What a circus.

"Listen, you two. Don't let people capitalize on your problems like this. Work on your own stuff. In private. Get healthy and strong. Get on solid ground. Have that therapist make a house call or two. You don't have to show the world how vulnerable you are."

"Will you think about it?" Blaine asked.

He stood slowly. "Sorry, but no. I wouldn't even consider it. In fact, in the twenty years I've been away, I've probably gotten too private to even do a movie, but—" He just gave his head a little shake. "I have my reasons that have nothing to do with anyone in the family, so let's retire the whole idea. Please don't ask me again." He locked eyes first with Blaine and then Bryce. "Seriously. Give it up. I hope you both do well, I really do. But we're not going to work together. Not ever."

In a way he was glad the surprise meeting with his half brother and stepsister had happened. He went directly to his hotel and checked out. He'd move in with Adele; she had more than enough room and the gated neighborhood had excellent security. When he phoned her to tell her he was coming, she was elated. He would explain why later. Then he went to the phone store and bought a new, upgraded phone. They put his memory card in the new phone and changed his number. First he called Lang to be sure his best friend and the company could reach him.

And then he called Katie, so glad to have an excuse. "Katie, how are you?"

"Dylan?"

"It's me."

"Well, I'm fine, but what about you? Are you all right?" she asked.

"Fine, but my cell number got out and I started getting unwelcome calls. I changed numbers and wanted to be sure you had the new one in case…in case you wanted to call."

"I don't want to bother you—aren't you making a movie?" she asked.

"I'm still talking about the specifics. These things don't usually happen fast. It's so weird to be here—so different and yet so much the same," he said. He wished he had explained in detail about his family, but that would take such a long time and it couldn't be done now over the phone. She might find it all difficult to believe. "It looks like it should work out. Are you all right? Really?"

"Sure. Of course. We…ah…went to the town Fourth of July picnic. The boys went fishing one Sunday with Conner. I guess that's all I can report."

"What about the bear, Katie? Any problems?"

"I guess she didn't like Jack's horn—we haven't seen her."

"But do you peek outside before you go out?"

She laughed and made him want her so much. "You bet I do."

"And the boys? Are they having fun?"

She hesitated before she answered. "If there's one thing they know, it's how to have fun!"

He wanted to ask her if she missed him. He was afraid of the answer, so he said instead, "I miss you."

"Aw, that's so nice, Dylan. I bet you're very busy. I bet you're running into lots of old friends."

"A few," he admitted, though he wanted to tell her it was more old enemies. "I'd rather be anywhere else…"

"Was it the right decision? Going to L.A. to make a movie?"

"I won't know until everyone agrees and there's a contract. You know why I'm doing this."

"You must be grateful that you *can,*" she stressed.

"Will you tell the boys I called and said to tell them 'hi'?"

Again there was a pause. "Listen, I know you'll understand this, or will at least try, but they don't know about movies and aviation companies and all that and…I don't want them to fix their hopes on you, Dylan. They're just little boys. They aren't going to get it the way I do—that you don't know when you'll see us again. Or if…"

"Can you believe this, Katie—that I *want* to see you again?"

Very quietly she said, "I can, but they might not. They're very impatient. They have trouble waiting for things like Christmas and birthdays. When you get down to it, I have trouble with that, too. Waiting. Wondering if it'll ever come." Then there was a moment of quiet before she said, "But you enjoy yourself—I'm sure all your fans will be so glad to have you back! Listen, I hate to cut this off, but—"

"Katie, write down this number, in case you want to tell me something." Then he reeled it off. "Call me if you want to talk. Anytime."

"What if I interrupt something important?" she asked.

"Then I'll call you back. But don't worry about that, just call if you want to."

"All right, then. I'm glad you called. I'd better—"

"I miss you, Katie," he said again.

In the quiet that followed, he wondered if she was thinking about what to say next. But...

"Be safe, Dylan," she said.

When they disconnected, he closed his eyes for a moment and took a breath. She wouldn't say it; she was afraid to say it. He could hardly blame her. Why would she pour more emotion into a situation that had no clear resolution?

He would think about that. Where he was going. And with whom.

Katie looked at the number she'd scribbled down. She could hear his voice in her head. *I miss you, Katie.* She lifted the folded tabloids from the kitchen counter and opened the one with Dylan kissing some blonde's neck.

"You'll be fine," she said. And then with sarcasm she thought, *Be brave.*

Conner couldn't count the number of days he felt grateful for finding Leslie. Their lives had converged at probably the most challenging of times for both of them—he was in hiding and she was escaping from a painful divorce. Yet now, just a few months later, they were living together in this little town, at peace in their relationship, their complicated lives settled. He even had his sister and nephews close by, which gave him no small amount of comfort.

But all wasn't cheery. Katie had grown quiet and distant. Well, he supposed that was to be expected—she'd had a fling with a guy who was just passing through and, unsurprisingly, he actually passed through. He was gone and she was left lonely. Again.

"Should I be worried about Katie?" he asked Les.

"Why? Because Dylan went to work?"

"Well…yeah, that. She seemed to be hanging tough for a while, but he's been gone a couple of weeks and it's like he took her sparkle with him."

She grinned at him. "How many women did you have short relationships with over the years, Conner?"

"But this is Katie," he said. "Unless she never mentioned it to me, I don't think she's had a guy she…" *slept with, laughed with a lot and who put a shine in her eyes*... "…liked a lot. Since Charlie. You know?"

"Why don't you give her a call?" Leslie suggested. "See how she's doing. Ask her if she wants to come over for ice cream. Or maybe we could bring the ice cream to her."

So he did that, he called her. And then he went back to Leslie, a pained expression on his face, and said, "I'm going out to check on her. Andy said she's in the bathtub. Crying. In the tub crying."

Leslie shot to her feet. "Wait! Just wait. Grab the ice cream. We'll both go. You can keep the boys busy and please, let me talk to Katie. I don't think this is a job for a big brother."

"Why not?" he asked indignantly. "I could hunt down the son of a bitch and beat the shit outta him."

She stared at him coolly, her hands on her hips. "There you go—reason number one."

Conner, not usually inclined to take orders from people, played it Leslie's way. He grabbed the ice cream from the freezer and then drove a little too fast to his sister's cabin. When they walked in and he went right to the kitchen to spoon up giant bowls for his nephews and himself, he was stopped short. "Les," he said, pointing to some newspapers on the kitchen counter. "Isn't this him? This is him!"

Leslie glanced at the papers. "Oh, man, this might be a little more complicated than I thought. I'll explain after I talk to Katie. You and the boys go up to the loft and stay busy for a while. Play video games and chow down."

Then she went to the bathroom. She knocked before she said, "I'm coming in." And in she went.

Katie was mostly concealed by bubbles. Her hair was piled on her head, her body submerged, her eyes red and swollen, and when she saw Leslie, a new flood of tears escaped. She tried to catch them with the wash-cloth.

Leslie sat on the closed toilet lid. Though she wanted to cry with her, she forced herself to be cool. Both of them blubbering away wouldn't help now. "What happened, Katie?"

"Nothing," she said. "Nothing at all…"

"And yet…?"

"He left, as he said he had to do—he has to earn money somehow. He said he didn't know when he'd see me again, that movies are a lot of work. I can't compete with Hollywood. Why would I try?"

"Are we crying over that? Hollywood?"

"Or a picture in a tabloid of him kissing some woman's neck?" Katie asked with a hiccup of emotion. "He called. He misses me, he says. By the picture I saw in one of those icky gossip papers, he doesn't miss me that much." She took a breath and gave her face a little scrub with the cloth. "Les, we didn't have any kind of agreement that after me, there would never be another woman. He admits he's that way. He wasn't callous about it. In fact, he was almost self-effacing. He called himself a bad bet—he said I'd be better off."

"Are you?" Leslie asked.

"I will be. I'm draining it out right now. The emotion…the disappointment…"

"Katie…"

"He might have left out a few details, but he never lied to me. There were things he didn't tell me, but then there were a couple of things I didn't tell him. In fact, one major thing."

Leslie reached toward the tub and captured one escaping curl of Katie's hair and tucked it behind her ear. "What, honey? What didn't you tell him?"

"Oh," she said, a fresh crop of tears rolling soundlessly down her cheeks. "That even though I didn't want to and didn't plan to, I fell a little bit in love with him.

I knew better. I knew it wasn't going to last. Because he didn't want it to…"

"Sweetheart…"

"If my heart hurts right now, whose fault is that? Not his."

"I could find ways to blame him."

"No," she said, "it's not his fault. I made the classic female mistake. When I realized how good we were together, I thought his agenda would change. I thought being with me would *change* him. And I wasn't kidding myself about how good we were. I was just kidding myself about the agenda."

"There are so many things a man can do to ease the pain and disappointment."

"Like promise to call?" Katie asked with an empty laugh. "Well, he did, and he was sweet, but it didn't help. Or maybe he should swear he'll be back when he won't? Like give hope where there is clearly none? He's right about one thing—once I get beyond this, I'll be better off. Because I need a lot more in a man than someone who has no faith in his own ability to stick around. Loser," she added, wiping a tear away.

"Um…why are you in the tub?" Leslie asked.

"The boys. They're all rough and tumble and bad unless I cry, something I almost never do. It really bothers them if they see me cry. They're such typical little men. They want to make it better."

Leslie laughed. "I've given Conner a couple of test cries, usually associated with ovulation, and you're right—men can't just listen and comfort. They need it resolved in five minutes. You're getting kind of pruny. Do you have a lot more crying to do?"

"I might, yeah. But maybe not for right now."

"Katie? Has there been anyone since Charlie? I mean besides that dentist back in Vermont..."

"No," she said, shaking her head and unplugging the tub drain with her toe. She reached for the towel and Leslie passed it. "I was considering the dentist because there wasn't much chance he was going to make me cry like this. You have to have a real emotional invest-ment in a man to cry your heart out when he dumps you or...or deploys. The dentist did make me cry for Char-lie, though. The blandness of my relationship with the dentist made me long for the commitment and passion Charlie always had for me. I mean, Charlie definitely had his character flaws, but there's just no substitute for knowing your man belongs to you completely. Oh, God, I missed that passion Charlie had for me." She stood up and wrapped the towel around herself. "Be careful what you pray for."

"Well," Leslie said, standing up and reaching for the robe on the door hook. "You'll forget Dylan in no time," she said hopefully.

"Sure," Katie said doubtfully. "Of course."

Leslie held the terry robe for Katie and for a moment, in wordless communication, they shared the same thought—it didn't matter if it was two weeks or two years. If the chemistry was powerful, if the heart shattered, healing was going to take time.

"Please take Conner home," Katie said. "Thank you

for letting me talk, but will you please get him out of here? And tell him I'm just not ready to go over this with him. Not right now."

"Sure, I understand. You know, he only wants to help."

"Yes, I know. And he'll have a terrible time understanding that there's nothing he can do for me."

"Sure. Absolutely." Then Leslie gave her a hug. "I'll talk to you tomorrow. Please, call me if you need me sooner."

"Of course I will."

They talked softly for just a minute more, then Leslie left Katie alone.

Leslie found Conner pacing in the living room, a very agitated expression on his face. The second he saw her he pointed at the newspapers and said, "Are you going to explain this?"

"Yes, Conner. We're going to leave now and I'll tell you about it. Boys?" she yelled. Two little heads popped over the loft rail. "We're going home now. Be nice to Mommy and stay out of her hair."

"She crying some more?" Andy asked, his little eyebrows scrunched in concern.

"Not so much," Leslie said. "But she might need quiet time. Be very sweet to her. Will you?"

They both nodded obediently and it made her smile. Those boys were going to grow up to take good care of their mother.

Once in Conner's truck, the first order of business was to explain that Dylan Childress was no ordinary biker or pilot. He was an ex-star who'd built himself some kind of life in Montana, away from the cameras and press.

"Then what was he doing here?" Conner wanted to know.

"I'm not sure," she told him. "Katie said he was looking at small airports around here to see if he could learn anything that would help his charter business, but she didn't mention he was leaving here to return to movies until after he was gone. I think it was his sudden departure that came as a shock, even though he'd been warning her that he had to go soon. And she really liked him. And here's the thing about women—we always say we're up for that fling, that we don't need commitment, and we're always lying to ourselves."

"Bull, I had flings…"

"I didn't say you men were lying to yourselves…"

"I never heard from women that they were all upset!" Conner said defensively.

She looked at him sharply. "Don't you have an ex-wife still pestering you from time to time?"

"Oh, her—well, that's not the same thing. She never said she didn't need commitment and she has problems." He shook his head. "Katie is completely normal." He glanced at Leslie. "Isn't she?"

"She is," Leslie confirmed. "And your completely normal sister kind of fell for the guy. It wasn't part of the plan, but stuff like that happens. I guess he didn't fall for her or maybe it wouldn't have turned out the way it did."

Conner growled.

"Really, Conner, I want to hate him, too. But as Katie said, it was an honest relationship—he never misled her. We didn't get into it, but I don't think she has any regrets. She's just having the hurt right now. You have to let her get through it. You can't fix it."

"I could punch the bastard in the face," Conner said.

"Hmm. Very sensitive. But somehow I don't think that's going to make Katie feel a lot better..."

He gave a deep sigh. "All I wanted for my sister was happiness. She's had such rotten luck, you know? Not just bad guy luck—but losing our mom and dad, losing Charlie when she was pregnant with the boys, being stuck with a brother as her only security, losing the hardware store, our inheritance... I just wanted her to have a real life. A good, stable, happy life. You know?"

"I know, Conner. I know."

"After Charlie, I couldn't call her after eight at night," Conner said softly, almost mournfully. "It used to break my heart. She'd go to bed when the kids did, because staying up and having a whole long evening alone, it was too lonely. She said she was never too lonely in the early morning or the afternoon, but the nights were always hard. She missed going to bed with her man at night. It never got easier to go to bed alone, she said. It's kind of hard to get used to the idea that your beautiful little sister has that kind of loneliness."

"Even though *you've* had some serious loneliness of your own?" Leslie asked him.

"Even though. So when I met that Dylan character,

I tried not to count on him too much, but there was no missing that her eyes were brighter. Her smile was pretty loaded, like she had one helluva secret. She was happy. And I'll admit, I hoped this was something that would work out for her."

"She did, too," Leslie said.

"She's okay now?"

"Conner, she might be a little emotional for a while. You have to let it go, let her grieve it in her own way and time."

"Yeah," he said grumpily. "You're probably right… So, did she say what she's going to do tonight? Since we left her?"

Leslie looked at Conner sympathetically. "She said she's going to bed early."

Grrrr came from the driver's side. "I'm going to have to beat the shit out of that son of a bitch."

Twelve

The phone didn't ring again for Katie, not that she expected it to. She did have this wild and uncontrollable wish that Dylan would call her every day or several times a day, to have him say he'd been a fool to leave her as he had, to promise to be back to see her because he couldn't stay away. She wouldn't even consider it, of course. She would say, *Fool me once, shame on you, fool me twice...* That she wanted to see him, that went without saying. But she wouldn't take that chance again. It couldn't possibly make the whole thing hurt less.

She had a few shameless problems over the following week. She couldn't stop herself from going to the grocery store in Fortuna and lingering in the magazine aisle and at the checkout, looking for a familiar face. He was still an item, it appeared, though there didn't seem to be any more kissing on the front pages. It was hard not to buy those papers, bring him home with her, but she resisted valiantly. Still, she kept the ones she had, tucked away in the trunk that held other keepsakes.

She had read and reread the articles, however. It was so like twenty years ago when her *Teen* magazine was shredded from use. One story said that Dylan had been living on his famous grandmother's Montana estate. Wow. You'd think he could afford jeans without holes in the knees, right?

She cried some, but not malignantly. She knew her twinkle was gone. In fact, she just didn't feel quite right—the whole ordeal had robbed her of appetite and unsettled her eating and sleeping patterns. No big surprise there—that's why the term *divorce diet* had been invented. Katie really didn't have weight to spare, however. If Dylan made her gaunt and thin in addition to everything else he'd done, she was really going to be pissed off.

She tried to push herself to spend a little more time with people, even if they did want to know what was wrong. Jack Sheridan always asked if she was feeling any better, which implied he knew all the reasons she wasn't feeling that great. She forced a smile and said, "Much. Thanks."

She sat with Leslie and her young neighbor, Nora, on Leslie's front porch and talked about everything from bad haircuts to having children and she found she could open up to Nora. Though young, she seemed so worldly. She had two little girls, nine months and two years, and was not only a single mom but a never-married single mom who had escaped a brutal relationship. Even though Katie had lost her husband to a war, she was not oblivious to the challenges Nora had faced. And it was Nora who said, "Reverend Kincaid really helped me get on my feet after I'd been dumped here without a dime to my name. Now I have two part-time jobs and can take my kids to both of them if I have to—I work at the clinic with Mel Sheridan and at the school with Becca Timm, the teacher, and some other mothers. But the most important thing is how practical and nonjudgmental Reverend Kincaid has been. I was very reluctant to go talk to a preacher after all the horrid things I'd done to get myself into my own mess."

Even with that glowing endorsement, Katie didn't feel inclined to seek counseling from the church. She was a little concerned about how the good minister might react to the fact that one of the things she grieved was the best sex of her life.

"I see him with his wife," Leslie said. "I have a feeling he'd be sympathetic. He looks at her like a starving man looks at a rib roast."

Katie giggled.

"You look like you could use a little milkshake or something," Leslie suggested. "Has this whole thing caused you to lose weight?"

"Possibly a pound or two, but don't worry. I'll gain it right back."

"Aren't you eating?"

"My appetite is a little off, but what do you expect? It'll come back. Soon, I think, since I'm starting to hate him."

"Really?" Leslie asked with a bit of excitement.

"Yes, really. What the hell was he thinking, telling me he doesn't date women with children because he's never going to be a family man, then not only dating me but shtupping me all the time. Did he really think I was taking him seriously? Wouldn't any woman think he'd shifted his thinking? What a fool!"

"Fool?" Leslie asked.

"If he's not going to get involved, maybe he shouldn't get involved. Hmm?" she asked, lifting a brow.

"Novel concept," Les agreed with a grin.

"Someone was thinking with his dick," Katie said, bringing a burst of laughter from both Leslie and Nora. "I was pretty hurt and lonely but I'm getting angry."

"I think I like where this is going," Leslie said.

"He ought to be ashamed of himself. At least I was sincere on all fronts. In for a penny, in for a pound. The jerk."

"You have a lot of your brother in you, Katie," she said. "Hungry?"

"Actually I am a little hungry. You have any cookies?"

Even a little bit of man-hate didn't completely restore her appetite. But then, fretting and feeling emotionally gutted didn't connect up to that good old robust habit.

It was a relief to see how well Conner and Leslie fit into the town; they had clearly found their place. And that helped Katie see this as a good place to raise her sons, even without a husband.

The second week in July passed and the weather was about as steamy as it was going to get in the mountains—a hot eighty degrees. After driving the boys to summer program, she headed for Fortuna. First she went to the grocery store's news rack and, thank God, Dylan Childress wasn't groping anyone for the paparazzi today. Then she went to the pharmacy aisle where she grabbed a pregnancy test. She didn't think it possible, but she just hadn't felt well and couldn't imagine it was all grief. She picked one up. Fifteen dollars? she thought in amazement. And who knew how accurate it was. She picked up a second for twenty-one dollars. And a third for seven and a fourth for twelve and a fifth for nineteen. "I'll send him a bill," she said aloud, and she walked to the checkout, head held high.

Realistically, Katie thought her period was overdue because of the stress, the sadness and upset of having a love affair go south without warning. She never kept track of her monthlies because she could feel it coming—a low backache, some cramps, tender breasts and bang—there it was. She thought she was at least a couple of weeks late, so a test to be sure she wasn't pregnant made sense.

An hour later she was peeing on a stick. The directions said it would be more accurate first thing in the morning but it was more likely to give a false negative when it was positive than a false positive if testing was done in the middle of the day.

Ding, ding, ding.

"Nooooooo!" she wailed. "No, no, no, no, no, no, NO!"

But yes. It said yes. And this was completely impossible—there had always been protection, always. Not only was she responsible about it, Dylan was obsessive! He was the guy who didn't want a family! God forbid he should end up paying the piper for all his screwing around!

She tried the seven-dollar test, though she didn't much have to pee anymore.

Bingo.

"No, no, no!"

She went to the kitchen and drank water. And tea. And more water. Then she paced around her clearing, holding it all as long as she could. She made it a couple of hours. She peed some on the twelve-dollar stick, some on the nineteen-dollar stick and saved the last for the big one—the twenty-one-dollar stick. Then she lined them up on the small bathroom counter and stared at them.

Bing, bing, bing. We have a winner.

She sank down on the bathroom floor and dug her fingers into her hair. *Oh, God, what in the world did I do to piss You off? Was it that no sex before marriage thing? It would be a more practical and effective lesson to have me eaten by a bear!*

And she heard noises. Squeaking. Jingling of chains. The play set. She got to her feet and ran to the kitchen window. Yes, they were back. Not playing on the jungle gym, but merely cutting across her clearing—Mom and the triplets. As if they owned the place.

Katie lunged for her air horn and ran right onto the porch, fearless. She blasted the horn and watched as they turned as one to look at her. "Get out of here," she screamed, giving the horn another long blast. "I am in NO mood!" And after an insulted grunt from Mother, they scuttled off into the brush.

Jack was just putting up clean glasses in the middle of the afternoon when the door to the bar opened. He looked up, half expecting his wife, who often took advantage of the quiet time before the dinner crowd showed up. But it was not Mel—it was the welcome face of a man he hadn't seen in some time. "I'll be damned," he said with a big grin. He came around the bar and approached a young man, about thirty years old, and pulled him into a fierce hug, hammering his back with a fist. Then he held him away and said, "Hey, Tom! You home on leave?"

"I'm out," Tom Cavanaugh said. "Six was enough for me. And my grandmother either has my help with the orchard or sells it. I vote for helping her. That orchard's been in the family a long time."

"How is Maxie?" Jack asked.

"Stubborn as ever, but as near as I can tell, tougher and healthier than you or me."

"I haven't seen you in a couple of years," Jack pointed out.

"I deployed a second time—I think that was the convincer. Plus, I never made it any secret, I was made to take care of apples. It's what I was raised to do."

"And we couldn't be happier about that. Let me find Preacher, he'll want to say hello."

Tom Cavanaugh grew up in Virgin River and had been a college student when Jack first arrived in town. It not only became a great refuge for him on his weekend and holiday visits home to Virgin River, but with his own plans to spend at least a few years in the military after college, he bonded with Jack and Preacher. Now at around thirty he was home for good, ready to take over the family business with his grandmother. Cavanaugh Apples.

He was halfway through his beer when Katie came into the bar.

"Well now," Jack said. "Look who's here. Katie Malone, meet one of the neighbors—Tom Cavanaugh. Tom just exited the Marine Corps and is home for good. Tom, Katie is new in town."

"It's definitely a pleasure," Tom said, his eyes lighting up a bit as he looked at her.

"Likewise," she said, putting out a hand.

"Glass of wine?" Jack asked.

"No, thanks, I'll be picking up the boys in fifteen minutes. So, Tom, you live here in town?"

"No, out about three miles down the mountain. I grew up on an apple orchard and that's where I'm probably going to be for the rest of my life."

"You say that with a smile," she observed.

"I like apples."

"Tommy here was raised on 'em," Jack said.

"Cavanaugh apples make some of my best pies," Preacher put in.

"So, you're looking a little better, missy," Jack said. "Got a little color in your cheeks."

"No surprise there," she said. "Remember that bear? She's been back and she acts like I'm renting space from her. I need a gun."

"What bear?" Tom asked.

"A mother bear with triplets. They like my boys' jungle gym."

"Hmm," Tom said. "I've seen her a couple of times. She's been in the orchard, poking around, and she's not a happy mother..."

"I have twin boys. I feel her pain. I think I need a gun."

"Katie, it takes a lot of gun to stop a bear her size. Can you handle a rifle?"

"That's one thing I haven't gotten around to, but I've got a permit for a handgun. Not that I have a handgun—not to be redundant, but twin boys... I did buy myself a really awful air horn—she hated that. But she took her kids out of my yard. After she made a noise that sounded as near to a growl as it could be. I don't think we're friends."

"I'll call Fish and Game," Tom said. "That little lady might have to be dealt with. Maybe relocated if she's going to be trouble. I'd hate for her to get shot."

"On the other hand, I'd hate to be eaten," Katie said.

Tom Cavanaugh grinned handsomely. "Maybe your

husband will show you how to handle a rifle. I knew a girl in the Marines as little as you and she's a crack shot. It's not always about size."

Oh, man, Katie thought. That was pretty obvious. And boy did young Tom have a wrong number. Wouldn't it be cruel to tell him, *I'm a knocked-up widow with twin five-year-old boys—run for your life.* "I'm widowed. I lost my husband in the war— Afghanistan."

"I'm sorry for your loss," he said immediately, dropping his head. "If there's any way I can help out—"

"That's very nice, but my older brother is right here in town. He's not off work yet today, but if I need him in a hurry, I can find him. And there's Jack…"

"There's always Jack," Tom said. "But if there's ever anything your brother or Jack can't help out with…"

"Thank you," she said. "Thank you for calling the game warden or whoever you're calling. And nice to meet you. I'd better go grab those boys…"

When you're the potential star in a movie, investors and distributors consider the weight of the cast in making their decisions about backing the film. Dylan had played the Hollywood game for three weeks, consenting to an interview about his consideration of a script, socializing with key people along with the producer and director and allowing himself to be photographed a few times. Lee Drake was still working on the contract, but he said it was moving in a very positive direction and shouldn't be more than a couple of weeks before he could pronounce it satisfactory and ready to sign. Once that happened, there would be even more prepublicity buzz that would lend itself to making money for the movie. He'd eaten too much rich food, imbibed too much liquor, ran into family members altogether too often. Bryce had faded into that background but Blaine and Cherise seemed to coincidentally appear at some of the same restaurants he happened to be dining in. Thank God his number was changed so they couldn't call him on top of all that.

He smiled as much as he could, but he hated it. At least the social aspect. He wasn't accustomed to that lifestyle anymore.

There was one exception to his discontent—he had been spending a little time with his grandmother. He filled her in on all the details that led to his reading of the script and negotiating of a contract. "Lang said that while business is still down compared to previous years, he has bid on a few charters and has rented out planes here and there—so they're hanging in there. With Sue Ann's help, they can manage Childress Aviation while I'm here working. Stu is minding the store, taking care of the runway, maintenance, fueling, that sort of thing. I need to get back there and get things stabilized before I commit to any kind of filming schedule."

"This is all so unnecessary…unless it's what you absolutely want."

"It's completely necessary," Dylan said.

"You're my only living heir," she reminded him. "And I'm loaded."

"I make my own way if I can," he said. "For all I know, you'll get pissed off at me for some reason and give it all to your cat. Then where would I be?"

"I don't have a cat…"

"Yet…"

It wasn't exactly an argument; it was more of an examination of boundaries. He appreciated her in many ways, was grateful for all she'd done for him, understood that after all her many years of hard work she was more than a little comfortable. But she was seventy-six. With any luck she would live to be a hundred and six. Besides, these were the boundaries *she'd* pounded into his head during their retreat to Payne, that he wasn't a little god who should have his way paid just because of some sense of entitlement.

She taught him to get over himself.

"I have only a couple of concerns about doing a movie," he said. "One is that I'll enjoy the acting and despise all the ancillary bullshit, not the least of which is my mother, stepbrothers and -sisters and half brothers and sisters moving in on me with requests. I don't want to get hooked, which will have me putting up with that kind of B.S. again and again. And the other is you thinking it's a mistake."

She shook her head. "First of all, I think you're past being the vulnerable kid star who doesn't really understand what's happening. Second, I'm an actor," she said. "I still work because I love it and also despise a lot of the ancillary bullshit. I do it because I *want* to. Millions of people who are trying to just get a part in a commercial would kill me to have a tenth of the opportunity I have had, and believe me, I don't take that for granted. But, Dylan, when I decide to take on a part, I'm happy. If this makes you unhappy, find another way."

"It's probably going to be six months of shooting," he said. "And it's a frightening amount of money."

"How are you handling the family?" she asked.

"I've said no, I've changed my cell number, I'm ignoring them, but I admit, they make it hard. They're everywhere, it seems."

"And your mother?"

"Cherise is the hardest to ignore…" She was his mother. He hated her and loved her. That she would use him was so painful. And so predictable.

"Yes, I can imagine," Adele said. "So, when do you leave for Montana?"

"In a few days. I'll fly back to Northern California where I left my bike. I've decided to rent a truck and haul the bike home. After the last few weeks, I don't think I'm up to a long-distance ride on the Harley."

"How long will the drive take you?" she asked.

"A couple of days," he said. "But I have a little unfinished business in Humboldt County…"

She lifted a thin, meticulously honey-colored brow and said, "Indeed?"

Oh, indeed.

Dylan had to see her once more. Katie. She didn't

want him, he got that. He'd called her, given her the new number, asked her to call and she hadn't—he got the message. His own fault, he admitted. And she didn't think their lives matched; didn't want to get mixed up with some Hollywood kid and he couldn't blame her. But it didn't feel right. It didn't feel complete. "There's a girl," he told Adele. "She doesn't want to be involved with an actor. Actors have rotten reputations for little things like fidelity. But I like her. I'm going to give her one more chance to reject me. I just haven't suffered enough yet."

"Listen, Dylan, there are lots of ordinary families who grapple with lousy relationships and plenty of actors who marry for the long-term, quite happily."

"I know. I just want to stop in Humboldt County and see her, make sure she's doing fine, that she feels the same way she did when I left—that she isn't interested. Because I think if we had a little time…"

But they didn't have time.

No matter how hard it was, no matter how tempted he was by her, he had to try to make her understand what he was feeling. He wasn't just some irresponsible pretty boy. A gentleman would find a way to say, "You're important and I'm going to miss you." To leave as though nothing that happened between them mattered, that was just wrong. He was going to fix that. Even if he was the last person she wanted to see right now.

Then he'd go back to Payne, lock down the little airport, leaving Lang, Sue Ann and Stu in charge, and he'd go make a movie. Why not? He'd save his company and he'd do it himself, not the way his extended family would have done it, not by taking handouts.

First mission—see Katie and apologize for abandoning her on a moment's notice.

He dreaded it.

He couldn't wait.

He was scared to death.

When he got back to Humboldt County a couple of days later, he rented a truck, loaded his Harley in the back and drove to Virgin River. He stopped off at Jack's for a beer and a meal, killing time and bolstering his courage before facing her. He was afraid if she cried he'd never be able to leave, to do what he had to do. If she was furious with his unannounced appearance, it might take him a lifetime to convince her he wasn't a low-life loser to treat her as he had and he'd never be able to leave her. If she threw her arms around him… yeah, he'd never be able to leave her.

He had a second beer and barely touched his dinner.

Katie visited Mel Sheridan, the friendly neighborhood midwife, who confirmed what she already knew—pregnant. In addition to an appointment for an ultrasound in Grace Valley to determine an accurate due date and a bunch of vitamins, Mel insisted on running a battery of tests for STDs. This was a very sensible precaution under the circumstances.

"Failed condom?" Katie asked Mel. "Seriously?"

"It's been known to happen," Mel said. "Or maybe

brief contact before or after the condom… Whatever it was, Katie, it's the real deal. Do we need to have a discussion of your options?"

"What options?" Katie asked.

"Are you planning on having the baby? Because I don't—"

"Yes," Katie said without hesitation.

"And the father?" Mel asked.

"Long gone," Katie said.

"I'm sorry. I take that to mean he doesn't know?" Katie shook her head.

"Do you want him to know?"

"What's the difference?" she asked with a shrug.

"There's the issue of financial support," Mel said. "The only time I don't recommend pursuing that is in cases of abuse or neglect or… Katie, you didn't make this baby alone and you don't have to shoulder all the responsibility alone. And there's the fact that he deserves to know, unless telling him endangers you or the child."

She took a deep breath. Dylan was passionate about not wanting children, but he was a good man. But what kind of father would a man like that make? Probably just an absent one. She was better off on her own. "I'll be fine," she said. "I appreciate your help." Then she bit her lower lip—but he was wonderful with her boys.

"If there's anything I can do…"

"I don't think there's anything more right now." Because she was going to tell her brother and Leslie. It was early, yes. And maybe it being early, Conner would stop twitching by the time she began to show.

A couple of days later, Katie asked Leslie and Conner if they could come out to the cabin after work for a beer. They sat on the porch and kept an eye on the monkeys on the swing set. Katie had tea while Leslie and Conner had cold beer.

"It really is beautiful out here," Leslie said. "So peaceful."

"I'm going to need something that's not in the woods, I think," Katie said.

"I was afraid you might be nervous out here," Conner said. "You can't see your neighbors, the boys are attracted to the forest and could get lost, you had a bear wandering around here…"

Do it just like a Band-Aid, Katie thought. *Rip it off, get it over with.* "I'm pregnant."

They both just looked at her in stunned disbelief.

"Talk about a conversation stopper," she said. "Total accident. Obviously my protection failed. But it is what it is. So, my timeline for finding a job, a house in a regular neighborhood with neighbors, near whatever school we decide on just got a lot shorter. Of course, I'd like it to be close to you guys, but I understand there just might not be anything available in your neighborhood. Who do you think is the best person to talk to about that? About available housing?"

They both just stared at her for a moment. Finally it was Conner who said, "Pregnant."

"Yep. Of course not very—it's early. I don't have an official due date because I'm so bad about keeping track of things, but there's only been one…" She cleared her throat. "It's early. That explains not feeling very well for the past couple of weeks…" That, and a battered heart. "But there was no point in waiting to tell you. Hopefully by the time I start feeling better you'll stop reeling from the news and maybe the boys and I can find a more suitable place to live before the start of school. Before I get, you know, enormous. Because I'm going to have to hunker down and nest. I think I'll be due around March first next year. But that's just a guess. And if there's a God, it's only one."

Conner leaned toward her, elbows on his knees. "Katie…"

"There's not a whole lot more to say, Conner. As you know, it was one-hundred-percent consensual, even though it wasn't planned. And yes, I'm on my own. I know it's asking a lot, that I've already asked too much of you, but I hope you'll be supportive. I'll take care of myself, I promise. I just want your emotional support, that's all."

Leslie put her hand on Conner's forearm. "Of course we'll do everything we can, Katie. Anything you need."

"He doesn't know?" Conner asked.

"There's no point, Conner. This was just a stop for Dylan and he's moved on. Dylan was not cut out to be a family man."

"Fine," Conner said with his teeth locked together in the back of his mouth. "That's fine. But you have to tell him. He can write a check. You shouldn't have to carry the whole load."

"Let's not go there yet," she said. "It might not seem so practical when he demands joint custody or something. I'd like some time to think about all the possible repercussions. And if it's not too much to ask, can we keep this between us for now?"

"Are you all right, Katie?" Leslie asked.

"Oh, besides that tired-all-the-time thing and getting a little green around the gills sometimes, I'm the picture of health. I'll admit I'm a little upside down emotionally, but that'll pass. And jeez, Conner, at least he didn't die. Huh?"

Conner's fierce expression didn't ease for a long time, but just the same Katie forced the conversation to houses, taking delivery of stored household goods from her old house in Sacramento, possible jobs Katie might be able to handle while pregnant. Conner was still kicking around the idea of a hardware store, smaller than the one they owned in Sacramento, but if he did open one nearby, that would solve a lot of problems.

As Conner and Leslie were leaving, Conner pulled Katie into his arms and held her close. "You never have to ask me to stand by you. No matter what happens in our lives, we always stand by each other."

"Thank you," she whispered. "I love you."

When they left, Katie pulled the boys inside and fixed them grilled cheese sandwiches, which they wolfed down in what seemed like seconds. Then she asked them to go to the loft and either watch movies or play quietly. "Mommy needs a nice soak in the tub."

The boys exchanged concerned glances.

"Just a soak," she assured them with a little smile. "And do *not* go outside!"

Thirteen

On the way back to town, Leslie spent a great deal of time trying to talk Conner down. "I know you feel very protective of Katie, but she's a grown woman who made adult choices and is now living up to them very admirably. She obviously wants to have this baby. Try to be happy for her."

"She look happy to you?" he nearly growled. "He needs to be accountable!"

"I think she'd be happier if things had gone a little differently—like if she'd had more time to develop a lasting relationship with Dylan. But, Conner, things don't always go the way we want."

"Humph," he grunted. "What kind of a man walks out on a pregnant woman?"

"Maybe the kind who has no idea she's pregnant," Leslie said. "I want you to do a little memory check—we made love before we established our future together. It could've happened to us."

"I wouldn't have walked away like he did."

She laughed softly. "Actually, you admitted later that had been your original plan. You had trust issues where women were concerned, you were a secret witness whose life had been threatened. You were going to bolt, but that didn't stop you from crawling into bed with me."

"But I stayed!" he argued.

"I repeat—Dylan has no idea there's a pregnancy! He's not an ass so much as another version of you a few years ago. We will give Katie love and support and stay out of her business. She can make her own decisions."

"Doesn't look like she's making really good ones," he grumbled angrily.

"If she heard this from you, she would be furious," Leslie said. "And you'd be lucky if she ever confided in you again."

"Let me get it out!" he said. "I'll get it out, I'll be done with it! Katie won't have to put up with this from me. I'll take care of her."

Leslie sighed. "Stop at Jack's," she said. "I'll get something of Preacher's to take home. And whatever you have to do to be done with this, do it. I don't want all this anger from you—I've never had to deal with this from you before. You get about fifteen more minutes, then I'm out of patience."

She soon realized how badly she'd chosen her words. It was almost six o'clock, the bar was at peak dinner hour when they walked in. There were only a couple of empty tables or bar stools. Sitting at the end of the bar with a beer and a dinner plate was Dylan Childress.

It was like waving the red cape in front of the bull.

Conner didn't look right or left. He stomped into the bar, grabbed Dylan by the front of his shirt, taking him completely by surprise, lifting him off the stool, and began to drag him out of the bar. Leslie screamed, "Jaaaccckkk!" Dylan hooked his boot behind Conner's knee and they both went down, toppling a table as they crashed to the floor. Just like a scene from the old West, people rose and pushed back tables and chairs to stay out of the way of a good old-fashioned bar fight.

And the fists flew, both men making significant, loud, crunching contact. They each got off two or three on the other before Jack, Paul Haggerty, Conner's boss and, fortuitously, Mike Valenzuela, the town cop, pulled them apart and got them outside. Dan Brady and Preacher came from the kitchen for backup. Most of the people who had been in the bar were more than happy to leave their dinners to get cold while they headed for the porch, enjoying the show. And quite the show it was, complete with Preacher in what could have appeared to be a bloody apron, except it was tomato sauce.

"What the fuck?" Dylan yelled through a split lip, spitting blood onto the street.

"You are the fuck!" Conner returned nasally, his nose having taken on a weird shape and now bleeding onto his shirt. "You don't treat my sister like the gum on your shoe!"

"No, I don't! Am I here? I'm here! Why do you think I'm here? She's a good woman. I care about her!"

"A little late, cowboy," Conner shot back. "Let go of me," he said over his shoulder to Paul and Dan Brady. "Let me kill him. I'll wipe up after."

"You just try, asshole," Dylan roared. "That fucker's crazy! Lock him up, will you?"

Jack and Preacher held on to Dylan. Mike V. stood between the opposing teams. "We don't exactly have a lockup around here," he said. "I could call the sheriff, however. But I'd have to give him both of you."

"I don't like their chances for family holidays," Jack said to Preacher. "Do you?"

"Did I do anything?" Dylan asked hotly. "I was having a beer and a meal!"

"And screwing my sister!" Conner shouted.

"Conner!" Leslie shouted from the porch. "Shut *up!*"

"You hurt her!" Conner yelled at Dylan, failing to take his beloved's advice.

"I'm back here to try to make amends!" Dylan yelled back.

"You're a little late, pretty boy!"

"You son of a—" And with that, Dylan threw himself against the strong arms that held him.

A piercing whistle shot through the air and everyone stopped yelling and moving. Right at the base of the porch stood Mel Sheridan and her partner, Doc Michaels. Jack lifted his eyebrows, wondering if that whistle had come out of his wife.

"Two choices, gentlemen," Mike Valenzuela said. "You can walk away quietly, get patched up and go home or I can cuff you and call the sheriff's deputy."

Dylan immediately stopped struggling. "I'm not the problem," he pointed out.

"Wanna get your lip fixed?" Jack asked.

"Pretty boy probably needs a plastic surgeon," Conner said.

"I'm about done trying," Mike V. said.

"All right," Conner said. "All right."

"Take Conner to the clinic," Jack said. "His nose needs to be…" he cleared his throat "…adjusted. This one can go to Preacher's quarters with Mel." Then to Dylan he said, "If you even bump into my wife, you'll have me to deal with and trust me…"

"Why would I bother your wife, man?" Dylan asked. "That was just self-defense, what happened. I just need a little ice. I'll settle up for my dinner and get out of here."

Mel walked over to Dylan and looked at his face, the bleeding lip, a small cut over his eye and rapidly spreading inflammation on the right side of his face. "I can probably fix those cuts with some tape," she said, turning his head left and right. "I'll go get my bag from the clinic. It could take me a few minutes to wade through all the testosterone in the street, so be patient."

Katie sat on the sofa in her little living room, wrapped in her soft, terry robe, giving her toenails a coat of polish. Her hair was piled on her head with damp tendrils trailing. She'd been in the tub long enough to cry a little bit; begging help from her brother yet again had taken a toll. Her eyes were a little red, her

cheeks pink. But fortunately Katie had never been one
to indulge in a lot of self-pity, so once she let some of
that emotion go, she just took a deep breath and moved
on.

Unfortunately, she knew she wasn't finished with
the crying. If being pregnant without a father around
wasn't hard enough, holding that newborn, alone, could
really rip a woman's heart out. There would be more
tears. Hard tears.

The knock at the cabin door caused her to immediately assume that either Conner or Leslie or the two of
them together weren't finished talking about it yet. But
when she opened the door, it was Dylan.

"My God," she gasped. "Have you been in an accident?"

"No," he said. "It was very deliberate."

"What in the world happened?" she asked, holding
open the door for him. He was inside before she realized that if his face weren't banged up, she wouldn't
have let him inside at all. She would have asked, "What
are you doing here?"

He stepped inside. "I came back," he said. Then with
a hand on his chin, he worked his jaw a little bit, clearly
uncomfortable. "I was getting up my courage to come
and see you, to talk to you about…I don't know. Our
relationship and the way I left you… That was wrong.
We should've had some discussion about how we'd stay
in touch, when we'd see each other or… Your brother
happened into Jack's. And he obviously has some issues
with my departure, also."

"Conner did that?" she asked, aghast.

Dylan nodded. "And he wasn't quite done, either."

Katie had not heard the rumble of the Harley. She glanced past him and saw a big white truck sitting in her clearing, the motorcycle loaded into the back.

"I rented a truck," he explained. He tilted his head, listening to the sound of *Avatar* in the loft. "Can we talk?"

"I guess so," she said. She curled up on one end of the sofa, pulling her terry robe around her legs, and he took the other end. And she waited.

"I don't really know where to start," he said.

She said nothing. Waiting.

"It wasn't my plan to get involved and then leave the way I did. With so many things unsaid."

She shrugged. "You said you were leaving all the time, that you had to go back to work. And I thought your explanation was thorough—that I was the best time you ever had and you were going to make a movie…"

He winced. "See? That was done badly."

"Well, I said I understood. You had to make some money."

"That's not the part I should've explained better—I should've told you how much you meant—for a little while, we were really close…really good friends."

"Not good friends, I think," she corrected. "Lovers, but not really friends. Friends would've been a little kinder to each other. And I don't need any more sweet talk as you're on the way out the door. It's inconsiderate."

He slid a little closer. "Katie, the decision to leave was sudden—the producer I'd been talking to finally came through with something. I hate the business, but I like acting, I'm good at it and I like the kind of money it can pay. It's just that there was money involved and it was the perfect opportunity to take a big payday back to Montana… If the whole movie deal could be worked out and it looks like it can be—"

"I know," she said.

"You know?" he asked.

"Even though you've been away from it for a long time, apparently the name Childress still gets people all excited in Hollywood and…" She reached over to the coffee table trunk and lifted the lid. She pulled out a few tabloids and tossed them on the sofa. "I figured that out pretty easily."

He glanced at the pictures idly. "This is what I hate," he muttered. "This is all B.S. This one here, with Jay Romney, this is the only one I actually posed for. The rest of them? I didn't even know there were photographers present. They might have even been taken with a cell phone and retouched with Photoshop for all I know. This one, I remember this," he said, showing her the picture with the pretty blonde. "But the caption is bogus."

"Hmm," Katie said. "So that one's real."

"It's a hug," he said. "I was so happy to see her.

Lindsey. I hadn't seen her in about twenty years. She was offered a chance to test for a part in this film."

Katie lifted her chin a notch. "How lovely for you."

"Seriously," he said, catching her sarcasm. "She's one of the few people I trust. She's good people. We didn't exactly keep in touch, but I've known her since she was thirteen."

"I recognize her," Katie said. "Lucky you."

"Katie, she's married with two kids. A nice person…"

"Well then, I guess we're all caught up," she said, standing up.

"Come on, sit down. I just want a chance to explain. I think you know most of what I'm going to say—I tried to say it before. I was feeling kind of serious and I told you how nervous it makes me to feel serious. That long history of family members who just can't—"

"Blah, blah, blah," she said.

He frowned, then grimaced because it hurt his face. "Okay, I guess you don't buy that."

"Oh, I buy it, Dylan. I also think it's a pretty convenient excuse to just bail out. You went to a lot of trouble to explain all this to me—that you just don't want a relationship. You wanted what we had. And we had it. I'm not holding you here."

"Katie, I called," he said. "I gave you my number—I didn't give it to very many people. I wanted you to call. I wanted us to stay in touch because maybe down the road… You mean a lot to me. I missed you like crazy. You're the one who said our lives just don't match."

"Listen, Dylan, I don't expect you to understand this—it's just not a part of your lifestyle and it's very old-fashioned, but I'm a mother and a woman who needs stability and permanence. This is my fault—I knew it was going to be a fling and I don't have flings. I don't have any practice at it. It was bound to work out the way it did. And I was bound to be unhappy about it. I didn't realize when I was involved with you that a part of me hoped things would be different with me, with us. Dumb. You told me up front, that would never change. So, don't worry—we're all square. You can hit the road with a clear conscience—you have more temporary girlfriends waiting."

He scowled. "Okay," he said. "Okay, you're pissed. I don't blame you. I don't have girlfriends waiting and I want to work this out with you. Maybe we can stay in touch or…something."

"Dylan, I'm not the kind of girl you want to stay in touch with. I'm looking for something a little more committed. This is not your problem. You don't have to make amends for just being yourself. I have no regrets about getting…" She almost said *getting knocked up by you,* but cleared her throat. "It was totally consensual. And I'm really sorry about Conner—he shouldn't have done that. It's inexcusable."

"And why did he?" Dylan asked.

"He must have felt kind of bad for me," she offered. "He's very protective."

"Why did he feel bad for you?"

"Probably because he thought my feelings were very

hurt, which they were for a while. He thought I was depressed but actually I seem to have a little..." She slid her hand over her belly. "I guess I have a little bug in me. I haven't been feeling so well. Better now, though. Nothing serious—just a temporary thing." *Should last about eight more months,* she thought.

"Katie, I wanted to be so much more romantic. I wanted to let you know how much you got under my skin and how hard it was to leave you, but I thought I might never leave. Every time I got near you, I just couldn't go. It was torture. Things *were* different with you!"

"Hmm," she said. "Well, as sorry as I am for you, I think you've done a noble thing, coming here to apologize, but you can leave now. I know this is going to upset your feeling of being unique, but they write articles about your type in all the women's magazines. Commitment phobia is almost a cliché."

"Nice," he said, sitting back. "May I have some ice before I go, please? For my face?"

She sighed. "I suppose. But then you have to go before the boys see you. They're zoned out to the movie in the loft, maybe even asleep already." She got up. She put some ice in a dish towel and brought it to him. "Let's not drag this out."

He pressed the ice against his eye. She could only see half his face when he talked. "The thing you don't get, Katie, it's not an excuse. I'm not *proud* of this. I probably qualify as some player—at least technically—because I don't get into steady things. You have no idea how much I wish it wasn't the case. My best friend is a married man with five kids, he's like family to me. Except for my grandmother, the only real family I have. His house is where I spend every long weekend and holiday. I would trade a kidney for his life even though he's always strapped for cash, usually tired, in constant demand at home, lives in perpetual chaos, but he's always got a smile on his face. I'd give anything for that life."

She wasn't sure if she was being played right now or if he was sincere. She took a chance. "Do you expect me to feel sorry for you?"

"It wouldn't hurt. And you might give me a chance to…I don't know…check this out, this thing we have. I want to. I've never met a woman so hard to leave." He took a breath.

"Okay, that's too obvious. What do you want?"

"A second chance?"

"Oh? For how many days or weeks this time?"

He got clumsily to his feet, holding the ice over his eye. "Okay, I deserved that. I won't jam you up anymore. Would it be all right if I stayed in touch for a while? Called? Maybe visited you sometime?" He wobbled a little.

She stood, as well. "Where are you going?"

"I thought it seemed pretty obvious you're all done talking here…"

"I don't know that you're okay," she said. "You're a little unsteady."

He pulled the ice pack off his eye. "It's just my balance with the ice over one eye. And the fact that your brother tried to beat my brains out."

"So, where are you going?"

"Not sure," he said with a shrug. "I passed by Riordan's and they're full up. Even that funky little trailer he let me have for a week is in use."

She just stared at him for a minute. "I don't think you should drive…"

"I'll be okay," he said, handing her the ice pack.

She groaned in resignation, handing it back. "You can have the couch. I'm going to get my children in bed before they see you. If you sneak into my room tonight, you'd better be coming to get me because the house is on fire or you're going to live to regret it. Are we clear?"

He looked down. "Can I take off my boots? Or should I be ready to run?"

"You take off anything else, you better run," she said, and she turned away from him, going upstairs. She hustled the boys into their room before they noticed him. And then the door to her bedroom closed.

Dylan felt the sunlight, then he felt the eyes. He opened one of his to four brown ones. "Y'know, you guys are sometimes a little creepy. The way you do that."

"Did you have a sleepover again?" Andy asked.

"And forgot your pajamas?" Mitch added.

"I had a sleepover," he said. "I was feeling a little

wobbly and your mother thought maybe I shouldn't drive."

"She said you had an accident," Andy shared.

"That's right," Dylan said. "Ran right into a big, stupid fist."

"Boys, go to the table," Katie said. "Your waffles are ready." When they left and she looked at Dylan, she made a face. He was more swollen and the skin around his eye was definitely black-and-blue. "The color is setting in," she informed him. Then she picked up four empty beer bottles from the top of the trunk. "Go ahead and help yourself to a beer." She carried them into the kitchen.

He followed. "I'll be glad to replace them. I had a little trouble sleeping. Did you have trouble sleeping?"

"Sleeping seems to be one of my gifts lately," she said. "I slept like a dead person. Would you like an egg or something before you leave?"

"Coffee would be nice," he said.

When she turned away from him to grab a cup, he eyed her backside. She was wearing some thin summer knit sweatpants that fit loosely around her hips and a short shirt, leaving her midriff exposed. He remembered her as tiny, but today she was looking thin. When she turned toward him with a cup of coffee he asked, "Have you lost weight, Katie?"

"I told you, I had a little bug. I'm not completely over it, but almost…"

"Katie," he asked, stepping closer. "Did I do that to you?"

"Probably," she said. "Egg?"

"Let me take you out to a big breakfast," he said.

"Boy, guilt really works on you, doesn't it? I'm going to have a little cereal, not feeling like a big breakfast."

"You've gotten too thin," he said. "Makes me want to feed you. And hold you."

"Wow, that's real talent," she said. "You know how to make a woman feel unattractive and desired in the same sentence. Do you want an egg or are you on the way out?"

He tilted his head. "Have you always been this cranky? Could you be a little nicer, please? Your brother beat me up and I'm concerned about you."

"I'm really just fine," she said in a calmer voice. "Meet me on the porch." She grabbed her glass of juice and headed out the door. She sat in one of the chairs and when he sat down beside her, she winced again just looking at him. "What are the chances Conner looks as bad as you?"

"I think he won," Dylan said.

"Lord. Men." She cleared her throat. "Listen, Dylan, I apologize if I've been less than friendly. But just how many times do you think I want to go through withdrawal? Because seriously, I am not interested in a close casual friendship with benefits. It's not who I am. I'm not comfortable with that kind of relationship."

"Did Charlie ask you to marry him after the first week?"

"No," she said. "After the first week he said he couldn't live without me. It was after the second week he begged me to marry him. But that has nothing to do with us, with now. Now I'm a mother first and I'm feeling a little protective. I'm not a good mother if I'm worrying about how some man feels about me."

He felt a smile come to his lips. "That's very reasonable."

"Thank you. No regrets, but I'm not getting involved with you. Again."

"I understand. But you don't hate me?"

"I don't hate you. I'll never hate you. After all, I loved you for three years when I was a girl. And that was before I even slept with you."

He smiled wider. "What if I wanted to be friends? Without benefits?"

"Big talk," she said. "We have history. We'd probably end up in the sack and I'd just get hurt again."

He took a thoughtful sip of his coffee. "Katie, I'd never deliberately do anything to hurt you."

"You know what? I believe you. But I'd end up hurt just the same and you'd be fine—off meeting up with old movie star girlfriends, et cetera, while I sit here alone in the woods wondering what happened. And the boys…"

"What about the boys?" he asked.

"Well, brace yourself," she said. "They like you. They were so excited to see you sleeping on the couch, it was almost impossible to keep them from waking you up. It's probably not so good for you to come in and out of their lives."

"Kind of sounds like I really screwed this up."

"This?" she asked. She shook her head. "We were attracted to each other, but there's nothing we can do about the fact that we're not headed in the same direction, except maybe make a clean break so we can move on. You have to go!" She touched his hand. "It's okay, Dylan. Let's just part friends. No hard feelings."

"I don't necessarily want to—"

There was a bit of rustling and a small bear cub rolled out of the bushes, followed by a second. Katie jumped to her feet. "Dylan, in the house, hurry up." She was ahead of him, heading for the kitchen. She went to the small cupboard above the microwave and grabbed the air horn and the bear repellant, a fancy hair-spray-size can of mace. "She is seriously getting on my nerves…." And then she was out on the porch again. "Hey!" she yelled. "Get outta here!" And she blasted the horn a few times, some short annoying pops.

Dylan stepped out on the porch, wide-eyed. "Holy shit, Katie! Get inside!"

Mama stepped into the clearing and puffed up, making her groaning, almost growling noises. That could've meant *You'll be my breakfast soon* or *Come with me, kids.*

Katie aimed the mace and the horn just in case, but she blew the horn again. The bear stood on her hind legs and her cubs ran behind her. She dropped back to all fours and disappeared into the shrubs, and a moment later Katie saw the four of them hightailing it up the path and into the forest. And Katie yelled, "I've got cubs, too! Bitch!"

He grabbed her arm. "Katie, good Christ, you shouldn't antagonize her like that. Just get out of the way."

"She's really got some attitude, that one. A guy I met at Jack's, some guy with an orchard, said she's been bothering them and he was going to call someone— like the game warden or something." Then she turned her big blue eyes up to his. "But I think maybe I'll find something a little more urban. Know what I mean?"

He ran a hand through his hair and shook his head. The boys peeked out the door to see if there were bears. "Go inside, please," Dylan said. "Get ready for school." When they were gone he turned to Katie. "All right, listen to me. I'm not leaving right away. I'm going to take the boys to school and drop them off. Then I'm going to run a few errands, make a couple of phone calls and come back here. You—stay in the house and do not confront that bear again!"

"I don't want you hanging around here," she said. "I'm not going to sleep with you!"

"Oh, absolutely not," he said. "But we are going to examine the potential for a relationship, you and me. It might not be easy, but—"

"But Hollywood waits," she said.

"Yeah, well, I probably won't be able to work and hang out here all the time, but I also probably won't be out of town any more often than a soldier. Right now I think you need me. So I'll take the boys to town and I'll be back."

She put her hands on her hips. "Don't you under-stand 'no'?"

"No," he said.

Fourteen

Right after leaving Katie's house and dropping off the boys, Dylan parked on the side of a hill that offered a spectator's view of a lush valley, but his interest was not the view. He had cell reception here. He called Lang. "How's everything going?"

"Going," Lang said. "I flew a couple of charters. They didn't pay enough, but they paid and it was work. We could use more. I was out of town most of last week, but it's money and I'm encouraged by the business."

"How's Mrs. Lang getting along?"

"She's doing all right, but then Sue Ann always gets along better without me than I do without her."

"Listen to you," Dylan said. "She's stuck at home with five kids, trying to help run an airport, manage the house and everything and you're whining about doing something you love to do—fly."

"I know," he admitted. "She could've done better. Boy, am I lucky she didn't."

"I remember when you met her," Dylan said. "It was like you saw her and glazed over…"

"Nah, I didn't really go into a trance until I talked to her. But I was in big trouble once I slept with her. Shew." Lang took a breath. "Thank God I'm home for a few days!"

"Eleven years later, still the horn dog for your wife."

"Hard to get bored with perfection," he said with a sigh.

Dylan just chuckled to himself. Sue Ann was pretty, but she wasn't a knockout. She was kind of soft and wholesome-looking, but she had a sharp tongue on her, like someone else Dylan knew. She didn't suffer fools gladly. She certainly didn't put up with any of Lang's shit. "I'm still trying to figure out how that works," Dylan said. "One look and not only did you know how you felt then, you knew how you were going to feel in twenty years."

"You see what you want to see, D," Lang said. "Like we're the perfect married couple? Hell, we've had some knockdowns. I've spent my share of nights on the couch. In fact, it's making up that really gets us into trouble—that's usually when we slip up and get pregnant."

"Didn't you promise her a vasectomy?"

"Yeah, when little D is two, and guess what? He had a birthday just after I got back from our ride. As soon as I can put together some days off, I'm going to get that done. We can't afford another one. And there are so many kids, I never get any time alone with my wife."

"Man," Dylan said. "No one's *ever* cutting on me..."

Lang laughed heartily at that. "We'll talk after you have five kids."

"Like that'll ever happen..."

"It's a pretty simple formula, Dylan. Once I found a woman I loved, I stopped worrying about whether I'd ever find a woman I loved. I ask Sue Ann what I want and she's only too happy to tell me. And then, my friend, she *rewards* me. It's a beautiful thing."

The reward he was talking about flashed in Dylan's mind, but the players certainly were not Lang and Mrs. Lang. It was Dylan and Katie, of course. The first image happened to be on the floor. His mouth watered. Then the bed, then the shower, then the bed... He cleared his throat. "Sounds like you know what you're doing. Even I think you have the perfect life. And everyone knows I'm impossible to please."

"I don't think that," Lang said. "I've told you what I think a hundred times, but you don't listen."

"Tell me one more time."

Lang drew an impatient breath. "When I found my woman, I focused on her. You'll never find your woman, because you're focused on your silly demons. Demons you barely remember from your childhood anyway. Demons that have nearly died of old age, by the way. Speaking of those demons, how's the movie business these days? And the *family?*"

Dylan was speechless. Had Lang said that before? Was he always living inside his own head, worrying about how certain things would make *him* feel, not thinking about how other people might feel? But no, that wasn't right, because he felt very bad about the way he made Katie feel and came back to apologize... came back to apologize because he hadn't been sleeping and he wanted a clear conscience. And while he'd been gone, Katie had grown thin.

Oh, God, he thought. *I was trying not to, but I found her. I can't stand it, it's so scary. But I found her. My woman.*

"Dylan?" Lang said. "How's the sick and twisted family?"

"They're everywhere you look in Hollywood, all angling for a break, an endorsement, a part in a movie. I exchanged a few unpleasant words with my mother and a couple of sibs, but otherwise I haven't talked to the rest of them. I'm sure that makes me the bad guy."

"Nah," Lang said. "You're the *all done* guy. Very reasonable behavior. It is perfectly all right to stay away from vampires."

"Silly demons?" Dylan heard himself ask.

"I've known you for over fifteen years," Lang said. "Those characteristics you've complained about your family having—that narcissism, envy, cruelty, lack of accountability. If you showed those traits, we wouldn't be friends." Then he laughed and added, "Sue Ann wouldn't let me."

Dylan laughed with him. "One question," he said. "What makes you think I'm obsessed with my demons? Why don't you assume I avoid attachments to save women the bad luck of getting hooked up with me *and* my demons?"

"You ever ask anyone if they're willing to take a chance on you? Because I asked Sue Ann. I told her I wasn't good enough for her, that I probably wouldn't amount to much, but I had a good temperament and was trainable. She thought about it and decided I was worth the risk."

"Would you have gone away quietly if she'd said she thought it in her best interests to keep looking?" Dylan asked.

"Nah, I probably would've asked at least three times. I let her domesticate me. Now she's stuck with me."

Again Dylan laughed. And air hung in the line— dead air.

"Dylan," Lang finally said, suspicion dripping from the name. "Where are you?"

He didn't answer at once. "Virgin River."

"Ah."

"I wanted to apologize for being such an ass, for leaving suddenly, for making her feel dumped, for hurting her feelings like that."

"Ah. How's that working out for you?"

"About like you'd expect," he said. "Katie's real pissed and her brother beat me up. But I rented a truck. Think you can manage Childress Aviation without me for a while longer?"

Katie was never one to follow orders. She didn't stay at home, locked in the cabin, as Dylan commanded. She thought she'd drive into town, visit with Mel Sheridan and ask if they could delay that ultrasound appointment for a few more days. Surely Dylan would be gone again soon. When she drove into town she noticed a truck parked at Jack's with a logo on the side—Cavanaugh Apples. Perfect, she thought. So she parked there and went to the bar. There he was, Tom Cavanaugh, having a cup of coffee with Jack and Preacher.

"I saw your truck, Tom," she said. "I'm so glad I ran into you!"

"Katie," he said, smiling so handsomely.

"I wondered, have you called the game warden about that bear?"

"I'm sorry, Katie. I'll do it today, I promise."

"She was back this morning, and she's very pissy. I mean, come on, I have kids, too, and I can hold it together better than she can." She looked at Jack. "I wonder if maybe we need to get rid of the blackberries."

"They've been there for years and there's never been a problem before. Besides, they're still pretty green... I wonder if it's the play set."

"Where is this place?" Tom asked.

"It's my place," Jack said. "Mel lived in it when she first got here and we bought it. It's ended up a rental cabin, not far out of town but kind of hard to see, off the grid."

"Show me?" Tom asked Katie. "Maybe I can figure out what's drawing her, even though I'm not sure what's attracting her to my place. Probably green apples and a broken fence. Between the green apples and berries, it might be a bellyache that's making her so cranky."

"Sure, I'll show you," she said. "But finish your coffee by all means."

"I'm done. I'll follow you." He stuck out his hand to Jack, then Preacher. "Later," he said.

When they arrived at the cabin, Tom parked behind Katie. He got out, pushed his hat back on his head and whistled. "I can see why you'd hate to give this up. What an awesome little cabin."

"It is," she agreed. "But I just can't let the boys play with bear cubs."

He laughed. "No doubt. Where do you see her most often?"

"Around those bushes," Katie said, pointing. "And she was crossing the clearing, headed that way." She indicated. "And when I ran her off this morning, she and the cubs headed up that way."

"You ran her off?" he asked.

"I have a horn now. And some mace that I hope to never use—I don't want the breeze blowing it into my eyes. I can't wrestle a bear if I'm half-blind."

"You're something," he said, laughing. "It might just be her path, the route she likes to take to where she's going. She might take off in another direction when the cubs mature. Or when she falls in love next time. In fact, if you walked straight down that hill for about a mile and a half, you'd hit the orchard and on the other side of the orchard, the river. Or, here's a thought—she might have changed her route to the river to avoid predators because it's hard to keep track of three cubs."

"I can't even imagine…"

"You could always get a dog."

"The dog would scare her away?"

"No," he said. "But she might eat the dog before she eats you."

"Funny," she said, but she did laugh. "Would you like some coffee on the porch? I happen to have some in the pot."

"That would be perfect," he said. "After we met the other day, I thought of a couple of things I wanted to tell you. And ask you."

"Oh? Well let me get that coffee. Come inside if you like."

He was right on her heels and while she was fixing the coffee and warming some water in the microwave for tea, he was looking around. "This is awesome," he said.

"It's perfect for me. With the boys' toys, TV and video games up in the loft, I can keep the living space picked up without them undoing my housekeeping one step behind me. A couple of kids can really wreak havoc on a house." The microwave dinged and she pulled out her hot water. "What did you want to ask me?"

He held the door to the porch open for her. "I wanted to tell you—I'm just back from Afghanistan myself. My deployment was my last assignment in the Marines and time to get out. And I wanted to ask you—" He waited for her to sit. "When did you lose your husband?"

"Right before the twins were born, so I doubt there's any chance you knew him."

"I was in Iraq three years ago," he said. "So, you've been widowed for a while."

"Five years plus," she said. "Charlie was in the army."

"Again, I'm sorry, Katie. On my way home to Virgin River, I stopped off to visit a buddy's widow. We've lost some real good men."

"How's your friend's widow doing?"

He shook his head. "She's having some real hard times right now, but she has family around. I think I might head back there to check on her after we harvest the apples."

That touched her; what a nice man, she thought. But then, some of Charlie's buddies had visited her.

"I guess it's not too soon for you to think about dating," he said.

She knew it was coming. She had sensed it from their first meeting. "Well, it's not. But it's an awkward moment—I'm kind of…" She stopped to think of how she should put this, exactly. "I guess the only way to describe it is, interested in someone."

He grinned at her. "I guess the best thing for me to do is hang around till you lose interest."

And then, with the most miserable timing, Dylan pulled into the clearing, parking beside Katie's SUV. He had his motorcycle propped up and strapped into the bed of the truck. The place was starting to look like a parking lot.

Dylan didn't seem to be intimidated by the presence of another man. He jumped out of the truck and sauntered toward the porch, his boots hitting the ground pretty hard, his thumbs in his pockets. He was smiling, but it looked pretty contorted given his bruised face. "Howdy," he said, sticking out his hand toward Tom. "I'm Dylan."

Tom stood uneasily. "Tom," he said. "Tom Cavanaugh. What happened, man?"

"This?" he asked, pointing to his face. "Katie roughed me up."

"I did not!"

"Accident," Dylan said with a laugh. "Always wear a helmet, man. Katie, I brought you a six-pack and some other stuff." And he turned and went back to his truck. He proceeded to take grocery bags into the house.

"That him?" Tom asked. "The one you're interested in?"

Katie scowled. "No," she said. "Dylan is just a friend. Passing through town. He'll be leaving soon."

Dylan stuck his head out of the door and said, "Actually, I thought I might stay a couple of days, if that's not a problem. Really great to meet you, Tom." And then he disappeared into the cabin again.

Katie looked at Tom. "Ever have one of those annoying visitors? The kind who just doesn't get it when they're not actually *invited?*"

Tom laughed. "Maxie, my grandmother, has a million friends. She never had a visitor she wanted to leave."

"Hmm. Maybe she'd like to have Dylan," she offered.

Tom laughed and stood up. "I'll call the game warden, Katie. Listen, don't become the bear's adversary. Stay out of her way. New mothers can be unpredictable."

Dylan heard the talk on the porch. *Is he the one you're interested in? No, just a friend, passing through town...* He chuckled soundlessly. He was still putting food in the refrigerator when he heard Tom's truck start up and back out of the clearing. And then Katie was there. "Oh, you're funny," she said. "I guess if I'd wanted you to stick around before I should've just told you to leave."

"Are you throwing out the dating net, Katie?" he asked.

"That's none of your business..."

"You should tell me so I can manage to be...ah... unobtrusive when young Tom comes calling."

"How about absent? Absent would be so much more convenient than unobtrusive."

His expression became serious. "Look, I don't blame you for not wanting to move in with your brother—I personally think he has a short fuse and a very crabby disposition. But I don't think you should be all alone out here. I'm cooking tonight—my special pizza. The boys will love it. I'll take the couch."

She put her hands on her hips. "I don't think so."

"Then I'll sleep in the truck. Or on the porch—I have a sleeping bag."

"Why are you doing this?"

"Being responsible? Helping out?"

"I'm not your responsibility," Katie said. "And you're confusing me. You're in, you're out, you're back, you're leaving…"

"I missed you," he said. "And I shouldn't have left the way I did. But I had to leave. And we're not done talking…"

"Don't you have to get back to work? Don't you have an airline and airport to run? A movie to make? The paper says you're living on a big estate in Montana— you won't be happy on a couch. Or a porch."

He scrunched up his eyebrows. "Estate?"

"Your grandmother's estate…"

"Estate?" he said again.

She sighed deeply. "Airline? You own the airport it operates out of? Your rich and famous grandmother's estate? Am I speaking a foreign language here?" she asked.

He was careful with his answer; he was not smiling. "I checked in with the company. They're maintaining in my absence. And the 'estate' is being watched over. Would you like me to take you on a nice long, exciting bike ride? That used to blow your whistle."

Her hand slid over her belly. "Maybe not while I still have the remnants of this little bug…"

"Shouldn't you be better by now?"

"Something's going around, so don't breathe my air. You don't want to catch it."

"I'm not too worried about that. I'd be willing to take my chances for a whiff of your air."

"As flirting goes, you might be losing your touch."

"Okay, tell me this. How do we make peace with your big mean brother so I don't get hauled off the couch and beat senseless in the dark of night?"

She couldn't help but smile at him. "Already on the couch, are you? I thought you were taking the truck or the porch."

"I'm trying to make up, Katie. Work with me here."

"Leslie and I will take care of you and Conner," she said. "Don't worry about a thing."

Dylan smiled broadly. He was feeling a sense of safety and familiarity. This was one of the reasons he hadn't fallen in love before, he realized. He was used to women who thought he was important, either as an actor or the owner of an airline. Hah—two six-seaters and a Lear! Or the owner of an airport—a relatively short runway paved onto his grandmother's back forty and a couple of Quonset hangers and a prefab building for an office. Oh, yeah, there was that wind sock. Suddenly he wondered how many people thought he lived on an "estate."

Katie wasn't that impressed. She wouldn't trade a thing for his importance. The two women Dylan admired most were his grandmother and his best friend's wife, and Adele and Sue Ann didn't need a man to define them, bring their value into focus. He was ready to add Katie to that group, but...

"When I explain that he has to be nice to you, what should I say you're doing here? Exactly."

"I told you. I'm trying to make amends for acting like an ass after having a very romantic fling with you. A fling that shouldn't be finished anytime soon."

"I don't know how that'll go over," she said.

"You don't have to tell him about the fling unless you want to. Know what I really wish, Katie?" he said. "I wish we could start over. I wish I could unsay a bunch of stuff and say some new things."

Her hand slid over her stomach again and she said, "Too late, I'm afraid. I didn't trust you too much before and I trust you a little less now."

He had work to do here, he realized. Serious work, regaining her trust. "Can I see those articles again? The ones you saved?"

"Knock yourself out," she said. "I'll call Leslie at work. We can decide what to do with you two imbeciles."

So while she headed for the phone, he headed for the trunk. And he listened to what she was saying.

"Well, he was on his way out here to apologize for being a jerk when Conner went after him, so now I've got this banged-up guy on my couch, trying to make amends..."

"Couch," he muttered under his breath with a smile.

"Do you think that's a good idea, getting them together? No, no of course not! Just the bare...you

know…And let's not push on that—that's up to *me!*
And tell Conner he'd better remember that! Yes, I told
him he's forgiven, but I don't think I want to get mixed
up with him again. But it's still inexcusable for Conner
to be beating him up like that! You should see his face!
Oh, really?" she asked, then laughed.

Dylan turned and looked toward the kitchen.

"Apparently you did some damage, too," she told
Dylan. "Broke his nose."

"Self-defense," Dylan reminded her.

"Okay, we'll do that later," she said into the phone.
"But you talk to him first—I don't want a repeat of this
insanity. And I definitely don't want that happening in
front of the boys."

Dylan was multitasking. He read the articles and
captions while he listened to Katie—there was a reason
why he never looked at the tabloids. It was all such a
bunch of crap. There was speculation about whether
he'd be getting together romantically with Lindsey, his
old costar. Now, that didn't hurt him in any way, but
what about her? She had a good marriage to a great guy
and a couple of little kids. This kind of reporting was
irresponsible and could create problems where there
were none. There were plenty of seedy stories out there
without victimizing her.

Katie and Leslie had moved on to the bear, the
summer program the boys were in and Tom, the guy
who was going to call Fish and Game. They started
laughing about something to do with Conner's nose.

Dylan read that he'd been living on his grandmother's Montana estate and a snort escaped him. It was a four-bedroom, two-bath, thirty-five-year-old ranch-style house. It was perfectly nice; he'd had the kitchen remodeled about ten years ago and replaced some carpeting. There were some real nice hardwood floors and he had landscaped the backyard a few years ago, adding a big patio and grill he could use about three months of the year. But *estate?* It was around twenty-four hundred square feet of house and except for the yard surrounding the house, it was raw land in the valley that was Payne. There was a barn, a shed, a corral, a pasture. And there was Ham, doing his chores, letting himself into Dylan's house to make a sandwich when he got hungry.

And damn, he wanted her there. Suddenly that's what he wanted. To take Katie home with him.

Katie was talking about someone who lived on Leslie's street—the girls, she called them. Apparently Katie had settled in and had girlfriends.

Dylan poked through the trunk. He lifted out a photo album and flipped through some pages. Baby pictures of the twins, from the first day to about three months, but the man in the pictures wasn't their dad, it was their uncle. The next album he recognized as a wedding album and that got him a little wound up. Being a fairly typical man, he'd usually only look at wedding pictures if torture were the alternative. But he wanted to see Katie all dressed up and he wanted to see the guy who caught her.

"Yeah," he said, smiling quietly. She was spectacular. She wore a strapless dress that fit her snugly to her hips and then did some billowing. No veil, just a lot of baby's breath in her hair. She was so natural that way that he was surprised to see shoes on her feet. And there was Charlie—tall and strong. And goddamn him, he was good-looking enough to be a movie star himself. Decked out in his uniform, covered with medals and ribbons, every photo of him gazing at Katie with absolute love and longing and the promise of making her cry out in pleasure every night.

And suddenly she was sitting beside him. "Our wedding," she said.

"It's a wonder the guy can stand up under all that brass," Dylan said.

"He was highly decorated. He took way too many chances, I'm sure of that. He got the Medal of Honor posthumously for acts of bravery and heroism that cost him his life, but saved others. We weren't married long, but I felt like I knew Charlie very well—he wouldn't have thought twice. Did you know that only a few living soldiers have been awarded the Medal of Honor? I saw one interviewed on TV. And you should see how modest and humble he is. I must admit, that's about the only time Charlie was modest and humble, when the army wanted to give him a medal, otherwise he was kind of full of himself."

"Really?"

"You know guys," she said. She turned the page. "We had six months together before he deployed, so he got to know the boys a little bit. But two months later he was killed."

"Got to know the boys?" Dylan asked.

She put her hand on her tummy. "In here. While they were in here, moving around, going crazy. We named them before he left. And the nicest thing—the president made sure there were two Medals of Honor—one for each of the boys. And three flags—one for me, one for each of them…"

And all this time Dylan had been pissing and moaning about a half-whacked family and the rigors of fame…?

Charlie Malone, hard act to follow.

Dylan picked up the tabloids that sat beside him on the sofa. "Katie, throw these in the trash."

"Why?"

"First of all, it's all B.S. Second, this crap shouldn't sit on top of Charlie's medals. It's sacrilege."

"It must be really annoying, seeing that kind of stuff printed."

"It would be if I ever bothered to look. I used to. When I was a kid it really bothered me. So—what did you and Leslie decide is going to happen to us—Conner and I?"

"Well, you're going to face the music. After I pick up the boys this afternoon, we're going to their house. The two of you will apologize, take an oath to stay out of each other's business and shake hands."

"Awww…"

"Just shake hands and talk about baseball or something. I honestly don't care if you hate each other till the end of time, you're going to act like adults around Leslie and I. Or else."

"Can I just remind you that I didn't attack him?"

"Uh-huh, so I hear. And you also had to be held back so you wouldn't retaliate. It is officially over, Dylan. Or you will be banished."

"But you said I could have the couch. You can't banish me."

She lifted one light brown brow. "Try me."

The phone rang and she got up to answer it. Dylan could only hear her side of the conversation but he realized two things immediately—it was that Tom fellow, and whatever he had to say did not make her happy. "What? Oh, no! Tom, that isn't a good thing. No, I don't like it but I feel trapped. And I'm very grateful that you let them know but... Honestly, if she were better natured, I might try to hide her..."

By the time she hung up, Dylan was standing, looking at her across the room. "What's the matter, Katie?"

She pulled a sad face and shrugged. "Tom did as he promised and called Fish and Game. They said they would put a plan in motion to relocate the bear but they couldn't guarantee anything. It's very unlikely the whole family would be relocated together. They might hold one or two of the cubs in captivity for a while, till they're more independent. Apparently relocating four bears is quite a tall order. So tall an order, they might just..."

"You seem pretty upset..."

"Shoot her…they might just shoot her. Even if they do move her, a mother shouldn't lose her children just because she got a little overprotective. And, God, brothers shouldn't be separated…"

He just smiled at her. She could be so tough, but there were some issues on which she was completely tenderhearted. "Let's go for a ride," he said.

"I told you, I'm not really feeling like the bike—"

"I know, no problem. We'll take the truck. Or better still—your SUV. You don't have anything better to do between now and when you toss me to that brother of yours. Let's head for the beach. Got an old blanket around here? We can stop and get some lunch to go, take it easy. You can tell me all about Charlie. How you met him, how you knew you wanted to take a chance on him, all your secrets."

"They're not secrets, Dylan. They're also not the sort of thing you should be interested in. What kind of guy wants to know about the first guy?"

"I'm interested in Charlie," he said. "But I want to know about *you.*"

Fifteen

Over a couple of deli sandwiches, bag of chips and unsweetened tea, Dylan learned that Katie met Charlie through a girlfriend. "She had a date with some soldier, set up by a cousin of hers or something, and she didn't want to go alone. So, before she even asked me if I'd go, she asked her date to bring a friend for her girlfriend. I was pretty annoyed with her, but I went. She never saw her soldier again after that night, but I married mine."

"You must've been a lot easier back then…" Dylan teased.

"He made me laugh," she said, amused. "Then he made me love him. Conner had a fit because I was ready to run away with Charlie after a week. I agreed to wait a few months and Charlie won over Conner."

"Just out of curiosity, how'd he do that?"

"Well, he didn't break his nose, for one thing. It did take a while, but Charlie worked hard at courting me. He flew from Texas to Sacramento every chance he got, not easy to do on a soldier's salary. Conner thought he'd lose interest, find a more convenient girlfriend, but Charlie kept coming back. He just wouldn't give up. He told Conner he'd never quit because he loved me."

Dylan reached for her, smoothing back her hair on one side. "I came back," he reminded her.

"I didn't expect that," she said. "But that doesn't mean I trust you."

"I know you don't. I'll be honest with you—I didn't know I'd come back, either. And here's a flash for you, Katie Malone—I'm not giving up, either."

She sighed and lay down on the blanket, on her back. "I think you might, Dylan. I'm pretty sure I'm not going to fit into your plans."

"I'm flexible, when you get down to it," he said, leaning over her, hoping he could wrap up this conversation with some meaningful kissing.

"Not about everything," she said. She touched the tender black-and-blue cheek under his eye. "Listen, I didn't plan this, but I guess since you're here asking for another chance, you should have the facts. There's a reason why Conner went a little crazy on you. It's not just because you left and I was sad. It's because just minutes before he ran into you at Jack's, I had told him…" She lost her nerve and bit her lower lip.

"What, Katie?"

"Well, the one thing you had long ago made up your mind never to do—have a family," she said.

"I've given that some thought," he said. "If the girl I want comes with a couple of kids, I'll have to rethink that." He shrugged. "I guess the real danger to you probably lies in my screwed up DNA. I'd really like to overcome that. I just don't know if I can."

"Right," she said. She turned on her side and balanced her head on her hand, her elbow braced on the ground. "As it turns out, we're going to find out just how screwed up your DNA is. Take a deep breath. I'm pregnant."

He didn't move. He couldn't breathe. His eyes got a little wide as he looked at her.

"You aren't going to throw up, are you?" she asked him.

He still didn't move. He leaned away from her and she sat up. "I'm very careful," he said. "That shouldn't have happened."

"Yeah, I'm careful, too. We had some bad luck, I guess. Failed protection? I think we got a little too... ahem...close before the protection got involved."

"My fault," he muttered. "I lost my mind. I lost control. I couldn't think and I—I'm sorry..."

"You're probably right about how it happened. I can promise you I didn't stick pins in condoms—I wasn't interested in having this kind of surprise. I already have plenty on my plate."

"Were you going to tell me?" he asked, and his voice sounded very hoarse.

"Absolutely, but when I was ready and not because I need anything from you. You've been very clear how you feel about this sort of thing, like you don't realize I'll have some DNA in this child, as well... And mine is excellent, by the way. So once I realized what had happened, I decided I could handle this just fine. But I'm an honest person and you deserve to know. How you respond is up to you."

He looked out at the ocean. He circled his raised knees with his arms and put his forehead down on his knees. He groaned. He took a moment, then he straightened, looked at her and said, "And how are *you* going to respond?" he asked.

She actually laughed. "Well, funny you should ask. I'm going to be a little nauseated in the mornings, be very tired in the afternoons and early evenings, grow enormous and then deliver. Then I am rather committed full-time for about twenty years."

"Do I have this right—you told your brother already, but not me?" he asked.

She took a breath. "First of all, you weren't here and he was. I had a phone number but this wasn't the kind of thing I wanted to tell you on the phone, at least until I was sure that was the only option. I would've gotten in touch eventually, you can be sure of that. But for the time being all I was sure of was that you were partying in Hollywood, kissing blond necks and stuff."

"I told you," he said. "A good friend, a hug. That was not a real kiss."

"So, I had to ask for my brother's emotional support. I'll get a job, pay my own freight, take care of my children and—"

"Is there any discussion about whether—?"

Her expression became fierce as she stopped him

by holding up a hand. "Don't even go there. You don't have to like it, but it is what it is."

"Go where?" he asked, confused.

"I'm having my baby, no matter what you want."

"I wasn't going to ask that! I was going to ask if there was any chance we could do it together."

"Not likely, if I'm here and you're in Hollywood," she said.

He ran a hand over his head. "I figured as much."

And like a mental collage, little snapshots of his childhood came to mind—his dad leaving when he was about five. A new man with a couple of weekend sons, older than Dylan, moving in. A new baby sister, another man leaving—but at least he took the weekend sons who had never missed an opportunity to pick on Dylan. He had weekend visits with his own dad but more often with his grandmother. His mother going away to make a movie, coming home six months later with a different man, this time with a stepdaughter older than Dylan and a new baby brother for his mother. That gave him five half sibs and just as many steps.

Katie lay down on her back again, her fingers laced over her abdomen. He looked down at that sweet face and knew it wouldn't be that way with her. It still scared him to death, but he wasn't afraid of *her.* But she had his baby in her and it was the idea that a single mother was better for that baby than an unhappy family life that scared him. He could not let his child have the kind of childhood he had. He just wasn't entirely sure how to guarantee that.

He leaned over her and put a small kiss on her lips and she opened her eyes. "You don't need a job, Katie. Your job is being a mother and you're an excellent one. I'll take care of the other details."

She almost smiled but not quite. "Does this mean you're actually happy?"

"Are you, Katie? Happy about it?"

"When I had time to think about it, yes. It's inconvenient and I still have to deal with some of those early pregnancy issues, but if I had a choice, I wouldn't change it. And I realize I do have a choice."

"And how long have you had to think about it? How long have you known?"

"Maybe a week. Maybe a little less."

"I have a favor to ask," he said. "Let me have that much time to get to happy. I'm a little shocked. And a lot uncomfortable. But I'm not an idiot—no one takes care of you but me."

She just looked at him for a long, meaningful moment and he knew there was so much missing from this situation. This must be so far from ideal in her eyes—he should mention marriage and love. There was a part of him that wanted to, even if he wasn't completely sure yet.

"I guess that's not too much to ask," she finally said.

Good thing Katie wasn't expecting an instant transformation from Dylan because she certainly didn't get one. He appeared to be in the same place. The idea of fathering a child must be terrifying to him.

She remembered Charlie. Not long after their honeymoon, he had a field training mission with the army. They'd been married a whole month when he left for two weeks. When he returned he walked into their small apartment, dropped his duffel and yelled for her. Bellowed for her, which was what he typically did. *Katie, baby, come get all over your man!* He could be such a caveman. There was a part of her that craved that kind of attention, a part of her that wished he could be a little more civilized. She was so in love she ran to him. He smelled to high heaven, of stale perspiration, mud, two weeks in the field, God knew what all.

She flung herself into his arms, then flung herself out of his arms and ran for the bathroom where she proceeded to hover over the commode, really on the verge.

"I know I smell bad, but that's a little melodramatic, don't you think," he said, standing in the bathroom doorway, unlacing his boots and stripping off his BDU. "Take it easy, I'll get right in the shower."

He was down to his fatigue pants, stinky bare feet and broad, delicious, tattooed chest, when she turned watering eyes up to him. "Charlie, I'm pregnant."

"Oh, baby!" he said, falling to his knees to take her into his arms. "Baby…"

"Charlie!" she yelled. "Shower, for God's sake! Please!"

"Yeah," he said, rising and getting rid of what remained of his clothes. "You bet, baby. Then we'll celebrate! Do pregnant women have sex?" he wanted to know as he turned on the shower.

He was one of a kind, that was for sure. It took a special woman to be married to Charlie Malone and his lifestyle. And it was going to take a lot of patience to make peace with Dylan Childress and draw him safely into her heart. She wondered if she had the time or the faith.

With her eyes closed, she thought about the differences between Charlie and Dylan…and their similarities. Both shockingly handsome, smart and confident men, at first glance you'd think they were alike. Beyond those obvious similarities they were opposites. Charlie was bold while Dylan was more reserved. Charlie grabbed what he wanted without the slightest hesitation while there were lots of emotional connections that still terrified Dylan. Charlie had waited a long time to really fall in love but once he recognized it, he was all in. Dylan had too many childhood ghosts to make that leap of faith.

Both men were phenomenal lovers; she could never have resisted either one of them.

She must have nodded off in the warm, beach sunshine because she felt Dylan curve around her. He was lying on his side, his arm casually crossing over her waist. His breath was warm on her ear and inhaled her scent, exhaling slowly. He nuzzled her softly. "Don't fall asleep, honey," he said. "We have to watch the time. The boys…"

She smiled and snuggled a little closer. He remembered they had to pick up the twins. And stop by her brother's house.

Yes, it was going to take a special kind of patience to let him know he'd be safe with her. And she would require a special kind of courage to take a chance on him. Green Berets were a piece of cake compared to movie stars.

Dylan sensed a sort of peacefulness about Katie as they left the beach and drove back to Virgin River. Or maybe it was just that she wasn't as uptight about this peacemaking confrontation with Conner as he was. He remained quiet while Katie talked about Dylan's mysterious special pizza for dinner, about how to make peace with her bear, about how the sound of the waves had been so relaxing she'd fallen asleep, but then she was so sleepy these days she could fall asleep standing up.

"I know I'm not very talkative right now, Katie, but it's not you," he said.

"I don't care, Dylan, because my mind is made up about how I'm moving forward. I'm sure when you work out a few things in your head, you'll talk a little more."

He turned toward her. "Exactly," he said.

When they pulled up to the little prefab schoolhouse, the boys were busy on the play set that Dylan had helped to erect. "Katie, when we get to Conner's house, can you get the boys occupied with something so I can talk to your brother without the boys around?"

"If you promise you're not using that as an excuse to get into a fistfight…"

"Look at my eye. You think I want to sacrifice the

other one? I just want to talk to him, but if he gets angry the boys shouldn't be there. If you want to, I can take you and the guys home and come back by myself for this talk."

"No—I'll find them something on TV they can watch. But behave!"

He didn't reply to that but he didn't feel that he was the loose cannon—behaving was his sole intention. And he knew the road to hell was paved with good intentions.

He and Katie got to Conner and Leslie's house before they were home from work. "The door will be unlocked," she said. "I'll take the kids in and get them settled in front of the TV with a snack. Conner has a few of their favorite movies and games here. Would you like something to drink?"

"How would he feel about me having a beer from his refrigerator?"

She flashed him a teasing smile, lifting her brow. "Need a little calming courage?"

"Baby, after what I learned about an hour ago, I should probably have a six-pack. I'll wait on the front porch."

He leaned against the porch rail and waited. This must be what it felt like to be a teenage boy who was meeting a girl's father when he'd gotten her in trouble, except it was probably the rare father who launched an attack. Even with all the siblings Dylan had, he'd never been close enough to one to feel that kind of protectiveness. In fact, he felt more protective toward Katie after knowing her for half a summer than he ever had toward one of his own family members. He wondered if that little bun in the oven was making the difference.

She finally brought him a beer. "Sure you don't want to come inside?"

"Nope," he said. He walked down the porch steps.

"Where are you going?"

He turned to look at her. "I'm not doing this in front of you, Katie. I mean, you might see us, but I'm not having this conversation for your entertainment."

"Trust me, I don't feel real entertained."

"If I'm away from the house, you won't be tempted to put in your two cents' worth."

"Well, jeez, you're a little bossy there, aren't you?"

"Making us a very well-matched set, when you think about it," he said, and he walked back to the street where her SUV was parked. He leaned against it. It was his own damn fault he had this mess to clean up and he was going to figure it out before it got any worse. When he thought about what Lang would do it didn't really help his situation much. Lang wouldn't hesitate to try to convince his woman to marry him, provided the woman had been Sue Ann.

Finally the yellow SUV that Leslie drove pulled up to the house and into the drive, all the way forward to the carport. Right behind her was Conner in his great big truck and Dylan thought, *I should've rented a bigger truck.* Conner got out of the truck and briefly glared at Dylan, and Dylan had to look at the ground in front of his crossed legs to keep from laughing. Conner had white tape across his rather swollen, purple nose.

Conner took his lunch tote into the house, but momentarily he was back, striding toward Dylan. Dylan just couldn't help it, he grinned stupidly.

"You look in the mirror, idiot?" Conner asked.

"So," he said, ignoring the taunt. "I've been told to work this out with you, so let's work this out. I learned about one hour ago why you lost your temper."

"Because you weren't here!" Conner returned rather loudly.

Dylan came off the truck and stood straight, meeting him eye to eye. "You want the women involved in this conversation?" he asked. "Because at the first sign of trouble, they're right in the middle of it, I guarantee it. I wasn't here because I had to go to work. I told Katie from the day I met her, I was going to have to go to work, but because she's Katie, I put it off as long as I could."

"And you abandoned her," Conner ground out between clenched teeth. "Left her pregnant and alone!"

"I didn't realize what was going on and I apologized. Listen, it doesn't really matter to me if you understand or sympathize or hate my guts, but I told her the truth, that I was not in the market for a girlfriend or steady relationship, that I was temporary here at best, and whether she believed me or not, she accepted that. At least when she had the chance to tell me to just hit the road then, she didn't. I don't know you, don't know anything about you, but you're at least my age and just barely hooked up with this woman," he said, lifting the chin toward the house. That's when he noticed Katie and Leslie sitting on the porch, watching them. He cleared his throat. "I'm guessing you had one or two situations like that in your time."

"That doesn't matter," he said. "This is my *sister*."

"Noted," Dylan said. "And now that I know the situation, I'll take care of it. And you better back off or you're going to screw it up for all of us."

"How do you plan to take care of it?" he demanded.

"That's going to be between me and Katie. We'll work it out."

"Don't you even think about making her do *anything* she doesn't want to do!"

Dylan couldn't help it, a huff of laughter escaped. In his mind he saw her struggling with the lug nuts, standing up to an angry bear, telling him, *Don't even go there—it is what it is*. "Are we talking about the same woman?"

"She was hurt," he said. "No matter what you said, the way you just dumped her, hurt her. Don't you do anything to her that makes her cry again. Do you get me?"

"I'm going to do the best I can" was all he promised.

"Your best better be some improvement."

Dylan was quiet for a long moment. He gathered himself internally. "I know you love her," he said with as much understanding as he could muster, "but you can't fix this for her. She has to deal with me because we made this situation together, Katie and I. If you don't back off, if we don't make our peace for her sake, it's going to get more complicated than it needs to be."

Conner was stubbornly silent, frowning.

At long last Dylan said, "So. How about those Red Sox?"

About an hour after Dylan and Conner shook hands and Dylan walked away down the street, Katie picked him up at Jack's. When he was sitting beside her in the car she said, "You couldn't sit on the porch with my brother and have a beer? A friendly conversation?"

"Not today, Katie," he said. "Soon," he added.

He wasn't real happy with the idea that Conner punched him before talking to him. Before they made their peace, Dylan had many things to come to terms with. That was only one of them.

When they were back at the cabin, he made his special pizzas, which were basically a simple bread dough covered with tomato sauce, lots of cheese, some pepperoni and on one, some mushrooms and black olives. He asked the boys to help cover them with stuff. The pizzas couldn't lose because the boys were involved.

After dinner, he took the boys outside and kicked the soccer ball around with them, though he was wearing boots to their tennis shoes. Then he sat on the porch and watched as they climbed all over the jungle gym. When Katie came outside and sat in the chair next to his he said, "I'm wearing them down for you." And he smiled.

"What are your plans, Dylan?"

"If you don't mind, I'd like your couch for a while. I need some time to figure out how to handle our… situation. I want to do the right thing. For many reasons."

"You do understand that it's not entirely up to you, right? I have no husband and three children to think about so whatever you come up with, I'll definitely listen. But you're not going to decide our lives for us."

"Can I have the couch?" he asked. "Or not?"

"You can have the couch and the kitchen. You're a good cook, as it turns out."

Right now Dylan didn't want to be distracted—he wanted to figure out how he felt and what he should ultimately do with his life. The day after his forced handshake with Conner, he drove down the mountain and checked in with Lang. All was status quo in Payne, Lang assured him. So he texted his grandmother, the agent working on his movie contract, Jay Romney, Lang, Sue Ann and Stu—*I'm staying in the mountains for a few days and cell reception isn't great. I'll check in when I can, but might be out of touch. No problems, just out of touch. I'll be in touch when I'm back in service. Thanks.*

And then he turned off the phone.

Over the next several days Dylan hung pretty tight to Katie and the boys, stayed close to the cabin except for errands. When he wanted to go off on his own he made Katie promise not to have a standoff with any wildlife, especially the bear. He went to the larger towns for groceries, more than happy to be responsible for dinner.

The one thing that kept him on the couch and from sneaking into Katie's room at night or from begging her to make love while the boys were at school was the fact that he felt he had their entire lives to figure out before he could think about things like that. He also thought there was a good possibility she might clobber him.

But Dylan had plenty of confidence in other things—like his ability to think rationally about business. He knew he was levelheaded and fair. And while he might have siblings who were assholes and idiots, he was a nice person and good with people. He played to his strengths.

On a night he'd taken Katie and the boys to McDonald's and afterward to a park to further wear them out, he thought he had it together. As they were pulling through Virgin River on the way to the cabin he asked, "After the boys have gone to bed, can we talk about things?"

"Well, butter my butt and call me biscuit! Only six short nights on my couch and you're ready to talk about our situation?"

And he laughed.

"I'm not sure I can stay up until after they're asleep. But I'll make a compromise—I'll meet you on the porch after they're bathed and rooted in front of a movie in the loft. Will that do it for you?"

"That will do it."

It was hard to stay on track with Miss Funny Bones teasing him, but he was determined. He had come up with what he thought was a fantastic idea. He was sure she'd be relieved.

She brought a couple of steaming cups of tea to the front porch and he noticed, not for the first time, she seemed to be looking better. He was only too aware of her brief fits of nausea, when a smell or something else would trigger a wave of it, but she no longer looked like she'd been ill or starving. It made him feel a rush of pride because although he'd never tell her, that had been his goal—to cook her at least one hearty meal a day and hopefully put back those pounds he'd robbed from her.

He took the cup she offered. He'd never been a tea drinker but this stuff Katie made didn't gag him. In fact this was one of the ways he always knew Sue Ann was pregnant again—she'd offer them tea. He and Lang would make gagging sounds and go get a beer or a Crown Royal on ice.

Behind them in the house, he could hear the TV in the loft. He obediently sipped his tea. "Are they almost ready to go to bed?" he asked.

"Almost."

"Katie," he said. And then he just looked at her. There were times he'd catch a glance and think he'd never seen such a pretty girl in his life. It made him frown slightly as he wondered if she was really that beautiful or just to him. After all, he thought Sue Ann was pretty but Lang was completely hypnotized by her. Well, as it should be. But Dylan had never been in that place before.

"After six nights on my couch, cat's got your tongue?"

And that mouth—she was relentless. Why did he love that so much?

"I've got a few ideas," he said.

"Well, let's have it. I can't wait."

"Let's start with that movie I'm supposed to make," he said. "That could come in handy under the circumstances."

"Oh?" she asked. "You said the whole idea was to get your charter business and airport on its feet."

"That was the whole idea, but now there seems to be more on the table. I could use a portion of that movie money for the baby."

It was as if she came to attention. Her neck straightened a bit, her eyes brightened. "Oh?"

"How about a trust for the…ah…baby. For his education. That sort of thing."

And as he watched, it seemed she showed first shock and then disappointment. The dusky night was darkening and he wondered if he hadn't seen quite right. Shouldn't she be thrilled?

"A trust?" she asked.

"Something put aside to be sure he's always taken care of, in case something should happen to either of us. You know."

"Wow."

He waited for some huge, grateful reaction, but it didn't come. After a few moments, he said, "It seemed like an even more important reason to make that movie than the company. I thought it would make you happy."

"That's really thoughtful."

"So…why do I get the impression you aren't too happy?"

"Oh, sorry. Thank you, that's so generous."

"Katie!"

"What?"

"What about this idea doesn't make you happy?"

Her eyelids fluttered closed as she looked down. She put her cup of tea on the porch and reached for his hand. "Let me ask you something, Dylan. Growing up, did you have a lot of half brothers and sisters?"

"You know I did. I told you all that…"

"Was there ever jealousy? Resentment? That kind of thing?"

"All the time."

"Was it ever directed at you? I mean, you were a child star. Did any of your siblings resent that they were not the stars?"

He took a moment to answer, but not because the answer wasn't on his lips. Where was this coming from? "Yes."

"And so how do you think Andy and Mitch will feel about their younger brother or sister and the big trust to ensure his or her future?"

He was momentarily struck silent. Then in an effort to recover he said, "I could do it for all of them."

She shook her head. "I think you're under the impression that I'm poor. Oh, I'm sure I'm not rich by your standards, but Conner and I were left a very successful store. It was destroyed by fire but there was insurance money, the sale of commercial land and both of our houses, more than enough to resettle and rebuild. There's some security there, though of course I'll work. Between Conner and I, we'll make sure the kids get everything they're entitled to—all of them, not just one of them. And I get it, that one is *your* one. I get that. But really, you don't want to do things to make him different. To make him, or *her,* enviable in his or her own family. In families everyone takes care of each other as much as possible."

"Fine!" he said almost angrily. "I'll give it to *you!* You take care of it. Spread it around any way you want to!"

She stared at him for a long moment. "That's very nice of you," she said. Her eyes got glassy. "I don't know how I can possibly thank you."

And then she stood up and went into the house.

He sat there, stunned. He had absolutely no idea what he'd done wrong.

He noticed that quiet slowly replaced the noise of the TV inside the little cabin. He heard the shuffling of the boys down the stairs as she herded them into bed. And her bedroom door closed.

Dylan was devastated. He'd spent days trying to figure out how to make this right, how to reassure her he was in this with her all the way. He was a responsible man and he adored Katie. He was terrified to tell her that, of course—she might ask him to get married and then what would he do? He wanted to, but he wasn't quite ready. He thought he might be in a little while, once he worked into the idea. Probably by the time he'd finished that movie and had the airline on track and the trust set up, he'd feel ready, but right now, the whole idea scared him. That didn't mean he didn't feel like it—it just meant he wanted to be ready. She was only about a month, maybe six weeks pregnant. There was time.

His dad had sent him a ten-thousand-dollar check on his tenth birthday because he'd promised to take him to Egypt and had gone alone, or more likely with a woman, leaving him behind. Ten thousand dollars to a ten-year-old. A kite and a day at the park would've meant so much more.

He remembered his grandmother had been furious about that.

Dylan asked himself, had he just done that? Could Katie think that money was to make her go away quietly? Because it wasn't! He wanted to take care of her! Them! He wanted to never lose her, them.

I've been thinking about it, he remembered saying. *If the girl I want comes with a couple of kids, I can deal with that.*

He sat down on the sofa and pulled off his boots, his belt, his shirt. He went to her bedroom, tapped softly a couple of times and entered. She slid over as he sat down on the edge of the bed. He could barely see her face, so he ran a finger along her cheek to the curve of her chin. "If you're crying, I'll hate myself forever."

"I'm not crying, Dylan."

"Katie, you need to be married to a man who has

some instincts about this whole situation. And I don't have any. Just when I think I have the one idea that will solve most of our problems, it makes you sad."

"It's not instincts you're lacking, Dyl. It's experience. You grew up in a household of this one and that one. There was a different group for every holiday and if I'm guessing right, a lot of jockeying for position. It can't have been real nurturing." He just shook his head. "We don't have to do that, Dylan."

"Katie, you're unlike any woman I've ever known. My feelings for you are…" He couldn't quite finish. "Strong. You have no idea how strong. I want to never lose you. But…"

"I know," she said. "We still don't have to make a life of spare parts and separate people, like a group home or something. We can still be one family."

"And if I don't know how that's done, exactly?"

She smiled at him and put a tender finger against his lips. "Here's a thought. I could trust you to fly the planes and you could trust me to do the mothering. Those things that I don't do very well, fortunately you do. And those things you struggle with?" She shrugged. "I happen to understand."

When he just scowled, drawing his eyebrows tight, she asked, "What?"

"And if it doesn't work out for us, for you and me? I want it to always be like it is right now, but if for some reason it isn't? Like if you come to your senses?"

She laughed softly. "I will still raise my children as a group, as a family, no matter what you choose to do. Now why don't you make sure the bedroom door is locked and come in here beside me, hold me for a while, do something you *know* you have a talent for."

He stood up and chucked his jeans, slipping in beside her with a big grin on his face. "I think we've just stumbled on an area of mutual success."

"Uh-huh," she said. "Stop thinking so hard, Dylan. You're wearing me out."

Sixteen

Luke Riordan enjoyed a late-afternoon beer with Jack, something he treated himself to now and then. He occasionally took a break from tending his son and his cabins if his wife was at home. Shelby was a clinic nurse in Eureka and worked three ten-hour shifts every week, which left Luke to play househusband, including cooking. This was a good thing. Shelby *liked* to cook. She was miserable at it, but no one had the guts to tell her.

"You're facing about three or four days of dinner by Shelby," Jack teased.

"I might get her in here one of those days," Luke said hopefully.

"I wish you luck. Are your cabins still booked?"

"Right up through fall. We have summer people—families and students and vacationers almost to hunting season, then we have hunters and fishermen through the holidays. Plus, a couple of my buddies are coming for a week this fall."

"No kidding?" Jack asked. "And who might that be?"

"Just a couple of guys from army days. We haven't been that good about staying in touch but every time we touch base, it's like yesterday. You know what I mean?"

"I have a few like that," Jack said. "They lifers like you?"

"No, short timers. Both were pilots, both got out at the first chance. One of 'em had some family store or something up in Oregon. The other one had a little bit of trouble in the army and our favorite uncle pretty much asked him to leave. Trouble of the disciplinary sort, if you get my drift."

Jack laughed. "Have one or two of those, too," he said. "Hunters?"

"As it happens both of them love to hunt. Fortunately for me, since I'm full of hunters during the season, it turned out the only time we could all get together was right before the season opens. We'll get in some fishing at least. But I'd put these two in the house if I had to. They're good guys."

"Let us know when you expect them and maybe we can round up a poker game or something," Jack suggested.

"Deal us in," Luke said, finishing his beer. "How's my tab these days?"

"I think you owe me a great deal of money."

"See you later," he said with a laugh, putting a couple of bills on the bar.

He'd only been out the door a minute when he was right back inside.

"Wait till you see what just pulled up outside," Luke said from the door. "I think it's a limousine."

"In Virgin River?" Jack asked. He came around the bar and went to the door and sitting in front of the bar was an oversize, cream-colored town car trimmed in gold with a driver in a black suit holding the back passenger door open.

"That a limousine?" Luke asked.

"Sort of. Not really," Jack said. "Fancy town car with a chauffeur."

A small woman got out of the car. Even Jack could tell she was dressed to the nines but he couldn't guess her age. Older than she looked by the way she moved, he thought. Her short hair was blond but almost gray; her face was soft and smooth-looking but had a look of experience, especially around the eyes. She walked to the base of the porch and asked, "Are you the proprietor, sir?"

He gave a slight bow, then stepped down from the porch to meet her on equal ground. The little thing was probably five foot one in her shoes. "I'm Jack Sheridan, ma'am, and this is my bar."

"Charming little place," she said with a smile. Her teeth were perfect and healthy. "I bet you have a wonderful time!"

"Just a simple place, ma'am. Would you like to come inside?"

"I'm going to have to make it another time. I'm looking for my grandson and perhaps you know where I might find him. His name is Dylan Childress and I believe he was last seen around here."

"I know Dylan," Jack said. "I bet you'll find him at his lady friend's cabin. In fact, it's my cabin which I lease to his lady friend and chances are—"

"Ah, yes, the lady friend," she said with a tilt of her head. "I heard there was a lady friend, but we haven't met."

"He's been seen around with Katie Malone," Jack said. "She's a newcomer here, but we love her already."

"What a nice recommendation. Can you tell Randy how to get to that cabin?" And she nodded over her shoulder to her driver. On that signal alone, he stepped forward.

"Easy enough," Jack said. "Go back out 36 almost exactly two miles. Right turn at a dirt road…not the best road, either. Go about two and a half miles back up the mountain until you come to a mailbox and newspaper drop. Take a left down the drive right up to the house. It's a small A-frame in a large clearing. Dylan and Katie's brother erected a jungle gym in the clearing for her kids and there are a couple of Adirondack chairs on the porch."

Randy nodded but the lady looked surprised. "She has a family?"

"Twin boys, five years old. I didn't catch the name, ma'am."

"Oh, I'm sorry, how rude of me! Adele Childress and please, just call me Adele. It appears as if I'll have to enjoy your public house another time, Jack. Right now I'd like to see Dylan."

"But I want your promise that you'll be back," Jack said good-naturedly.

"Absolutely! It looks charming."

And then she let Randy help her back into the car. In a moment, they were pulling out of town.

Luke whistled. "You don't see that every day."

"No shit," Jack said.

"You aren't going to call him, are you?"

"I should," Jack said. "I have a feeling this will come as a surprise. If he'd been expecting her, Randy wouldn't have needed directions."

"Yeah, but don't," Luke said with a decidedly evil grin. "I mean, come on. Can't we have a little fun?"

"Give it up—you won't be there to see it. Think of Dylan!"

"Yeah, who *is* Dylan?" Luke asked.

"The grandson of Randy's boss!" Jack said, heading back into the bar.

Dylan was just a little self-conscious about how easy it was to chill him out. A little romp in the sack with Katie and all his rough edges and worries were smooth and soft. But he was only a little embarrassed by that because he was cognizant of how simple it was to soothe him, and no one had ever soothed him like Katie could. Suddenly all the problems and complications of the earlier days seemed unimportant. As he sat on the porch watching the boys on the play set, feet up on the rail, hat tilted over his eyes, he thought, *Nice—I have a woman with my bun in her oven, she loves me, she's going to keep me on the right path.*

He heard the phone in the cabin ring, heard Katie answer. Then she was at the door. "Dylan? It's Jack Sheridan and he'd like to speak to you."

"Keep an eye on things out here, will you?"

"Sure," she said. "Oh, God, Dylan—the boys are upside down again!"

"They're fine," he said. "They prefer to be upside down. I'll be right back."

A few moments later he was back on the porch, but the expression he wore was odd. He looked puzzled and maybe unhappy. "I'm not sure there's any way to prepare you for this…"

And just as he said that, a long and classy Lincoln town car pulled into the clearing. It looked like a modern version of Cinderella's coach.

"Dylan?" she asked, standing from her chair.

The uniformed driver jumped out and went to open the back passenger door. Adele Childress stepped out. She was wearing cream-colored slacks that matched her car, low heels, a cinnamon blouse with a silk scarf under the collar and around her neck, the color of her slacks. She wore a gold chain belt and matching necklace. Her hair and makeup were perfect. Dylan smirked. This was her going-into-the-mountains attire.

Katie ran her hands down her pants, which were jeans with a short T-shirt that exposed her flat belly and navel.

"You look great," Dylan said to Katie.

She ran her hands over her hair at her temples, patting it into place.

"You're beautiful," he told her. "Don't be intimidated by flash."

He crossed his arms over his chest as Adele approached the porch. Unlike Jack had done by stepping down from the porch, Dylan held his ground.

"I would have called ahead, but you haven't answered any of my texts or voice mails or emails," she said.

"Because as I explained, I was going to be out of cell contact for a few days and would be back in touch when possible."

Katie whacked him on the shoulder and bounded off the porch steps. "Hi. I'm Katie Malone," she said. For a second she was flustered, wondering whether to curtsy or shake hands. She put out her hand.

"It's a pleasure, Katie," Adele said, taking her hand. "Adele Childress. How wonderful to meet you. And those must be your sons."

"Mitch and Andy," she said. "Boys. Come and say hello to Dylan's grandmother, Mrs. Childress."

They seemed to climb down from the jungle gym a bit reluctantly, approaching warily.

"Are they shy?" Adele asked.

"Not in the least," Katie said with a laugh. "Maybe they're afraid they'll get you dirty. And I'm sure they've never seen a car like that."

"How in the world do you tell them apart?"

"It comes with time. Dylan can tell the difference. Would you like a glass of tea on the porch?"

"That would be lovely, Katie." She turned to look at her driver. "Randy?"

"I'm fine, ma'am," he said, going to the trunk which produced a cold drink.

Katie bent at the waist and focused on her boys. "Say hello, boys." One at a time they said a very quiet "hello." Then they began to back away, making Katie laugh. "Go ahead, you can play. Come up on the porch, Mrs. Childress. I'll get you a cold tea."

As Katie went inside and Adele stepped onto the porch, Dylan threw an arm wide, indicating the chair he had just vacated. She sat down and said, "Thank you, dear."

"My pleasure," he said. Then he jogged down the porch steps and into the clearing where he grasped the driver's hand in a firm and welcoming handshake. Then he was back to the porch. "Now," he said to his grandmother. "What are you doing here?" He leaned a hip on the porch rail and folded his arms against his chest again.

"Wouldn't I welcome as hearty a greeting as the chauffeur received," she said, indignant.

"We both know this wasn't Randy's idea. So? Your purpose?"

"Just a little recon, Dylan," she said. "You mentioned unfinished business of the female kind and Lang said he was fairly sure you were here about a woman. And I was out of the loop."

"I can't believe you did this," he muttered.

"I can't believe you expected less," she replied. "I ask very little of you—just that you stay in touch. There are all kinds of things happening in your life and I was…well, curious. Concerned."

"Gran, I'm of age. I'm self-supporting. Some things I like to work out for myself."

"Was I born yesterday? The only time you don't call me regularly or at least take my calls is when something of magnitude is going on and you're afraid you'll tell me more than you want to. That doesn't happen to us often. And I suspect this is the first time it involved a woman." Dylan remained stubbornly silent. "So, this is serious?"

He gave a nod but said no more.

"Excellent. She's very pretty, seems nice."

"There's no guest room here, Gran," he said.

"I've made arrangements," she said. "It happens I have an old friend in the area. You remember Muriel St. Claire."

He chuckled and just shook his head. "Of course. Muriel lives around here? Why?"

"Hell if I know," Adele said. "The town isn't exactly…much. It's even smaller than Payne."

"I like small towns," he said.

"Now, there's a surprise I was unprepared for. When I took you to Payne, you saw it as a prison sentence and couldn't wait to get out of there."

"Not prison," he said. "Rehab. And you were the first to leave."

"Not until I knew I was leaving you in safe hands. Now, Dylan, what's going on?"

"When there's something to tell, you'll be told," he said. He loved and trusted his grandmother, but some things were personal. Confiding in her about business matters was one thing, but with matters of the heart, a man of thirty-five did not go to his grandmother for advice.

She sat back. She gave him a small smile. "Sometimes I look at you and can't help but see my son in your eyes."

Katie came outside with a glass of tea and a napkin. "Here you go, Mrs.—" She looked into the yard to find the car doors all open on the Lincoln and saw one of her boys behind the wheel. "Boys!" she called. "What are you *doing?*"

The driver stood up from the passenger side of the car and looked at her over the open door, smiling. "They're all right, ma'am. They asked permission."

"They're going to get that car all dirty!"

"Not to worry, ma'am—I keep it clean."

"Don't worry, Katie," Adele said. "Randy's on top of things. He's very protective of the car. Now sit down beside me and tell me all about yourself."

"Prepare to be grilled," Dylan said, pushing off the rail. "Just because she asks you something doesn't mean you have to answer." He went inside the cabin.

"Testy," Adele said.

"Why is he so testy?" Katie asked.

"I invaded his space. He sent me a text message

saying he'd be out of touch for a while and I would hear from him when he's ready to be back in touch. Well, something like that. I waited as long as I felt like waiting. At first I was worried something had gone wrong with that movie he was considering, but when I called Lang and he said it was probably about a wo—about you, I decided we should meet. And why not? If you're struggling to decide whether Dylan is worth your consideration, you should have a look at his baggage." She took a small sip of her tea. "That would be me, Katie. The baggage."

Katie laughed. "Well, I'm sure he doesn't consider you baggage at all."

"At the moment, I'm sure he does. Where are you from, Katie?"

"Sacramento." She gave Adele a quick run-through of her history. She knew she was revealing more than she'd been asked, but if she were meeting the girlfriend of one of her boys, she'd want to know these things and they weren't secrets. While she was talking, Dylan returned to the porch with a beer. "The boys and I came here to hopefully settle near my brother. Uncle Conner has always been an involved uncle. I met Dylan on the way into town when he helped me change a flat tire. And we became friends."

"You haven't known each other all that long, then?" Adele asked.

"Long enough, Gran," he said.

"Please, Dylan, I wasn't being critical!" Adele looked at Katie. "And now you're very good friends..."

"Adele," Dylan warned.

"I hope so," Katie said with a smile.

"Very good friends," Dylan assured his grandmother. "So, Gran. Just how long can we expect to enjoy the pleasure of your company?"

"Not long, I'm afraid. A few days. A week. Whatever." Dylan groaned.

Adele Childress wondered if she should dare even hope that her grandson was finally wising up and settling down with a good woman. Katie Malone was instantly likable. Like Adele, she'd been through some tough times but managed to somehow hold her family together, work and maintain a lovely disposition as far as Adele could tell.

Adele looked out the car window. "Are you sure you know where you're going?" she asked.

"Yes, ma'am," Randy said.

"It's nothing but country out there. Or trees."

"Yes, ma'am, that's what it is."

"Are you *mocking* me?" she asked sharply.

"Yes, ma'am," he said.

She grunted.

A little while later he said, "Look ahead. That's Ms. St. Claire's house."

All Adele could see was a two-story farmhouse with some outbuildings around it. There were a couple of lights in the windows and some flickering candlelight on the front porch. When they pulled up the drive to the front of the house a couple of people emerged from the darkness and she recognized Muriel. She was stand-ing beside a man Adele didn't know. He was a very handsome, tall, silver-haired man with a wide chest and strong shoulders.

This was Muriel in her country incarnation. Adele and Muriel did not share this trait. Muriel liked roughing it; liked to ride, hunt, garden and poke around farm sales and buy antiques. She was one of those do-it-yourselfers while Adele was just the opposite—anything she could throw money at worked for her. And Muriel was wear-ing jeans and boots. Adele couldn't remember owning a pair of jeans, even while living in Montana.

Randy gave her a hand out of the car. Randy had been her driver for years, since his wife died a long, long time ago. He was nearly seventy himself, but he didn't seem it; he was fit and colored his hair, which was still thick and plentiful. He'd never been one for a lot of outdoor sports so his skin was taut, but he had a trim beard.

In Hollywood, seventy wasn't old unless you wanted it to be. Adele hadn't started playing the matronly or grandmotherly roles until five years ago. She had an excellent surgeon and colorist. She was, after all, a bit younger than Carol Burnett.

"Oh, darling," Muriel said, rushing toward her, arms open. "It's so wonderful to see you!" They embraced and Muriel immediately introduced her gentleman. "This is Walt, my neighbor and boyfriend. Walt, this is Adele Childress. We've known each other for—"

"Very long," Adele cut in. Adding up years always

made her weary. "I appreciate the hospitality, Muriel. I hope it's not a major inconvenience."

"It's none at all. There's a guesthouse, and there's a bedroom in the house on the second floor. Now, bear in mind, it's an old farmhouse that I restored, so there's only the one bath upstairs, claw-foot tub. I have no trouble sharing it. You decide if you want to put your driver in the guesthouse with a private shower but no tub or take it for yourself and I'll put him up in the house."

Randy was pulling suitcases out of the trunk and lining them up beside the car. "Let Miss Daisy have a look at the guesthouse," he said. And then he added, "Ma'am."

Adele tsked. "Impertinent," she muttered. "Pain in my ass."

"Her knee bothers her—that tub won't work as well as a shower," Randy said.

Muriel laughed. "Put her bags in the guesthouse," she advised. "You'll have everything you need, even a refrigerator. The shower is perfect for you, the mattress is fairly new, there's a flat screen, and if you need anything more than you find in the refrigerator, the front door is always unlocked. And you," she said, looking at the driver.

"Muriel, it's Randy. You remember Randy?" Adele asked.

Muriel stepped closer. "You grew a beard!" she said. "I can't believe it's you. My God, you two have lasted longer than most marriages!"

"Through no fault of hers," the driver said. "Ma'am."

Muriel laughed, covering her mouth. "Well, then, come up on the porch. Let me get you both a drink. Walt and I had dinner, not knowing exactly when you might be here, but saved you some in the warmer. And don't worry—Walt cooked and he's gifted. Now, about that drink?"

"Make mine vodka on the rocks with either a couple of olives or a twist of lime, whatever is handy. Make it good and strong—I just saw my grandson."

"Beer," Randy said. "Any old beer. Can or bottle, just cold. Nothing fancy." And then he pulled off his black jacket and tossed it into the car, rolled up his white sleeves, unbuttoned his collar and carted the suitcases off to the guesthouse.

"Sit right here, Adele," Walt said, placing her beside the table that held a few flickering candles. Then he pulled a couple of chairs near the grouping, but when Randy had delivered the suitcases to the guesthouse and arrived on the porch, he immediately pulled one chair away, to the end of the porch, not too far but isolated nonetheless.

"Antisocial," Adele muttered by way of explanation.

Muriel brought drinks, handing Adele hers first. "One heavy on the liquor for the lady. Now what's wrong? I can't believe Dylan gave you trouble!"

Adele took a sip. "Ah, nicely done," she said, praising the drink. "Dylan doesn't make trouble, just his personal brand of contrariness. He's independent, the ingredient that allowed him to become successful, and I approve of that. He appears to have himself a lovely lady friend, a serious one, and I find myself hoping he won't mess it up. It's the first time he's lingered around a woman's front door for weeks on end, ignoring all other business. And yet he has nothing to say? He's still suffering from that old fear of commitment."

"Your friend Muriel has the same issue," Walt said.

"Yes, but Muriel's fear comes from another place—she's afraid she's not good at commitment. Dylan is afraid he has inherited an inability to commit."

"I'm right here," Muriel reminded them, motioning for Walt to pass her drink from the table.

"Having you show up unannounced must put him at ease," Randy added from his much darker side of the porch.

"I only want to help," Adele said. "I only want Dylan to be happy. I could resolve ninety percent of his problems if he'd let me."

"Let him make himself happy," Randy said. "He'll appreciate it more."

Adele turned her head in her driver's direction. "Do you wish to join this conversation? Then pull your chair closer!"

"The one thing you insisted he learn," Randy went on, completely uninhibited by the sharpness of her tone, "that he make his own way, learn to think for himself, not follow the crowd and definitely not expect happiness to come from taking the easy way or handouts from his rich parents or grandparents, whether it comes in the form of money or influence. Well, he learned it. And now you better live with it."

Adele looked pointedly at Muriel, frowning. "We've taken some rather long road trips. Apparently I've been flapping my jaw to a person with a dangerous memory."

Muriel just laughed. "Take it easy, Adele. You're among friends."

"Then I hope you won't mind if we stay among friends for a while. Just a few days. Long enough for me to try to crack that nut I half raised."

"You stay as long as you like. Weeks if you need to. It's not fancy, but it's very comfortable."

"Groaning like that was rude," Katie chastised.

"Shhh," he whispered, kissing her. "Talk later…"

Adele hadn't overstayed her welcome that first visit. She had Randy take her to her friend's home where she'd be staying, Dylan made a spaghetti dinner with garlic bread, the boys showered, watched some TV in the loft, then were tucked in. Then Dylan tucked Katie in.

"Don't go to sleep until we talk," she insisted.

"I'll be awake awhile," he murmured, kissing his way down her neck. "Katie, have you noticed what happened to your boobs?" He held them in the palms of his hands. "They're *magnificent!*"

"They're temporary," she said. "And sore."

"Does this hurt?" he asked, gently kissing them.

"No. Thank you for being sweet to them. They're…" She felt her panties sliding downward and Dylan's fingers where there had been silk. "Oh, God…" And then his hands were again on her breasts, tender and soft, and something else was where the silk had been. "Dylan…" she whispered.

"Yeah, baby?" he asked, probing. "You want something?"

"You. I want you."

"Are you sure?"

"Hmm. Sure. Any day now…"

He laughed and then covered her mouth with his just as he slid into her. He held her still, filling her. He moved a little, carefully, slowly.

"Don't tease me," she whispered.

"Easy," he said. "Let's go easy. I don't want to disturb anything…"

"You're going to disturb *me*," she said. "Come on…"

He seemed to consider this for a moment. Then he grabbed her behind the knees, bent her legs to take him deeper, licked a taut nipple before latching on to it for a solid fit, and he pumped his hips. She threaded her fingers into his hair to hold him against her breast, dug her heels into the mattress to push against him, moving with him. She began to moan and cry out his name and his hand came up to gently cover her mouth. The boys were sound asleep and the door was locked, but still… He slipped the other hand down between their bodies and had barely made contact with that erogenous button when she blew apart, shattered, pushing against him for a moment as everything inside her clenched around him in hot spasms.

And he went with her, coming so hard and long he thought he might've lost consciousness for a second or two. When it let up, he let her nipple slide out of his mouth and he rested his head there on her swollen, tender breast, panting.

She laughed softly and began to run her fingers through his hair. "That's more like it," she whispered.

He lifted his head. "You're a very demanding woman."

"I'm so sorry," she apologized with a big smile and very sleepy eyes. She was limp as a dishrag. Happy. And not sorry in the least.

He brushed the hair away from her face. "It's a good thing I didn't know about this unprotected sex business before now," he said. "We'll have to try something that has no latex in the equation after the baby."

She didn't open her eyes, but she smiled. "That sounds suspiciously like plans, Dylan. Could you possibly be a little excited?"

"Oh, sure, a little. And a lot terrified."

"That's understandable." She opened her eyes. "You have to tell Adele."

"I will when I'm ready. I love Adele, but she can't just show up uninvited and throw her weight around."

"But you love her," Katie said. "And she might look like a million bucks, but she's not that young."

"She'll be dancing on my grave," Dylan said.

"She's going to have a great-grandchild. My guess is she didn't think she ever would. Tell her."

"I'll tell her when I'm ready," he said.

Seventeen

Dylan wanted to languish in bed with Katie, but he was up, putting on the coffee she wasn't drinking these days. His first overnight in her house, she had been the first one up, dressed, making coffee, greeting the day. But that probably had been the night he put the curse of sleepiness and morning sickness on her.

The cabin was very quiet and he didn't put on his boots. He wanted Katie to sleep as long as possible. When the coffee was brewed, he took a cup outside to the porch. He moved quietly in his stocking feet; there was a little movement in the trees at the edge of the clearing and he spied a fawn, nibbling at the grass under a tree. This was so like home....

He remembered how shell-shocked he'd been when Adele had yanked him out of his mother's eight-thousand-square-foot house and toted him off to parts unknown. Adele had had a maid help pack two suitcases... Dylan had never traveled with so little. Adele had said to Cherise, "The boy's in trouble. My son is deceased, you're filming in Sri Lanka for the next six months, there's no one but staff to look after him and his best friend is dead...do yourself a favor—don't argue with me. Give me a chance. I failed his father, maybe I won't fail him..."

Cherise had replied, "I should call my lawyer..."

And Adele had said, "Have your lawyer call my lawyer. You know I only want Dylan. Whatever *you* want is undoubtedly easier."

He remembered like it was yesterday.

Dylan was pulled out of his concrete world where everything was about him and taken to what seemed, at first glance, a jungle. An amazing, beautiful, astonishing wilderness, but still... Nothing in those suitcases worked for him so some grizzled old ranch hand who worked on the property drove him in an old pickup truck to the next big town to buy Wranglers, what he called a proper belt, some boots and most important, underwear that wouldn't embarrass him in the high school boy's locker room.

Dylan chuckled silently. In Los Angeles he had to have designer boxers, silk. In Payne he couldn't drop his drawers unless he wore tightie whities. Really cheap tightie whities.

Ham washed his new clothes a dozen times so they wouldn't look new. "One pair o' new ain't a bad thing," he had said. "*All* new'll prolly get you beat up. Get out in the barn with those boots—work 'em over. And while you're scuffing 'em up, muck them stalls."

"Great," Dylan remembered saying. And he had caressed his face. Get beat up? His primary job was to keep himself ready for the camera. If he was always ready to perform, he could have any other thing he wanted. In. The. World.

He'd been an actor since the age of six, starting with commercials, so he *acted* like a Montana kid in worn jeans, scuffed boots and really bad underwear. And while he was acting, he blended. While he blended, he started to like where he was—but he kept that to himself for as long as possible.

He had noticed things, however. It had been early spring when Adele snatched him and before he'd been in Montana long his shoulders had grown bulky from pitching hay and mucking stalls in the barn; his face had tanned and his hair was streaked from the sun, his Wranglers were worn in the knees and butt and he'd seen the shy appearance of new babies around his property—fawns, lambs, one foal, a couple of calves, cubs.

And old concrete jungle superstar Dylan Childress began to fall in love with the country, with nature.

The fawn at the edge of the clearing came into full view; the doe behind him was still half-hidden in the trees. And Dylan heard rustling in the kitchen. He put his coffee on the porch floor beside his chair and, moving slowly and quietly, peeked in the cabin. Andy was rooting around in the refrigerator.

"Psst," Dylan whispered. When Andy looked at him he put a finger to his lips, warning him to be quiet. Then he crooked a finger for Andy to come to him. He very quietly led Andy to the porch. He sat down and brought Andy to stand between his legs and pointed toward the deer. "Look," he whispered.

Andy let out a little excited gasp.

"Mother and child," Dylan whispered. "The kid's getting pretty big. You should see 'em when they're brand-new, when they can hardly stand up."

"He looks little to me…"

Dylan chuckled softly. "He's doubled in size since he was born, probably last spring. He'll be on his own before long, but they'll have to move down the mountain where it's warmer before the snow comes. I used to love the spring at home—not just because the weather got nicer but because… Look," he said as more deer became visible. "There are more."

"Home?" Andy asked.

"I live in Montana," Dylan said. "It's kind of like here—mountains, woods, wildlife. I have a couple of horses, some chickens, some cows and goats, a mean old bull. You'd like it."

"I never been on a horse," Andy said.

"You're kidding me!"

Andy shook his head. "Or on a cow," he added.

"Well, we don't ride cows, we just milk 'em. I only have a couple milk cows and I don't even know exactly why. Because they're breeders, I guess." Andy gave Dylan a totally perplexed look and Dylan laughed. "They have calves. I sell the calves."

"Why?" Andy asked.

He delayed his answer. "We don't want to talk about

that… The chickens lay eggs—that's fun. I eat a few, sell the rest. They're trouble, though. Wildlife want to eat the chickens and keeping them safe can be a pain. So, I have a couple of barn dogs."

"I never had a dog," Andy said.

"Kid, I think you've been deprived," he said with a laugh.

"You going home, Dylan?"

"You ready for me to go home?" he asked, giving the twin a little squeeze.

Andy shook his head. "Wish't I could ride a horse," he said.

"You ever been on a plane?" Dylan asked.

Andy nodded vigorously. "Two times. Moving away, moving back. It was big. And we had to be still and quiet."

"Never been on a little plane, huh?"

"Nope. At Disney I was on a elephant…"

"Was it pink? Because if you were on a pink elephant, maybe you should keep that to yourself."

"You ain't going home, are you, Dylan?"

"I'm in no big hurry," Dylan said. "I get a kick out of you and Mitch. And I bet you get a kick out of me."

There were now five deer in the clearing. Dylan pulled Andy onto his lap. "I do have to think about getting home one of these days," he said, half to Andy and half to himself.

He considered how awkward the situation he found himself in was. He was here because of Katie and he was not ready to leave her. But she was all that kept him here. There was no denying the beauty of the Virgin River area and the town appealed to him, but he wasn't one for sitting around on a porch, someone else's porch at that, whittling and counting deer. He had a home, one he'd been living in for twenty years, in a town he happened to love.

"There's seven," Andy whispered. "Look at 'em."

"You ever live around so many wild animals before?" Dylan asked. Andy just shook his head. "When I was a kid and moved to Montana, I didn't know anything about wild animals. I'd never been on a horse. But a friend of mine who worked on the property, he taught me to ride, took me off on a trail ride, showed me how to camp, how to shoot a shotgun, then a rifle, how to make it from the house to the barn in a blizzard, how to—"

"Huh?" Andy asked, twisting his head around.

Dylan chuckled softly. "Sometimes we had blizzards so fierce in Montana you wouldn't want to set out for the barn to check on the animals without a rope tied to the house—you could get lost just hiking across the yard. My friend Ham showed me all kinds of survival things. You ever been in a blizzard, Andy?"

"I don't know," he said.

"The answer is no, no blizzards," Katie said from the door. She came onto the porch with her glass of juice. "Look at the deer!"

"That's what we're doing," Dylan said. "We started with one youngster, obviously a scout for the group.

Keep your voice down. Where's Mitch? I don't want him to miss this."

Katie smiled at him. "Andy, go get your brother. Very quietly, don't bang the door or the deer will run." When Andy was inside Katie sat down on the porch steps and looked up at Dylan. "Are you talking about going home?" she asked him.

"I was telling Andy about Montana. Everything I have is back there. But, Katie, I'm not going to bail out on you. I gave you my word. I'm going to find a way to prove to you that you can trust me." He took a sip of his coffee. "I have to run some errands and make some phone calls today. I can drop the boys at summer school for you. Will you promise not to go a round with the bear while I'm gone?"

"Promise," she said.

Mitch came flying out the door, eyes wide, Andy on his heels. "Whoa!" he said. "How long have they been there?"

"A few minutes," Dylan said. "Come here, let me tell you about my horses. I have two—did you know that? And a few cows."

"And a bull and chickens," Andy added.

"And goats and a couple of barn dogs," Dylan said. "It's a lot like this place, except I live in a valley and look out at the mountains instead of living in the mountains and looking down at the valley...." And by the time he was telling them about blizzards in Montana he had one twin on each knee.

And he knew *exactly* what he had to do.

* * *

Dylan hadn't been to his grassy hill alone since leaving those texts that he'd be out of touch for a while. He turned on the phone somewhat reluctantly and saw what he expected—a ton of voice mails, emails and texts. Of course there were quite a few from Hollywood and while he was curious, he didn't want to waste a lot of time going through them.

He called the one person who hadn't left him a ton of messages.

"Yo," Lang answered.

"Hey. You real busy?" Dylan asked.

Lang laughed. "You have reached Childress Aviation—busy is the one thing we're not. What's on your mind? Take your time."

That made him wince, that the company was far from busy. But he pushed through the worry. "I haven't told you anything about Katie Malone," he said to his best friend. "You probably saw the kids in the car when we stopped to change her flat—twins. Five-year-old twin boys."

Lang groaned. "You know, that's one thing I've always been grateful for—that we had ours one at a time. They're hard enough that way."

"She had them and raised them almost entirely alone. Well, her brother has always supported her where he could—good male role model for a couple of little boys. Her husband was killed in the war before they were born. He was a highly decorated Green Beret, a hero, a Medal of Honor recipient."

Lang just whistled.

"I said something about how hard that must have been to bury her husband while her twins were about to pop," Dylan said. "And I asked her if she had any regrets about falling for this risk-taking soldier and you know what she said, man? She said she was grateful for every second."

Lang was quiet for a moment before he said, "So, you found her. The one."

"I found her. There is no one like her in the world. And she's pregnant."

There was a chuckle that came all the way from Montana. "You always did get ahead of yourself."

"I have a lot to prove," Dylan said. "You probably know this already, but I don't have one freaking medal to my name. I have a lot to prove to her. To myself."

"It's going to come naturally, you'll see."

"The boys have never been on a horse or in a small plane. They've never reached under a hen for an egg, and they don't know what a blizzard is."

"I can't count the number of times I wished I didn't know what a blizzard was. They make me wonder how you talked me into this place," Lang said.

"And times like spring in the mountains when you thank me. We have to flip for who gets to chase wildlife off the runway, it's so much fun. I've heard you say you'd never raise your family anywhere else."

"That's what the snowplow is for, chasing the wildlife. Those twins ever ride in a snowplow and chase a big, mean old moose off a runway so a plane can land?"

Dylan laughed. "I think that's a no. Here's what I want to do. I want to bring them to Payne, just to show them where we live. How we live. I want them all to know what it's like there because when a woman with kids is having your baby, you don't ask one person to marry you—you ask a family to marry you. But here's the thing you need to know up front—if she can't see her way to living in Payne, I'll live wherever she lives."

"Absolutely," Lang said.

"She might just say no to everything," Dylan said. "If she does, then I pull up stakes and live wherever she lives because…" He let his voice trail off.

"Because you're going to have to be a part of that." Lang finished that sentence for Dylan.

"Yep. That's how it is," Dylan repeated. "That puts our company kind of up in the air, ha-ha. But first things first."

"Want me to bring a Bonanza down to pick you up? You and the family?" Lang asked.

"Nah, Katie can't handle it. I took her up in a little Cherokee and she got sick, so it's going to have to be something bigger—I'm pretty sure if she isn't drinking coffee she's not taking Dramamine. I'll talk to her and let you know when we're headed that way. If we're headed that way."

"How is Adele handling the news about the baby?" Lang asked.

"Oh, so you know she's here, huh? Did you encourage this idea of her surprising me in Virgin River?"

"I swear to God, I did not!" Lang insisted. "I did laugh about it, but I didn't cause it to happen."

"Well, Adele doesn't know yet. This isn't the kind of thing you want to tell your elderly grandmother until you have plans, and my plan is to do anything Katie wants, not anything Adele wants. Help me out a little and don't tell Adele yet."

"I can do that for you, bud. And, D? Something you haven't given me a chance to say."

"What's that?"

"Congratulations."

Katie was sitting on the porch when the town car pulled into her clearing. Randy parked beside Katie's SUV. He jumped out to open the door for his passenger.

"Well, good morning," Katie said. "How are you this morning?"

"Lovely, thank you," Adele said. "And you?"

"It's a beautiful morning. I'm afraid Dylan isn't here."

"Where has he gone off to?"

"He said something about errands, but I have no idea what errands. Can I pour you a cup of coffee?"

Adele stopped at the steps to the porch. "What are the chances you have tea? Any tea will do."

"You're in luck if you can tolerate Earl Grey. Randy?" she called. "I have a pot of coffee. Or there's tea or juice."

"Not to worry, ma'am. I'm taken care of."

Katie laughed and looked at Adele. "I love him. What does it take to get one of him?"

"Well, millions. And a very strong disposition—he sometimes annoys the sanity out of me. He's full of sass."

"Is that so?" came from the yard.

"I'll have trouble with the millions, but I have twin sons—putting up with sass happens to be my specialty. Have a seat, Mrs. Childress. I'll heat water."

"Please, call me Adele. And Earl Grey will be splendid."

"Well, have a seat, Adele. I'll be right back."

Katie shook her head and smiled as she busied herself making tea. It was hard for her to imagine this grand dame twenty years ago. There was something about her... She liked to appear difficult while really, she seemed to end up being quite accommodating.

Five minutes later Katie took Adele a tray with her tea. "I'm sorry, there are no proper teacups in the cabin so you have a mug, saucer, a spoon, a little cream and sugar..."

"Perfect," Adele said. She took a sip before doctoring her tea. "Ah, nicely done. I never minded a tea bag," she said, as though she did. "It's absolutely fine." She took another sip. "I think I'm glad Dylan is busy elsewhere. It gives us a chance to get to know each other."

Katie chuckled. "Should I prepare to be grilled?"

"Isn't he a brat? I thought maybe I'd tell you about Dylan. What do you suppose you'd like to know?"

Katie shrugged. "I'm not sure." She thought for a

second. "He gave me this long explanation about growing up all Hollywood and I wondered…is it possible he's never before dated a woman with children?"

"I suppose it is," Adele said. "It's a fact that his parents changed partners so often it left him convinced no one in his family was capable of long, stable relationships. And it must be said, before his father's death, my son, Dean, wasn't the best parent. After all, I wasn't a crackerjack mother! But when Dylan's friend died, I panicked. I gave thanks that I hadn't lost Dylan, then snatched him away from his contract, his series, his family. I took a legal beating for it, too, but it was money well spent. We were very lucky. Living in Payne called on Dylan's strengths and he came around, though it was miserable at first."

Adele rested her cup and saucer on her knees and looked at Katie. "I think it would be hard for you to imagine the household he grew up in. What chaos. I don't even know how many children there were in total—Dylan has not one full sibling. They're all a mess, to the last one. All born and bred in Hollywood, all screwed up, all in various stages of romance, divorce, legal trouble, rehab, whatever you can imagine. Except Dylan. He began to appreciate the simpler expectations of the small Montana town where he lives, got an education and built himself a little business. I can't say why he tars himself with that same brush— he's nothing like the rest of them."

"How in the world did you find that little town?" Katie asked.

"I made a few phone calls and someone knew the place—that it was in a beautiful setting, that it was rustic and not a particularly easy place to live. Mother Nature is a difficult taskmaster in that part of the country, but she rewards the brave and strong with astonishing natural beauty. Now, I was at a time in my life that living with any sort of challenge did not appeal to me in the least. But Dylan? Oh, my…" Adele sipped her tea. "Has Dylan talked much about what it's like to be a Hollywood kid? A child star?"

"He talked about it some, but I admit, it's hard to imagine."

"Imagine this," Adele said. "As long as you're in demand, as long as you have the right ratings, you can have anything you want. While you're a success, people live to please you and there are practically no limits. What's particularly hard for a child star to understand is that success is very fragile. And the second you slip, the party is over. The fall from grace is fast and hard, you can no longer get away with bad behavior. The pressure to do well is astronomical. Yet Dylan probably had no idea how much pressure he was under." She shook her head. "Even with all the hard work, big money, fame and recognition, it's a very difficult and artificial life, but it was all he'd known.

"I took Dylan to a place where he could learn how the America that worshipped him actually lives. And to see what they really thought of him—not as a star but as a kid who had trouble reading, couldn't play sports very well, had never had to make his own bed, et cetera.

I intended for him to be laden with chores rather than the memorizing of scripts, which by the way, someone always read to him to be sure he remembered the right lines."

"Does he still have trouble reading?" Katie asked.

"I believe he learned to compensate while in Payne. They had a school librarian who had worked with some minor dyslexia in students and she stepped in when asked by his English teacher. Payne—small town where people worked together. They didn't have much money, couldn't generate much by way of tax dollars, so they put muscle into their community spirit."

"Sounds like this place," Katie said with a smile.

"Dylan was mesmerized by that rugged beauty. I was not—it was too harsh and unyielding for me, but... There's a hand on the property because there are animals to take care of, and I needed him to show us the ropes. Dylan and I wouldn't have the first idea what to do if a herd of elk got in the yard—later he had to clear a herd to build the runway." She smiled. "Look what he's managed to do. Isn't it amazing?"

"Does he know how proud you are of him?" Katie asked.

Adele scoffed. "I have a tendency to be a bit rigid. Unsentimental." There was a snort and some muffled laughter from the direction of the town car and Adele shifted her gaze sharply in that direction. She muttered something that sounded vaguely like *pain in my ass*.

Katie laughed softly. They were like an old married couple.

"I hope he knows how much I admire him," Adele went on. "Talk about taking a sow's ear... Well, he's turned himself into a rancher, businessman, good neighbor, friend... I failed his father. I was a hardworking actress while raising Dean and I left him with staff, indulged him, sometimes pulled strings for him and did whatever it took to shut him up. What I ended up with was a great actor who was so completely self-indulgent he was doomed to hubris. He thought he was invincible and thus died in an alcohol-related car accident." She tsked, shaking her head. "Such a loss. Tragic. So you can see my desperation to rescue Dylan. It was bloody awful, let me tell you. I almost killed us both just learning to drive a Jeep around Montana's snow-covered roads! Not to even mention the debacle of me trying to feed a moose buck an apple like I thought the thing was a docile pony! We had three years of adjusting to each other, the land and homestead, the people. And then he went to college and set me free. Thank God. But you can be damn sure I never let him get far from me—I insisted we stay in close touch and I spent considerable time in Prescott, where he got his degree."

Katie couldn't help but laugh at the image of a teenage boy holding on for dear life while his grandmother, who had probably always had a driver, learned to handle a Jeep in the snow, or facing off with a huge, antlered buck. And how about a frisky college freshman putting up with regular visits from his grandmother?

"You were so devoted to him," Katie said. "I hope he's that devoted to you."

"Most of the time," she said. "He does get his back up when I don't shrink into the background like a good little granny."

Katie reached for her hand. "Oh, I think Dylan knows better than to expect that."

Eighteen

It was just after lunch when Dylan phoned Katie at the cabin. "Hey," she said, "where are you?"

"I just stopped by Jack's to call you. I'm having a hard time getting everything I wanted to do done. Are you feeling okay?"

"Sure. Fine. I can't wait to hear about all the things you're trying to do."

"Oh, you might be surprised. You aren't wrangling a bear or anything, are you?"

"No, of course not. But, Dylan, your grandmother came by this morning. You missed her."

"Add that to my list—I should see her," he said. "Will you be okay till dinner time?"

"Well, I don't know," she teased. "I might lose my head and chop down some trees or something…"

"I'll be satisfied if you stay away from the wildlife," he said. "I'll bring the boys home. I should finish everything by the time their program lets out. I can bring us dinner from Jack's."

"Are you sure? Because I don't mind…"

"Take a nap or something. I'll see you a little later."

When Dylan went back to the bar from the kitchen he said to Jack, "I'll need some more directions. I missed my grandmother this morning and she's staying with Muriel St. Claire. Can you tell me how to get there?"

"Sure thing," Jack said. He wrote out the route on a napkin. "You're running all over the place today."

"It's turning out that way."

He went first to Muriel's to see his grandmother, happy to see how comfortable she was in Muriel's home. Muriel was out riding with the man in her life, Walt Booth, which left Dylan to have a relaxing visit with Adele on the front porch. He didn't have to say much—Adele went on at length about how much she enjoyed Katie. "I do hope you're smart enough to see you have a winner there," she said to Dylan.

Then Dylan headed for a home under construction in the mountains between Virgin River and Clear River…all these rivers…yet another thing this place had in common with Montana. The house appeared to be nearly finished and he recognized Conner's truck parked outside. Unfortunately there were other vehicles as well and Dylan had hoped to catch Katie's brother alone. But with no alternative, he went inside.

The house was filled with the sound of hammering, power saws, air compressors and the scraping and sliding of equipment and large slabs of building materials. There were men putting up drywall, installing hardwood planks and cutting ceramic tiles for the floor. He found Conner in the kitchen, fitting granite counters. "Hey," he said. Conner looked up. "Got a minute?"

Conner's first reaction was to frown. He wiped his hands on a rag from his back pocket. "Your face is looking better."

Dylan almost laughed. "I think yours is improved."

"Just don't improve it any more. It hurt like a bitch."

"I came to ask you a question. Want to step outside?" Dylan asked.

"Let's just do it here," Conner said. "In case I need backup."

"You won't. I hope we've made our peace for Katie's sake. And for Andy and Mitch."

"As long as you treat her right, I'll be fine."

"I'm going to try my hardest to, Conner, I give you my word. Did you know those boys have never been on a horse? Never had a dog? Never been for a ride in a small plane?"

Conner sighed. "What are you getting at?"

He shrugged. "I have a horse, a dog, a small plane..."

"Yeah? And how should this interest me?"

"If it wouldn't make you go totally crazy, I'd like to take them back to Montana with me for a couple of days. I have things to attend to there—property, animals and a business. I think they might have fun—it's a good place. I want them to see where I've lived the last twenty years. I want them to know me. The real me."

"Twenty years, huh?" Conner asked.

"That's right. It's a great little town and it's a good

place for boys to grow up. Maybe a good place for tomboys, too."

"Does Katie want to go?" Conner asked.

"I haven't asked her yet. I'm asking you to go along with this before I ask her. Because after I show her my home, I'd like to ask her to marry me. If you give your blessing."

"Seriously?" Conner said dubiously. "You're asking my blessing? Why?"

"Because you're the most important person in her life besides the boys. And because we started a family, which means we're going to be family, you and I."

"Are you saying you love her?"

Dylan noticed that the place had gone kind of quiet. Not so much drywall, hardwood or tile was getting done. He was afraid to turn around and find a gallery of workers hanging on his answer. "You know what, Conner? I'll tell you about anything you want to know, but that thing? I'd really like to tell her before I tell you. All I want is your permission to show her my home and propose. And I want the boys to go, too."

Conner took a step toward him. "Listen, if you're not in all the way, you don't have to do this, marry her. Because I can take care of my family and I will…"

"Let her decide, Conner. I've never been married, never been a father. But I have an idea what it takes and I'll do my best."

"Do you have any idea how important Katie's happiness is to me?"

"I can guess," Dylan said. "Do you have any idea

how sorry I am that her father is deceased? Because I can't imagine he'd be any tougher to please than you."

Conner gave a huff of laughter. "You might want to take that back—my dad was a pretty grumpy old coot, even when he was young."

"Big surprise," Dylan said. "I guess the apple doesn't fall far from the tree."

Conner thought for a minute. "We should probably go have a beer. Talk about some particulars. Like how you're going to take care of her with a business that isn't doing too well. And what you're going to say if she doesn't like where and how you live."

"I don't hear a lot of pounding or sawing," Dylan said. "Does most of Haggerty Construction now know I want to marry my pregnant girlfriend?"

"I'd have to say yes, if they don't know now, they soon will. Let's go. You're buying."

"Fine," Dylan said. "Jack's?"

"The only game in town. See you there. I'll pack up my tools."

Dylan walked toward the door. He turned back and faced about six men, all very large, all wearing tool belts, all looking like they'd prefer more gossip than a chance to beat him up. "Get back to work," he said to them. "That's all I'm giving you." And then he left and drove back to Virgin River.

Dylan was nursing a cup of coffee when Conner finally showed up. The bar was still empty, the dinner crowd not yet arrived. Conner sat up on the stool beside

Dylan and said to Jack, "Give him a beer. And run him a tab."

"I'm picking up the boys and taking them home."

"No, you're not. I checked in with Leslie—she's going to take the boys home for you."

Dylan stiffened. "Hey, I haven't run this plan by Katie yet. I'd rather Leslie not fill her in on our discussion."

"Relax. Les is going to tell Katie that we're having a beer together. Hopefully she'll see that as a good thing."

"Leslie is a nice lady," Dylan said. "So here's a pertinent question—you planning on marrying Leslie?"

"That's between us. And by the way, she's not pregnant..."

Jack stepped in front of them, delivering a couple of beers. "I have some experience with this if you're interested."

"No," they said in unison.

"Jeez," Jack said. "Have it your way." And he moved away and went into the kitchen.

Conner turned toward Dylan. "I take it you've never found yourself in this position before?"

"Nope," Dylan confirmed. "You?"

"Nope," Conner said. Then he shrugged and added, "Can't say why. I've never proven myself to be all that smart."

Dylan laughed in spite of himself. "Katie thinks you walk on water..."

"She's biased. So, what's your plan, big shot?"

"Well, it's simple. I have a meeting in L.A. tomorrow

night—should be quick. Then like I said, I have to go back to Montana—I think the kids will like it. It's a lot like here, but rougher sometimes, like in winter. Winters can be brutal. It's small, nice people, good schools, clean air, very big sky…"

"Right. So—suppose they like it?"

"If they like Payne and like me, that could make life pretty easy since we should all be together."

"In Montana…"

"Where to live is up to Katie, all right? If she can't stand the idea of being away from you, we'll work with that. I can probably find some kind of job around here…"

"What's this crap about you being some kind of big star?" Conner asked.

"A long, long time ago. I'm a has-been, and frankly I like it that way. I wouldn't want to raise the twins in Hollywood. Or this new one, either. I'd rather raise them on egg and milk money."

"And what the hell does that mean? Egg and milk money?"

"My little airport can probably support a couple of families just on plane storage, maintenance, a few charters, the occasional instruction. The airport is on my ranch, which is about sixty acres—a few cows, some chickens, some goats. I have a hand who likes taking care of the animals. We sell eggs and stock—he bought us a bull several years ago. The little bit of laying and breeding we do just about covers his salary. I lease some grazing land to a rancher but Ham, that's my hand, he has a big summer garden at my place. We hunt and fish. We process our kill and eat it all winter."

"You're not rich?" Conner asked.

"Nope."

"No big star money?"

"Nope. But I get by pretty well. The way I live—it's healthy."

"And you fly? Leave home a lot?"

"Less often than a commercial pilot. And it's a tight community—we all look out for each other. I live in the valley and we have lots of wildlife—ours can be a little more challenging. We have the occasional grizzly—a lot more aggressive than black bear, but they tend to like the mountains. We have moose, deer, elk, coyote, mountain lions, bobcats, wolves. We have dogs who wake us up if the wolves or cats start pestering the chickens or goats. We keep the barn and pens secure against predators. Why buy a chicken or goat to feed to wolves?" Dylan took a drink of his beer. "Boys and girls grow up strong and healthy."

Conner put his elbow on the bar and leaned his head on his hand. "I think I want to see this place."

"Fine," Dylan said. He smiled. "Summers," he suggested. "Maybe every other Christmas."

Conner just laughed. "You going to leave pretty soon? If she agrees?"

"I bought tickets. I took Katie up in a little plane and she puked, so I bought tickets. I think she'll be okay on a jet. We'll have to drive to Redding and fly into Butte.

My best friend's wife will pick us up. So...after I get back from L.A. in a few days," he finished.

"A few days?" Conner asked.

"I'll get back from L.A. Wednesday afternoon. I have tickets to leave Friday, be back Monday. Can you live with that?"

"We better have another beer. You can tell me more about your plans."

Dylan smiled. "I guess we better."

Dylan pulled into the clearing at the cabin and found that Katie was watching the boys on the jungle gym. She sat on the porch with her air horn beside her chair.

The boys ran to him, shouting his name, grabbing on to his legs. "Play catch?" Mitch asked. "No, soccer," Andy said. "Or kick ball."

"First I want to talk to your mom and put this dinner in the house, all right? Go play for a little while."

They reluctantly let go of him. He grinned as they went back to the swing set. He couldn't help thinking, *They like me.* He mounted the porch and bent to give Katie a kiss on the forehead.

"What in the world is going on?" she asked. "Having a beer with Conner? Leslie bringing the boys home? What are you up to?"

"Surprise," he said. "I'll tell you in a second." He took the brown paper bag with Preacher's fried chicken in the house and came back outside, sitting in the chair beside her. He pulled a folded piece of paper out of his pocket and presented it to her.

She unfolded it—it was a ticketless travel voucher to Butte. "What is this?"

"Well, Katie, I want to take you and the boys to Montana. I want to try to show you what my life there is like. I want to introduce you to my best friend and his wife and kids. I want you to see the town. I think the boys would like to meet the animals."

"Four tickets," she said. "Coming back to California after just a couple of days?"

"I want to check on Lang and the company, too. I didn't think you had anything else you had to do."

"You have our names spelled exactly right for travel. The birthdates are correct. How did you know I was Katherine Marie Malone?"

"That was dicey—I had to look at your driver's license. I figured if you caught me in your wallet, I'd get the air horn, or worse. And you keep the birth certificates in the trunk along with Charlie's medals."

"Hmm. And this has to do with Conner how?" she asked.

"If Conner and I are going to be friends, I didn't dare take you out of town without talking to him—he'd have the Feds running me down. Here's what I have to do," he said, pulling out another piece of paper, another ticketless reservation. "I have to make a quick trip down to L.A. for a meeting with those movie people I've been working with. Jay Romney, the producer who made this offer, is an old friend and when he wants to meet, it's the least I can do. The man has tried to help me in any way he can. One meeting—and it should be quick. I'll be gone one night. When I get back, we'll pack some bags. You won't need much—the weather is about the same as here. And I can get booster seats and whatever from Lang."

She got a worried look on her face. "Is your movie deal all put together?"

"That's what we're going to find out."

"Do you hope...?" she asked.

He gave her cheek a soft caress and smiled. "What I hope is that you and the boys have fun with me in Montana. I'm kind of proud of it."

This time Dylan didn't wear business meeting clothes to see Jay Romney in L.A., although he now had them. He did wear decent jeans with his boots, however. And he had asked specifically to meet in the office, not in a restaurant or at Jay's lavish Brentwood home. He also asked if it could be just the two of them, sans directors, lawyers, agents or administrative assistants.

When he walked into the office at four in the afternoon, hopefully the last meeting of the day for Jay, he couldn't help but appreciate the rich decor—the Moroccan leather furniture, the polished rosewood, the original art and the view—Jay sat on top of Hollywood, overlooking the lesser movie gods. It made him smile; there was a time Dylan aspired to something like this.

Jay stood from behind his desk. For someone who worked and lived in this modern opulence, Jay was a pretty simple man. He was the father of grown children, he was bald with a ring of brown hair around his dome and even though he surfed, ran and worked out, he had a bit of a paunch.

What the majority of the glittering city didn't understand about Jay—he was a genuinely decent guy. That didn't make him a patsy; he was a fierce negotiator. But he had unshakable ethics and his values ran deep—the only reason Dylan ever talked to him at all.

"Something about this meeting feels wrong," Jay said.

"Not at all, not at all," Dylan said, approaching, putting out his hand. "Good to see you."

"Drink?" Jay asked, moving from behind the desk to the buffet that doubled as a bar.

"I think so, yes," Dylan said. "What's the special tonight?"

"A very expensive, aged single malt or a cold beer," Jay said.

Dylan laughed. "That cold beer sounds pretty good. Do you know how many planes a person has to board to get from Virgin River to L.A.?"

Jay opened two cold bottled beers and handed one to Dylan, without the chilled glass, without the linen napkin. Then he half leaned, half sat on the front edge of his desk, facing Dylan. "What's going on?" he asked.

Dylan tipped back the beer first. "I want to start by telling you how grateful I am. Not for a potential movie deal, Jay, but to have you for a friend. You're one of the very few people in the business I'm proud to have call me. It must be hard sometimes, dealing with all the stuff you deal with, when you're driven by such rigid scruples."

Jay laughed. "All right, all right. You could've just sent flowers. Or a case of that single malt."

"I came to tell you that I'm not an actor. I'm a pilot and a rancher."

Jay took a moment to absorb the shock. Then he said, "You might be a pilot and rancher, but you are by God an actor. One of the few naturals I know. I saw you when you were ten—"

"You saw a kid who couldn't read but could memorize anything, but I wasn't sure what was going on around me, I just wanted to please people. Do you have any experience with dyslexia, Jay? Mine wasn't too serious—I now realize it was moderate. But I wanted to make my mom and dad happy, and while all the other kids could read what the teacher wrote on the blackboard and snap out answers, I had to fake it. I had to manipulate people into telling me what I was attempting to read. Since I realized the rest of the world was way ahead of me, I've had a terrible fear of failure. You're right, I became a very good actor. Did you know the scripts for *Rough Housing* had to be read to me? That I memorized them from hearing them?"

Jay leaned away from him a bit, surprised.

Dylan laughed. "Isn't it just typical—the celebrity news managed to capture every single incident of me drinking underage and getting with a girl, but they never knew I could barely read. I could almost read if you gave me a lot of time, but who had a lot of time?"

He shook his head. "Sometimes I think those were funny memories, sometimes tragic. But the bottom line is—I don't act anymore."

"I thought you were into this idea?" Jay said.

"I was, I definitely was. I have a little airline that's limping along and it looked like easy money. I figured I could probably hang by my toes for six months— or put up with the gossip and insanity that can get so mean in this town. But then something that has nothing to do with airlines or movies happened to me—the last thing I expected. I met a woman." He could feel the silly, boyish look on his face. "She has twins and now she has one on the way. I don't want to make a movie, Jay. I want to go home. I want to take care of my family the best I can in a safe place." Then he laughed at the absurdity. "A safe place full of blizzards and grizzlies. Much safer than Hollywood."

Jay looked at Dylan for a long moment, then he tipped back his bottle of beer and took a deep swallow. "Sounds romantic," he said with sarcasm.

Dylan laughed. "Yeah, doesn't it? I hope she doesn't tell me to go pound sand. But she likes me, I know she does. She doesn't have a lot of faith in me yet, I'm working on that angle. I might've talked a little too much about not being the marrying kind." Dylan leaned toward Jay and said, "Jay, I'm not an actor anymore. I'm a pilot, rancher and father."

"How you going to stay afloat? Adele?" Jay asked.

"She offers all the time, but we have an understanding—we both work and try to take care of ourselves.

If she ever needed me, I'd move heaven and earth for her—she's my only real family. And I know she'd do anything for me. But what I hope will keep me above water is a little boost in the charter business. Just enough to let the economy recover. See, there aren't many businesses who still hire air charter. There's professional sports teams and there's the entertainment industry."

Jay lifted an eyebrow.

"Bells and whistles went off when you offered to send a jet for me—I realized I could've brokered that deal. I've spent so many years avoiding this place, I forgot how much money is thrown at services. You need a really competitive charter contract? I'll cut you a deal."

"You're in Montana," Jay said.

"I can put an airplane in L.A. Better still, I can put an airplane at Burbank or Long Beach, crew ready, convenient and low stress. What's your pleasure? Will a Lear make you happy? If you want something bigger, I just let a BBJ go—bet I can get her back. That would be sixty seats in a luxury jet. We could tear out seats and put in a screening room or pool table. Or, maybe you want a charter contract out of Montana—we're pretty flexible about where we can pick up and deliver."

Jay thought about this a moment. "What have you got for equipment?"

Dylan smiled. "What do you need for equipment? Six seats? Twelve? Sixty? It's a buyer's market, Jay. Whatever you need, I bet I can get cheap right now and operate your charters at a better price than you're getting now. And I bet you have friends with similar needs."

Jay just smiled slyly. "Pilot and businessman," Jay said.

"And, with any luck, family man."

"But no matter what you say, you are an actor. A natural. I think you got it in the DNA."

Dylan smiled because it was nice to hear about some positive stuff in the genes. "Thanks. My dad smiled down on you for saying that. But I'm not acting right now. I'm looking for work. I love what I do and want to keep doing it. So, if you have any ideas..."

"Feel like a pizza?" Jay asked. "We could go to my favorite pizza dive. I could bring my BlackBerry. There won't be any stars or photographers."

"Perfect. Before we go, I think we have a couple of phone calls to make. Like the agent, the lawyer, the director, all the folks looking to get into a new film...."

"You call your agent—"

"Adele's agent," he said with a laugh.

"Good," Jay said. "That'll cut down on the screaming. I'll have my assistant get in touch with the rest of them tomorrow. We'll still get a movie out of this and you'll be jealous as all hell."

"I feel bad, bailing out on everyone like this," Dylan said.

"Yeah? Well don't. They wouldn't feel bad if they bailed on you."

"There's just one thing you have to know before we

break bread," Dylan said. "I was never really into the idea of a movie. I wanted to be—I thought I could be. My heart's in another place. But I've operated my company successfully for fifteen years and if you book a charter, I won't be breaking it to you over pizza that I've changed my mind. It's what I do. And we're real proud of our little company."

Jay slapped him on the back. "I get it, Dylan. I get it. Let's see if we can scare up a little business over pepperoni and sausage."

Nineteen

When Dylan returned to Virgin River, there was no stopping off at Jack's on his way to Katie's cabin, he was so anxious to get back to her. It was after four o'clock and it appeared all the kids had been picked up from the summer program—the school looked quiet. He hoped there was food in the cabin, but if not he would take them all out to dinner. When he drove into the clearing, he saw the monkeys on the jungle gym and Katie's horn beside her empty chair.

He parked and pulled his duffel out of the truck and the boys came running to him, shouting his name.

He never thought he wanted this—coming home like this. He dropped the duffel and grabbed the boys, tossing them up in the air one at a time, laughing at their excitement.

"Are we going tomorrow?" Andy asked.

"To ride the horses?" Mitch asked.

"Not tomorrow. The next day," Dylan said. He was just about to say, "Where's your mom," when she stepped out onto the porch. "Go play while I take my duffel in the house and get a soda."

"Then wanna play catch?" Andy asked.

"I have to talk to your mom for a while," he said, ruffling the boy's hair. For identical twins, Dylan marveled at the differences in their personalities—Andy was so silly and rambunctious and Mitch was the serious one. "I need a little time with her."

Katie didn't greet him with the same enthusiasm as her sons. She smiled for him, but seemed to wait tensely. Fortunately she didn't stretch it out. "So?" she asked, looking up at him. "The movie?"

"No movie," he said, giving her a kiss on the forehead. "Something way better. Some potential charter business for the company. I wish I'd thought of it a year or two ago, but I was so intent on avoiding Hollywood and its high maintenance stars, I didn't take a closer look."

"Huh?" she said.

"I turned down the movie—I don't want to do a movie. But production companies fly their stars and executives around in private jets—sometimes little planes, sometimes bigger ones. I talked to the producer, who I consider a friend, about letting us bid on some of his charter needs and he gave me a couple dozen names of people to contact for more work on his recommendation." He grinned. "Just the thing we need."

"Isn't that a little far from Montana?" she said, confused.

"Not a problem," Dylan said. "It obviously wouldn't be cost-effective to fly from Montana to Southern California every time a charter is booked, but if there's enough work there, I'll just put a plane and crew there. Lang and I don't fly every trip. We have a lot of other things to do."

She let out her breath slowly. "Is that something you do? Put planes in other places?"

"Only when there's lots of business in one location. We kept a plane and crew in Seattle for a software manufacturer several years ago, till they stopped spending so much money on charters. We can park a plane in L.A., send a pilot down on a commercial flight and put him in a hotel. This could be—" He looked at her closely. "Have you been worrying about this?"

"I don't understand very much about how your company works," she said. "For that matter, I'm not sure how you work. I thought you'd be coming back to tell me you had to spend six months in L.A. and I'd be doing it again, having a baby alone. And I know you want me to go to Montana to check out where you live for a reason—probably so we could live there. But I'm not sure I'm ready for that kind of change. It bothers me. I don't want to be six or seven months pregnant, the mother of twins, in a blizzard when I've never seen a blizzard and—"

"No," he said gently. "No, baby, no. When I promised to take care of you, I never considered sticking you out in the middle of nowhere, alone, while I went off to do something else. Katie, I want you to see my home so you understand—I'm not some movie star. I'm a pretty ordinary guy. Let's not plan any further than that right now. Let's just plan what you'll pack. The tickets are round-trip."

She considered this for a moment. "No movie?" she said again.

He shook his head. "Does that disappoint you?"

"Having you all to myself? I think I can live with that."

"That's the answer I'm looking for. You can have all of me in a variety of different places. If that big lug, Conner, makes you feel safe, I guess we'll probably live down the street from him, but we're going to have to work on his manners…."

She let a little huff of laughter escape.

"I can't believe he made me buy him beers," Dylan said. "He's such an oaf." He looked around "Do you have groceries or do we go out to dinner?"

"I don't know. I've been too busy worrying about you being a movie star to pay attention. Go forage in the kitchen and let me know. You're the cook, anyway."

"Okay," he said. "Go play. Let me see what I find in here."

She went out the door and he dropped his duffel beside her bedroom door and went to the refrigerator. He opened the door and did a quick inventory. They had milk, eggs, bread and sandwich stuff; there was some leftover taco meat and hot dogs. In the background he heard Katie ask her son what he was up to. Then she asked, "Where's your brother?"

Dylan listened; he heard the mumbling of a small boy.

"No, he didn't," she said. "He wouldn't do that. How long ago did he say that?"

Dylan lifted his head.

"Which way?" she said in a panic. "Which way did he go?" And then he heard her yell, "Andy! Andy, come back here!"

He closed the refrigerator door and went to the porch. He saw Katie kneeling in front of Mitch. She stood up and yelled for the other twin again.

"What's going on?" Dylan asked.

Katie threw a panicked look over her shoulder. "Andy isn't in the yard. He told Mitch he wanted to see where the bear lived." Then she turned toward the back of the house. "Andy Malone! Come here at once!"

"I'm sure he's close." Dylan jumped down from the porch and met her in the yard. "You go that way, I'll go this way," he said. "Don't go into the woods. Stay in the clearing."

They separated, Dylan going down the drive toward the road, Katie going toward the back of the cabin, circling it. He couldn't imagine anyone, even an adventurous five-year-old, tromping through the thick brush and trees if there was a road handy to walk on. Dylan and Katie were both shouting his name in every direction. Mitch quickly joined in, calling out to his brother. In just minutes, they met back at the front of the cabin.

"He can't have gone far," Dylan said. "We weren't in the house five minutes. How far can a five-year-old go in five minutes? Get Mitch inside and keep calling for Andy in the front. I'm going to look around the back, behind the blackberry bushes, along that trail where you've seen the bear and her cubs heading home."

Katie had a wild look in her eyes. "Dylan, I've told him a hundred times…"

"Just stay cool," Dylan said. "Just look for a sign of a direction he might've taken and call out for him. Don't panic."

He went around the tree line surrounding the cabin. There were a couple of trails, mostly overgrown, into the forest. He knew that to go in one direction was down the hill toward the orchard. Another direction was up into steeper terrain. Another was toward the road and town. He walked a bit in the more overgrown path, deeper into the bushes and trees because it was tamped down here and there. He heard Katie calling and he called from time to time, but this all felt so inadequate. He added a rather paternal warning to his call. "Andy, if you're hiding, you have two seconds to come out or you're in big trouble!"

Not so much as a rustle.

If he was nearby, Andy should have heard them call his name—but he hadn't responded. He hadn't called back. Had it now been ten or fifteen or twenty minutes? How far and which way? He looked at his watch. It was just barely after five—they had at least three hours of sun, but it would start to get dark too soon, especially in

Robyn Carr

the woods. He went back to the cabin. He broke through the heavy brush into the clearing.

Mitch was standing on the porch by the cabin's front door, looking scared and upset, as if he bore the weight of this disappearance, as if it was all his fault. Dylan wondered if he was feeling the pain of separation, as well.

Dylan called out to Mitch. "Mitch, do me a favor— empty your school backpack for me. I need to borrow it. Hurry up." And then he went to his Harley, parked at the tree line beside his leased truck. He opened up one of the side pockets and began to pull things out just as Katie came back into the clearing. "Katie, I want you to call Conner and Jack Sheridan and tell them Andy is lost. Give them the details. Tell them we need to search in the woods around the cabin before dark." His saddlebags were stuffed with emergency and camping gear; he pulled out a large flashlight and Katie gasped. "Just make the calls—it's dark back in the trees."

He found a silver emergency thermal blanket and the thing he was looking for—a large, sheathed, serrated hunting knife. He pulled it out and affixed it to his belt. It wouldn't do him much good against an animal, but it was handy when it came to tangles of vines or illegal traps, if there was such back in this forest.

Mitch brought him the backpack. The kid's eyes were scared as he handed it to Dylan, so he crouched and ruffled the kid's hair. "Don't worry," he said softly. "We'll find him. Now can you go get me a couple of bottles of water from the cabin? Please?"

He nodded and ran to the task. Dylan loaded up the little backpack. It was much too small to wear on his back, but he could sling it over one shoulder. It wasn't a good idea to go more than a hundred yards into unknown territory or strange forest without a little emergency gear handy—you never know when you might have trouble finding your way back.

"Water?" Katie said, having overheard him ask Mitch. "You're taking water? Oh, my God!"

"Katie! Easy! It's in case I get lost. I don't know this area any better than you do! Did you call Conner?"

"He's coming. Jack said he'll round up some people. Oh, God. That knife!"

"It's for stubborn branches or tight spaces. Now you can call to Andy from the clearing close to the house but I want you to keep Mitch close—we don't want two of them lost." He looked at his watch. Had it been almost a half hour? Not good. "I want you to tell whoever comes first that I'm going that way—the direction we saw the bear and her cubs go. There's a path, a little overgrown, and it's not near a road. Tell them Andy's been missing from the front yard since just before five." He walked toward the porch and Mitch bolted out the door with two bottles of water. He smiled and gave Mitch a pat on the shoulder. "Thanks, buddy. Stay with your mom, please."

"Can you find him?" Mitch asked.

"Sure we'll find him." Then he turned to Katie. He gave her a quick kiss. "Keep your head. Don't panic.

Just stay close to the house with Mitch. If Andy turns up before I do, try blasting the air horn as a signal."

"Please, Dylan," she said softly. "Please."

"If I'm any judge of this place, pretty soon there will be a bunch of guys helping. You can keep calling to him—maybe he'll get turned back in the right direction and hear you. Listen carefully in case he calls back, but if he does, don't go running into the woods. Sounds bounce around in the forest and you might go in the wrong direction. We don't need you and Mitch lost. If you hear him, just call back so he has something to walk toward. Got that?"

"Got it."

He turned and loped into the forest, a five-year-old's backpack slung over one shoulder. It had been a long time since he'd ventured into uncharted territory like this and about ten years since they'd had someone lost in the mountains around Payne. Never a little kid.

He pushed on, going mainly uphill. He could hear Katie calling Andy's name, her voice getting more and more faint as he walked. When he could barely hear her, he began to call out Andy's name. After each time, he would stop and listen, but nothing came back at him.

He had nothing to go on except a narrow, overgrown path, but all around it was thick overgrowth and he thought if he were a little half pint like Andy, he'd take the path rather than tackle the thickness of the woods on each side. He went up, then around, then down, then up, leaving markers along the way—three stones in a triangle, a branch cut with the knife, a pile of pine cones. The path was winding upward around a hill. It was getting dark back in the trees and he couldn't hear Katie anymore; there were no other voices calling out.

His watch said six; some of the trees were so tall the sun was almost completely blocked. He got out the flashlight and began to step a little more softly, carefully, shining the light on and off the trail, calling Andy's name, telling him to make a sound. "Say something so I can find you," he encouraged. And sometimes he just said, "I'm coming, Andy. I'm coming."

Dylan thought he should've been ready for something like this—Andy was the curious and impulsive one. Adventurous. Mitch was more methodical; a plotter. Mitch was the thinker, Andy was the doer. Andy was the one who would get some harebrained notion like finding out where the bear lived and then just walk into the forest. He could've gotten turned around, tried to go back to the cabin but instead went deeper and deeper. He wasn't sure when he came to know them so well, but he knew he was right.

He looked at his watch. Six-thirty.

There would still be light on the roads and in town, but back here it was deep dusk, quickly growing darker by the minute. He called, then listened, then walked, then called again.

And he finally heard something. He shined the flashlight into the trees and what did he see but the bear family on the left side of the trail. Shit. Mama glared into the light, her eyes reflecting yellow. She made a sound. It didn't sound like an angry sound, more like a bored *I dare you* sound.

And there, on the right side of the trail, not nearly far enough away, he saw him, facedown beside a dead tree, burrowed half under the rotting trunk. He could be dead, he was that still.

Dylan crouched, sitting on one boot heel, partially concealed by a big bush, watching Andy and Mama Bear and her cubs. He knew she could smell him, but as long as he didn't get any closer she apparently didn't much care. He turned off the flashlight and listened carefully so he could hear if she approached him, but they all just waited in silence. His eyes adjusted to the darkness and there she was, surrounded by her three big balls of fur, right on the other side of the path. Andy wasn't separated from the bears by more than twenty feet. He might as well have been right on top of them.

And then Andy lifted his head briefly. He tried to move but it appeared his foot was caught by the heel, stuck in a crack in the dead tree, holding him there. Dylan smiled—Andy was playing dead. Although it must've hurt to have his ankle twisted as it was, he was facedown and still. He didn't see Dylan. He put his head back down and Dylan didn't move.

Another half hour passed while the night darkened and Mama settled herself in a semisheltered batch of bushes, rotting trunks and big trees. She was licking her pads and claws like a contented zoo animal. And finally she quieted. Dylan gave her another ten minutes.

Then he dared to do the only thing that came to mind. He tried to get to Andy.

He took the longest and quietest strides toward the boy that he could manage—a good twenty long strides through the growth. He fell to the ground, covering Andy with his body. "Don't move, no matter what," he whispered.

"Dylan, I—"

"Shhh," Dylan shushed.

And then he heard her; sticks were breaking, leaves were crunching. Was she curious or angry? Then he could smell her, like she'd been in the garbage somewhere. And he heard her sigh and snort. She was dangerously close and he prayed Andy wouldn't move or speak. And then there was a movement, a rustle very nearby, and then a sharp, scalding, terrifying streak of pain shot across his back and he reared suddenly in agony, a loud "Ahhh!" coming out of him despite his intention to be silent. He heard lots of rustling, but no additional clawing—thank God! That once was about all he could take. He heard the bear talking, cubs mewling. Their sounds didn't seem to be getting closer; he prayed she felt invaded and was moving away.

Andy was trembling beneath him; he must be frightened to death.

"Don't move," Dylan whispered. "Play dead."

Andy stilled. There was not the slightest movement beneath him. The poor kid, only five and faced with life or death.

Dylan held positively still despite the pain that

blasted across his back. The bitch had gotten one good swipe and it hurt like bloody hell, but his heart was still beating. He had not posed a threat; she probably just slapped him to see if he was alive, then hustled away, but until he waited her out he couldn't be sure. He tried to slow his pulse so he could be sure of what he was hearing. She could have gone back to her cubs and settled in to sleep, in which case she was far too close and getting Andy out of here might wake her.

"Andy," he whispered. "I have to move a little. I have to see if she's near us. Don't you move, no matter what."

"My foot's stuck," Andy whispered back.

"Shhh," he said. Then he listened. Nothing.

He lifted his head slowly, looking over the thick trunk of the felled tree carcass under which they hid. He glanced into the surrounding forest in her direction, but he didn't see her. She could have moved a little and still been near, but he couldn't smell her. He lifted his head further and looked in other directions, but there was no sign of her. That didn't mean she was gone. In fact he could run into her on his way back to the cabin. But he was hurt and so was Andy; they couldn't stay here any longer.

"I'm going to move," he said softly. "Don't you move a muscle."

He gingerly pulled himself off Andy and knelt beside him. He wiggled the little tennis shoe, stuck in a slit in the tree trunk, and as he moved Andy's foot, Andy tried to stifle a cry. Then with a quick motion, he just pulled the boy's foot out and left the shoe wedged there. He moved the boy's ankle. "Hurt?" he asked. And Andy nodded, not even turning to look at Dylan.

He leaned down and whispered, "I'm going to try to carry you out of here—no talking. At. All."

Andy nodded, his head still facedown. Dylan slowly and cautiously rolled Andy over onto his back, then lifted him into his arms. With great effort, he rose to his feet, wincing with pain. He just had to stay upright long enough to get Andy home and fortunately it was mostly downhill and not steep. He gripped the flashlight in the hand that was under Andy's knees, but he didn't turn it on until he'd made his way down the path for a few minutes, each step slow and careful so he wouldn't trip, then he lit the way. "Andy," he said softly. "If anything happens, if we run into trouble, take the flashlight, stay on this path down the hill—it winds around, but leads back to the cabin."

"'Kay," he said softly.

As Dylan walked a little farther, his breath came harder and he grunted a little with the effort.

"I can walk," Andy said.

"Not with one shoe and a sore ankle," Dylan pointed out. "You'll cut up your foot and make your ankle worse."

"I can go piggyback," he suggested.

"Not gonna work, buddy," Dylan whispered. "I have a scratch on my back."

"From the bear?" Andy asked.

"She must've been scared that I'd hurt her cubs or something," Dylan said. "We have to rest a second,

Andy," he said, setting the boy down briefly. He was dizzy and hoped it was from anything but blood loss. His watch told him it was eight o'clock. He'd dropped the backpack back by the dead tree and thus the water, so he'd have to keep going without it. He could feel the wet and cold on his back. The best thing, he thought, was to get where he was going as quickly as possible; get Andy to his mother, get some medical attention. "Okay, bud, let's go," Dylan said.

"I want to walk," he said.

"The sticks and stones on the path will tear up your foot," Dylan said, attempting to lift him again.

"I can walk until it starts to hurt my foot," Andy said.

Dylan thought about this briefly. "All right, walk in front of me." They proceeded that way, but it didn't take Andy two minutes before he started limping, trying very hard to conceal it. "Okay, pal," Dylan said hoarsely. "Come on, let me give you a hand." Andy turned and Dylan picked him up, but this time he pulled Andy up facing him and Andy wrapped his arms around Dylan's neck and his legs around his hips. He held him up under the rump. "That's a little better," Dylan said. And they set out again.

Dylan's watch told him it was eight-thirty and just as he read that, he noticed a glow up ahead. They'd be coming to a clearing and the final rays of the setting summer sun would have lit the way—he just hoped it was the right clearing. He didn't feel lost and he had seen what he thought were his markers, hoping they weren't someone else's.

"Getting there," he said to Andy.

He felt Andy lean away from him and wipe his cheek; the kid didn't even cry out loud.

"Do you have any idea how brave you are?" Dylan asked him. "You were still and quiet with that big old bear practically on top of you. You're the bravest kid I know."

"I was backing away like you said and tripped over that stupid tree," he grumbled.

Dylan actually chuckled. "You did good," he said.

"I'm gonna be in trouble," he said.

"Aw, you might escape trouble—your mom is going to be so glad to see you. Never do it again, though. Never."

"'Kay," he answered. "I have to pee."

"Hold it," Dylan said. "Really, I see light. If it's not the cabin, we'll take a break and a whizz."

"'Kay."

The path came down the hill right behind the blackberry bushes and he saw that it wasn't the setting sunlight, but headlights. The clearing was full of trucks and SUVs, all with their headlights trained on the forest in every direction. There were only a couple of men in the clearing, among them the town doctor and Conner. Jack's wife was there, too, probably anticipating Andy's possible injuries. Wouldn't they be surprised. Katie was in the clearing, pacing. Leslie was on the porch, doing likewise. He put Andy down.

"Mom!" he yelled and ran, limping, to her. "Mom!"

"Andy! Oh, my God, Andy!" She ran to him and snatched him up in her arms. Mitch burst through the front door from the cabin, charging across the porch and yard to his brother.

Dylan just smiled.

And then he sank to his knees.

"Andy's bleeding! Andy, where are you bleeding?"

"I'm not," he said. "I don't think I am. I didn't get hurt, only that bear scared me."

Mel Sheridan ran to them and with Katie, they were examining Andy's face and hands, looking him over, finding nothing.

Then Conner was striding toward Dylan. "You get a little dehydrated, bud?" he asked calmly.

Dylan just shook his head, looking up at Conner with glassy eyes. It was as if all the adrenaline that got him down the hill and back to the cabin with Andy had drained out of him, leaving him weak. Andy must've gotten blood from Dylan's back on his hands before he wiped his cheeks and eyes. Dylan had a brief and crazy notion that he was glad he couldn't see his back. In fact, he decided he didn't want to ever see it. He started to shake a little bit and looked down, trying for composure. Shock. He was going into shock.

Conner stood over him. It took him only a second. "Doc! Mel! Over here!" Then he gave Dylan a little support under one arm. "Christ, man, you got mauled. Here, sit down—let's get you looked at."

"Don't look," Dylan rasped out. "Bet it's awful."

Cameron Michaels was assisting Dylan on his other side. "Easy does it," he was saying. "We'll get the gurney over here."

"I can walk," Dylan said, more than aware how weak his voice was. "And don't tell me what it looks like."

"I'm going to wet your shirt before I cut it off," Cameron said. "I want better lighting than this."

"Better than this?" Dylan croaked. "I thought it was daylight with the cars."

"If we help, think you can make it to the cabin?" Cameron asked. When Dylan nodded, Cameron said, "Let us do the work. You're weak."

"That five-year-old is heavy," Dylan said. "Big for his age. Plus, he had to pee." The men chuckled as they pulled him up. "God, I'm out of shape," Dylan muttered, letting them lead him to the porch.

"Mel, will you grab my bag and a set up for IV Ringers?"

"Gotcha," she said.

"Tell Katie…" Then his voice trailed off.

"Tell me what, Dylan? I'm right here."

He looked around until he saw her, his eyes watering from the pain, stress and weakness. "Katie," he said. "Blow that horn, honey. Bring in the searchers."

Dylan had an impressive four furrows down his back, from his left shoulder blade to his right lower side. A mean slash. Deep enough to bleed heavily and leave an impressive scar, but once an IV had been started and he was rehydrated, he was no longer so weak. A tetanus shot, some IV antibiotics and morphine put him on the right side of the living. And all the men who had come to search for Andy admired his wound.

"That is shit hot," Jack said. "I don't think anyone around here has been mauled in twenty years."

"Not bad, for an actor," Preacher said.

"He was acting dead," Andy pointed out to them for at least the tenth time. "We were acting dead together. But that bear didn't like us anyway."

"That bear's days are numbered, I'm afraid," Jack said. "Unfortunately for her, you can't get away with that, even though that is a very shit-hot scar. I have a battle scar, but it's nothing like that."

"It's on your ass," Preacher reminded him. "And it's the size of one round. Like maybe as big as a dime."

"Yeah, but I bet Dylan can still sit. It was no picnic, let me tell you."

"He'll never let me hear the end of it," Conner sulked.

"Got any more of that morphine, Doc?" Dylan asked. "Poor old Conner here could use a little something to ease his pain."

"We played dead," Andy said yet again. "Dylan was on the top, that's why he got the scratch. That bear isn't friendly." He looked up at his mother. "Are you mad?"

"Yes," she said. "I'm going to hug you all night long, but tomorrow I think I might yell at you all day long."

"You don't have to," he said. "I'm not going to do that again."

"I might still yell…."

"I think I'm going to have to break up this party," Cameron Michaels said. "Dylan, I want you overnight in the hospital. Just one night, though the wound will probably bother you for at least several days, maybe a couple of weeks. I want to watch you for fever, infection, bleeding. I think we got ahead of it, but humor me. One night."

"Can't I just call you if I feel infected?" he asked.

"One night," Cameron insisted. "We don't know where those bear claws have been."

"Someplace nasty—she had a terrible smell about her, like she'd been feeding in the dump. I was going to take Katie to Montana on Friday."

"That might have to wait a week or so. I can write a letter so you get transfer credit on your tickets. You want to walk to the Humvee and lay on the gurney on your stomach?" he asked.

"After I have just a minute alone with Katie," he said.

"You two kiss good-night, then let's get going," Cameron suggested. "We can give your grandmother a call from the hospital and tell her about all your excitement and that you're fine."

"Boys, come with me," Conner said.

"Dylan?" Andy asked. "Are we gonna ride the horse?"

"Maybe next week," Dylan said. "As soon as my scratch feels better."

And slowly the cabin emptied of people. The sound of trucks and SUVs departing began to fill the night.

Dylan sat backward on a kitchen chair, straddling

the chair so as not to disturb the antiseptic wash on his wounds. Katie stood in front of him. "This is not what I planned," he said.

"This isn't what anyone planned, Dylan. You saved Andy's life, I'm sure of it. I don't know how I'll ever thank you."

"That's not what I meant, but you don't have to worry about thanking me. See, I was holding a little something back because I had this grandiose plan for Montana. I was going to show you the place, the ranch, the airport, and you guys were going to have such a good time. I'd see you fall in love with it like I did. I'd get to watch the boys experience new things and get all excited. And then at night, when they were tucked in and asleep, I'd take you out on the back patio. I was going to show you that big, black sky at night—you can't believe how many stars there are. And then I was going to tell you—I can't live without you, Katie. I just can't."

"Dylan," she whispered.

"I love you, Katie. I've never loved anyone before, not like this. I can't be away from you for a day without thinking about how much I want to get home. And I don't really care where home is—you can pick the moon for all I care. But, Katie, please, pick me. Marry me. Because you're my life."

She ran a hand along his cheek. Tears came to her eyes. "I thought you were more hit and run."

"Yeah, what do I know," he said with a laugh. "You amaze me every day, Katie. I want you in my life forever, through everything. I swear, I'll make you happy or die trying."

"No dying," she said, shaking her head. "Been there, done that."

"Marry me," he said. "Let me take care of you and the boys and whoever you have in there. Love me. Choose me. Let me be your one."

"Dylan, you are The One. You sure you want me? I don't travel light."

"Oh, I'm sure," he said, pulling her mouth down to his for a kiss. "I've been wanting you since I found you in that wet T-shirt on the side of the road. You make my mouth water and my brain freeze—you are almost too much for my heart. I love you so much. I want you and your twins and your brother and Charlie's medals. I want all of you. I want everything that's part of you— your past, your present and your future. And I want you to be *mine*."

She smiled despite the tear that rolled down her cheek. "I love you right back. Love you too much to even say how much, it's that big. It's bigger than you can imagine. And once I say yes, you're totally stuck. I'll tell everyone I know, including Conner, and there is absolutely no way out."

He grinned at her. "I don't want out, baby. I want *in*."

Epilogue

It took three weeks for Dylan's back to heal enough for him to fly with Katie and the boys to Montana and by then it was already well into August. They were picked up at the airport by Sue Ann Langston, or Mrs. Lang as Dylan liked to refer to her. She called him "D." Sometimes she called him Big D because her two-year-old son was Little D. "Sorry to have appropriated the name, Katie," she said. "I didn't think Big D would ever get around to it!"

Katie found Sue Ann to be a complete delight—happy, friendly and very, very talkative in her excitement at meeting Katie and the boys. She told Katie everything she could think of about Payne on the ride from the Butte airport, including, "The weather has been awesome, the kids have been swimming at the lake whenever they can talk me into taking them and Lang is already working on a couple of charter bids out of L.A., trying to figure out what type of equipment is most cost-effective to put there."

"Already?" Dylan asked.

"And nothing from your friend Jay, yet. Two of the industry people from your list jumped right on the opportunity. Dylan, this might just work out."

Katie thought she was prepared for the beauty of the landscape since Dylan had described it so thoroughly and given her many comparisons to Virgin River. But she was stunned by the magnificence that was Montana and overwhelmed by the majesty of the mountain peaks and rich, green valleys. The drive to the valley that was Payne over the mountains gave views that caused her to gasp every time they came around another curve.

"And you look at this every day?" she asked Dylan.

"When I'm in town. Flying in here is awesome," he said. "Sue Ann, pull over at the next lookout."

A few minutes later Sue Ann brought the car to a stop at a wide space on a mountain road that overlooked a broad expanse of valley dotted with ranches. A stone wall bordered the lookout to keep people like crazy five-year-old boys from diving down the side of the mountain. Dylan jumped out and held the door for Katie, then the boys.

She stood at the wall and looked down. "My God," she whispered reverently. "It looks like a postcard."

He came up behind her, slipping his arms around her waist. Sue Ann joined them.

"See that small house at the far end of the valley?" Dylan asked her, pointing. "Just a small house, a barn, a couple of storage sheds you can barely see, a corral… that's my place. And way down there on the other side of the pasture, way past the house, you can see the runway, hangars and a few planes."

"All that is yours?"

"Kind of," he said. "It's mine and Adele's. I borrowed from her to build the airport though I paid her back for that. She still owns the house and land, and put my name on the deed along with hers. You know her, she won't take rent. I tried to buy it from her and she said if I argue any more, she'll take her name off the deed altogether. She wants me to be here because I built the business here—she wanted to do something for me. It's the only thing I've ever gone along with."

She turned around to face him. "Why have you been so stubborn?" Katie asked.

"I had a lot to prove," he said. "I wanted to show Adele that I grew up, that I could be responsible. I didn't want her fixing things for me." He kissed her.

One of the boys made a gagging sound and Sue Ann laughed.

"They never stop doing that," Mitch said.

Andy looked up at Sue Ann. "He's gonna be like our dad. Not our real dad, who died and went to live in heaven, but *like* our dad."

"You okay with that?" Sue Ann asked with a smile.

"Yeah," the boys said in unison. "We like him," Mitch said. "He's fun when he's not kissing all the time."

Dylan looked at Sue Ann over Katie's head. "It's a tough audience."

Katie had turned back to the view. "Dylan, do you have a lot of cars?"

"Just a truck and a Harley," he said. "It looks like an invasion down there."

Sue Ann cleared her throat. "Yeah, there was really no keeping people away, once they figured out you were going to be in town. I could apologize, but there was nothing I could do, so I asked Lang and Ham to just get out the grill."

"Who are they?" Katie asked.

"Oh, you know," Sue Ann said. "The town."

When they finally arrived at Dylan's house it was almost dinnertime and there seemed to be a huge community there to greet them—employees from the airport, neighbors, friends. Katie was introduced to a couple of teachers from the town elementary school, two pilots who worked for Dylan, their families, a rancher who used Dylan's pasture for grazing along with his wife and kids, and many others. Ham, a grizzled old guy with fingers bent from arthritis, merely nodded and gave a grunt when introduced and Dylan said, "He does speak, but not overly." But apparently he knew child-speak because her boys wandered off not ten minutes later and she found them in the corral, each on his own horse with Ham managing the lead. There were a lot of other kids sitting on the rail, cheering and shouting instructions.

Most of the welcoming party was gathered outside because the weather was beautiful—seventy-five degrees with a pleasant breeze. The grill was lit, burgers and hot dogs cooked away, lots of side dishes were put out and there was plenty of lemonade and tea to drink, brought in huge thermoses. There were a few women in the kitchen, making sure things were cleaned up and tidy, and Katie slipped past them to take a look at the rest of the house.

Dylan had been honest, it wasn't fancy, but she was charmed by it just the same. He had collected the kind of rustic furniture that would be at home in a log cabin, including a plush leather sectional in the living room. He had a big TV—he must like either movies or sports. His bedroom held an ordinary double-size bed— nothing of the hit and run bachelor here—no king-size bed or mirrored ceiling. This house had what people called a mother-in-law plan—another master bedroom on the other side of the house. This was probably a requirement for the old days when Adele and her grandson shared the house and Katie bet that Adele took the master with the bath. There were two bathrooms—one small master bath with a shower, and a hallway bath with a tub. And although there was a large kitchen table and breakfast bar, the dining room was void of furniture. Apparently Dylan didn't entertain much.

Still, she liked the house. She liked the big, clear, beautiful land it sat on and the mountains that rose to the west. When she went back outside, her boys came shrieking and shouting toward her, barking dogs following them. "We rode horses," they were yelling.

She crouched. "Did Ham talk to you?" she asked.

They both nodded. "He told us everything we had to do," Andy said.

"He made us brush them after," Mitch added. "And stay away from their feet."

She laughed. Bribery, she thought. Clever.

The two things most of the town wanted to see were the claw marks on Dylan's back and Katie's ring. Since they'd had time before they could travel, Dylan took her to Eureka to shop for a ring—he couldn't get her locked in fast enough. It wasn't a real big ring, but it was a ring she picked for herself and she thought it beautiful. And the claw marks on his back had healed into a mean-looking, slightly raised red welt and won the admiration of the men here just as it had in Virgin River.

"Awesome," someone said.

"Very cool," said another.

"You're going to get a lot of mileage out of that."

The sun began to sink over the mountains in the west and suddenly, without warning, the party was over. Everyone packed up, wiped countertops, swept off the patio, closed up the grill, put outdoor chairs back where they belonged. They said quick, unfussy goodbyes. Like a parade, trucks and SUVs drove away from the property.

Two hours later, Katie had her boys showered and settled in the mother-in-law room. Dylan had lit a fire in the pit on the patio and he was waiting for her, his long legs stretched out in front of him, taking in the big sky. When she joined him, he pulled her chair close to his.

"Tomorrow I'll take you to the airport first and give the boys a ride. Then to town. Not much of a town, but we like it. There's a couple of good schools—elementary and high school. We have some excellent parks—soccer and football and softball. This town really gets into their sports, especially those the kids play. I'll take you guys into the mountains and some of the national parks, just to see. If we had more time, we'd check out the Grand Tetons, Yellowstone, Jackson Hole. I'll show you where Ham took me to camp the first time. I thought it was the end of the world but now I realize it's ten minutes up the road. By the time we've done that, we'll have to get back to Virgin River."

She looked up at the sky. "What if we didn't?" she asked.

He sat up straighter. "You want to stay a little longer?"

She turned toward him. "What if we just called Conner, Leslie and Adele and asked them when they'll have time to come up here? What if we just stayed?"

"Stayed?"

"Stayed."

"Katie, you have a car, I have a Harley, and there's all that stuff in the cabin. All the clothes, TV, toys... stuff. Enough to fill up a U-Haul, at least."

"What if I asked Conner to gather up that stuff and bring me my car and your Harley. We can afford to fly Conner and Leslie home, right?"

"I think I can swing that. Are you saying…?" he asked softly.

"We should settle in. I should start nesting before it snows, which I'm told happens kind of early here. They were kidding when they told me August, right?"

He laughed. "I hope so."

"I don't think I'll ever get the boys away from the dogs and horses."

He smiled. "I knew those animals would come in handy eventually. I love you, Katie Malone. But you have all that precious stuff—Charlie's medals, wedding pictures…"

"What if we made some new wedding pictures? Something simple, sweet and as soon as possible."

He smiled at her and pulled her a little closer. "Sounds like a plan."

"And it's Katie Malone Childress," she said. "If you're sure."

"I'm sure," he said. "This is the life I've always dreamed about. The life I didn't think I could have."

"Oh, you can have it, Big D. Just try to get away."

* * * * *

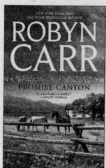
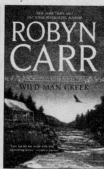
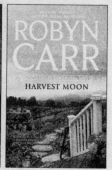

PRESENTING...

More Than Words

STORIES OF THE HEART

Three bestselling authors
Three real-life heroines

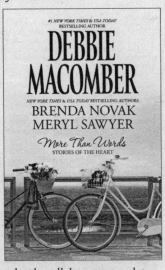

Even as you read these words, there are women just like you stepping up and making a difference in their communities, making our world a better place to live. Three such exceptional women have been selected as recipients of Harlequin's More Than Words award. To celebrate their accomplishments, three bestselling authors have written short stories inspired by these real-life heroines.

Proceeds from the sale of this book will be reinvested into the Harlequin More Than Words program to support causes that are of concern to women.

Visit
www.HarlequinMoreThanWords.com
to nominate a real-life heroine from your community.

REQUEST YOUR
FREE BOOKS!

2 FREE NOVELS
FROM THE ROMANCE COLLECTION
PLUS 2 FREE GIFTS!

ROBYN CARR

32978	VIRGIN RIVER	___ $7.99 U.S.	___ $9.99 CAN.
32974	SHELTER MOUNTAIN	___ $7.99 U.S.	___ $9.99 CAN.
32942	HARVEST MOON	___ $7.99 U.S.	___ $9.99 CAN.
32931	WILD MAN CREEK	___ $7.99 U.S.	___ $9.99 CAN.
32921	PROMISE CANYON	___ $7.99 U.S.	___ $9.99 CAN.
32917	SECOND CHANCE PASS	___ $7.99 U.S.	___ $9.99 CAN.
32899	JUST OVER THE MOUNTAIN	___ $7.99 U.S.	___ $9.99 CAN.
32897	DEEP IN THE VALLEY	___ $7.99 U.S.	___ $9.99 CAN.
32896	A VIRGIN RIVER CHRISTMAS	___ $7.99 U.S.	___ $9.99 CAN.
32870	A SUMMER IN SONOMA	___ $7.99 U.S.	___ $9.99 CAN.
32868	THE HOUSE ON OLIVE STREET	___ $7.99 U.S.	___ $9.99 CAN.
32768	MOONLIGHT ROAD	___ $7.99 U.S.	___ $9.99 CAN.
32761	ANGEL'S PEAK	___ $7.99 U.S.	___ $9.99 CAN.
32749	FORBIDDEN FALLS	___ $7.99 U.S.	___ $9.99 CAN.
31310	REDWOOD BEND	___ $7.99 U.S.	___ $9.99 CAN.
31300	HIDDEN SUMMIT	___ $7.99 U.S.	___ $9.99 CAN.
31290	TEMPTATION RIDGE	___ $7.99 U.S.	___ $9.99 CAN.
31286	WHISPERING ROCK	___ $7.99 U.S.	___ $9.99 CAN.
31271	BRING ME HOME FOR CHRISTMAS	___ $7.99 U.S.	___ $9.99 CAN.

(limited quantities available)

TOTAL AMOUNT	$ _____
POSTAGE & HANDLING	$ _____
($1.00 for 1 book, 50¢ for each additional)	
APPLICABLE TAXES*	$ _____
TOTAL PAYABLE	$ _____

(check or money order—please do not send cash)

To order, complete this form and send it, along with a check or money order for the total above, payable to MIRA Books, to: **In the U.S.:** 3010 Walden Avenue, P.O. Box 9077, Buffalo, NY 14269-9077; **In Canada:** P.O. Box 636, Fort Erie, Ontario, L2A 5X3.

Name: _____

Address: _____ City: _____

State/Prov.: _____ Zip/Postal Code: _____

Account Number (if applicable): _____

075 CSAS

*New York residents remit applicable sales taxes.
*Canadian residents remit applicable GST and provincial taxes.

MIRA | HARLEQUIN®
www.Harlequin.com

MRC0312BL